First published November 1967
Second impression January 1968
Third impression April 1979

DOWN
AT THE
VICARAGE

BY WINIFRED EASTMENT
(S. O. Green)

ILLUSTRATED BY
JOHN CLARKE

Republished by
EGON PUBLISHERS LTD.
19 BALDOCK ROAD, LETCHWORTH, HERTS.
First published in 1967 by
Letchworth Printers Ltd., Letchworth, Herts.

By the same author

WE PRAYED FOR PEACE
Under name Winifred V. Phillips

WANSTEAD THROUGH THE AGES
Under name Winifred V. Phillips

HEART TO HEART (bedside book)

FORD END VILLAGE HISTORY
(Women's Institute circulation)

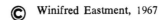
ISBN 0 905858 08 5

Printed by Inprint of Luton (Designers & Printers) Ltd.,
95-115 Windmill Road, Luton, Bedfordshire.

TO
HENRY'S MEMORY
ALSO TO
" JOHN " AND HIS BELOVED FLOCK

CONTENTS

ILLUSTRATIONS

INTRODUCTION

" Fool! " said my muse to me, " look in thy heart, and write."
SIR PHILIP SIDNEY.

VICARAGE life is essentially an amalgam of variegated experiences, conforming to no set pattern yet geared inevitably to the orderly cycle of the Church's calendar. It contains all the basic ingredients for a full feast of the most unlikely dishes.

The experiences may at times be solemn, sobering and sad; at others trying, trite and trivial; but more often, thank goodness, they are happy, human and hilarious. These present jottings, garnered mainly from our personal observations in a small country parish, are concerned chiefly with those elements that fall within the third category: the happy, human and hilarious.

For the incumbent, of course, the familiar round can now and then become frustrating and depressing to the point of soul-desolation and near despair. This is where a wife, if she is reasonably alert and resourceful, can prove her asset value by being ready with a metaphorical hypodermic, to inject the necessary booster. She will pray that it may be sufficiently potent to recharge his sagging spirit, restore his lost perspective and revive his normal sense of humour. If so, he will then be able to set off once more along his chosen path with accustomed serenity and buoyant step.

In my opinion, the parsonage experience, measured against *any* background and weighed against the sum of its undisputed problems and difficulties, is a singularly rewarding assignment, which I would not have missed for all the tea in China.

Since our retirement I have lived over and over again, in imagination, those amusing, homely incidents that at the time afforded us such rich entertainment and furnished us often with a privileged view of the minor eccentricities of human nature.

In my reminiscent moments I have often found myself smiling

broadly, as if acknowledging a crowd of friendly, genial ghosts assembling for a parish reunion. The recollections have sometimes evoked spasms of convulsive mirth, which one has felt inclined to share. In fact, the inclination to do so became eventually a compulsive urge, which refused to be satisfied until I set to work trying to record incident after incident in the train of nostalgic events.

It was Lord Mount-Edgecombe, I believe, who claimed that " the remembrance of the past is infinitely more agreeable than the enjoyment of the present." I confess that my recollections covering the period of my husband's rural incumbency are " infinitely agreeable," although I have no notable quarrel with the " enjoyment of the present "; and if these reminiscences should succeed in amusing the reader—perhaps to the point of encouraging a few irrepressible peals of laughter—I shall feel handsomely rewarded and the labour will seem justified.

The picture is to some extent a composite one; a few items contributed by other vicarage families have been added to the hash.

The characters are (I hope!) impenetrably disguised; but the anecdotes, with hardly an exception, are substantially true.

It was abundantly clear from the very beginning that in the parochial field we had everything to learn. We were soon thinking of ourselves and—in private—even speaking of ourselves as " the Greens "; and when it came to writing this book it was natural enough that I should feel inclined to take cover behind the pseudonym *S. O. Green*. But, on second thoughts, *why* take cover? So I decided to come right out into the open and face the firing squad.

CHAPTER 1

Enter the Greens!

WE had hardly paid off the taxi and crossed the threshold of our new home when the telephone bell rang. I looked questioningly at John and murmured " Good heavens, so soon? "

Standing there nervously surveying the strange surroundings, I must have looked absurdly miscast for my new rôle. I was still wearing my frivolous honeymoon hat and clutching a bunch of wild flowers in one hand, and in the crook of the other arm I clasped an unwrapped fireside companion set. The simple explanation for the inclusion of this odd item in our travelling kit is that, in the course of our honeymoon ramblings in north Cornwall, we had stumbled across an attractive little studio stocked with pleasing examples of the local arts and crafts. We had both fallen for these hand-wrought fire-irons, and on the impulse had decided to make them a practical souvenir of our new-found bliss; so I had treated John to a poker and tongs, and he had reciprocated with shovel, hearth-brush and stand. But wrapping paper, like most other commodities at the end of the war, was in terribly short supply, so we hadn't questioned the unblushing nakedness of our trophy as it was handed to us with only a bit of string tied at each end to hold the component parts together.

Now, within minutes of our arrival at the vicarage, I was struggling to disentangle myself from the mountain of assorted luggage and parcels while John, bracing himself for this unexpectedly swift initiation into his pastoral office, strode briskly towards the telephone.

" This is Mrs. Turnpike " announced a casual voice at the other end. " Can you let me have twenty pounds of gooseberries to-morrow? Bottling and jamming; not dessert. Put them on the 10.15 bus, as usual."

John, who would probably have been less taken aback if it had been the rural dean requesting his attendance at a chapter meeting that very afternoon on the top of Mont Blanc, stammered: " I think you've made a mistake, madam. This is the *vicarage*. This is the new vicar speaking."

" Oh, really? I don't think I knew the old one had gone. I always have my fruit from your garden," she went on imperturbably. " You won't forget, will you? The name's Turnpike, Hill Road, *Lower* Bellpull; 10.15 bus tomorrow; my daughter will meet the bus—with the pram, you know; bye-bye! "

Of course, we *didn't* know. How could we be expected to? But with these bewildering instructions our customer's voice trailed off.

John mopped his brow, fumbled for his note-book, and, under the impressive heading " Garden produce," jotted down the details of our first greengrocery order.

This, I reflected, was a distinctly odd introduction to vicarage life. Clearly, flexibility was to be an indispensable qualification for success in our new appointment. From now on we must learn to expect the unexpected.

(For the record, I suppose it should be mentioned that dear Mrs. Turnpike's esteemed order was duly executed—right on time. And this, on sober reflection and subsequent reference to available statistics relating to picking capacity per man-hour in comparable branches of the fruit-growing industry, seemed no mean achievement for a couple of well-past-middle-age townies with no previous experience whatsoever of gathering fruit of *any* description, let alone that most vicious and intractable member of the whole fruit family the gooseberry.)

We had set to work with the unquenchable zeal of children attacking a forbidden project, confident of complete mastery of the situation in no time. After all, picking fruit was simple enough we thought!

I do not doubt that it was the sheer novelty of the game that provided the incentive to go doggedly on long after approaching dusk; common sense, severe backache and the most painful and gory lacerations of arms and legs should have warned us that harvesting fruit can be a much overrated pastime. My nylons (fool that I was not to have removed them!) were in shreds; our flesh was mercilessly punctured by ubiquitous thorns; and John had badly snagged his only decent pullover.

From these initial errors we soon evolved a rational picking technique and sported protective clothing, and thus equipped we emerged virtually unscathed from the most spiky and off-putting bushes. Just a simple matter of know-how!

Meanwhile, being ignorant of the current market price of gooseberries, yet vaguely aware that the sale of all produce at that time was subject to controls, we telephoned the nearest food control office to find out. The answer was a trifle chilling, and we calculated that, on balance, after allowing for replacement of my nylons, a supply of embrocation for our backs, a bottle of T.C.P. and some bandages for our surface wounds, we were just sixteen shillings and tenpence down on our first transaction.

Surely, we consoled ourselves, with a little more experience we would eventually discover how to break even. An actual profit was something to which we hardly dared to aspire.

*   *   *   *   *

Moving into a parsonage house to take up a new living must always be an experience approached with mixed emotions. It is not merely moving into a new vicarage—most of them, anyway, are far from *new;* generally they're depressingly old and rambling, with an air of shabby obsolescence and faded elegance; but, of course, I did not mean literally *new.* It is moving into a new community; into a position that is highly vulnerable from all angles and at all levels, a position for which the incumbent and his wife—if he has one— may or may not be adequately prepared and equipped. In accepting a beneficed living the incumbent becomes a larger-than-life target for every shade of criticism, and occasionally undeserved abuse. He may find himself the unsuspecting tool of existing pressure groups. To preserve parochial integration and harmony in his (as yet) unexplored field, it is an advantage to be a diplomat of a fairly high order—adept at reconciling warring factions and ever willing to placate the malcontents without yielding ground. Woe betide the greenhorns, for the overall requirements of the office are very exacting !

Preparedness depends, naturally, on such obvious factors as family tradition in the " cloth " (we had none), previous experience in a beneficed living (this was our first), sound briefing from the outgoing incumbent (ours was sketchy in the extreme, as he had been there so short a time and had been handicapped throughout by illness), and stray snippets of friendly advice—coupled usually with dark warnings!—gleaned from more widely experienced brethren (easily our most promising source). Beyond that, a touch of intuitive caution or E.S.P. could doubtless be invaluable in fore-warning of the occupational hazards of the office (and we were certainly not conscious of any specific promptings of that sort).

Even the most rigorous training at the hands of the wisest of parish priests under whom one may have served as curate is only as valuable as secondhand experience can ever be; and the most profound counsel, offered in all good faith, is limited in its scope and validity by the fact that—like individuals—no two parishes are exactly alike in character, tradition, temperament, churchmanship, and so forth. It so happened that John, who in his forties had aban-doned a business career to enter the Church, had, in serving his two curacies, struck the extreme opposites in tradition, and he couldn't possibly have relied on either as a practical yardstick for measuring the particular requirements of a country parish of his own. Imponderables such as these take time and patient probing.

Our emotions, therefore, as we crossed the threshold into a new home and a new life ranged over a singularly wide and incalculable field of possibilities. Uppermost was the exhilarating thrill of responsibility springing from a vocational zest. Here, we felt, was a challenge. We dared to be hopeful; we wanted to be friendly; and we expected it to be no sinecure. We strove to stifle the lurking doubts as to the adequacy of our qualifications for the assignment, for we were deeply—agonizingly—conscious of the solemn implica-tions of the work that lay ahead.

A niggling upsurge of vague misgivings had tended to cloud the last lap of our journey home. That first naïve confidence was slowly giving way to disturbing questionings. What, for instance, would the parishioners be like?—friendly and approachable or frigid and off-putting? What would they, in their turn, think of the " new " man? Would the parochial atmosphere be happy and united, or would we meet the backwash of past feuds and discordant jang-lings? Why, by the way, had the last man left? Had he drawn big crowds, emptied his pews, or merely jogged placidly along? Were the young people here drifting, or had they in fact drifted? What of the organizations and cultural facilities within the parish? Would it be the familiar pattern of responsibility being always shouldered by the same " few," or would things here be animated by a lively community spirit fed on local pride, with everyone competing amicably to do his bit for the common weal? And, turning to domestic issues, would the parsonage house prove manageable and economic to run or would it be the proverbial " barn of a place," in a mouldering state of disrepair, with obsolete plumbing arrangements or virtually none at all? We knew, for instance, that in some of the neighbouring parsonages pumped water and primitive sanitation had not yet been replaced by mod. cons. Would the upkeep of the place—in our case an imposing gentleman's residence, with three floors, two stairways and a cluster of outbuildings, including stabling for three horses—become an insupportable financial burden?

These and an endless train of similar speculations will surely assail the most seasoned of spiritual campaigners on moving-in day, and cause a touch of pallor. We, as bare initiates not only into the *mystique* of pastoral responsibility but also into the manifold complications of sweet domesticity, could surely be excused if we turned a bit green under the gills and wondered how on earth we were ever going to chew all that we had so optimistically bitten off. The answers to our questionings were soon to be supplied; on some issues, in fact, all too soon.

Meanwhile here we were, right down to earth and face to face with stern reality. For the past ten days in north Cornwall we had been lazily reclining on the crest of a pleasant wave of wedding recollections (packed church, augmented choir, red carpet, bells, vestments, a subsequent sea of familiar faces crowding into the nearby hall, nervous speeches, facetious farewells, and final escape from the confetti battle, choking and spluttering over the bits that had lodged in our throats), interrupting romantic reveries only for the occasional game of golf. But, as the last of our modest stock of golf balls sailed perversely off course through a badly sliced drive, over the steep cliffs and into the swirling Atlantic rollers below, we had resolutely agreed that golf was now too expensive a hobby for us; we must hit on something more commensurate with a clerical stipend.

So, with golf now definitely " out," we had turned to musing on the furniture and fabrics of our new home, devising a dozen possible arrangements for our prized pieces—where to put this to advantage and how best to display that. We relished the prospect of setting

B

out our wonderful array of wedding presents. We envisaged the vast vicarage apartments made habitable and entrancing by our ambitious experiments in do-it-yourself *décor*; and, in the idle contentment of the rest of our holiday, we thoroughly enjoyed, in imagination, adding all the little finishing touches to these fanciful schemes.

Looking back, one hopes that pride of possession was excusable in those early summer days of 1947, when post-war shortages and restrictions, having reduced supplies of everything to the stark minimum, rendered house-furnishing—even on the most modestly conceived lines—a fabulously difficult and costly business. It was the age of docket and coupon, and—tell it not in Gath—of *black market* dealings; every hard-won acquisition became a prized trophy and fictitious values were liable to go to the head. But these grim days, we reminded ourselves, would pass and the future was everyone's oyster.

In anticipation of setting up home, John and I had experienced the sportsman's thrill of stalking secondhand furniture with the patient skill and low cunning of seasoned hunters. We had our accredited " spotters " widely deployed over London to the north, south, east and west—with a roving commission over the Home Counties as well. They had kept us regularly informed of forth-coming sales and private disposals, whereupon we had descended like shock troops ahead of the massed assault, snapping up bargains often before the main forces had even been briefed. Not that *all* our purchases were, in fact, bargains; sometimes they were quite the reverse, as when a whole herd of white elephants would be in-separably bracketed with the real *pièce de résistance* and a shocking price demanded for this " choice collection "! At least it was always *something* to help fill the vast vacuum in that " barn of a place."

We had the grace to blush in recalling the amazing generosity of many sympathetic friends—particularly old-age pensioners—who had lavishly pressed upon us their precious coupons so that the innumerable vicarage windows could be modestly curtained and some of the more shabby chairs chintz-covered. We prayed that their noble sacrifices had been celestially recorded for their ultimate benediction.

We had remembered—with renewed giggles—our first crude attempt, as an engaged couple, to make an inventory of the odd chattels we already possessed: the nucleus of our future home had consisted, incredibly, of three pianos (two uprights and a boudoir grand), four Chippendale chairs, and—a bed-pan! At this unexpected revelation from John I had raised a rather surprised eyebrow. " It's been in the family for well over 100 years," he had boasted; " it's a really *beautiful* one; genuine copper, with a delicately chased design [could he have meant " chaste "?], and a long black handle; I once had a good offer for it, but I wouldn't part with it for worlds "! Finally the penny had dropped, and I had said " Oh, you mean a *warming* pan "; and John had looked frankly puzzled and asked " Well, what did you suppose I meant? " My supposition, I confess, had run to something more functional than ornamental, and rather intimate.

We had also recalled the amusing carpet incident—amusing in spite of its macabre associations. In this connection our country scout, stationed on the outer perimeter of the diocese, had spied two likely carpets rolled up and lolling drunkenly against a battered wing chair in the window of an antique shop—remote and rather hush-hush. To acquire floor covering of any description, let alone honest-to-goodness Wiltons (practically new), was at that time a major conquest, so thither John and I raced—by hired car, which greatly diminished the bargain element whatever the outcome.

The owner of the antique shop—a strikingly whimsy woman both in manner and attire—welcomed us effusively and began to haul the rolls clear of the indescribable miscellany of hideous fern-pots, rusty old lamps, faded pictures, Victorian wash-hand stands and chipped china figures—all keeping incongruous company with a few really lovely pieces of cut crystal and a gem of a walnut bureau.

Unwinding a few inches of the first carpet in the cramped space of her mad medley, she felt convinced that this was *just* what we were looking for; it would look simply *handsome*, she burbled, in a large, well-proportioned room! We could better judge their undoubted merits, John had suggested, if we might be allowed to see them fully extended somewhere. " Ah, yes, of course," implying approval of such an original thought; " come to the back yard—there's plenty of space there," she suggested pleasantly.

Together we tugged the rolls through the low, narrow doorway into a spacious courtyard, where we were soon satisfied that carpets such as these—now spread out and seen to advantage—would do *very* nicely, thank you (apart from the sting inflicted by the swingeing price she was asking!).

There was a glimpse of a pretty garden beyond the yard; it looked cool and inviting, tempting us to linger; but the carpet lady begged us to excuse her seeming hurry, as she had arranged to bury her husband's ashes in the back garden that very evening—by the herbaceous border—and she had asked a few friends round for the ceremony. Our stammered sympathy was cut short by the widow, who briskly concluded the carpet deal and busied herself with the bill. Her matter-of-fact tone and utter composure encouraged the suspicion that burying human ashes—even her husband's—was almost a routine task with her. One could imagine her, at the end of the day's transactions, mechanically checking the till, perhaps popping dust covers over her stock, bolting the shop door, and then toddling off, with unaffected simplicity and absence of fuss, down the garden path, armed with ashes and trowel, to perform the solemn rite.

Ah well, one must be tolerant about other people's idiosyncrasies! We collected our carpets and left her to her unconventional party.

All these and a stream of other amusing reflections had passed in kaleidoscopic confusion as we browsed contentedly on the warm, scrubby clifftops; but the most idyllic musings have to come to an end, and now we were back from honeymoon and installed in the parish of Upper Bellpull, an enchanting little relic of feudal England lying peacefully on the north-easterly side of Essex, with farm after farm of arable land stretching in compact acres towards the east coast.

*   *   *   *   *

We had cleverly dodged the nerve-shredding chaos and initial discomforts of the actual move-in. My brother had magnificently volunteered to supervise the whole exercise. He would be there, he promised, to meet the vans, refresh the men, check the stuff and generally get things ship-shape for our arrival—a piece of social service which we had accepted with manifest relief and enthusiasm, not to mention gratitude.

The "stuff," acquired from so many widely separated sources and stored temporarily in a dozen different repositories, had first to be listed, then assembled and checked in a central marshalling yard, and subsequently reloaded for delivery to its ultimate destination. How this staggering feat of organization was accomplished in the short space of forty-eight hours remains an undisclosed mystery. John and I could only suppose that a local task-force of considerable size and much previous experience had been heavily bribed into service with the removal men: curtain-hanging, lino-laying, shelf-fixing, sorting and distributing must have cost my brother a small fortune in tips and refreshment. The undeniable fact is that an atmosphere of surprising calm and orderliness, amounting almost to mellowed comfort, awaited our homecoming.

My brother's supreme achievement was the provision of a stylish cold luncheon (wedding presents in striking evidence!), with *everything* laid on, even to a huge bowl of luscious strawberries—colossal, sun-warmed, mouth-watering specimens, worthy of the top award at any county show. And these, my brother assured us, were but a fair sample of the prodigious quantities awaiting our pleasure in the vicarage garden—such quantities, in fact, that if we chose to live exclusively on strawberries for the whole of next month there would still be a fabulous surplus. And, from his brief explorations, he estimated that we were likely to be just as surfeited with all the other kinds of fruit out there. This forecast was soon to be confirmed by the gooseberry episode already related, and all the other prolific pickings that were to become a daily exercise. Clearly the advantages of a country living were not to be despised! Not that our garden ever again yielded a comparable harvest. Perhaps that initial experience was all part of a deep, seductive conspiracy to woo us by first impressions! In any event, gathering bumper crops is not the whole story; there is the marketing, which involves climbing, bending, sorting, weighing, packing, invoicing, and in our case, as we hadn't a car or even a carrier-bicycle, the actual *carrying*.

*   *   *   *   *

With the first meal over, John and I strolled up the drive to bid a fond farewell to our capable mover-in. Then we paused self-consciously on the doorstep, casting a nervous eye over the new scene, feeling rather like a couple of raw recruits on the parade ground for the first time and praying fervently that our initial *gaffes* might mercifully be few and not too conspicuous and resounding. Not, of course, that the miniature estate that comprised the vicarage gardens and glebe in any way resembled the chilling aspect of a typical parade ground; far from it!

Our first impression was of a veritable private paradise, with spacious lawns, bold herbaceous borders, rambler-covered arches, a fascinating strip of woodland nestling under the shade of half a dozen gigantic old elms, and the wide sweep of a semi-circular drive, bordered by lilacs, laburnums, syringa and laurels; then, away to the south, a vast kitchen garden and all the soft fruit. Beyond a low, red-brick wall the large orchard stretched away out of sight. Frankly, we were slightly overawed.

The silence was suddenly shattered by a chorus of rasping, raucous squawks. At the top of those giant elms was a colony of rooks' nests, from which the noisy tenants appeared to be taking careful stock of us—their new neighbours—and expressing their unanimous disapproval.

We had good reason to pray that our howlers might not be too numerous, for we hadn't exactly passed the introductory stage (some six months earlier) with flying colours. We still blushed, for instance, at the recollection of our first *faux pas*, committed with naïve innocence during that exploratory chat with John's predecessor when we went to scan the horizon before accepting the living.

He, the outgoing incumbent, combined immense dignity, age and erudition with an astonishing rotundity. He was almost completely spherical.

Summarizing his fragmentary remarks on the parochial set-up, he had said to John: " By the way, I'll leave you my terrier "; and John, gazing uneasily on the overfed brute sprawled half inside the fender, had guardedly replied: " That's very good of you, but we hadn't thought of keeping one; actually we prefer cats "; whereupon the portly old gentleman, scenting facetiousness, had shot him a look of blistering severity; but, quickly realizing that poor John was being anything but facetious, he hastened to correct the misunderstanding—though not without a touch of asperity: " I mean *terrier*,* not terrier "!

John, as if coming out of a coma, agreed fatuously, " Of course, of course, *of course.*"

The portly old gentleman, by the way, was an engaging personality, reminiscent of a character out of Trollope. His enormous frame seemed to be upholstered with latex foam, which rippled and rolled as he laughed and coughed, which he did quite a lot, as he had both a keen sense of humour and chronic bronchitis. As a

* Fr. register, court-roll.

concession to age and some cardiac disability he received his visitors seated. His impressive girth and the foam padding may also have had something to do with it, since the physical exertion of getting himself in and out of his fabulous armchair-cum-throne must have been a supremely exhausting exercise for him; far better, in the circumstances, to stay put. If you can, imagine a human jelly, poured into the mould with an unsteady hand and tending to over-flow. I was fascinated to watch his entire being ripple as he laughed; and he had large, guileless, saucer eyes, which imparted a look of unruffled geniality and well-being. He might have been recast from the traditional man in the moon.

He had an exaggeratedly precise enunciation—every syllable given full measure and a little extra for effect—and this lent tremendous weight to his utterances.

John, from a totally different mould, was his physical antithesis.

Well, that was our initial howler. It was by no means the last.

*   *   *   *   *

Now he—the retiring incumbent (and his terrier!)—had gone. *We* were in nervous possession, and nearly every time the telephone rang it was for red currants, or raspberries, or more gooseberries, or were the loganberries ripe yet?

It didn't seem to make sense. We came to the conclusion that John's predecessor, for all his massive dignity and erudition, must have been a remarkably astute fruit salesman, and we were finding ourselves the reluctant heirs to a well-established greengrocery business—albeit as a side-line, but nevertheless very arduous and demanding.

One thing was quite certain: he, the portly old gentleman, was obviously no tree climber, so we assumed that he was the business brain behind a flourishing enterprise, with willing servitors to do his practical bidding. For instance, not only the tree-climbing and fruit-picking but also the weighing and carrying must have been delegated to a far more nimble and mobile understudy. Who, we were curious to find out for future reference, was the " dog's-body "?

*   *   *   *   *

As we bade him farewell that day we gained the impression that the old man was rather kindly disposed towards us and genuinely anxious to be helpful. Was it only imagination, or did we *really* detect a look of mild pity in those large saucer eyes? His benign, unwavering gaze rather reminded one of a Botticelli angel!

We have ever since referred to him by the affectionate abbreviation the P.O.G.

CHAPTER 2

First things first

THE final arrangements for John's institution and induction were arrived at only after some spirited controversy with the hierarchy and a reluctant reversal of the bishop's original plan. It had been fixed for Saturday, June 14, at three o'clock in the afternoon—an eminently suitable hour one might think. Instead, it took place at eight o'clock in the evening.

The eventual retiming hinged on *cricket*. Not that the bishop suddenly remembered an engagement at Lord's which he was unwilling to forgo; or that John had been unexpectedly selected to represent England that very day. Candidly, John hardly knew a bail from a stump, a lamentable piece of ignorance that cost him more than one black mark in his new parish.

No, it was total unawareness at administrative level of the obsessional, if not idolatrous, local attitude to cricket that caused the rumpus and raised enough dust to threaten open mutiny on the part of the entire congregation. Mercifully, the gravity of the error was pointed out by the P.O.G. in time for the printers to amend the hour, but not in time for his lordship to reshuffle his episcopal undertakings.

It all came to the surface by seeming chance when John had had that meagre briefing from his predecessor. Just as we were leaving him (and that was as hastily as we could politely contrive after the *terrier* incident!), John had said something about his induction, and the P.O.G. had intervened with a sharp " *What* day did you say? "

" Saturday, June 14, at three o'clock," John repeated.

" *Three* o'clock, did you say? That won't do; it can't possibly be at three; quite out of the question. It must be seven-thirty at the earliest—preferably eight." This in a tone of unchallengeable finality, as if he had successfully vetoed a highly contentious issue before Convocation.

John, naturally perplexed, gasped " Why not, for heaven's sake? In any case, it's *got* to be three. The bishop himself fixed it; you can't upset his lordship's arrangements."

The P.O.G. fixed John with a sad, pitying gaze. He seemed to be trying to devise some means of measuring his abysmal ignorance without exposing him to undue embarrassment.

At last, with a patient sigh and using that slow, precise enunciation of his with telling effect, he said: " My good friend, it wouldn't make the slightest difference if it had been arranged by the king himself [his tone implying that " the king " was only a split-second substitution for " Almighty God "]; it cannot—I repeat *cannot*—be at three o'clock. Barring rain, there'll be a cricket match on. The earliest you could be inducted would be seven-thirty, and even then it would be a close thing. They draw stumps at seven. Better make it eight, to be on the safe side; and think yourself lucky it's not an away match."

" But surely," protested John a trifle touchily, " they could put off a cricket match for once, for an induction,"

" *Put off a cricket match?* Did I hear you say ' Put off a cricket match '? " groaned the P.O.G., verging on apoplexy. " Are you crazy? You just don't understand. Cricket here is the inalienable sacred cow. For cricket there is a deep, burning and inextinguishable passion. In all local issues cricket ranks as top priority. *Never* forget that! "

Still John didn't seem fully convinced, for after a moment's reflection he persisted. " Well, even so, I don't see why *their* cricket match should affect *my* induction—not to that extent; let those who play cricket do so and let the church people attend the service."

Then the P.O.G., with monumental patience, explained the whole intricate situation in detail. " But don't you see, they're all one and the same! The organist owns the pitch and is also captain; the tenor soloist is the only reliable spin bowler; both the baritones —they're brothers—are far the best bats the team can produce; all the rest of the choir, with the exception of the women and girls, are in the team. Both churchwardens are bespoke—the people's keeps wicket and the vicar's umpires. The leader of the sopranos is both scorer and tea hostess; the rest of the field's made up of ' other ranks '; and the entire village turns out to watch. That, let me tell you, is the established pattern here—as unalterable as the laws of the Medes and Persians. You violate local custom at your peril. No, you've only one course, my friend, if you don't want an entirely deserted church—apart, that is, from the bishop, yourself, and any who may turn up from your last parish. You must contact the bishop at once; point out his (!) mistake and ask him to switch his standing evening engagement and come along to Upper Bellpull at eight o'clock. Then you'll get a reasonable congregation—provided they're not too whacked from the afternoon's exertions."

This was as good as an ultimatum, which John didn't relish. That evening he telephoned the bishop—not without some apprehension. The bishop at first demurred; then, as John's miserable dilemma communicated itself to him, his lordship gave way and agreed to the alteration with a breezy " Very well then; I see that difficulty; *first things first*, I suppose! Make it eight, but *I'm* booked elsewhere. I'll get in touch with the suffragan and see how he's fixed."

And, replacing the receiver, I heard John growl " Well, that's a fine opening gambit with my new father in God! "

* * * * *

All this, I felt, ought to have given John the right cue for his first encounter with the organist and choirmaster, but unfortunately he missed it.

They came face to face by the vestry door the day we moved in. The organist introduced himself and, after a friendly exchange of greetings, asked hopefully " Do *you* play? " John, enchanted to have met someone so soon with kindred tastes, admitted smilingly that he did, adding with becoming modesty: " Just a little, you know; more or less to amuse myself. Of the two, I prefer the organ, though I *do* play the piano as well. Have you a one- or two-manual here? "

By now the organist's jaw had dropped to its utmost capacity. He seemed rather to have lost interest in the conversation, commenting vaguely: " Oh! What *we're* looking for is a good leg-break bowler; Bolt's not too dependable these days; in fact the whole field's getting a bit slack. Last Saturday Pelican missed three absolute sitters; said the sun dazzled him. It cost us the match," he ended, a shade mournfully.

John's non-committal "Oh!" couldn't have been very comforting.

*   *   *   *   *

As there were only three clear days between our arrival and the induction, the tempo of life became pretty feverish; it developed, in fact, into a crazy nightmare of unpacking luggage, lining cupboard shelves, washing wedding-present china and glass to which wisps of straw packing still clung, switching over furniture that had been inadvertently deposited in the wrong rooms by our well-intentioned movers-in, and hunting desperately and incessantly for such odds and ends as the tin-opener, bread saw, scissors, ink, emergency tool kit, first-aid ditto, picture cord, spare plugs and light bulbs, soap, saucepan scourers, and service sheets for Saturday —and the hundred and one other things that never count until you can't find them.

To achieve complete apple-pie order in three days was an impossibility; superficial tidiness in the main rooms must suffice as long as the study and cloakroom were immaculate to receive the bishop—even if he were not the diocesan!

I had been warned to expect two coachloads of friends from John's old parish, and they would no doubt want to make a tour of inspection: I must remember to make the more chaotic corners officially "out of bounds."

Light refreshments, I knew, were to be served afterwards in the village hall by the social committee, but I had to prepare at the vicarage for personal friends and relations—and for any of the sixty-odd members of the coach party who might elect to wander in to be fortified after their long journey. I had rations for *two*, but those wonderful, prolific strawberries would provide an excellent standby. Who in their senses would hanker after buns and cakes when they could have lashings of strawberries and Jersey cream? (The cream was in the nature of a house-warming present from a neighbouring farm.)

We were also expecting our first weekend guest—our ever-faithful old friend Fergus. He, a heart-and-soul supporter of John's pastoral mission, just couldn't bear to miss the induction, although it meant travelling all the way from Scotland; so a two- or three-day stay seemed clearly indicated.

Faced with this somewhat formidable programme, it was hardly surprising that I—a new bride—began to show signs of wilting.

With all these hectic preparations going on, there was little time for us to go out and meet any of our parishioners in the highways and byways, or to take our topographical bearings. We had, of course, carefully inspected the church, which was lofty, spacious, and scrupulously well kept. It had fairly recently been wired for electricity, which was an immense relief to me, for I find the slightest hint of paraffin unbearably nauseating.

The few sporadic attempts I had made to get the vicarage boiler-cum-cooker going had proved abortive. My efforts had produced only ominous clouds of acrid smoke, which had seeped stealthily into every room and polluted the whole atmosphere, so the popular roast and two veg. were definitely " off " until such time as I could give my undivided attention to the collective mysteries (to me) of dampers, draughts, riddlers, and the vast array of odd knobs. In any event, cold collations more than sufficed, for there was scarcely time to breathe, let alone to eat.

The only available hot water—for *all* purposes—was from our medium-sized kettle, heated on the little table electric cooker, a new and unfamiliar toy to me. That soon fused. As mechanics we were quite hopeless and helpless. Having been accustomed to gas, everything here was an unopened book to me, and my incurable paraffin phobia completed the present domestic impasse. The village boasted nothing as practical as an electricity repair service, so our immediate outlook was a trifle bleak. However, with an upsurge of pioneer spirit, we were resolved not to be defeated by these minor (?) initial contretemps—just grit your teeth and accept them for what they are, mere teething troubles! Once Saturday was over we'd jolly soon get to grips with *everything*! (Meanwhile, the nice organist—evidently an all-round man—came to our rescue and soon fixed the fuse.)

* * * * *

On Saturday we rose with the lark, in eager anticipation of the day's events and reasonably confident that everything was under control.

Such optimism made no allowance for the totally unexpected arrival of the boudoir Schiedmayer! This treasured instrument had been in store somewhere near Norwich ever since John had bought it, two or three years ago. We had once been to visit it and had simply *longed* to have it out from its impersonal and overcrowded surroundings; but, much as we *yearned* to have it in our immediate possession, to admire it, to caress it, to *play* it, we could have thought of a more convenient moment for the carriers to deliver it than at nine-thirty on the very morning of the induction. Not that they were to know, of course!

There was I, leaping round the house, placing family photographs and wedding presents in prominent positions, while John was engrossed in checking service sheets and the less familiar details of the induction ceremony, when suddenly a huge pantechnicon rolled up, parked itself in our drive, and released its team of four baize-aproned stalwarts, followed by a trolley, rollers, lifting tackle and—after some delay—the piano.

Judging by the fabulous build of the foreman, I should have thought that his three associates and the lifting tackle were entirely surplus to requirements. Beside this giant of a man everyone and everything seemed absurdly dwarfed; one felt that, had he chosen to do so, he could easily have carried at least a couple of grand pianos under each arm and another on his head without the slightest strain or discomfort. However, they were all in it together and clearly intended to share the honour of lifting and transporting our Schiedmayer.

Naturally, our own current domestic operations had to be hastily suspended while we shifted tables, chairs, mats, a few delicate ornaments and anything else that was in the way, so that the piano could be safely manœuvred into place opposite its future companion—my upright Cramer.

Because the less massive members of the moving quartet had a silly habit of getting under the giant's feet (just like Gulliver's encounter with the Lilliputians, I kept thinking) it all proved a prodigiously slow job, for which the subsequent cup of tea seemed a paltry gratuity. In any event, an ordinary man-size cup was an implied insult to Gulliver, but, as we hadn't a vessel commensurate with the noble stature, he had to make do. I refilled it seven times.

The minute the men had gone we lifted the lid to peep at the keyboard; then we simply *had* to try it out. John gave an impromptu recital, while I hunted for dusters and furniture cream to remove the incriminating collection of finger prints and general evidence of prolonged storage, which tended to mar the ravishing beauty of our latest treasure.

Naturally the temptation there and then to try the two pianos in duet was irresistible; chores must wait; meals must wait; visitors must wait; even the bishop, if need be, must wait; we simply *had* to play our two pianos. Alas, they hadn't yet been tuned to identical pitch, so there was an undeniable element of discord in our otherwise harmonious and exciting performance. The minutes slipped by, and an hour or so later we awakened with a start to the day's tight programme. Reluctantly we closed the lids and rushed guiltily back to our respective tasks, in real panic now, stepping up the speed of every gesture in a desperate attempt to overtake the clock. We sighed for automation!

In next to no time *everything* began to happen. Our relatives arrived, having picked up Fergus in London and piloted him safely to port.

The air became thick with ecstatic comments on our " *lovely* vicarage," our " *magnificent* aspects " and our " rare good fortune " to be starting married life in such superlative surroundings.

The two coaches drew up and out poured a stream of smiling friends, whose generous loyalty had brought them all this way in support of their former curate.

An inconspicuous and slightly battered car turned in at our gate. Out stepped the bishop, and John hurried forward to relieve him of the case with his robes and pastoral staff. They, in earnest conversation, disappeared into the study with a tray of sandwiches and coffee, and I saw them no more until in slow solemnity they processed up the aisle, led by the crucifer, the robed choir (still red-faced and rather breathless from recent exertions on the cricket field), the archdeacon, a handful of neighbouring clergy, and our two wandless wardens. (Why they were so obdurate on this little matter of wands we never fathomed.)

I had never seen John look so white, serious and resolute.

* * * * *

In the fairly packed church our supporting parishioners from London provided a solid wedge.

I, not having been told where I was expected to sit and seeing no one eager to usher me into a reserved place, led the family party nervously to a pew half-way down the church, hoping that my identity might remain undisclosed for as long as possible.

I needn't have worried. Suspicion and attention were splendidly diverted!

Among our visiting "fans" was a middle-aged lady whose sonorous voice and pronounced eccentricities in dress singled her out in any company as someone of more than usual importance and intriguing personality. In build and features she closely resembled Queen Victoria.

Need I add that she had long entertained a secret admiration for my husband? To my mind she had displayed remarkable magnanimity and dignity when John's engagement to me was announced, and now her attendance at his induction could only be interpreted as eloquent testimony to a wholly generous and forgiving nature.

Her eccentricity in dress ran to wild excesses of beautiful lace: it ornamented all her gowns, here, there and everywhere; it hung in festoons, dripped in cascades, and sometimes whirled around in flounces and frills. It even developed at times into boleros, shawls and floating panels. But for this very special occasion—and doubtless in honour of my husband—she had draped herself bewitchingly from head to foot in yards of exquisite needlerun cream net, surmounted by a mantilla-like headdress which fell in delicate folds over her shoulders. By any standards it was a fabulous creation; and, to offset her drapes, there were discreet touches of *diamanté*.

As the natural spearhead of the visiting contingent, she led the way with an air of regal confidence up the aisle to the pew nearest the pulpit.

Inevitably she became (and remained!) the cynosure of all eyes. To the unsophisticated villagers she must have been simply terrific.

It was very unfortunate that they made the mistake—the excusable and possibly *obvious* mistake?—of thinking that this was the new bride, the new vicarage lady, and *ipso facto* the leader designate of their Mothers' Union branch.

Of course, I was not to know of this sensational misunderstanding until afterwards in the adjoining hall, when the new vicar and his wife were required to take their places on the platform and the secretary of the P.C.C. advanced gallantly towards the lady in lace to escort her thither. " Will you please come up now, Mrs. Green, and take the seat next to your husband?"

Without flinching or betraying a trace of emotion she had pointed across to me: " Over there, in the fawn coat and straw hat "; and I, in relatively drab and disappointing contrast, was thereupon dragged from obscurity and piloted towards the platform—reluctantly enough, for innate shyness makes limelight anathema to me.

* * * * *

The distracting spectacle of the lady of the lace had not, I am thankful to say, seriously diverted my thoughts from the deep significance of the service of institution and induction.

It was from first to last a tremendously moving experience, with moments of rare spiritual ecstasy—as if here, for me as well as for John, was an occasion of self-dedication; and there was no mistaking *his* air of unreserved surrender to the cause to which he had felt called. We dared to believe that ours was a pre-ordained marriage partnership, and that the care of this parish was to be, as far as is humanly possible, a shared responsibility between us.

Coming out of church, the last three lines of the closing hymn echoed reassuringly in my ears:

" *Ponder anew*
What the Almighty can do
If to the end He befriend thee."

So armed and sustained we could surely cope.

* * * * *

Now in the hall, with the welcoming speeches over—including, of course, a few homely words from the bishop—John and I circulated among the throng, trying not to knock too many elbows and upset cups of scalding tea in unsuspecting laps. Altogether we managed to have a word or two with nearly everybody; we sensed a friendly warmth, although in most cases it was very shyly and haltingly articulated—if at all. Everyone seemed to be sheltering under an assumed cloak of reserve, and conversation proceeded mostly by fitful, stilted monosyllables, but we plugged away, for these were to be our new friends and neighbours and we looked forward to getting to know them and breaking down that reserve. As foreigners we did not expect to be *accepted* under twelve years; but it was decidedly heartening to be cordially *received* on sight. Surely a good omen this.

C

Their liberal hospitality must have greatly impressed the London visitors, semi-starved on rationing, some of whom spoke years later of the wonderful refreshments at John's induction! I was soon to discover that the local farmers' wives enjoyed an unrivalled reputation on the kitchen front. Their skill was legendary, and the provision of prodigious quantities of professional-looking cakes and pastries, scones, pies and savouries—all bearing the stamp of glossy-magazine perfection—was an assured feature of every social function in the parish, be it bazaar, garden fête, whist drive, jumble sale or Christmas party. I was also to discover, however, that what was less assured at some of these events was an adequate attendance to warrant their fabulous generosity; usually piles of delectable cakes and confectionery, surplus to requirements, would finally have to be auctioned or sold for a song. Here was an opportunity *par excellence* to replenish the family cake tins to capacity—and who doesn't love a bargain?—but, alas, it was clearly at the expense of these large-hearted women. They were wizards. How did they do it? Admittedly food-rationing had a very different connotation for them (thanks largely to sundry occupational concessions), but their baking was sheer wizardry nevertheless.

*   *   *   *   *

Perhaps it was not surprising that the following day had a touch of anti-climax about it. The clamour and excitement of the official welcome had died down and we faced our first day in full harness. It did not pass entirely without incident! It was, in fact, the only occasion when my husband prayed publicly for me in church—at evensong. To this day he vows that he did nothing of the sort; nothing, he protests, was farther from his intention; why flatter myself with such a silly notion? Surely the new appointment wasn't going to my head? John's shocked disclaimer was all very well, but let the facts speak for themselves.

Sunday morning had started with a further minor domestic crisis, for returning from the early celebration with a sharpened appetite and deep thirst it was shattering to find that we were without electricity. What we imagined to be a general cut turned out to be another fuse. To our shame and mortification we still hadn't a clue how to fix it. With the brand-new electric kettle temporarily unusable we must fall back on the old tin one, and this meant that the cook-and-heat stove *must* be coaxed into action. I piled on the kindling and anthracite, only to be rewarded with a vulgar belch of smoke, followed by clouds of increasing density. Soon the scullery was as impenetrable as Piccadilly Circus in a good old pea-souper; the features of John and Fergus became ghostly and then were obliterated; my eyes smarted painfully and streamed like miniature waterfalls. I pulled it all to pieces and started afresh, reversing all available knobs. It didn't make any difference, except that the fog thickened.

Then Fergus, licking his parched lips thirstily, offered his services. Together we poked, pleaded, coerced and threatened. Nothing happened, except that we soon looked like a couple of chimney sweeps and the smoke was now swirling in choking clouds *everywhere*.

We broke our fast with bread and butter and marmalade—and cold water! Then I launched a renewed attack on the recalcitrant cook-and-heat. It was playfully named, by the way, the " Wonder-matic," which, to say the least, seemed a gross misnomer; as a joke it literally misfired. True, the P.O.G's housekeeper had extolled the virtues of the " Wondermatic " in terms of reckless extrava-gance: " You'll find the stove's a perfect *pet*; it bakes *everything* to perfection, and you'll have loads—simply *loads*—of hot water day and night; it's a little *gem*; it needs no *coaxing*; just stoke up well, see that the dampers are right, and turn that knob to ' oven '; you'll be *delighted* with it! "

What more glowing testimonial than that?

An hour later I was still kneeling, almost prayerfully, in front of it, imploring it to do *something* for goodness sake. It did, and caught me unprepared with a sudden terrific roar as the thing got exuberantly under way, and I assumed that the chimney was on fire and the vicarage about to be gutted. Dante's Inferno wasn't in it! Very quickly, however, the conflagration settled down to a steady glow and all seemed set fair for a roast dinner *at last*. Before the brute had time to change its mind, I rushed to get the joint from the larder and fill the saucepans for the vegetables. The whole job lot, I calculated, would more or less cook itself while we were at matins.

Returning at mid-day—starved—there was no appetizing aroma of roast beef to greet us; in fact, no aroma of anything—only a melancholy pile of dead embers and a stone-cold oven. So for

Dante's Inferno wasn't in it !

dinner—as for breakfast—we had bread and butter, but supplemented by as many strawberries as we could wish for.

After that Fergus and I set to work in deadly earnest on the " perfect pet," the " little gem " that so stubbornly defied us. " Come on," I rallied him, " don't let it master us; we'll get this fire going or perish in the attempt."

By teatime we were able to boil a kettle on it, and that first cup of hot tea was like elixir to a dying man.

Now for that ill-fated joint of beef! Let's eat in style, after evensong! So into the oven it went for the second time and off we three trooped to church.

It was after the third collect that John offered that memorable prayer for me, by tacking on to the customary intercessions for the royal family and for the sick and aged in the parish an unmistakably fervent plea for the *inefficient*, the *unsuccessful*, and *those who try to help them*!

In case Fergus had missed this handsome tribute to himself as my assistant stoker I nudged him. He was shaking uncontrollably, so I opened my eyes and peeped. His face was purple, presumably with the tremendous effort of stifling his mirth. We found ourselves sniggering guiltily instead of paying reverent heed to our devotions; and, with thoughts straying permissively over the whole sequence of the day's happenings, I'm afraid that I, for one, missed the entire relevance of poor John's sermon.

But no prayer could have been more convincingly answered, or more swiftly, for when we got indoors an aroma like a Dickensian Christmas greeted us. Everything was going merrily. By eight-thirty we were tucking in ravenously to slightly dehydrated roast beef, new potatoes, peas, and, as a bonus award for patience and perseverance, Yorkshire pudding; and, of course, strawberries to follow.

I begged John never again to make a public example of me. He, after that indignant disclaimer, lapsed into thoughtful silence, broken later by the profound observation " It only goes to show that Providence is *always* working "—with an affirmative nod of his head.

* * * * *

On the practical level, the outcome of this episode was John's gift to me of a standard model electric cooker, which was to prove our domestic salvation, and the installation of an immersion heater, which enabled us to resume the normal hygienic practices, such as bathing in more than a saucepan of water and washing the smalls at home instead of running up crippling laundry bills. A washing machine, at that juncture, was an undreamt-of luxury, and the existing vicarage copper was a museum piece of unspecified vintage which, judging by its frightening rash of rust marks, had outlived its usefulness by at least a couple of decades. It was a colossal thing —a real monstrosity. It stood submissively by the capricious " Wondermatic," and was as ironically misnamed. The copper was naïvely called the " Wizard." It was designed to be hand-filled and baled out, but actually the baling out didn't count, as it leaked persistently of its own accord. On the one and only occasion when I tried to use it the scullery floor was completely awash before I realized what was happening, and, of course, my wellington boots hadn't yet been unpacked. But for all practical purposes even the leak was of small consequence, for when I had gone to light the furnace underneath the " Wizard " had misbehaved in much the same way as the " Wondermatic "—only without ever going to the lengths of suddenly roaring up like mad and then settling down to a humdrum combustion. The " Wizard " declined sullenly to give *any* spectacular performance beyond the smoke-belching, at which it excelled with the minimum of encouragement.

CHAPTER 3

Full cycle

THE thing about vicarage life that for a long while greatly puzzled and eluded me was why the seasons flashed by with such bewitching haste. And not only the seasons, I realized later, but also the *years*. Life for me had never moved at anything like such a wildly relentless tempo. Then eventually it dawned on me, and the explanation seemed so simple and obvious: we were now living in the almost hypnotic atmosphere of the crowded, unbroken sequence of events that constitutes the parochial—and the Church—calendar.

Here we were caught up in an inexorable round of festivals and feasts, pageants and plays, parties and outings, rallies, displays, conferences—moving inevitably and inescapably towards the annual church fête in our garden; and all these events were dominated, of course, by the major religious observances of Advent, Christmas, Lent, Easter, Ascension, Whitsun and harvest thanksgiving. We found ourselves gyrating helplessly on this traditional roundabout, driven by a mysterious hidden force—ceaseless, compulsive and at times almost overwhelming. In a sense, time almost ceased to exist as we were carried around like little robots on a rotating table. It was useless, in moments of panic, to cry " Stop the calendar; I want to get off! "; it never stopped, never even slowed down. In fact, routine involvement in so much advance planning actually created the impression that we were living six months ahead of schedule.

Some events had a way of overlapping. No sooner were the Christmas decorations taken down and the crib packed carefully away for next year than we were engulfed in the welter of parish parties—so numerous that they, in their turn, ran right into the Lenten course. Then close on the heels of Easter and Whitsun came

39

the veritable epidemic of summer outings, geared to an established local pattern: Sunday school, Women's Institute, Mothers' Union, choristers and bellringers, British Legion, day school, all leading up to the two major events: the annual garden show and—most dreaded of all from our point of view—the church fête, invariably on the last Saturday in July, *always* in the vicarage garden. And this, we were fully convinced, recurred with greater frequency than any other annual event!

*   *   *   *   *

Now the art of running a fête, as everyone knows (even John and I know it *now*, though in our raw apprentice days at Upper Bellpull we paid dearly for being naïvely ignorant!), is to pin-point all the capable people to whom the work can be safely delegated, and then just to parcel out the jobs in suitable lots. The basic blueprint is familiar enough to every fête organizer:

Fête secretary .... Mrs. X
Fête treasurer .... Mr. Y
Social organizers .... Mr. and Mrs. Z
General purposes committee .... A, B, C, and D
Stallholders .... Mesdames F, G, H, I and J
Refreshments .... Mothers' Union
Produce .... Young Farmers' Club
Sports .... Current schoolmaster
Sideshows .... Anybody left over after the above assignments

Follow the accepted pattern and then the success of the thing is more or less a foregone conclusion. Even the most inexperienced incumbent, by adopting the master plan, can scarcely go wrong—provided, of course, that he parcels it all out in such a way that the selected victims are never allowed to suspect a plot; rather, they must be encouraged to believe that their particular appointments are a special award for tested ability and competence—even virtue—if not actually for personal charm and good looks.

With all this properly attended to they all rush wildly to action stations and become busily involved. Meanwhile, the incumbent and his wife have only to keep the date free from other engagements, make a point of " looking in " affably during the afternoon, patronize each stall with strict impartiality, flowerily compliment the workers on their superlative efforts, drink endless cups of tea, indulge in a brief moment of small talk with as many people as possible, and, in due course, *she* presents the prizes to the successful competitors and *he*, in a telling but suspiciously stereotyped piece of oratory, thanks everyone for having worked like beavers to achieve this *wonderful* result, which will allow the treasurer and finance committee to breathe freely again for another twelve months. " It's been a *magnificent* corporate effort . . . "; a solemn little pause, then " Shall we sing the Doxology? "

(The important thing to remember is *never* to win the treasure hunt prize himself; it looks too much like a " fix "; and it's safer not even to enter for the pig bowling, as rivalry in this field can be intense, and most villages have their acknowledged bowling champs, who don't take kindly to the threat of relegation.)

With these pleasant little duties fulfilled, both the incumbent and his wife disappear discreetly from the untidy scene, making way for the labour force to move in unimpeded and get down to the formidable task of removing all trace of the fairground atmosphere.

Encouraged by the vicar's grateful tribute, the clearers-up brace themselves to begin dismantling stalls and sideshows and sweep up lolly sticks, ice-cream tubs, sweet wrappers, empty cigarette packets, smashed coconut shells, and all the other littering evidence of the recent revels. Incidentally, John and I never ceased to marvel at the good will and energy with which they attacked this final chore. In less than no time the vicarage garden would be restored again to reasonable order and all the portable equipment stowed safely away for the next occasion.

To revert, however, to fête organization, at Upper Bellpull procedure by way of the conventional master plan was undreamt of; they favoured their own formula of administration, and seemed most reluctant to abandon it.

Towards the end of April or early May there would be a P.C.C. meeting, when the item on the agenda reserved for " Any other business " would invariably inspire an innocent " Oh, we haven't decided about the fête yet, have we? " It was a purely formal cue and one that was never missed; the quick reaction was almost electrifying. There and then, with the minimum of fuss and by a unanimous vote, the issue would be settled: " . . . last Saturday in July in the vicarage garden; at 2.30 p.m. *You'll* get on with that,

then, sir ? "—directed straight at John—and, as if to set the seal of
certain success upon the whole project, it would be followed by the
magnanimous reassurance " And *we'll* see that there isn't an away
match that day."

There were two distinct schools of thought on this particular
point: John and myself v. the rest. The popular local argument was
that a *home* match would provide such an irresistible attraction
that it was bound to draw multitudes of spectators from far and
wide, who might be civil enough to patronize our fête during
the cricket interval. Conversely, John and I could only see a cricket
fixture—either home or away—on the day of the fête as a rival
enterprise, calculated to leave us miserably short of helpers to man
the sideshows and stalls, and much more likely to lure away our
local regulars than to draw in itinerant casuals from among the
cricket " fans " who owed no allegiance whatever to our parish.

But to the end of our days at Upper Bellpull these were to remain
two hopelessly irreconcilable points of view: the cricket tradition
remained inviolate, while John and I were obliged to press-gang
members of our family—who had come ostensibly to support the
effort and enjoy a country revel—into supervising the coconut
shies, the donkey rides and clay-pigeon shooting, regulating the
queue for the fortune teller, and so on. As a novelty, they pretended
to like it.

It was because John was thus invested—albeit unsuspectingly
in our early days—with the unenviable rôle of major-domo of the
fête that we found ourselves living six months ahead of time. When
other people were pleasantly engrossed in the seasonal occupations
of mid-winter—plum puddings, presents, parties, postman's knock,
pantomimes, and so forth—we would be heavily preoccupied with
the fiddling details upon which the success of our summer fête
depended—band, bunting, balloons, barbecue, baby show, bran
tub, and the rest. We would be perpetually racking our brains for
those elusive *new* ideas to make this year's fête something *different*;
always on the look-out for original features that would attract a
" good press." And the perennial bugbear was *entertainment*.

After the usual sequence of sleepless nights and abortive inquiries
we always fell back with tired resignation on last year's stereotyped programme, which, incidentally, was also the year before's
—and, in fact, had never been known to vary materially throughout
all the years of fête history.

Experience taught us eventually, however, that the occasion always provided its own highlight—something least expected and totally unrehearsed. Once it was the electricity failure half an hour before teas were due to be served. Upper Bellpull had no gas supply, so there was a wild scramble in all directions for oil stoves and paraffin cans; meanwhile, as a second line of defence, the Scouts and Cubs were bundled off to the little village store to buy up all the available bottles of pop.

No sooner were the paraffin stoves beginning to warm up and the pop to be uncorked than the power was restored and chaos was complete.

Once it was a hurricane that intruded upon the peaceful village scene, with all the stealth, strength and speed of a homicidal maniac, and, in a matter of seconds, reduced it all to a shambles of over-turned seats, collapsed stalls, ruined produce, torn tarpaulin, and general devastation. For a while, as the screeching wind lashed itself up into a climax, everything appeared to be airborne, floating here and there at the mercy of every frolicsome gust; then it sub-sided with dramatic suddenness as the heavens opened and released a deluge of torrential rain, which quickly threatened to inundate the garden and sent everyone rushing to take cover. In the blind scamper for shelter, people were colliding head-on and tripping over guy ropes, and the vicarage porch became a solid jam; soon the whole of the ground floor gave the impression of a communal vapour bath as more and still more drenched and steaming parishioners came crowding in for protection from the humid desolation outside.

Mercifully, it wasn't far short of closing time when this catas-trophe happened, so there wasn't very much left on the stalls and what there was had already been reduced to give-away prices. On that occasion it was not only sweet-wrappers, lolly sticks and such-like litter that had to be collected up afterwards; flags and bunting had to be disentangled from the hawthorn hedges, stall draperies retrieved from the gooseberry bushes, a couple of smashed kiosks pieced together again, and a whole mad miscellany of remaining stock rescued from the waterlogged lawns.

The only consoling aspect of the disaster, as far as John and I could estimate, was the sudden suspension of the cricket match and the frenzied stampede of both players and spectators into the refreshment hall, where the eleventh-hour demand for sustenance became so terrific that every crumb was sold at full price and the tea takings beat all previous records. No home-made cakes going for a song that day!

But the unavoidable cancellation of the rest of the programme put paid to the widely advertised barbecue, and we were left with a hefty consignment of chickens, pounds of sausages and a trayful of mutton chops—all surplus to requirements.

The rummage stall, which I regarded secretly as an odd and incongruous feature to include in a garden fête, never failed to produce an amusing incident or two. I had initially questioned the suitability of displaying mountains of old cast-offs at so elegant an event as a garden party, but it was pointed out that, clothes rationing having reduced every woman's wardrobe to the irreducible minimum, bargain-hunters from miles around—if not from neighbouring counties—would assuredly move in, like an army of locusts or the hosts of Midian, in search of wearable garments, no matter how old and unfashionable provided they would just hold together for a few months longer; there was an insatiable hunger for a change of apparel; they were willing to pay the earth; the rummage takings invariably beat all the rest put together! To meet the situation, and deal with sporadic warfare between the contending invaders, it was necessary to have reserve forces of counter assistants—commando-trained. It was a revelation to me.

How was it, I wondered, that great piles of rummage were always sent in, in the face of an acute clothes shortage? After a good deal of close observation I realized that a well-organized system of regular exchange had been set in motion and continued to operate with mounting success—on the principle of a lending library, only instead of books garments circulated smoothly and conveniently until they reached a state of disreputable shabbiness and had to be withdrawn from circulation. The rules were simplicity itself; when Mrs. A reached the point of revulsion for her third-year spring costume it would enter quietly into circulation at the next rummage sale, and be snatched up smartly by Mrs. B, who saw it as something refreshingly new and captivating; and it was quite on the cards that Mrs. A would go home happy and satisfied with Mrs. B's discarded outfit. To the purchaser it was always something *new*, and as there were never enough coupons for *really* new rigouts the exchange system worked admirably. I joined in the racket with a good heart and zest; but I had to be careful, naturally, to choose the occasions when it would be discreetly safe to wear my secondhand bargains. To make assurance doubly sure, I always disguised the basic style by the cunning addition of fresh trimming. I came to feel that it was an implied compliment when I spotted *my* cast-offs being paraded in the village by new owners.

Of course, it was a system that, like every other scheme in which the human element plays a predominant part, had its inherent weaknesses. To quote a handy illustration, there was the blue dressing gown affair.

This bewitching creation, in a violent peacock blue woollen material adorned with massive embroidered motifs in shades of red and puce, had been sent to me as a personal gift—in a generous assortment of other cast-offs. Most of the items were acceptable enough, but this thing had little to commend it; basically it was *not* my colour anyway, and the thought of relaxing with sprays of vivid chrysanthemums accentuating my undulations, was more likely, I felt, to raise than to reduce my blood pressure. John's withering appraisal: " God bless my soul, has rationing brought you to this? " clinched it. Also a few incipient moth holes had not escaped my notice, so it was to be the next rummage sale for the blue woollen dressing gown.

This prize was marked (scandalously, I thought) " Ten shillings; special bargain; all wool " !

At the end of the day, when human resistance and vitality had reached zero, my sister tapped on our bedroom door; there she stood, as you will surely have guessed, with the peacock blue dressing gown spread over her arm and a triumphant smile spread across her face. " Here, dear," she burbled, " this is just a little birthday present in advance; I wasn't going to let *that* go; all wool, my dear —if ever there was a bargain; just your size, I feel sure; and so cosy! " The speech ended, I was formally presented with the inescapable dressing gown. I shuddered as I beheld afresh that awful, flamboyant embroidery, plastered on like lumps of filigree liver— in shades for which I have a congenital loathing. Ugh!

I made the idiotically obvious remark: " You got that from the rummage stall, didn't you? "

" Yes, dear; and only ten shillings! How did you know? "

" *I* gave it, because when it was given to me I considered it unbearably revolting."

The incident had reminded me of a rather similar experience suffered by the wife of one of John's colleagues. She, as a lady of

Repository of all the parochial cast-offs.

very substantial means and impeccable taste, had furnished their large rectory exquisitely and extravagantly, with particular emphasis on curtains. She had invested in rich ruby red silk damask for the immense bay and french windows in the lounge. Having spent so recklessly she felt that they ought to last till the end of her days, but after the tenth year their fascination began to wear thin. Two years later she felt that it was psychologically bad not to have a change; she rather regretted having spent so extravagantly in the first place. The following year they were taken down and sold at a silly price to a local antique dealer, who displayed them to great effect. Her replacements were in a less exclusive range altogether, but the ghost of the ruby silk damask continued to haunt her as friend after friend told her excitedly of the simply *magnificent* curtains in Foxley's window: " *You* would *love* them; *do* go and have a look; it's the most *sumptuous* material; they'd look superb in *your* lounge," quite forgetting (or perhaps never realizing?) that that was where they had in fact hung for the past decade and a half! Their enthusiastic remarks began to make an impression; next she found herself strolling past Foxley's, glancing surreptitiously at the familiar ruby silk damask. Of course, she eventually succumbed and bought them back at a price that paid Foxley handsomely for the privilege of being in business.

But to revert to the fête, my serious grouse about the rummage racket concerned its method of assembly, sorting, pricing, and temporary storage until the day of disposal. Here again there was an established precedent at Upper Bellpull which from time immemorial had never deviated by one iota; and who was I—serving my novitiate, so to speak—to suggest radical changes?

The acknowledged supervisor of rummage knew her job and had done it with glowing success for years past; but it was not *her* house that had to accommodate the avalanche of stuff till the appointed day. This honour, like so many others, was reserved for the vicarage —and here was the rub.

For days—nay, for weeks—before the great event mysterious consignments would find their way to the vicarage, deposited stealthily on the doorstep or tucked under cover in the outer porch. This went on with gathering momentum until, as the day drew near, we could never get in or out of our home without first removing barricades of old clothes—some just dumped loose and unwrapped, some stuffed in higgledy-piggledy bundles in outsize cartons or in badly wrapped brown-paper parcels with odd areas unblushingly revealed. There would be the occasional donor who took pride in the condition and general appearance of her contribution, and *her* garments would be handed in personally, neatly pressed and on hangers, with repeated apologies for a missing button. A few hyper-cautious ones, fearful of leaving anything on an unguarded doorstep, would poke a scribbled note through the letter-box: " Look in the potting shed " or " Parcel in coal bunker," and then, like participants in an exciting treasure hunt, John and I would rush out there, expecting to find something of vastly more than average value, only to discover a disillusioning pair of old gum-boots, or maybe a box of outmoded nightshirts (*circa* 1850), a feather boa and a jet-trimmed toque.

Once we came home from market to find a gigantic imitation toadstool in the porch—like one of those old-fashioned rotating piano stools, only more acutely domed and bearing a rash of leopard spots in white paint. Beside it, and obviously a part of the same consignment, were a couple of enormous cardboard boxes bulging with obsolete Brownie outfits, Brown Owl's full kit, and a massive assortment of pixie " props." The Brownies had recently been disbanded, and the vicarage was, by established custom, assumed to be the natural shoot for all accumulated clobber.

All these piles of jumble, once cleared from the doorstep, had to be parked somewhere—*somehow*—until the day before the fête, when the official stallholder and her task force would descend on us, and then the whole job lot had to be transferred from its temporary storage in the butler's pantry to the kitchen for sorting and pricing. Admittedly, it needed a really spacious apartment for this exercise, but I could without difficulty have thought of many better uses for our domestic H.Q. than as repository for all the parochial cast-offs—some still bearing the marks of quite prolonged and intimate human contact! However, according to precedent, there they had to remain until business began the next day—piled high on the table and the tea trolley; draped over every available chair, the clothes horse and the airing rack; even carpeting the floor to a depth of several inches, leaving John and me only the already crowded dresser at which to have stand-up meals until the whole affair was over, our kitchen derequisitioned and the normal amenities of the domestic quarters restored exclusively to us. The obvious—and only—advantage of this annexation of the home front was when the odd *couturier* model, still in reasonable condition, found its way unaccountably into the mixed bag; *I* had the benefit of a preview, and if the vital statistics were right—well, the " first come, first served " principle seemed fair enough.

It was through this arbitrary method of handling rummage that one year John lost his best black shoes. They had been sent to the local cobbler for repair, and when they were ready the cobbler's small urchin had been told to take them down to the vicarage. His —the small urchin's—habit was to tear up the front drive, make a full-scale assault on the door bell with the frenzied insistence of a hunted refugee seeking asylum, and then dump the shoes on the step and bolt off home. By the time we had raced to answer the bell not a soul would be in sight, but there, to dispel the possible illusion of having dreamt it all or that the house was haunted, we would find our mended shoes. Evidently on this occasion the child had deposited them there when we were out, then mounting consignments of rummage must have been piled up and up over John's shoes. When we returned the usual debarricading had to be attended to, and undoubtedly John's personal property was inadvertently swept up in the armfuls of other stuff and shot into the butler's pantry with the conglomeration already there, with never a thought of examining it for unintended personal items. It was much later on, when the usual post-mortem on the fête was being held, that the rummage supervisor referred to the high quality of the things sent in this year . . . " I remember there was a really *good* pair of black shoes—freshly mended; they looked as if they had come straight from the cobblers! "

John managed not to swoon in the presence of the P.C.C. He just accepted the loss with a philosophic " So that's where they went! "

In theory only is a garden fête a *garden* fête. In practice it is a full-scale invasion of all invadable territory—both indoors and out—and a cool commandeering of all borrowable chattels—both spare and in current usage—likely to be of assistance in the mounting of a successful show. Put another way, it is a sort of gigantic public take-over (without bid) of the entire parsonage property, together with its fixtures and fittings, equipage and appurtenances, occupants and staff. Every square inch of land and of floor space is requisitioned for the duration; in short, the temporary suspension of the parson's freehold is assumed without question.

D

This explains why the vicarage folk seldom become noticeably infected with fête fever.

John's study naturally became operational H.Q.—the nerve centre of bustling activity—and here, between periodic tours of inspection outside, he sat at the receipt of customs, and was an easy target for all the " slings and arrows of outrageous fortune." He was relentlessly besieged from first to last by battalions of harassed, clamant officials: " Have you any more small change? They've run out of silver on produce "; " Where's the reserve stock of coconuts hidden? We're down to the last six "; " Has anyone remembered to go to the station to collect the baby show judge? " " D'you think we ought to begin marking down? Business is a bit stagnant "; " Whatever shall we do? *Blue* raffle tickets are being sold for both the iced cake and the basket of fruit "; " Can you take over the ' mike ' yourself, Vicar, while the man's at tea? "; " For heaven's sake, where do you keep safety pins? The ballerina's tights are loose—we must do *something* "; and " Quick, Vicar, ring for an ambulance; somebody's tripped over a tent-peg— caught her head on the rockery—bleeding like mad! "

At times the burden of administration became overwhelming and John would tear his hair and emit a few groans.

The drawing room was always entirely monopolized by the man with the relayed music and sound effects. He arrived soon after breakfast, shifted all the furniture, opened windows on to the lawn and proceeded to conjure with mile after mile of flex, planted loud-speakers up in the trees, and saw that a comfortable armchair was left close to his mike. One point on which John and I remained adamant was in refusing to allow our pianos to be moved into the garden, as everyone seemed to expect.

The dining room served a dual purpose: first as store room, accommodating all the fancy stock-in-trade waiting to be displayed on the stalls; then as extra dressing room for the dancers in their quick-change numbers, when they hadn't time to rush upstairs to strip.

The entire first floor—embracing four large bedrooms and the usual offices!—was assigned to the dancers, their dressers encouraging mammas and supporting friends. They would distri-bute themselves comfortably over the whole area and monopolize the bathroom and toilet as by right. So we were not only bereft of peace but also stripped of privacy, and yet, somehow, the shock of invasion soon wore off and we became resigned to temporary dispossession.

Experience taught me the wisdom of timing the spring clean for the week after the fête, so that in one stupendous effort all the residue of make-up—powder, cotton-wool, sequins, hair-grips, safety-pins, ribbons, mislaid combs, etc.—that littered the whole house could be removed at one fell swoop.

Entertainments took place on the strip of specially trimmed lawn by the drawing room window. Here was the perfect setting for nymph-like ballet scenes; it was singularly inappropriate for strenuous hornpipes, reels and " taps."

The cats always made an early and dim assessment of the entire situation and took themselves off immediately after breakfast to the bottom of the orchard, where they remained out of harm's way until nightfall.

John's chief concern and the cause of his biggest headache was *entertainment*. Fête-goers expect to be amused; they have usually spent most of their money within the first hour, yet they tend to linger in the hope of eleventh-hour bargains, and in any event are loath to leave before the raffles have been drawn. *Good* entertainment involves long-distance planning; so soon after Christmas John would take his first soundings, writing round to all the known schools of dancing within a twenty-mile radius hoping to enlist the services of a full ballet class or, failing that, of at least half a dozen star pupils. There was a spot of low cunning behind this dodge: if you got the whole ballet school to come they usually had hosts of friends and relations in tow and their presence would add substantially to the volume of trade on the stalls!

The simple secret of success was to get in first, for we soon discovered that organizers of *all* the outdoor functions in the neighbouring areas had a perverse habit of choosing the same day for their big event, and *all* were obsessed with the same idea about entertainment. I always felt that it reflected singularly poor liaison work between the various organizations. Surely a joint master plan to stagger the fêtes, bazaars, flower shows, etc., would have removed this perennial nettle.

However, John usually got off to a good, early start with his bookings. If, despite this, he was a bit too late to bespeak a likely ballet school he would switch his attention immediately to morris dancers, Scottish dancers, Territorial or Salvation Army bands, variety concert parties, P.T. teams, women's youth and beauty groups, a ventriloquist or a Punch and Judy show—in roughly that order. There was usually something diverting for our patrons.

As I have said, every fête produces its own highlights, and one year the *contretemps* was a classic affair. John's wily and nearly completed negotiations for a troupe of child dancers broke down abruptly, leaving us at the last moment without any prospect of entertainment.

A Sunday school teacher heroically undertook to put on a one-act play—obviously almost unrehearsed—by the little boys from the mission Sunday school.

Having failed, at such short notice, to find a script with an all-male cast, she chose—rather surprisingly—something called " The Cowboy's Wedding," which required two female impersonations. It was a piece of spectacular melodrama offering unlimited scope for sham violence and shooting. Little heed was paid to the gabbled dialogue in untranslatable Americanese.

The producer, by a seeming miracle, managed to assemble her cast in good time and get them into their cowboy costumes, and this, from my own somewhat limited experience of rounding up juvenile actors, was in itself a major achievement. The dressing room, I had found, often became the storm-centre of wild scuffles and sporadic warfare among the players—sometimes with gory casualties that left the company impossibly depleted.

The dressing room on this occasion was a cramped corner behind the laurel bushes. Crouching cautiously out of sight, she got the excited performers as ready as they were ever likely to be. They were formally announced over the " mike," and then briskly took the stage—or, more accurately, that reserved strip of lawn by the drawing room window. The audience settled comfortably, in a state of relaxed expectancy.

For raw young actors they displayed superb *sang-froid*; not a trace of stage fright. They seemed, indeed, in their element as trigger-happy gunmen, taking reckless aim with consistently deadly results. After all, playing at cowboys was second nature to these lads.

However, an important character in this stirring drama was a coal-black mammy, whose function was to prepare and serve the wedding feast. The part was assigned, quite unaccountably, to an undersized shrimp of a child, about ten or eleven, streamlined and bespectacled. Heaven only knows why the most diminutive boy in the village was awarded this larger-than-life rôle . . . though, in view of what transpired, it could have been because all others had modestly declined! Anyway, what this little midget lacked in natural proportions was handsomely—nay, extravagantly—made up for by ingenious upholstery. There was a perceptible gasp of surprise as we beheld him . . . a convincing dark-skinned dame in full bustling skirt and whiter-than-white cooking apron, a wonderfully contrived wig of black darning wool, brass curtain rings dangling from his ears, and his normally pale face shining like polished ebony under its veneer of stove-black. Altogether it was a startling achievement. His matronly bosom—inevitably the focal point of the laborious transformation—was a *tour de force*. With such authentic feminine contours the impersonation Oscar seemed unchallengeably his!

The little chap's eyes shone with dedicated zeal as he threw himself vigorously into his part—alas, all too vigorously as it turned out, for his strenuous exertions precipitated what was at first a slight, almost imperceptible, dislodgement of his ponderous bosom; then it became obvious to everyone that his undisciplined bust had slipped its moorings and was getting rapidly out of control in its descent.

At first he was happily unaware of impending disaster; then a niggling, suspicious discomfort provoked some furtive fidgeting and a few surreptitious hoists. The upholstery gathered momentum, and in less than no time the black mammy appeared in an advanced stage of pregnancy. There was no sign of panic; just a moment of unbearable suspense. Mercifully, his Scout's belt, concealed beneath his gingham, staved off complete catastrophe; even so, we could almost *feel* the heat of his blushes under the stove-black. To his credit he finished the part with superb courage and both hands firmly clutching the rebellious bosom—now hovering in the lower abdominal region.

Of course he was a riot. The rest of the cast—even the " bride " —suffered total eclipse. The audience was convulsed; the standing ovation deafening. The subsequent local write-up put our village prominently and permanently on the dramatic map. After that episode John and I never really worried unduly about entertainment; we felt that we could always tap that unpredictable source

His bust had slipped its moorings.

of *local* talent and be pretty sure of something sensational gushing forth.

                    *   *   *   *   *

It is a foregone conclusion that when any small village community ventures into the illimitable possibilities of amateur dramatics plenty of hilarious mishaps—and not a few near-disasters —are bound to crop up in the course of production; it's all part of the game, and surmounting the unforeseen obstacles is a challenge to ingenuity, resourcefulness and tact. Upper Bellpull was no exception; its most crippling blows included eleventh-hour laryngitis when the lead hadn't an understudy, and a refractory curtain that got stuck halfway and remained obdurate until the caretaker and his wife got to work with a couple of clothes-props. Possibly this was why most of the local excursions into the field of drama were left to the younger element—children from the day and Sunday schools. Whatever the reason, the adults, for the most part, seemed to shun the footlights with a deep, incurable horror. John thought it was due to a paralysing selfconsciousness; but it could, of course, have reflected a streak of innate laziness, which easily convinced them that they simply *couldn't* act—because, in actual fact, they much preferred to sit back and be entertained. In my opinion there was a good deal of latent talent there, which, if only put to the test, would have produced some surprisingly good results.

There had been one notable attempt—actually before our time— to stimulate local interest in play production. A handful of warweary fire-watchers had got together with the idea of infusing a spark of new life in the village, and at the same time ensuring a bit of harmless fun for themselves at rehearsals. The schoolmaster was actor-manager-producer. The allocation of parts had occasioned quite a lot of bad feeling—groundless, of course. The people being awarded dubious rôles—suspicious characters or actual villains— made the mistake of taking it as a personal affront; *nobody* wanted to be the purple villain, or the blousy little minx, or the unctuous Rev. Giblett, or Lord Polstrip, with a propensity for social misdemeanours and shady deals; and they had one and all betrayed tight-lipped resistance at the bare mention of the half-demented champion and admirer of Mr. Giblett—Miss Annabel Tufts, who in the play had to be convincingly odd without being wholly certifiable. " *I'm* not going to let people think I'm nuts " said one after another. The deadlock was broken by a generous offer from the official " prompt," who was loath to see the project die before it was born, so to speak. " Oh well, I don't mind how potty people think I am; I'll do it," she volunteered, " though I've never acted before in my life, so don't expect anything spectacular. I'll just be myself! "—and with this effortless approach she achieved an outstanding performance.

There was no comparable reluctance on the part of the children, whose main attraction to drama lay, of course, in the fun of dressing up. Putting on a juvenile performance, then, was far easier in every way, though never without incident.

I recall the occasion when, at roughly ten days' notice, John wanted a Nativity play for the Sunday school prizegiving. With so little time for preparation we were simply floundering in orgies of improvisation; no production could have been more seriously under-rehearsed, with only a single full-dress assembly on the morning of the event.

Costumes consisted chiefly of bedspreads and curtains, snatched hurriedly from their usual places; some useful effects were contrived with sheets and strips of tinsel; shepherds looked realistic enough in cut-open potato sacks, secured with knotted rope. A good deal of sparkling illusion emerged from our own eleventh-hour efforts—John's and mine—in the manufacture of wings, crowns, haloes and harps from whatever odds and ends of material we could lay hands on in the vicarage.

We laboured at fantastic speed and without a thought of demarcation disputes—from teatime until past midnight—on our makeshift assembly line in the kitchen. As fast as I cut out thin cardboard wings and haloes John dabbed away with gold paint and frost, as if his life depended on it. I raked up a few broken strings of coloured beads, and these applied to the hastily contrived cardboard crowns looked almost as precious as the stones they were supposed to represent

These modest accessories, together with the bedspreads and curtains, seemed likely to ensure a recognizable picture of the traditional Bethlehem scene. For Mary, the Blessed Virgin, we had decided that a swathed sheet surmounted by a Mothers' Union blue veil would meet the needs realistically enough.

It was due to take place on a Saturday. At the morning's rehearsal we were totally unprepared for the sudden chaotic stampede which instantly disrupted everything and, in a split second, cleared the stage of the entire cast—at the sound of one magic word: " *Meet!* " One irresponsible shout, and the whole carefully contrived tableau simply dissolved, and in its place a wildly uninhibited rabble jostled and elbowed for positions at the windows and door of the village hall—mesmerized, it seemed, by the assembling hunt. One minute these unpredictable children were grouped soberly, nay angelically, round the manger, the shepherds at a reverent distance from Mary and the Babe, Joseph beside her, and the three kings and their pages (holding the bedspreads well up off the dusty floorboards!) doing obeisance in the foreground, and the chorus of heralding angels mounted on draped stools—the *perfect* tableau till someone had recklessly yelled " Meet! " Then kings, shepherds, angels and the Holy Family, gathering up robes and bedspreads, clutching haloes and crowns, and heedlessly endangering fragile wings, pushed and shoved like a lawless mob to get the best grandstand view of huntsmen leading the horses from their boxes, hounds racing hither and thither—barking in excited chorus—and the milling crowd of followers, manifestly impatient at a single moment's delay, getting into formation and then moving off at a spirited canter towards the river. It was a spectacle that these country children must have seen dozens of times before, yet it still proved irresistible. It certainly reduced our rehearsal to tatters.

(To digress, my own introduction to the novelty of a hunt meet resulted in a joke against me which I shall never be allowed to live down. In fact, even at our parish farewell gathering on John's retirement the story was publicly recounted as one of the highlights of his reminiscences—to the considerable amusement of everybody except me. I just blushed.

One fine autumn Saturday morning, when I was busy upstairs bed-making, John's genial voice reached me: " Hi, the meat's come," to which I yelled back unconcernedly " Good; pop it in the larder, darling."

His guffaws made the rafters rattle. " In the *larder*? You don't get me, sweetie; it's hounds, huntsmen, gee-gees, and the whole full-dress show. Come *on* . . . and *buck up;* they'll be moving off in a jiffy.")

To return to the interrupted Nativity rehearsal: it took a very long time and repeated threats of final cancellation to round up the cast again, and even so we failed utterly to recapture any semblance of the solemn atmosphere of that original tableau. The brittle thread of concentration had snapped.

The actual performance was a greater success than we had dared to expect, but two incidents are engraved on my memory to this day. One concerned the dressing of the three kings, a duty that fell to my unfortunate lot. The " kings " were primary schoolboys, roughly of an age around nine or ten. They were bubbling over with silly excitement and giggles. In vain I pleaded with them to " stand still, for goodness sake, *if you can* " while I encased them, each in turn, in a sort of winding sheet as a basic garment, overlaid with gaily striped stoles worn cummerbundwise, with the inevitable bedspreads floating majestically from the shoulders and the jewelled cardboard crowns providing an authentic finishing touch. They were to carry gilded dummy chocolate boxes as their offerings. Because of the obvious insecurity of the improvised costumes and the constitutional inability of the wearers to exercise care and caution in their movements—and, of course, to avoid any foreseeable disaster should they tread on each other's bedspreads!—I had painstakingly safety-pinned them right, left and centre until they were as tight as mummies, and no doubt just about as uncomfortable. This miracle, mark you, had to be achieved on the stage itself, as the only tiny dressing room—normally the school canteen kitchen—was choc-a-bloc with the female cast. As I stood back to survey the final effect, word went round " Quick, the curtain's going up "—and at this psychological moment Melchior decided that he needed to be excused and his plight triggered off an epidemic: both Gaspar and Balthasar promptly claimed to be in the same embarrassing predicament.

What was I to do with these securely trussed and well-pinned lads, especially as the hall lacked indoor accommodation for such crises, and their escape could only be effected by a bold descent from the platform, in full view of the audience, into the body of the hall, then toddling down the length of the centre gangway to the outer door, and from there—amid torrential rain and blustery wind!—away through a sea of mud and puddles to the distant lean-to, with bedspreads trailing forlornly in the wet grass?

I had to make a split-second decision. I hope I made the right one. It was *not* the pilgrimage I have just outlined.

The other memorable incident concerned the little blonde fairy who portrayed, very earnestly and coyly, the Blessed Virgin Mary.

Looking back, one can see it as a piece of very bad casting; she was altogether too young and inexperienced for the part. She would have made an enchanting little Christmas-tree figure, in frilled muslin, with tinsel star and wand. Anyway, draped demurely in her ground-length white cotton gown, and looking sweetly sincere beneath her Madonna blue veil, she marched resolutely on to the stage—with Joseph following a shade sheepishly—and planted herself squarely before the footlights, facing the audience; and here she paused purposefully before delivering the grim ultimatum " I can go no farther! " in a totally unemotional, dead-pan voice that evoked an out-of-place titter.

In spite of everything, we felt reasonably satisfied that the essence and beauty of the Christmas story had not failed to touch the hearts of an attentive audience. It was also gratifying to reflect that the children, too, by identifying themselves even in this crudely simple way with the central figures of the Nativity in the Bethlehem stable, had no doubt gained something of lasting value from the experience.

I can imagine that their lusty, uninhibited singing of " We three kings of *Orientar* " would have struck a jarring note in the purist's ear! But what child playing his first eager rôle on the stage—however modestly cast—cares twopence for pernickety critics?

CHAPTER 4

Internal rumblings

JOHN always favoured the human approach to the solution of any seemingly intractable problem in church or parish—with a show of unruffled patience if the situation seemed about to hot up. These tactics came fairly easily to him, for he is patience personified. More than one parishioner has said to me: " Your husband doesn't seem like a parson; he's so *human*." (Food for thought there, surely.)

To gain a controversial point or to win support for a parish project, his policy was broadly to open fire with a captivating smile and engage in a little homely chat on some unrelated topic—perhaps a faintly ingratiating note could sometimes have been detected. Then he would take sudden calculated aim at the real target, hoping to disarm his opponent before he was fully aware that a shot had been fired. His manner was always conciliatory, and it usually paid off; the victim would find himself yielding—perhaps rather ruefully, perhaps with smiling compliance, but at times, I honestly believe, without even suspecting that a point had been conceded.

There was, of course, the odd occasion when this disarming strategy failed. A case in point concerned the problem of trying to ensure that he was clearly audible to a congregation that insisted on sitting too far back in church. It was more than a trifle unfair, John felt, that worshippers who perversely shunned row after row of front pews and huddled themselves together in a gregarious bunch towards the rear should complain that the vicar's voice didn't always carry, overlooking the fact that the acoustics were far from perfect anyway. The simple and obvious answer was " Friend, come up higher! " Besides, as John pointed out, a strong *forward* movement on a broad front would also do something to promote a closer sense of fellowship; narrowing that yawning gap between pulpit and people would create a more intimate atmosphere. It would certainly reduce the constant strain on his vocal cords!

He made an impassioned plea one Sunday, but nobody seemed anxious for promotion. There followed a tactfully worded paragraph in the parish magazine; this, too, was silently ignored. So there was nothing for it but a touch of his guileless diplomacy, his invariably successful " human approach "; he would pin-point individual worshippers and smilingly *invite* them personally and persuasively—if necessary cajole and coerce them—to come and sit nearer the front and so " help to create the atmosphere of one big worshipping family "!

He singled out initially the one or two regulars who were most firmly and distantly entrenched in the very back row; but his " human approach " in this instance produced a surprisingly *human* response, though *no* concession: " No, I can't come any nearer Vicar, because me tummy rumbles so "!

John, who was not slow to assess the validity (or veracity!) of any proffered excuse, made a quick calculation that all the others, under pastoral pressure, might feel constrained to hatch up equally embarrassing reasons for remote location—perhaps better left undisclosed. The plea of internal rumblings was novel, but hardly convincing. It was transparently clear that, as they had *always* sat at the back, they had no intention of being dislodged. And, after all, had they not warmed and polished these back pews with loyal devotion throughout the years? The bare thought of shifting now to a strange new position was a chilling prospect, not to be entertained for a single moment.

John chalked up total defeat on that issue.

On another occasion he had a notion about persuading the choir to process up the centre aisle to their stalls instead of emerging, in accordance with present custom, from an obscure door in the chancel, which required a few obstructions to be dodged and dignity to be sacrificed. Here again his guileless " human approach " misfired.

He buttonholed a group of choristers after practice one night and engaged in a few pleasantries about their important rôle in the coming deanery choir rally; then he switched pointedly to the real objective: " There's no question, a *robed* choir adds tremendous dignity to the whole service; how fortunate we are here, at St. John's, in this respect; but, you know, it could be even more impressive if you processed from the *west* end. I would *very* much like to see that given a trial."

This time, without dissimulation or recourse to any elaborate excuses—intimate or otherwise—the suggestion was summarily squashed: " That we'll *never* do! "—nor did they, because, you see, the traditional entry by way of the chancel had satisfied them from time immemorial, so why change now? It's daft!

" Fair enough " grunted John, and, under his breath, " Let custom prevail and avert a split." He knew a resistant-to-change climate when he met one! Indeed, prompted by a touch of Darwinian philosophy, we both knew we must " adapt or die "; and we were not courting death!

*   *   *   *   *

It was, in fact, apparent from the outset that the attitude at Upper Bellpull left no margin for interference with the *status quo*, as witness the classic example of the cricket tradition. A seemingly innocent remark dropped by the people's warden, apropos of nothing in particular, in our very early days, " We can be led *a little*, but driven not at all," was rightly interpreted by John as a kindly warning, commanding the deepest respect. As it happened, this was one hint that John scarcely needed; it reflected a point of view with which he already heartily concurred. He had little patience with the all-too-common tendency of new incumbents to embark straight away on fanatical schemes of sweeping innovation almost before they've had time to take a deep breath, as if the existing pattern of worship and administration was a symptom of spiritual immaturity or parochial inefficiency—just waiting for their clever diagnosis and treatment. John's view was that such an approach to a new parish (unless, of course, it was known to be spiritually supine and in dire need of full-scale resuscitation) was both tactless and provocative, likely to hasten both the early failure of the "new" man and an irreparable split in the ranks of the laity. Broadly speaking, he favoured the view " It's *their* parish; for generations they have been creating this image; *my* personal preferences and prejudices are of small account measured against their own wishes —provided always that there is nothing glaringly and gravely amiss and the parish is not allowed, through complacency, to become spiritually static." In short, he was all for giving the observer's rôle a good run.

Just as there are no two parishes exactly alike, so there are no two incumbents exactly alike. It is hardly surprising, then, that the newcomer to a living should be cautiously scrutinized and weighed up—maybe with a tinge of apprehension—by those who in the days ahead will have to depend on him to minister to their spiritual needs and, to some extent, to their general welfare.

Will he pass muster? What is the measuring rod? Who is qualified to use it?

A fragment of conversation that I overheard one day in a bus queue had at the time caused me to ponder deeply on the attributes and qualifications commonly looked for in the parish priest. Was there a readily identifiable picture? I wondered. It didn't take long to convince me of the utter unreasonableness—indeed sheer futility—of looking for a minted image.

The bit I had overheard began " My complaint is, the *average* parson . . . " in a tone that clearly betrayed more than a hint of anti-clerical bias. *Average* parson indeed! Trying to envisage him got me nowhere, because, obviously, he doesn't exist. There is no tailored model, and it would be tragic if there were, because *your* idol could be anathema to me; *your* paragon my weakling; *your* perfection my mediocrity, and vice versa. Will he be scholarly, erudite; or sporting, practical? Dynamic, lethargic; dogmatic, tolerant? Bluff, sensitive; fluent, halting? Theologian, showman, saint, or humbug? A good shepherd or a bookish recluse? A capable administrator with a financial flair or a dreamy mystic living almost out of this world? Or, perhaps, a composite figure, embodying some of the best and a few of the worst of all these characteristics? Perhaps a personification of the Vicar of Wakefield, or a pathetically inadequate Mr. Gilfil? Or, to scan other random fields of history and fiction for the illusory figure, would you compare him to Chaucer's poor parson, or the immortal George Herbert—" holy, just, prudent, temperate, bold, grave "? What about Jane's odious Mr. Collins, Edmund Bertram, or the debonair Henry Tilney? Or the familiar figures of the Barchester set? Or the rich galaxy of William Addison's country parsons? Or even the mad, lovable, fanatical creation of Norman Collins—Father Headlam Fynne; not to mention Rose Macaulay's endearingly dotty Father Chantry-Pigg? Each in his own way is a mere caricature of the species as a whole; where, then, to place the emphasis? On rigid conformity to doctrine, adherence to liturgical accuracy, the immaculate ordering of special services, the undeviating fulfilment of the spiritual office for which he has been specifically ordained—as the rigorists would naturally contend? Or, rather, on powerful oratory and personal magnetism? Or on efficient administration, with active participation in public affairs, outside causes, and social services—in short, on *practical* Christianity (to draw a loose distinction where no possible distinction should exist!)?

Average? No; the very word removed from the field of statistics and applied to human beings loses its validity. Human nature—even parsonical human nature—is of the alchemy of oddities and idiosyncrasies; robust failings and solid virtues; trends and traits; spiritual aspirations and animal instincts; a handful of basic ingredients, which we go on stirring endlessly in our attempt ultimately to produce a worthy mixture.

So, with such a diverse range of possibilities, the " new " man at the parsonage will inevitably evoke curiosity. He knows only too well that he has to stand comparison with his immediate predecessors, if not, in fact, with all the neighbouring clergy for miles around. Time alone will tell whether he will come up to expectations. But if, all other qualifications apart, he has a genuine concern for his fellows—if, in fact, he loves *people*—then his prospects are good; but if not, all the gimmicky brilliance and academic degrees in Christendom will never fit him to be the shepherd of his flock; he had better by far seek another vocation.

Meanwhile, all the speculation is by no means on the part of the parishioners. The " new " man himself engages in it. Every speculative doubt they may have had in relation to their new incumbent is for him multiplied in ratio to the parish population, for he has to get to know and assess each individual. What new incumbent has ever succeeded in taking an accurate first reading of the parochial pulse, I wonder?

These are the people whose joys and sorrows he must now share to a convincing degree; whose confidence he must be prepared to receive and hold inviolate; whose guttering faith, maybe, he must try to rekindle; whose problems and quarrels he must endeavour to resolve; and in whose occupational interests and hobbies he would do well to prime himself. To avoid the more disastrous pitfalls of pastoral visiting, individual circumstances must be quickly committed to a mental dossier.

In the widest sense of the word he must, indeed, be " all things to all men "—rejoicing with those who rejoice, sorrowing with those who mourn, and trying to work up a responsive exuberance with those whose excitement runs high over sport, travel, art, science, gardening, or what have you—even if his own exclusive obsession is philately or chess. Mass technique won't do; the individual approach is essential. And here lurks a subtle danger! Through a laudable eagerness to identify himself with his people, the poor parson, reared usually in a different occupational and cultural climate, can easily come unstuck and reveal himself as a dyed-in-the-wool greenhorn; and from the depths of any such initial ignorance all the erudition and pastoral virtues that he may subsequently display will never fully reclaim him. Once out of his depth he is as good as sunk!

One of John's friends—transferred during the war from a dockland parish to a small farming hamlet—suffered this sad fate and he has never lived it down.

This man was so anxious to prove himself one with his farming community that he thought it would be a good idea to invest in a cow and a pig. When a sceptical farmer in his congregation asked " Can you milk? And how will you feed the pig? " he had innocently replied " Oh, my daughter will milk the cow; she comes home at weekends. And I should think the lawn is large enough for the pig to graze on! "

John, when he heard about it, murmured " What a pity; what a pity! He's such a sound theologian, and a jolly good chap; it's just his I.Q. that's got stuck in the groove! "

*　　*　　*　　*　　*

John conceded happily, and without any compromise of conscience, that any unavoidable change in the *status quo* must be at least democratically approved, if not unanimously welcomed. Acting on this principle, he launched his first tentative suggestion to the P.C.C. that a thorough overhaul of the organ was absolutely necessary (its chronic asthmatical symptoms left no doubt about this) and that it would be an obvious advantage, while on the job, to dispense with hand-blowing and go over to automation.

From the outset he had sensed an inherent risk in total dependence on the services of a village lad who, strong and muscular

E

though he be, was subject to such human frailties as over-sleeping, playing truant, falling sick, or just missing his cue through over-absorption in his current western; and the unpredictable performance of a hurriedly recruited understudy could carry equal risks. Besides, there were always those midweek occasions—notably funerals—when organ music was specially requested, and John's own willingness to play found no matching willingness to blow—the boy being at school—and everyone concerned was faced with a musical deadlock.

Furthermore, there was always at the back of John's mind the devastating experience of one of his neighbouring colleagues, rector of a small parish at the other end of the deanery. At that church hand-blowing had always operated satisfactorily enough—*until the awful occasion.*

In that village was a " character "—an elderly woman who was troublesome, interfering and full of queer kinks, but accepted by everyone as just quietly but decently dotty. She was also suspected of religious mania. Her eccentricities found expression in a variety of ways, mostly harmless, but particularly in her addiction to phenomenal millinery.

She favoured two contrasting styles—summer and winter.

The basic summer model, in yellowish straw, was fashioned on the lines of an immense cornucopia, simply dripping with lush fruit and flowers, with just a relieving touch of foliage. This was the hat that she wore regularly from Whitsun till harvest, when, as a fitting symbol of her personal gratitude to her Creator's unfailing bounty, she would add a bunch or two of artificial berries and a miniature sheaf of wheat, or even a solitary ear of ripe corn in carefully contrived prominence.

The winter model seemed to be a touching memorial to a succession of family pets—fur, claws, beaks, wings, tails, all dominated by a gaping jaw with menacing fangs and a glassy stare.

Nobody paid too much attention to these creations; they were too well known. And nobody was unduly concerned about the wearer until the Sunday when she " went right off."

It began at matins. The rector sank to his knees in private devotion during the hymn before the sermon. He was a quiet, dreamy, rather absent-minded type of man. He got up and walked thoughtfully, with downcast eyes, towards the pulpit and began to climb the stone steps. There was a sudden, holy hush! He pulled up with a mighty jerk as he suddenly became aware that his pulpit was already occupied—by the cornucopia and its wearer.

She was now earnestly invoking that " the words of my mouth and the meditations of our hearts be always acceptable in Thy sight, O Lord . . ."

The entire congregation seemed to be in deep freeze, but the rector, for an alleged dreamer, reacted with remarkable speed and presence of mind. He turned smartly from the pulpit, walked to the lectern and announced calmly " We will now sing the closing hymn, No. 291." (By no means inappropriate—" Oft in danger, oft in woe "!)

The sidesmen took their cue and began to receive the offertory; and then, with a brief blessing, the congregation dispersed and the hat wearer was persuaded that it was all over; everybody had gone home and her powerful homily was being wasted on empty pews.

There followed a hurried consultation between rector and wardens. Suitable precautions must be taken at evensong; someone must be posted to watch the north and south doors; and, as an extra precaution, a Justice of the Peace would be asked to attend.

The cornucopia failed to appear and the service proceeded without incident until halfway through the *Magnificat*, when the organ suddenly groaned and then stopped dead.

The blower at that church was a reliable old pensioner, and it was at first feared that he had had a seizure. Someone left the choir and rushed to the back of the organ, and someone else followed proffering a little bottle and hissing " Smelling salts; smelling salts! "

They found not an exhausted blower overcome with his official exertions but an invincible old warrior clinging stubbornly to both ankles of the hat lady, who, in turn, was equally stubbornly making efforts to free herself and get into the chancel.

Under combined operations she was quickly overpowered.

The blower explained afterwards that he had suddenly caught sight of her stealthy figure creeping quietly in by a disused vestry entrance; in a split second he had to decide whether to let the *Magnificat* rip and go and grab the intruder or vice versa. He decided that at all costs the intruder *must* be stopped, and that's why they found him in the throes of a deadly rugby tackle behind the organ—and why there was a protracted hiatus in the accompaniment of the *Magnificat*.

Who could deny, then, that John had his reasons for wanting to replace a human blower with an electric switch?

*   *   *   *   *

The suggestion did not arouse the opposition John had anticipated. A fund-raising campaign was launched without delay.

Collecting money for special purposes in a very small parish is naturally a burdensome undertaking and must normally be accepted as a long-term project. In this instance, however, it was accomplished in record time and with an encouraging show of zealous co-operation—probably because the vexatious asthmatic condition of the organ had been tolerated for too long and, in the nature of things, could at any moment become acute, perhaps beyond resuscitation. So for the next six months the village buzzed with activity; a dozen or so small cells were at work within the one parochial hive, organizing whist drives, jumble sales, bring-and-buys and coffee mornings, supplemented by competitive trading schemes and a direct begging campaign.

Our main contribution from the vicarage—apart from John's massive postal bombardment—was a series of musical evenings in the drawing room, for which we enlisted the generous help of several talented professional friends from town.

On paper this brain-wave was simplicity itself: one just telephoned a pianist or a singer and begged her (or him) to be a dear and come down to entertain the parishioners, and help us to get a decent organ. We were never refused.

In practice it had its drawbacks and complications. First, there would be the local advertising, ticket selling, programme production (by hand, of course, as the takings would not justify pukka printing); there would be the retuning of the pianos on the day; and then hospitality—all of which could be counted on to keep me pretty busy. Last, but by no means least, there was the painfully strenuous exercise known as " arranging the seats." We soon discovered that " arranging the seats " was only the culminating feature of a large-scale furniture-moving operation that took the best part of the day and left us in grave doubt, after all, as to either the brilliance or the simplicity of our brain-wave. All superfluous objects—such as radiogram, music cabinets, pedestals and fernpots, occasional tables, draught screens, footstools, vases and anything else capable of getting knocked over or providing a booby-trap—had to be cleared out lock, stock and barrel, and pushed into some temporary accommodation. How? Where? Naturally one aimed at presenting a reasonably attractive and lived-in atmosphere when the audience arrived—not a bare barn or museum-like vault.

Then the remaining weightier pieces—the pianos, Chesterfield and large armchairs—all had to be manœuvred into the most space-saving sites, and finally all the other chairs lined up in tight rows to form a nice compact auditorium. We reckoned that twenty-five was our total capacity, and this meant hauling extra chairs from upstairs and a final half-dozen hard wooden ones across the lawn from the vestry.

Having wedged them all in nice symmetrical lines, it at once became evident that nobody could possibly worm his way between; nor could any member of the audience, once in and packed sardine-wise shoulder to shoulder, risk a deep breath or bat an eyelid, let alone move an elbow or dive for a handkerchief. A sneeze, we calculated, could cause a corporate disaster; a faint lead to mass hysteria.

So the whole pattern—in depth and breadth—had to be dissolved and reset to allow at least unimpeded access to the seats, even if this meant that front-row patrons would now be only a couple of inches from the performers and a source of distracting annoyance to them.

Altogether it was an exhausting, muscle-testing drill; and after the show it all had to be shifted back again. In this way John and I became quite experienced furniture movers.

The recitals, musically and financially, were an unqualified success. Usually it was a pianist who came down; once we had an ambitious recital for two pianos, and on this occasion the final rousing ovation, as the Queen of Sheba arrived at her appointed rendezvous with synchronized precision on both pianos, nearly raised the roof. John and I felt gloriously rewarded for all our heavy preliminary chores. On another occasion a promising young *lieder* singer entranced our parishioners as much with his personal charm as with his well-modulated voice and sensitive interpretations.

Possibly the most musicianly performance of them all was by a well-known B.B.C. recitalist who, even in those early days, was sedulously building up a solid reputation as an interpreter of modern works.

She was stand-in for a friend who was indisposed, and we had not met her previously. John had arranged for a car to collect her at the nearest railway station—eight miles off. As time slipped by and she failed to appear, I became frankly alarmed and agitated. She was expected at four o'clock; the evening meal was timed for six-thirty, and at a quarter to seven we telephoned the car-hire man, who admitted that he had completely overlooked the booking.

At seven o'clock she arrived—herself a trifle flurried and distressed at not having been met as arranged. After a fruitless hunt for the car that wasn't there she had finally managed independent transport.

This charming, friendly and delightfully animated young lady was also, we discovered rather too late, a chronic dyspeptic, committed to the most rigid diet—no fats or fried food, no rich pastry or cream! This rendered my studiously planned menu a total write-off before it was even served (filleted plaice fried golden brown; blackberry and apple pie with oodles of cream; cheese savoury). Fortunately I had a reserve stock of eggs—her staple food.

For this intimate little occasion our pianist very sensibly avoided her beloved modern idiom and treated us instead to a conventional feast more suited to our plebeian tastes—some crisp, rhythmical snacks of Scarlatti, a discreet portion of Beethoven, and a really generous serving of Schumann and Chopin to round it off.

She was handsomely applauded; somebody's frilly-skirted little maiden shyly presented a bouquet; and then, with a sigh of relief, we three relaxed in front of a colossal log fire, sipping hot cocoa.

We wondered what on earth was the matter when our visitor made a sudden beeline for the door, murmuring apologetically as she vanished " It's the heat; it makes my eyes burn; do you mind if I run and take them out? "

This failed to register with either of us, and we positively gaped in bewilderment until she came back and enlightened us: " I wear contact lenses "—a literally unheard-of phenomenon to us until then. How lamentably ignorant can one be?

These musical ventures helped substantially to swell our organ fund, and may even have done something to our prestige; but our other naïve money-raising experiment—for the same project—proved far less remunerative and, if possible, ten times as exhausting. It died a natural death and we made no effort to impart the kiss of life. Briefly, it was a paper salvage campaign.

In a madly exuberant moment we launched this waste-paper scheme—almost to a fanfare of trumpets. It was given terrific publicity, but never in our wildest flights of imagination had we foreseen the simply terrifying avalanche of old newspapers and magazines, obsolete books, flattened cartons, torn letters, crumpled bags and similar litter that was about to descend upon the vicarage to the point of total inundation. " Good prices paid " the trade advertisements seductively promised! The scheme was seized upon, apparently, by every household in the parish as the opportunity *par excellence* to rid itself of a lifetime's accumulation of despised literature: shelves, bookcases, attics and cellars—not to mention odd trunks and outhouses—must have been thankfully and hilariously emptied as word spread: " They're collecting waste paper down at the vicarage—for the organ."

A promising initial trickle soon swelled into a steady, ominous flow; it came by the armful, by the sackful; pushed along on bikes, in prams and packed tightly in car boots; then came loaded—nay, overloaded—cars and cattle floats piled high and overflowing, and finally, as testimony of unsurpassed zeal, a string of lorries in convoy, stacked with empty chicken-feed bags. We were deluged, and no mistake!

The willing (all-too-willing!) donors shot their consignments in higgledy-piggledy dumps—first in the garage, till that was crammed from floor to rafters; then they annexed the stable and quickly filled up the three stalls, naturally *on top* of our existing stocks of coal, coke, kindling and logs. The residue made a mountainous deposit in the stable yard, effectively blockading the entrance to the orchard, until such time as the salvage people came for the entire hoard—and paid us their " good price."

In the event they took two bites at this cherry. First they turned up noisily and unloaded about a million (repeat, *about*) empty sacks, and critically surveyed our vast paper collection. Then, accusingly, " You 'aven't bundled 'em; they must all be tied up in bundles before *we* can 'andle 'em. See yer next week. O.K. ? "—and away they roared to attend to other " good price " transactions. John and I stared at each other—speechless, transfixed.

From then until the following Wednesday we did little else but haul, straighten and tie into big bundles our paper avalanche, an exercise that was in no way expedited by the fact that John is constitutionally incapable of *touching* a piece of printed paper without pausing to peruse it. As I continued silently and wearily the penance of bundling and tying there came periodic drifts of unrelated snippets: " Fancy, this *is* an interesting article—*Tit-Bits*, 1903 "; or " I say, just listen to this. Did *you* ever take the *Girls' Own Paper*? Terribly stuffy, and what hideous fashions! " A prolonged silence usually meant that he had lost himself utterly in a turn-of-the-century *Strand Magazine*; or " D'you remember what that other book by Jules Verne was called—not *Round the World*, but *Under* something or other? "

The following week the salvage men came back for our prodigious, but now orderly, consignment.

The organ fund benefited to the tune of approximately £3, and I always felt that it was *we* who paid the " good price " for that particular exercise!

*   *   *   *   *

To mark the organ restoration a special service of church music was arranged, with the cathedral organist as the main draw and our own choir in the supporting rôle, with a few imported choristers from neighbouring parishes. Our choir could always be counted on to lead the congregation with assured competence. They were well trained and as keen as mustard. In this respect Upper Bellpull was singularly fortunate. It was heartwarming in our earliest days to find that a good, dependable choir was an outstanding feature of the local set-up. Many of the older choristers had been singing together since boyhood; their voices blended well and their zeal was unquenchable. With the help of a few female voices, and the usual handful of small boys, a really well-balanced team had evolved. Year in and year out their loyalty never wavered. We could always be sure of something special for festivals, and their reputation as Christmas carollers was established for miles around.

Their custom on Christmas Eve was to tour the whole parish between teatime and midnight, halting every few hundred yards to proclaim the glad tidings in the ageless, well-loved tunes, and also to partake of occasional yuletide hospitality—just to keep out the cold! In acreage it was a large and straggling parish; the singers, wending their tortuous way along the country lanes by the light of their flickering lanterns, might have been taken for a band of stalwart pilgrims treading the Bethlehem road. In rendering this felicitous service to the parish they had often to contend with anything but felicitous weather. I have seen them muffled to the chin, stamping their feet and slapping their thighs as their breath froze on the icy air; I have watched them singing with heart and soul in the teeth of a challenging gale; and I remember that on one occasion they were clearly heard but only dimly seen as we peered at them through an almost impenetrable fog; it was quite eerie, for they resembled a chorus of ghostly heralds, trying vainly to locate a perversely elusive star. But, come rain, come storm, our singers never failed us on Christmas Eve, and having covered their formidable itinerary they would always be back on time and trooping into church for the midnight mass; and every year our hearts overflowed with renewed gratitude to these dedicated choristers who helped immeasurably to recapture once again for us all the true spirit of the Nativity.

It was their custom on reaching the vicarage to come right in and group themselves in the soft, warm glow of the candle-lit hall—festively decorated, of course, with its garlands of ivy, holly and mistletoe. John and I, and any guests who happened to be staying for Christmas, would join heartily in the singing, and we were always invited to choose some of our favourite carols. Their repertoire was equal to any demands.

For us this was one of the highlights of the festive season. We simply revelled in it. To this day every detail is crystal clear. We would come back from the blessing of the crib and the lighting of the Christmas tree aware of a steadily rising elation as the hours slipped by. Our custom was to have tea by a roaring fire, with lashings of hot buttered toast—really swimming in butter, and be bothered to indigestion for once in a while! The next *big* moment would be the arrival of the carollers; so from teatime onwards we used to be on the *qui vive* for their coming, straining our ears to catch the first welcome note wafted across the fields on the night air. A carpet of snow enhanced the scene.

I could usually time their approach almost to the minute—just as I got the first batch of mince pies out of the oven and the whole house would be pervaded with the rich, spicy aroma of Christmas baking.

To the end of our mortal days this picture of cosy good cheer and anticipation, translated in an instant into a humble act of worship and praise as we all sang heartily, will remain a treasured memory —like an exceptionally fine cameo in a wholly choice collection.

There can be no doubt that our village choir deserved all the unsolicited tributes it received—at least *nearly* all. There was one notable exception!

A new parishioner, who had recently moved down from the industrial north, was happily adjusting himself to the radical change of surroundings and custom. He was looking forward keenly to his first Christmas in the romantic wilds of the countryside.

On Christmas Eve he was exchanging seasonal greetings with his nearest neighbour over a glass of sherry. Presently the carol singers began.

The newcomer pricked up his ears and listened intently, then commented almost extravagantly to his host on the remarkably fine singing of our church choir. " In my humble opinion," he enthused, " you'd have to go *miles*—even oop in Manchester—to hear singing like that; and fancy, in an out-of-the-way little place like this! I bet there's not another choir in the whole diocese to coom oop to it." With his generosity suitably stirred, he fumbled for his wallet and took out a note. He waited expectantly, but the carollers failed to knock. The singing died away and he finally popped the note back in his pocket.

His host, with whom John and I spent Christmas Day that year, confided to us the unpremeditated hoax that had fooled his new neighbour; but he simply hadn't the heart to disillusion the poor chap himself. The singing that evoked such generous comment (and impulse!) was, in fact, from King's College Chapel—the service of the nine lessons and carols—in a repeat programme on a portable radio in a guest's bedroom overhead!

Actually, our own choir had for once not managed to reach the extreme border of the parish where these people lived. I felt that they deserved that handsome donation all the same—at least the new parishioner had had his money's worth.

*   *   *   *   *

Now that the organ was restored and electrically blown, John felt that it was incumbent on him to get into practice again so that, in an emergency, he would be in a position to stand in.

Requests for hymns at funerals inevitably posed a problem; who would *sing* them? Without a choir (and in mid-week it was impossible to assemble ours—mostly busy on their farms) and with a relatively small congregation—mostly choked with emotion, and even without the emotion far too shy to let their voices be heard above a whisper—it devolved almost entirely upon John to keep the singing going, and he considered it better, in the circumstances, to dispense with hymns altogether. He had tried to discourage the custom, but here again custom dies hard. If they wanted hymns, then hymns they should have—if it was within his power.

An added complication, if the funeral was on a weekday and the organist at work, was to find anyone willing to deputize; hence John's decision to rub up his organ playing.

He must have found it quite exhausting to shuttle between his stall and the organ manual—praying one minute, playing " Abide with me " the next, then scurrying across to the lectern for the reading, and darting back again to the organ for " Now the labourer's task is o'er " before taking off again with seemingly indecent haste to precede the cortège out to the churchyard.

As this was a small voluntary service which John, out of kindness of heart, rendered when asked to do so, we did feel it was a bit tough when one family of mourners subsequently chided him for " dodging about like that." One of them spoke of the vicar's " shocking irreverence—dashing from place to place in the middle of a funeral "; an " insult to the dead " they had summed it up.

Poor John, I thought; why vilify him? *He* hadn't wanted to elaborate a solemn occasion with frivolous gymnastics; it was *they* who had asked for a choral valediction for their dear one—fully aware that the official organist was not available. Having forced considerable mobility on John, it seemed strangely illogical to criticize his peregrinations.

But then logic is not an outstanding quality in the human animal, particularly when he is immersed in grief.

*   *   *   *   *

Generally, of course, these little personal favours were appreciatively received; so much so that even I was prevailed upon now and then to " officiate at the organ "—in the hackneyed terms of press reportage—if all other sources of musical supply failed and the occasion warranted it.

Briefly, the occasions were baptisms, and at least one family thoughtfully saw to it that I was given an annual assignment—to keep my hand in, I suppose.

It was not usual to ask for hymns at a christening; but on the rare occasions when they were, John—ever loath to disappoint— would cheerily promise to "fix something up." He did draw the line, however, in this particular rite, at *personally* filling the dual rôle—priestly and musical. As he said to me, just imagine holding the baby, offering prayers, sprinkling the water, handing the infant (probably crying lustily by now) into the godmother's arms, then charging up the aisle to accompany " 'Tis done! that new and heavenly birth," then scurrying back to the font for the final blessing! No, he wisely foresaw the possible consequences of such a mad mêlée, and was adamant. But one day he sounded me on the issue: " I suppose *you* wouldn't be able to manage No. 327 for the Dansons' christening next week? "

Clever psychology that, to question my ability to manage! He knew perfectly well that it is not in my nature to dismiss a challenge lightly. Having tried my hand at so many unfamiliar tasks since coming to the vicarage I was prepared to have a stab at the organ.

But I had never played an organ in my life, and made only the most modest pretensions even on the piano. In any case, anything in the nature of a public performance was liable to reduce me to a nervous wreck long before the event, so the prospects for the Dansons' affair were not altogether propitious; but, with an assumed boldness, I agreed to help them out. Under my breath I was saying " I'll play the organ at that baptism, even if I die in the attempt."

Happily, I survived—as, to my infinite relief, did the christening party—but of course I cheated. With my legs tucked safely out of harm's way, and with all the terrifying stops pre-arranged for me by John, I just set to work with a determined *legato* touch and masterly concentration, mentally ticking off the verses as we finished them—all six!—for I was desperately anxious to give them full measure, but not " pressed down and running over." The real handicap, I found, was the distance separating singers from organist: there *they* were, so far off that they looked like pygmies grouped round the font in the west end, and here was *I*, in glorious but trembling isolation, away up in the chancel, in direct polarity, like a solitary exile in outer space. The gap between seemed unbridgeable as far as sound was concerned. Whether, in fact, I *did* " accompany " them, or whether I raced ahead or trailed miserably behind, I never knew; the important thing was that the baby was duly christened, the parents thanked me (!) very charmingly and were civil enough to invite me to do the same for their next offspring —and so on throughout the years we remained there.

So, although I cannot claim to be an organist, I've certainly had my delirious moments! And that is not counting the occasion when, again in response to John's frantic appeal, I played one Sunday afternoon for evensong at the mission church.

Normally John himself presided over the wheezy old harmonium on which the mission congregation depended for its hymns. Even in its youth this had been a heavy-going, reluctant brute, requiring undue coaxing and coercion; with advancing age—and being condemned to live in an atmosphere of perpetual dampness—its stubborn resistance moved towards a threatened climax. It became for John a severe test of both mental endurance and physical strength to play, pedal *and* sing (for there was no choir here and only a handful of inaudible worshippers), and then to pray, preach and read lessons. After a serious operation he was no longer able to cope with the organist's rôle; a deputy *must* be found. So once more, where angels might well have feared to tread, *this* fool rushed in, without any previous experience of harmonium-playing.

Obeying John's exhortation not to stop pedalling whatever happened, I put everything I'd got into that frenzied footwork; no Olympic cyclist ever pedalled with greater abandon and grimmer intention. Naturally, I had insisted on choosing my own hymns; I had no intention of being caught out with six sharps or five flats or a bewildering rash of accidentals.

Together we made it, though I ended up in a tropical bath of perspiration—the combined outcome, I suppose, of the awful nervous tension and the furious pedalling.

It was just as well that I hadn't known in advance that the rickety old rotating stool which so uneasily supported me had been adjusted to its utmost thread; one extra wriggle, one more violent pressure and I would have been deposited flat on the floor in front of the congregation.

$$*\quad *\quad *\quad *\quad *$$

Recalling some of these crazy incidents, perhaps it is not altogether surprising that one night John wakened up shaking with laughter from a madly realistic dream in which he thought he was attending a county dog show in our village hall, only all the canine competitors were grouped in choir formation, surpliced and wearing their medallions, with our organist earnestly conducting them in a Bach cantata.

*   *   *   *   *

Speaking of the village hall, and also of the musical aspect of our varied activities, reminds me that as a reluctant accompanist at the Women's Institute I did not last very long. I was appointed in the first place, of course, only because all other likely candidates were known to be even less reliable on the keyboard than I was, and it seemed to be the considered opinion of the committee that even my bit of reckless strumming would be a shade better than the depressing effect (once suffered and never forgotten) of an *un*accompanied mob all contending for survival in what could only be described as a choral free-for-all—some sharp, some flat, a few racing ahead of the main stream, and others lagging painfully behind under the natural handicap of a built-in tendency to *ritardando*, while the acknowledged *prima donna* and her official understudy were both hopelessly outmanœuvred from the start by the combined forces of dissonance and mixed *tempi*.

Now " Jerusalem," I had always contended, was one of those deceptively simple tunes with an astonishing capacity for wrong notes, and I claimed my full quota. In fact, the trial canter under my uncertain leadership was quite excruciating. The next time, with mounting confidence, the way to " England's green and pleasant land " seemed slightly less hazardous; but my third appearance was completely marred by an unforeseen calamity, and this was virtually the beginning of the end.

The village hall piano, it should be explained, was a rare museum piece, picked up many years ago for an odd pound or two in a sale room and mistakenly regarded by the hall managers as a fantastic bargain—an acquisition that merited the most loving care and treatment. In fact, its numerous shortcomings included a defective sustaining pedal and an invincible colony of moths; there was also a discordant rattle in the upper register, and several of the ivories were missing. To complicate matters, a good number of the notes didn't respond at all, so that any performance on it—be the pianist a *virtuoso* of world class or the veriest beginner practising five-finger exercises—was bound to sound a trifle hiccoughy and disjointed.

However, accepting these deficiencies at their face value, one did one's humble best.

On this ill-starred occasion, before a full muster of our own members plus a strong contingent from a neighbouring Institute, I began very nervously, and it wasn't until we came to the bit marked in the score " (all available voices) "—" Bring me my bow . . . my arrows of desire . . . my spear . . . "—that I really let out the throttle in readiness for the dramatically sonorous " Bring me my chariot of fire "; and then, as I crashed down with everything I'd got on that dominant chord, there was an almighty clatter and out fell the lower front panel (I thought the whole inside was coming too!), dealing me a vicious swipe across the right shin—so vicious in fact, and unexpected, that I jumped up as if I'd been shot, yelped with pain, and, alas, took the name of the Lord in vain!

The singing stopped dead in its tracks. I glanced round and saw row upon row of gaping mouths, whose owners looked like startled waxworks.

It was several seconds before animation returned—with a round of stifled titters. Eventually, with that panel parked at a safe distance, I made a fresh start and this time we all got home without further incident. But their overall reaction didn't escape me; I was made to feel like a wanton vandal out to wreck their prized piano. I thought it best to tender my musical resignation before they had time to sack me!

CHAPTER 5

Hospitality

ALTHOUGH the routine of our new life followed a certain rough formula, we realized very clearly—especially after the initial gooseberry episode—that we must always be on our toes for the possible bolt from the blue, and, like Baden-Powell's scouts, *be prepared*—for strange callers and even stranger requests.

Significantly enough, it was a troop of boy scouts who put us to a searching test one bank holiday Monday when we had prayed to be left alone and undisturbed. It was our practice to seize on these so-called " leisure " days to make up arrears of chores, and on this occasion John and I had set to work after breakfast on an extra big wash.

We had been at it most of the morning, side by side at the old stone trough, rubbing, rinsing, wringing and squeezing blankets, until the inevitable pangs of hunger and sheer exhaustion reminded us that we were already late with dinner.

I broke off to prepare a quick snack. We had eaten only a mouthful when the door bell clanged. John, his washing apron hastily snatched off, got up to answer it. After a rather protracted conversation, he came and asked me a trifle apologetically " Could you possibly cook a potato for a boy scout? I haven't actually committed you, but . . . "

This odd request seemed to merit closer investigation, so I went to the door.

It had been drizzling with rain for the last half-hour and it was now coming down in bucketfuls. Indeed, the heavens had opened.

Standing on the doorstep, a vision of bedraggled misery, was one of the most diminutive scouts I have ever seen, looking for all the world like a dejected little tadpole that had escaped from its jar when the floods came.

Poor, pathetic little creature! Who could possibly refuse him the consolation of a boiled potato? Indeed, who could deny him the even greater comfort of a full meal, plus shelter from the deluge? Certainly not I; but the minute my expression registered capitulation, and he heard my " Oh, of *course*; come in and I'll soon see to it for you," his shrewd little face broke into a roguish, triumphant grin. He inserted two fingers between his teeth and produced a shrill whistle, signalling to his companions—yes, all fifteen of them!—who had been artfully crouching down behind our hawthorn hedge to come out and show themselves.

We were suckers all right! Their meal was as good as served; well, at least morally guaranteed.

I had to admire their clever psychology in choosing this wan little starveling as their emissary—a heart-moving specimen if ever there was one. Most of the others were bonny, tough, capable-looking lads—far less likely by their physique to evoke ready sympathy in any situation.

Having, by diplomacy and subterfuge, won the first round of the contest, one of the older scouts volunteered the information that they were on a weekend hike, but were returning earlier than planned owing to the poor weather. They found themselves landed at Upper Bellpull with no prearranged site for their mid-day halt, and it seemed pointless to push on till they were completely bogged down in rain and mud. Unanswerable logic!

" It's most awfully decent of you," he reiterated time and again, so that I could be in no doubt, " to offer (!) to cook our vegetables for us." They had their own potatoes and some bully beef. " If you could just spare a piece of bread [a *piece*, mark you, between sixteen of them, counting the tadpole!] it would be jolly acceptable." This was accompanied by a melting smile.

Whether his story was reasonable or feasible John and I were not qualified to judge, lacking all knowledge of scouting *mystique*, though I must confess I had always imagined that inclement weather —particularly drenching rain—constituted a challenge which all good scouts welcomed with boundless enthusiasm as a heaven-sent opportunity to demonstrate the special skills of scoutcraft. I had supposed that in such a predicament they got camp fires going merrily in next to no time, with a solitary match, soaking wet kindling and sodden paper, plus a touch of their particular brand of magic. And I had further supposed that while this miracle was still receiving applause they piled on the wizardry by producing a

F

delectable steaming hot stew out of a black cauldron suspended from a tripod over the fire—amply justifying all those proficiency badges that decorated their shirt sleeves like a rash of vaccination scars. Or was I confusing them with gipsies?

Anyway, the situation now confronting us had grown in alarming proportions since the tadpole's initial request to " boil a potato."

The lads quickly unpacked about twenty pounds of potatoes and began to peel them. They used their bowie-knives to good effect and worked with practised speed.

It really needed a bath-size pot, or better still a commodious tank, to cook this lot. I calculated that with my mini-saucepans it would take at least four boilings. Thank heaven I was no longer at the capricious mercy of my old " Wondermatic " cooker! Even with electricity I could not see any chance of their meal being ready under an hour and a half.

I gave them all the bread I had, except for a couple of slices to toast for our own breakfast next morning. All this *would* happen on a bank holiday, with shops closed and no deliveries!

Had they, I inquired tentatively, thought of a sweet course to follow? " Well, no; not r-e-a-l-l-y! "—with another melting smile.

A quick search in my store cupboard produced four three-pound jars of home-bottled plums, and they agreed that a pint or two of custard to go with them would be simply *fab*.

John, meanwhile, had visualized our large, carless garage as a possible refectory. We opened it up and arranged the tool chest, two wooden benches and an assortment of orange boxes in some semblance of homely comfort; no curtains, admittedly, but plenty of cobwebs.

In due course our uninvited guests threw their impromptu party, and a very jolly, well-disciplined crowd they were. The sounds soon issuing from the " refectory " left no doubt as to their conviviality; they sang a few rollicking songs and washed down their bully and potatoes, plums and custard with gallons of tea. I noted with envy how liberally they were supplied with their own tea and sugar, mentally comparing their unstinted reserves with our silly little domestic ration.

Finally they crowded into the scullery—and overflowed into the yard—to wash up the dishes, their tin plates and my saucepans. I must admit that they were remarkably slick and thorough with their chores.

Then their appointed spokesman rewarded us with a most effusive extempore speech of thanks (or could it, I wonder, have been a set piece, well rehearsed and committed to memory?), supported by plenty of squeaky " hear, hears " from the younger element.

The rain had now stopped. The scouts lined up, saluted gravely and trudged off in good heart, and, if it is true that an army marches on its stomach, equipped now to break all marching records.

John and I glanced at the cold remains of *our* abandoned meal— Welsh rarebit, hard and congealed on our plates. We had only enough bread for breakfast and barely enough milk for two cups of tea. We foraged around and managed to rake up a belated snack of sultana cake and raw apples, hoping to make good the deficiencies tomorrow.

We learned subsequently that our scouts had paid an uninvited call the night before at one of the nearby farms just as the farmer and his family were about to sit down to a cooked supper. Here the boys had benefited to the tune of hot cocoa *ad lib*, lodging for the night in a large, dry barn, and a substantial ham and egg breakfast —the tadpole again, I suppose, having been used as bait.

*   *   *   *   *

We were to learn before we were much older that a country parsonage, especially if it is set fairly close to a main road, is only a few degrees less public than a road house. We were fully prepared from the outset for the vicarage to be the natural hub of parochial life; indeed, we earnestly hoped that our home *would* be so regarded by our parishioners, for what better way to get to know them and for them to get to know us? And it was spacious enough in all conscience.

But a time came when we wished that we could have canalized the flood stream of callers into a manageable flow—better spaced and better timed! Too often we were inundated and found it difficult in such crowded waters to know how to cope with the influx. It was when the tide of callers lapped simultaneously at front door and at back door, and the telephone bell tinkled incessantly, that we *longed* for a competent janitor. By the time we became fully alive to an almost impossible situation it was rather too late to do much about it. With foreknowledge we could at least have introduced fixed "office hours" for interviews, form-signing, banns, etc., although even this precaution, being in the nature of an innovation, might have proved unpopular; and, of course, it would have been no answer to the problem of promiscuous droppers-in, such as our scouts.

It also took time for us to tumble to the fact that many callers deliberately resorted to the subtle dodge of timing their visit to synchronize with our meals—though *not*, let me hasten to add, for the most obvious reason, but simply to be sure of finding us in. At first we accepted it as an exasperating coincidence that the very moment we began a meal somebody was sure to knock, usually on a genuine enough pretext—to have a tobacco form signed or a baptism arranged, or to ask permission for a headstone.

John took to going to the door flapping his table napkin significantly and chewing with exaggerated emphasis, but this broad hint would be sure to bring the unabashed—nay, triumphant —admission, " Oh, *good*; I thought I'd be sure to catch you in at meal-time!" Occasionally the opening gambit would be "Forgive me, Vicar, but I though it would be *wiser* to call at dinner-time . . . "

Wiser? We took a rather dim view of this brand of wisdom; but the offenders, bless them, seemed happily convinced that they had acted on a supremely brilliant inspiration.

Clearly there was much purposeful planning behind it all. We learnt to accept it as just one more occupational hazard.

*   *   *   *   *

"Being prepared," in its practical application, meant acquiring and maintaining an adequate stock of iron rations in the larder, for there were no shops—apart from the small village store—to rush to in an emergency. On official rations for two it needed more than a magician's touch to build up even modest reserves. In fact, while rationing lasted I never discovered how to equate the accepted principles of hospitality with the hard facts of bureaucratic parsimony.

As soon as I realized the amount of entertaining that our position legitimately called for I applied to the local food office for a supplementary allowance of basic commodities. Here I drew a blank, so I then addressed an impassioned plea to Whitehall, but with no more satisfaction. In polite official language it was pointed out that the Rationing Act made no provision for privileged treatment for parsonage houses—though how parsonage houses differed in principle from business establishments, which *did* qualify for supplementary allowances, I failed to see. Looking back, this discrimination was manifestly unfair to clergy wives and inflicted real hardship on them, since, in the normal course of things, they simply *had* to contrive refreshments (at times amounting to full board and lodging for a couple of days or more) for visiting preachers, lecturers, delegates and area organizers of recognized societies, as well as for members of minor conferences and committees at the vicarage; let alone for the customary social entertaining that is an essential and, to my mind, a very important feature of an incumbent's work. The tricky situation was aggravated by the fact that ours was a section of the community that had no canteen facilities to help out, so the strain on personal rations was all the greater. And, of course, the more remote the country parish the more obvious the need for hospitality, for rarely could a visitor, after conducting his service or delivering his lecture, return home the same night, however anxious he was to do so. He would find himself immobilized by impossible bus and train services, with no workable connections; so hospitality was axiomatic.

Much as I loved this aspect of our work, it frequently posed a problem which I found all but insoluble.

Among the minor crises on the social side that nearly turned my hair white overnight was an incident arising from the visit of a party of change ringers (and their friends) to our tower.

It was fixed for a Saturday evening, and on the same afternoon I had already received a group of lads from a youth club in John's old parish. I had been warned that there would be seven in the youth club party; it turned out to be nine, as they hadn't counted their leader and the man who drove them down. For several weeks I had saved with miserly care for this little affair. I gave them a picnic tea on the lawn, and after their departure at sundown I hurried back to the kitchen to scrape together some semblance of a feast for the bellringers and their companions, who, like the lads, were coming from a distance. I confess that I have always accepted the challenge of a tight corner as an occasion to prove my mettle, and I would certainly have felt that I had badly failed John if I had not managed to produce *something* out of the bag.

At about nine o'clock John piloted the ringers across the lawn for their snack and I encouraged them to make short work of my brave pile of tomato and egg sandwiches, biscuits and coffee.

We all munched and chatted animatedly, and I learnt quite a lot about change ringing. Suddenly their leader glanced anxiously at his watch, jumped up hurriedly, and said " Well, that was very nice, Mrs. Green; thanks a lot. We must now buck up back to the tower and *send the other half over!* "

The other half? I nearly swooned. It surely couldn't be yet *another* party to feed. Well, it surely was. Being reluctant to overcrowd us, they had thoughtfully (?) split up for refreshments.

This time I felt completely sunk, with little prospect of rescue. However, a frantic rummage in the larder produced a few more biscuits and the uncut cake that was intended to serve John and me for the coming week. An even bigger problem was how to slake their thirst, but the surprise discovery of some powdered milk saved the situation—only poor John had to sit by with a sickly fixed smile on his face and watch his week's sugar ration disappear lump by lump into the ringers' cups. And sugar, I need hardly say, was his incurable weakness.

*   *   *   *   *

It didn't take many experiences of this sort to convince me that the only possible answer was to step up production on the home front, using every ingenious dodge. I must make a point of always being early off the mark at every bring-and-buy-sale, ready to pounce on the odd quarter of tea or half of margarine, or some precious sugar; by hook or crook I *must* build up a food bank. It entailed a marked sharpening of the old wits.

Then, with such prodigious quantities of fruit and vegetables in the garden, the pickling, jamming, bottling and chutney-making prospects were highly promising. Every grain of sugar that could be hoarded—with sometimes a welcome contribution from bee-keeping friends!—was stowed furtively away in my secret *cache*, and from time to time I made the necessary hush-hush withdrawals for a jamming orgy. (I have never to this day divulged the location of that hide-out to John, to whose sweet tooth the knowledge would have been refined torture.)

In this way our shelves began gradually to look like the well-stocked grocery section of a departmental store, with rows of assorted jams—strawberry, plum, raspberry, greengage; jar after jar of marmalade—*all* denominations; a dazzling variety of jellies —quince, wild bramble, red and black currant, apple and ginger; damson cheese and lemon curd. As the stock grew, so my silly pride swelled. Countless pots of chutney were lined up beside pickled onions and tomatoes bottled for Christmas consumption. As for fruit sterilizing, there were soon enough bottles of all sizes to feed an army corps: plums by the bushel—Victoria, Early Rivers, Black Monarch, the *lot*; raspberries, currants, pears, pulped apples, and the inevitable gooseberries. My sterilizing gear was seldom out of commission throughout the summer months.

Inordinate pride in such elementary skills richly deserved the deflation it eventually suffered. John's best man, for instance, coming to visit us for the first time, took one incredulous look at my fabulous collection and commented " Good heavens, are you preparing for a siege ? " and, seeing the thing from his angle, I began to wonder uneasily whether perhaps I *had* rather overplayed my hand at victualling. Yet always at the back of my mind was that compulsive urge to " be prepared." Besides, although John was normally a notoriously small eater even *he* was known to have his demanding moments, and I didn't want to be caught out when one of his strangely unpredictable pangs suddenly seized him and the inner man simply *groaned*—and groaned very loudly!—for sustenance. To my lasting embarrassment, this once happened when an eminent historian condescended to address our small community on the subject of a ruined priory in the vicinity. Having unwound nearly a mile of manorial rolls—like a giant stair-carpet down the entire centre gangway—and got himself well launched on the causes leading up to the dissolution of the monasteries, a Philistine voice *whispered* in my ear—in tones clearly audible to everyone in the first few rows, if not to the whole hall—" I'll have a lightly boiled egg with some brown bread and butter and a pot of strong tea when we get home; I'm absolutely starving—*sinking*."

Poor John, his own dissolution seemed imminent!

But to return to the kitchen front and my struggle to win a proficiency badge, I was instead taken down a peg by two dramatic mishaps. Being a " new girl " to domestic science, I suppose it was hardly to be expected that my experiments would be disaster-free; yet somehow I had launched out in sublime confidence of total success.

I came downstairs one morning to be met by a steady cascade of deep purple liquid gushing from a store cupboard in the kitchen; there was already a sizeable puddle on the new lino. Opening the cupboard gingerly, as if half expecting a gremlin to pounce on me, I was horrified to see that two bottles of Black Monarch had blown their tops, distributing the mashy contents impartially over everything; the inside of the doors and the shelves were simply plastered with fermenting skins and pulp, and there was a widely scattered array of stones, as if someone had been pretty handy with a catapult. A very beery smell pervaded the place. This mess took a lot of cleaning up, and the moral of it did not escape me.

The other bottling calamity, incredible as it may sound, narrowly missed decapitating our gardener—and this, of all times, at Christmas, the season of peace and good will!

On Christmas morning I took down a large-size bottle of tomatoes, gloating smugly over their uniform size and symmetrical packing. Despite endless persuasion, the metal screw top remained obstinate and unyielding. Each of us in turn—and that included our four guests—had a go, but it wouldn't budge. In the end we appealed to a young neighbour whose manual strength, as a builder and carpenter, was likely to be superior to ours.

He grinned reassuringly, " Oh yes, certainly! That'll be quite easy; give it to me, I'll shift it." But even his Herculean grip made no impression on the metal band. Slightly subdued, he suggested taking it across to the little shed in his uncle's garden (uncle was our gardener). " We'll use a vice on the job."

" How very good of you," I beamed; " I won't start grilling the bacon till you bring it back."

Presently there was a blood-curdling yell, followed by the confused sounds of general panic. It must have circled the village. It nearly paralysed me.

Explanation? Well, with the aid of the vice they had finally released the tiresome band—plus the contents of the jar—with such alarming suddenness that both operators thought they'd been shot; the younger man instinctively dropped the jar, saturating himself with a shower of disintegrating tomatoes, and the unfortunate old chap made an ill-calculated dive for the door. It was, alas, a low door—*very* low. He caught the top of his cranium a hideous whack on the lintel and then, blindly pursuing his headlong escape, he landed plonk in the middle of the chicken run, roaring blue murder as he tore his leg on some rusty wire.

Even if we hadn't lost our tomatoes I doubt whether we would have had the heart to enjoy them at the cost of poor old uncle's lacerated scalp and damaged calf.

One of our more experienced parishioners to whom I confided these tragic happenings said " Surely you always unscrew the band by half a turn before storing." Why ever hadn't I thought of that before? I made a mental note in readiness for the approaching bumper crop of raspberries. Every metal band in *that* lot was half-turned back. But events proved that I lacked the practised, delicate touch in " half " turning.

It was I who made the initial inroad into this batch. Fancying a fruit breakfast one morning, I took down a jar and was delighted to find how very easily *this* screw top came off. In fact, the glass lid came with it. I had a liberal helping, sprinkled with extra sugar, for they were unusually tart—in fact, distinctly acid.

It happened to be our shopping morning, by bus about eight miles away. Hardly had we paid the fares when I began to feel strangely uncomfortable and dizzy. A couple of hundred yards farther on I was nervously looking for a possible escape route. At the next stop (heaven be praised, near a deserted field), I poked John savagely and hissed " We're getting out here." He looked a bit puzzled, but had the good sense not to reason why, but to obey. I was rendered prostrate, and to my dying day I shall never forget the shattering symptoms of my first and only experience of fruit poisoning. It triggered off a neurosis that dogged my footsteps for long after.

*   *   *   *   *

I had invariably found the countrywomen's cookery advice absolutely dependable and given so willingly to help me over the initial hurdles of housewifery; so my final bottling setback was the penalty paid for once disregarding their sage counsel and tinkering with more dubious methods—recommended in this instance by a charming West Indian lady who was visiting the parish to give a recital of her mystical poems!

During lunch before the meeting she raised the subject of vegetable preservation—in particular runner beans. We grew scarlet runners almost by the ton; why hadn't I thought of bottling them before? Still acutely conscious of my embarrassing fruit-poisoning episode, I reminded her that one couldn't be too careful, especially with vegetables; they should *always* be canned under high pressure, *never* bottled.

This, our poet insisted, was a complete fallacy—just another old wives' tale! She herself had already bottled *vast* quantities of runner beans by the simple sterilizing method—just as one would do fruit. "I assure you," she went on rather convincingly, "it's one hundred per cent safe; I wouldn't be likely to jeopardize the lives of my husband and children, now, would I?" Without having met them it was hard to judge, but I supposed she wouldn't; so, on this seemingly good authority, I became a convert and, for the next four or five weeks, John and I gathered, sliced and bottled runner beans unremittingly until we had amassed enough for winter consumption for the rest of our lives; and John warned me that he wouldn't be answerable for his actions if I asked him ever to pick another runner bean. It was certainly a prodigious job and, surveying my stores for the umpteenth time, I preened myself on gradually becoming a model housewife—albeit a late developer.

Within a week or two of the campaign I received from the West Indian lady's curate husband a frantic warning about the potential dangers of eating *bottled* vegetables; botulism, he assured me, would be the likely consequence and he couldn't think why his wife had passed on such reckless information without first checking her facts. He hoped we hadn't already died or been subjected to the indignities of a stomach pump. He concluded: "I am writing *immediately* to warn you; my wife only mentioned the matter casually at breakfast today!"

I was glad to put his mind at rest; luckily we hadn't started on our beanfeast. I hinted, however, that he might profitably encourage his wife to stick to her mysticism.

Seeing these incidents as possible ill omens or strange warnings, I let my bottling craze die a natural death, and by now I was dabbling in a new skill—butter making.

Calling one day on an elderly parishioner, I was puzzled by her ceaseless shaking of a milk bottle, like a baby endlessly brandishing its rattle. Answering my curious gaze, she explained the simple know-how of saving the cream from the top of the milk for several days and allowing it to thicken in a warm temperature; she was

then able to get several ounces of good, rich butter—after prolonged and vigorous shaking. " Why don't *you* try? " she asked.
Why indeed? Butter rationing was a severe handicap; in fact, it was
becoming an almost forgotten luxury with our weekly allowance
now down to a paltry ounce or so. I jumped at the old lady's invitation to a full-scale demonstration—skimming off the cream, shaking,
salting, repeated washings, until it was at last ready for final patting
into professional shape. She stressed the immense importance of
endless washing to extract the buttermilk.

Before long I was making a regular six to eight ounces a week,
and when Christmas came round we got a beginner's thrill in dispatching to members of the family in London a modest sample of
vicarage creamery butter—gorgeously patted.

I continued to churn out our weekly supplement until butter
rationing ended, but from the outset the process in *our* dairy was
rationalized and physical exertion reduced to the minimum. With
a rotary whipper to hand no laborious bottle-shaking for me!

Was there ever butter of such superlative quality?

*   *   *   *   *

By now the experimental fever had got me in its grip and I became
an avid collector of unusual cookery books. A surprise gift of a
pound of sugar enabled me one day to plan a special treat for John.
His sweet ration was never enough and he longed for some old-
fashioned coconut ice—in bulk! Now he should have it—a really
good thick slab or two. A friend gave me a tested recipe, " absolutely fool-proof " she assured me somewhat pointedly. Following
instructions, I tipped the sugar and a tin of condensed milk into a
saucepan to bring to the boil. As it boiled it changed colour. It was
soon darkish brown and sticking hard to the side of the saucepan.
In short, it had got burnt before my very eyes.

The grievous loss of this precious sugar bonus served to convince me that I still had a long way to go before qualifying as a
competent cook. A would-be consoler said gently " Of course, you
put it in a *double* pan."

Of course, I hadn't! However, there was a mollifying sequel.
Determined not to waste that sugar if I could possibly help it, I
threw into the burnt mixture a sprinkling of everything to hand—
cocoa powder, vanilla, margarine, ground walnuts, a drop of fresh
milk and a blob of syrup. When this appeared cooked I poured it

into flat tins and prayed that it might prove friable and toothsome. John's enthusiastic verdict was " I say, what jolly good *fudge* this is! " I suppose it was by no means the first, or the last, tolerably successful recipe to be discovered literally by accident.

*   *   *   *   *

Despite the unequal battle against rationing, we can truthfully claim that some of our most valued and heart-warming recollections are those associated with vicarage hospitality, for it brought us into close contact with a steady stream of vividly contrasting types and personalities—people whose interests, professions, philosophies and talents covered an immeasurable field of human endeavour. It afforded John and me countless opportunities to explore and widen our own horizons, far beyond the limited range of parochial boundaries.

Our diversely qualified visitors included—besides, of course, bishops, boy scouts and bellringers—lecturers representing every line of country and shade of opinion—orthodox and otherwise, among them being a brigadier on occultism, whose experiments in astral projection made a fabulous story; a naval V.I.P. on Arctic exploration, whose personal exploits among ice-floes added an immensely authentic note to his talk; and a film actress specializing in Dickensian impersonations, whose own successful role in *David Copperfield* sparked off an animated discussion at supper. She, by the way, was a brilliant raconteuse, whose stream of amusing anecdotes deserved a far bigger audience than just the two of us at table.

Also among the visitors whose company added so richly to our vicarage experiences were two Mirfield fathers and a religious from an Anglican order at Whitby—all three busily conducting a mission in our parish. Their immense capacity for sheer hard work (including, as voluntary overtime, the scything of our huge orchard, waist-high in overgrown weeds and grass), and their genius for establishing personal contacts in the most unpromising quarters, soon made us humbly aware of the tremendous vocational power under which they laboured.

Then there were representatives of educational and hospital boards; inspectors of police and a prison governor; members of variety concert parties, a ventriloquist, a puppeteer, and musicians of all ranks—vocal, instrumental, highbrow and lowbrow; and we were honoured by travellers and missionaries from all corners of the globe; also a frighteningly erudite member of the B.B.C. " Brains Trust," and an eminent poet whose outstanding merit had recently taken her to Buckingham Palace to receive the coveted gold medal for poetry from the Queen. In short, it was a truly mixed bag—all coming to make some valuable contribution to the social or cultural life of our rural community.

To cope with it all one needed to be fairly versatile, so, in wild attempts to make good the more glaring deficiencies in our education, John and I would engage in diligent eleventh-hour swotting before a V.I.P.'s arrival—like a couple of sixth-formers cramming madly on the eve of "A" levels. Of course, it didn't get us very far and more often than not it proved, in the event, a sheer waste of time. Usually one penetrating probe on their part was enough to pierce the thin veneer of our mugged-up " learning," though I must say they were generally much too civil even to make the exploratory incision.

Poetry, for example, is not my strong point, but what valiant efforts I made when the poet was coming for the weekend! With a book of her modern verse in one hand and a spoon in the other as I stirred the white sauce, I strove vainly for success in either department; in fact, the rival claims of sonnets and sauce rendered me nearly schizophrenic—I neither captured the spirit of the poetry nor achieved the velvety texture that a delectable sauce requires. And I really needn't have bothered, for the dear soul never once referred to the muse, or even betrayed anything so alarming as a faraway look. Very practically she contributed to the repast a bottle of claret and a fine Stilton cheese.

The brigadier, whose specialized subject had, not unnaturally, filled me with apprehension because of my own total ignorance of experimentation in the super-normal, was surprisingly down-to-earth and delightfully homely, more anxious it seemed to come out to the scullery and give me a hand with the washing up than to pursue the abstruse theme of his talk, let alone to give a private demonstration of transmigratory phenomena.

The thing I always regretted was that I did not profit from the ventriloquist's visit to glean a few tips about *his* fascinating art. As a child I had sometimes fancied myself talking saucily through the lips of a ventriloquist's doll, even making a few overt experiments in front of a mirror; but I had been a confirmed failure. And now, having actually entertained a professional, I had stupidly let a golden opportunity slip by!

For all our valiant efforts to become thoroughly *au fait* with the relevant background of our distinguished visitors, John once revealed himself as *most* inadequately briefed when a certain M.P.— ex-R.A.F. and multi-decorated—came to lecture. This bigwig, apologizing for his early departure, said: " Must get away now, Vicar; so sorry to leave you, but I'm flying to Italy tonight," which evoked John's classic inanity, " Oh, I quite understand. Ever been up before, or is this your first flight? " The heroic M.P.'s moustache twitched dangerously, and out of a deathly silence someone whispered tersely in John's ear: " Bomber pilot . . . Hamburg . . . Cologne . . . Bremen! "

*   *   *   *   *

At the other end of the scale, social favours were not unknown from the occasional small fry with a half-term holiday on hand and no clearly defined plans. On one occasion, just as we were leaving the house to keep an important engagement, a young friend of about nine or ten turned up, unheralded, on a brand-new bike and accompanied by his current buddy, both fully intending to spend their weekend leave with us! " Yours is the best garden to play in, Uncle John, that's why we chose you; you don't mind, do you? "

This enterprising child, having had but one trial run in his own back garden on the new bike, calculated that a ride to Upper Bellpull—a distance of nearly forty miles—was a wizard idea, especially with the prospect of full board and lodging on arrival. Without disclosing their plan, the boys had set out confidently and had pedalled straight to the cathedral, where they asked for " Uncle John." The puzzled verger discovered eventually that they wanted the vicar of Upper Bellpull.

" But he doesn't live here, sonny," said the verger.

" Well, n-o-o-o; actually I know he doesn't," admitted Tim, " but we've lost our way and I thought the bishop would know. I'd like to see the bishop, if you don't mind; he's a friend of mine! "

The alleged friendship, I might say, rested on the briefest possible encounter—in fact his lordship's attendance once at Tim's church for a confirmation service, at the time when Tim was the youngest, newest and smallest chorister present, and had attracted episcopal notice only by his diminutive stature. But let that pass.

The verger put the boys on the right road. Tim assured us airily that nothing exciting had happened on the way, except when they rode up a one-way street against a strong stream of down-flowing traffic, and then some men had been terribly rude and called them *awful* names.

Our standing engagement had to go by default, after much apologetic telephoning on John's part. Our immediate concern was (a) to telephone the boys' parents, who by now, we calculated, would be distractedly contacting the police, who in their turn would soon be sending out search parties with tracker dogs, dragging rivers, and having photographs thrown on television screens; and (b) to give the boys an adequate meal. The best I could muster on that ill-starred day—with stocks in the larder at an all-time low—was a dreary issue of sardine sandwiches (bread and scrape with a vengeance that day!) and a bag of ginger nuts, bushels of apples, and an issue of crisps if they fancied them. They polished off the lot in a brisk, businesslike way, plus enough lemonade to float a battleship.

On another occasion—one of those singularly rare Sunday afternoons when John, having no official duty, had settled for a quiet forty winks—two slightly older boys from a neighbouring boarding school presented themselves. John received them. They were total strangers to him, but, after a somewhat unfruitful exchange of greetings, he concluded that he was *supposed* to know at least one of them. He invited them into the lounge. I was busy in the next room with some urgent correspondence for the four o'clock post. As an undercurrent to the breakneck tap-tap of my typewriter I could just hear (and wished I couldn't) the faint drone of voices, with occasional long pauses, indicating, I supposed, the points at which conversational ammunition ran out.

Presently John, looking positively haggard, came to me with a garbled story. Apparently the boys' spokesman had introduced himself as "Nigel, Mr. Cook's son," and his friend as "my pal Julian," adding: "Daddy told me that if I had a free Sunday afternoon and didn't know what to do why not go and see Mr. Green at Upper Bellpull?"

Well, why not?

Now we knew Mr. Cook only slightly, having maintained a tenuous link after meeting at some public function. We were in no sense indebted to him, and we were unaware that he even had a

son, so we felt it was certainly a bit steep to inflict the child and
" his pal, Julian " on us for an afternoon because they were at a
loose end. However, while I got tea ready, John endeavoured to
make a bit of conversational headway, only to find himself getting
deeper and deeper in the morass: the stock questions he asked
about Mr. and Mrs. Cook, and the Cooks' house near the golf
links, and the Cooks' landscaped garden, and the Cooks' trip to the
States (from which they had just returned when we made their
acquaintance), brought all the wrong answers and much bewildered
headshaking. The situation was getting out of hand. By the time
these abortive exchanges had reached the craziest levels of Mad
Hattery, and puzzled frowns furrowed all our brows, John decided
it had gone far enough and virtually asked Nigel for his credentials:
" Nigel, do you *really* know what you're talking about? In fact,
are we all speaking of the same people? "

Closer investigation revealed that we *weren't*. Nigel, it trans-
spired, was the witless son of another Mr. Cook altogether, whose
claim to John's acquaintance was even more slender than the first
Mr. C's. *This* man had once lived near John in his pre-clerical days
—countless moons ago.

On reflection, the boy, Nigel, may not have been as witless as in
some respects he appeared. He contributed at least one shrewd
observation, which I haven't forgotten. For want of a new topic, I
was firing stock questions at the boy: "Do you like school? Rugger
or soccer? What about the athletics record? What size staff have
you?" When he volunteered the information that their staff included
two women teachers, one of whom was, allegedly, " *terribly* old
and not a bit of good," I dived in to champion old age and decrepi-
tude, suggesting " If she's as old as that, no doubt she's past it."
And he flashed back, without a hint of facetiousness, " Oh no, I
should say she's never reached it "!

*   *   *   *   *

It would be impossible to pin-point all the highlights of vicarage
entertaining, but one deserving of at least passing mention con-
cerns the occasion when we all—guests and hosts—had to achieve
entry by a break-in, after a prolonged period of uncertainty on the
doorstep. It was not without a touch of melodrama.

The rural dean had come to preach at the harvest thanksgiving—

on Friday night—and a little supper party had been arranged for
him and a few other guests after the service.

As the R.D. was affably shaking hands with the departing
congregation, I scuttled ahead to get the food on the table and the
coffee made.

But I couldn't open the front door! The key slipped into the
lock all right, but it wouldn't turn a fraction. I tried shaking the
door, but it was so firmly jammed that I feared the worst: there
must be intruders; no doubt they counted on these delaying tactics
to facilitate a get-away in the event of disturbance.

I am no heroine, so I waited anxiously until reinforcements
arrived—John and the rural dean, a handful of my relations and
three or four local friends. Somebody suggested getting in through
a ground-floor window, but every one had been cautiously latched
before I left.

The menfolk, after a sober survey, agreed that the easiest window
to enter—in fact the *only* one that I knew was *un*latched—was the
toilet, immediately above the front porch. It only needed a ladder
(and a fearless climber!); ours was missing from its accustomed
place in the shed. John remembered using it recently for apple-
picking, so two of the party set off into the dark jungle of the
orchard to track it down. There was a protracted interval, during
which we were all shivering and I was becoming inanely repetitive
in my apologies to our guests for keeping them on the doorstep.
The searchers returned without the ladder, and only then did I
remember having lent it the day before to someone else who wanted
to pick fruit. Off went John to the borrower, who was profoundly
sorry to have caused us this trouble; he really *had* returned the
ladder the same day, but had parked it in the disused stable—wasn't
that right? By the time John had retrieved it from there we had
nominated (though *not* by drawing lots!) which one was to climb
up and break in: the obvious choice was our farming friend, who
had earned distinction as an outstanding Civil Defence hero during
the war.

Up the ladder he shinned with acrobatic skill, opened the lavatory
window and disappeared within, encouraged by applause and a
cheering chorus from below. The obvious catastrophe which I, in
my anguish, had envisaged was neatly avoided! Familiar as I was
with the lie of the land, I had failed to see how he could *possibly* miss
an ignominious descent into the lavatory pan. However, with

G

precious little room for manœuvrability, he landed safe and sound —and dry.

Thus the ice was well and truly broken for a very pleasant, informal little supper party.

Oh, by the way, everything in the place was safe and intact; no sign of a burglary. Somebody had inadvertently dropped a normally unused catch, which could only be released from within.

*   *   *   *   *

It was ironical and a little sad that the visitor who had travelled the farthest in a determined effort to make our acquaintance had to be denied even the most frugal token of hospitality because of the total unexpectedness of his arrival and unfortunate mistiming.

One Sunday afternoon, as John was on the point of leaving the house to take a service and I to fulfil a parochial enagagement, the door bell clanged. As I answered it, a gaunt, elderly stranger—hatless and very informally attired—stepped " right in " and, in an unmistakable American accent, wished me a singularly hearty "*Good* afternoon, ma'am," seizing my hand and shaking it village pump-wise with painful vigour.

To my routine civility "I expect you want the vicar" he responded with a most genial smile: "Not specially, ma'am; I guess *you'll* do. I'm James Dupont, from Texas. You *are* Mrs. Green, I guess?"

I assured him that he'd guessed aright; but who on earth, I was racking my brain, was Mr. James Dupont, from Texas, with his devastatingly friendly approach? I was at a total loss.

Bit by bit it emerged that he had read some little article of mine in a regional magazine; he had felt sufficiently interested (or curious?) to want to meet the author if the opportunity occurred. I had never felt more honoured—or more embarrassed. Surely I must have seemed in reality a trifle disappointing at the end of such a long trek.

However, John and I were simply obliged to keep our respective appointments, and the best I could do was gently to usher Mr. James Dupont towards the door, with an invitation (accompanied by *my* bewitching smile) to come some other day, when I hoped he would give me the pleasure of offering him a taste of English hospitality. It was a forlorn hope, as he was off to Liverpool next morning to embark on the homeward journey.

That was the nearest I ever got to having a " fan " following, and, to avoid possible misrepresentation, it should be made perfectly clear that even Mr. James Dupont did not cross the Atlantic solely to make the personal acquaintance of Mrs. S. O. Green, of Upper Bellpull. Actually he had been cruising around the country for four or five weeks, visiting friends and long-lost relatives, and ours was " scheduled as the last port of call, ma'ma "—only he, of course, pronounced it skeduled!

* * * * *

Easily the most remarkable of all our surprise visits—and the one with the most far-reaching and unforeseeable repercussions—occurred one Sunday evening in the dank gloom of a November mist.

John and I were enjoying a last-minute warm by the fire before evensong. He answered the faint knock at the front door; after a moment's disjointed mumbling he came back and begged me to come. " There's a mad woman on the doorstep " he said.

In the second in which it took me to get there she had slumped down and was in a semi-kneeling attitude on the doormat.

She was youngish—around the early twenties I estimated—in hiking attire and hatless. She seemed to be losing consciousness.

We carried her into the nearest room—John's study—and endeavoured to extract a few facts before she passed right out. She professed not to know who she was or from where she had come. She had no idea where she was, but she insisted that she had wakened up shivering with cold on the floor of the church and had managed to make her way to the nearest house.

(Actually, ours *wasn't* the nearest house to the church door; in fact the vicarage was completely hidden from that angle, and this is a point that provides a very significant factor in the final outcome of the strange episode.)

She said she couldn't remember *anything*, and she complained of violent pains in the head. She *thought* she was Jane Smith and, very vaguely, that she had some connection with a training college, but " everything's so hazy " she kept repeating. Then she gave up trying to talk and seemed almost in a state of coma.

With evensong less than half an hour off, we had to think and act quickly. Our nearest doctor was five miles away and the district nurse two parishes away. Abandoning all thought of church, I hastened to get blankets and hot water bottles for the girl; also a warm drink, but she was unable to take it.

Meanwhile John was urgently telephoning for aid and trying to find possible colleges from which she might be missing. He was also closely watching the clock for the service he was due to take. After three fruitless calls he contacted a college, about twenty miles from Upper Bellpull, whose student roll included a Jane Smith. She had not been seen since breakfast; they were not unduly alarmed as Jane suffered from wanderlust and frequently absented herself for a whole day.

It was the vice-principal of the college who spoke to John. She had little doubt that our foundling was her missing Jane; she begged us to hold on to her until she could come over with the car to collect her.

John then fetched a neighbour to give me moral support in this unpredicatable situation while he was in church.

It seemed an eternity before the vice-principal arrived, bringing the college nurse with her. It needed only the briefest examination to convince the nurse that Jane was very ill and could not possibly be moved except by ambulance direct to hospital.

She and the vice-principal began a series of telephone calls to secure ambulance service and a hospital bed without waiting for a doctor's chit, after trying unsuccessfully to contact one or two surgeries in the college area.

Eventually they were assured that an ambulance would shortly be on the way. There was nothing we could do now but wait patiently and sip coffee.

At this juncture I asked the vice-principal her name so that I could introduce her to my neighbour.

" My name's MacDougall," she replied, whereupon I suffered the surprise of a lifetime; there was an instant flash of mutual recognition, and I gasped " Heavens above, are you really Meg? " and she, equally incredulous, blurted out " Sally! It can't be you."

But indeed it *was*. We embraced and tried to calculate how long since we had last met—or even heard of each other. It was at least thirty years ago, when she was a gauche, hockey-playing undergraduate and I a flapper emerging diffidently from a secretarial college to offer my untested services to the world of commerce.

In those far-off days she had spent many a Sunday with my family, entertaining us hilariously with her irrepressible fun and mimicry.

The transformation was fantastic and amply excused my failure to recognize her on sight (as, indeed, she had failed to recognize me). Here was a woman of singular grace and poise, a sparkling personality, distinguished, perfectly groomed, with snow-white hair ; but she was still the irrepressible Meg, bubbling with high spirits, despite the acquisition of her doctorate.

The cultivated rôle of vicar's wife slipped from me like a loose cloak and Meg made no pretence to hide her wild excitement at this improbable meeting. Of course, she was unaware that I had married, and probably the last place she would have expected to find me, anyway, was in a parsonage.

We yarned reminiscently until the ambulance came, while nurse kept a professional eye on Jane. John got home just ahead of the ambulance and thought that I must have taken leave of my senses as I presented him effusively to Dr. MacDougall (whose very existence he had never heard of before !). " John, this is *Meg* ; can you believe it ? Isn't it *fantastic* ? "

Jane was duly transferred to a stretcher and whisked off to hospital ; Meg drove the nurse back to college ; my kind neighbour departed and no doubt gave a startling account of events to her family ; and then John made one of his strangely prophetic observations: " I wonder *why* Meg had to cross your path again in this incredible way, after all these years. There *must* be a purpose in it ; we'll know it some day."

I couldn't sleep for thinking of this out-of-the-blue encounter. The next day I telephoned Meg to inquire about Jane Smith and was told that she was still in hospital and the doctors were completely foxed by her case ; nobody could get much out of her, but she was known to have been dreading her finals—due to begin in a few days. They were considering the possibilities of a self-induced illness.

I telephoned several times that week ; she was still in hospital and her mysterious illness undiagnosed.

(My own theory, from the moment I saw her slumped on the mat, was that she had been doped, and some factors that came to light afterwards tended to confirmed this possibility, though it was never officially acknowledged.)

Well, all the excitement died down for the next twelve months or so, and we gave little thought to Jane Smith—or even to Meg. We were all busy people.

Then one day, like a minor bombshell, John's prophetic " purpose " was revealed and my strange encounter with Meg after that interval of over thirty years was seen as a *purposeful* gesture by the hand of providence.

A young parishioner of ours came for John's advice and, if possible, influential help at an extremely critical stage of her career. Owing to certain very unusual circumstances, her professional future hung precariously in the balance; her academic path had become blocked through no fault of her own. There seemed no conceivable way out of the impasse, despite her undoubted natural ability and promise.

John had no doubt as to the best course to recommend, but hadn't a clue how, in her situation, it could be accomplished. He certainly had no influence whatsoever to exercise on her behalf.

At this point 1 was called in. Had I any likely suggestion to offer? Our young parishioner looked terribly despondent as she saw her chances of a good career being denied her. Just as a deep depression was moving in on all of us there came a flash of inspiration and I yelled the name—*Meg!* There seemed a faint hope of solution through Dr. MacDougall's personal intervention.

A meeting was arranged at the vicarage between Dr. MacDougall and our young friend. The peculiar circumstances of her dilemma were carefully examined and the merits of the case assessed. Dr. MacDougall, accustomed as she was to dealing with students in the mass, was not slow to spot the girl's rare potentialities. The right course was mapped for her; the appropriate wires were deftly pulled and obstacles removed. To this day we (and the girl herself) are absolutely convinced that her particular problem *could not have been solved through any other agency.*

At the time of writing our former young parishioner is herself vice-principal of an important school in the Dominions, fulfilling handsomely that early promise—and it all hinged on the discovery one wintry night of a stranger in a state of collapse on our doorstep!

Dr. MacDougall passed right out of our orbit once more. We have not seen her since. Providence, or the hand of God, or fate—call it what you will—had been served.

The sceptic, of course, is at liberty to doubt that Jane Smith was *purposely* guided to our doorstep that night, completely hidden as it was from the main road; the fact remains, however, that with a row of cottages ablaze with lights so close at hand (surely a more obvious refuge in her plight) she groped her way in the dark to the vicarage—with such significant consequences.

*　*　*　*　*

There was another unforgettable visitation—this time on the eve of the festival of St. Michael and All Angels—when the vicarage calm was chaotically shattered by a caller with maniacal tendencies. He laboured under the delusion that he was sent to rescue us from hordes of evil spirits plotting to attack and destroy us on the following day. " I *must* save you," he pleaded earnestly, and was prepared to do so even at the risk of fearful retribution on himself. " I may have to suffer physical torture, or possible annihilation," he reflected sadly.

To the best of our ability we tried to pacify and reassure him; he submitted to brief incarceration locked in our garage—with sustenance, rugs and pillows—while we endeavoured to sort it all out with the authorities. At last he departed, with sandwiches, cake and apples for the road, perfectly happy in the belief that he had valiantly fulfilled his mission. If he came in like a lion he certainly went out like a lamb—and a very docile one!—to undertake his " next job . . . a *very* difficult one this time." In curiosity, we asked where. " Oh, I can't tell you that, because I'm never allowed to know where I have to go next until I get there," he confided darkly.

*　*　*　*　*

It mustn't be supposed that it was only members of the laity who were liable to swoop with impulsive suddenness on us. The clergy were equally capable of unpredictable calls.

Our peace was disturbed one drowsy summer afternoon by an extra impatient clanging of the doorbell. This time the clergy had arrived in force—four strapping young priests.

Of this quartet only two were personally known to John; they were all allegedly in strict retreat—engaged in a three-day period of intensive self-examination and spiritual discipline at the Diocesan

House. There had come a point, apparently, in their ascetic exercise where the claims of the spirit and the groanings of the flesh had met in head-on collision. In short, they sought sustenance! Hunger, they claimed, had proved their Waterloo; with engaging frankness, " We're all suffering from night starvation. How about it? What can you manage? "

Banking on John's hospitable sympathy, they had seized on their afternoon free session to trudge over to Upper Bellpull to replenish. There was no time to lose; they were committed to be back—and shrouded in silence again!—by four o'clock.

The hospitable spirit was there right enough, but I had no magic wand. I pointed out, as tactfully as I could, that had they warned us by telephone there was no knowing what I might have been able to " manage."

As it was, these four supposedly ravenous men, dropping virtually out of the blue, had to be satisfied with hunks of shop-bought seed cake, a packet of bisuits and four doughnuts (intended for our own tea). They washed down these meagre crumbs with oceans of tea, and for the return hike John sacrificed a slab of his rationed chocolate.

Having responded—albeit frugally—to our " needy brethren ", they admitted that it was a bit of a phoney story! The gnawing hunger was a prearranged leg-pull—I suppose to test our resourcefulness, or maybe to measure our credulity.

How gullible can one be?

*   *   *   *   *

One hideous bloomer in my vicarage career, which to this day I cannot recall without pangs of acute embarrassment, stemmed from a kind offer by the leader of a neighbouring youth group to come over and put on a variety show in aid of our church funds.

This kind Mr. Bellamy suggested that it would be a good idea for him first to pop along and inspect the available facilities. A date was fixed for this preliminary visit.

On the evening he was expected John had suddenly to see to some brief matter in church, so he instructed me: " If Mr. Bellamy should arrive before I get back, just ask him in and try to keep the pot boiling till I get there." Simple!

It was a lovely June evening, warm and cloudless. Mr. Bellamy cycled over. He was a very tall, well-built, affable man of about thirty. We had never met before.

I explained that John would be back in a few minutes and invited Mr. Bellamy to come in and sit down. As he was about to do so, I added—having spotted halfway down the drive a small blonde fairy leaning on her little bike and eyeing us wistfully—" Oh, don't leave your little girl outside; do bring her in, too. I'm afraid we haven't any children here for her to play with, but I'll find her some picture books."

Mr. Bellamy beckoned and called " Joan, Mrs. Green would like you to come in, dear," and as Joan reached the porch he gravely presented her, " My wife, Mrs. Bellamy—Mrs. Green! "

Who would have dreamt it? Never could there have been such a bewitching pocket Venus. Her head just about reached her husband's waist. She was dressed in the briefest of cycling pants, a T-shirt, little white socks and sandals, and a blue Alice band held her golden locks in place.

Having dealt her—unwittingly—such a shocking insult, I felt it was now incumbent on me to offer something more sophisticated than a lolly by way of refeshment! A leisurely sherry seemed to restore equilibrium all round.

These dear people demonstrated their magnanimity by subsequently putting on a first-class show and never referring again to my classic *faux pas*.

*   *   *   *   *

In the field of social entertaining there was one vital point of difference, I discovered (belatedly, alas!), between town and country custom: in a word, *tea time*. I wish I had been forewarned. As it was, a puzzling experience awaited me when I first launched out as tea hostess to the wife and daughter of one of our farming parishioners. It hadn't occurred to me to specify the hour. Tea time to me was *tea time*—namely four o'clock.

I duly prepared the customary light spread and then sat waiting in state for their arrival. An hour passed and no visitors had turned up. After another three-quarters of an hour we assumed they had mistaken the day and decided to go ahead on our own.

I was just beginning to preside over a trolley slightly overloaded for two when our friends came along. Their smiling composure betrayed no hint of embarrassment at their late arrival. In fact they were so completely at ease that there was only one conclusion to be drawn: tea time in the country means six o'clock at the earliest; more probably seven.

Just as they were leaving the mother said: " Now *you* must both come and see us, and I'll show you what a real farmhouse tea is like! "

Ruefully, I wondered just how far short of the approved standards of hospitality my light " four o'clock " had fallen. I found out with horrible certainty the next week when John and I returned the call.

One glance at their groaning table and we knew that a " farmhouse tea " and a conventional " four o'clock " are not to be confused. They are two distinct functions: one an over-satisfying banquet, from which one staggers full to repletion; the other, by comparison, a token fast—just going through the polite gestures of eating and drinking but with negligible intake.

We were regaled with a menu as long as your arm, beginning with colossal plates of ham—home-cured, and what superb ham it was! This was accompanied by a proportionately massive bowl of salad, loaded with eggs. I thought I must be seeing double; there were piles of crisp home-baked bread, fluffy scones, lashings of their own dairy butter, jam, cheese, rich fruit cake, tartlets, biscuits, and the most perfectly baked Victoria sandwich I had ever clapped eyes on—thickly butter-iced; there were fabulous fancy pastries, and, as a finishing touch, a giant bowl of fruit salad and whipped Jersey cream.

I realized that, by contrast, I had plumbed the depths of frugality in *my* entertaining. My hostess mentioned casually that rationing in farming areas had never been as rigorously enforced as she imagined it had been elsewhere. How right she was if this feast was any indication!

We made a mental note there and then, for future reference and digestion's sake, always to take suitable precautions before keeping farmhouse tea appointments—at least a two-day total fast!

In due course I was invited into many a farmhouse kitchen, and I never ceased to marvel at the astonishing up-to-dateness and perfection of the equipment, and, of course, the clinical spotlessness, that characterized them all. No fuggy Dickensian atmosphere here;

every kitchen resembled a colour-supplement model, with no labour-saving device lacking. I silently saluted their progressive attitude on the distaff side.

*   *   *   *   *

It would be ungracious, and indeed very unfair, if I failed to mention that our parsonage " feeding of the five thousand " was from time to time substantially eased by the numerous little gifts in kind which found their way unobtrusively into our larder from well-disposed members of the farming fraternity; perhaps it would be a dozen new-laid eggs, a carton of cream or some butter, or perhaps a jar of honey—deposited mysteriously at the back door. Once it was a magnificent turkey—such a giant of a bird that it had to be partially dismembered before it would go into our doll-size oven; and what an unforgettable bird that was! Or it might be a basket of mushrooms, a pheasant, chicken, duck or hare.

As for the hare, alas, that kindly intention brought us irretrievable disgrace!

Colonel Banks, meeting John for the first time, had said affably " I'll send my man along shortly with some game."

A few days later I espied a tough-looking stranger, in leather leggings and a down-turned tweed hat, with a gun under his arm and a dog at his heels, strolling unconcernedly across our lawn. A corpse of some kind hung stiffly from his free hand. I was too dull to associate this unfamiliar figure with the benevolent colonel, and I screamed " John, quick! There's a man with a gun in our garden; he must be a poacher; what do we do? "

John, bravely unarmed, approached his adversary with assumed nonchalance.

" With the colonel's compliments, Vicar," said the colonel's courteous gamekeeper, handing John the corpse—a nauseating spectacle, still dripping blood. I felt a bit sick and turned away.

John, nothing if not prompt in expressing gratitude for any favour received, dashed off a letter of thanks—for the " lovely *rabbit,* which I assure you, Colonel, is most acceptable! "

As the letter dropped with an irrevocable thud in the post-box poor John suddenly came to: " John Green, you're the biggest idiot in Upper Bellpull; that rabbit was a hare."

We didn't receive any more game from that quarter. I suppose

Colonel Banks saw the futility of casting any more gastronomic pearls before the vicarage swine.

*   *   *   *   *

Generosity was unquestionably a fixed habit with these kindly if somewhat shy and emotionally undemonstrative country parishioners. We ourselves had ample evidence of it, and we were told, on reliable authority, a classic story concerning the P.O.G.'s exceptionally fruitful visitation, which illustrates the point in the grand manner.

A year or so after his retirement he came on a round of Christmas visits to old friends in the neighbourhood. He ended up, towards late afternoon, at a certain farm noted for its extreme liberality. Here was waiting a fine plump turkey, which they had prepared for the old gentleman's Christmas box.

As he was about to leave, the farmer's son jumped up to carry the bird out to the boot of the car. But the P.O.G. showed signs of agitation and uncharacteristic alertness. He begged " No; no! *Please* don't bother to come out. *I* can manage that quite well."

But the young man knew his manners and couldn't think of allowing the P.O.G. to stagger out under the weight of a twenty-pound bird, so he became insistent.

" No, really, sir; I couldn't possibly let *you* carry it;   *do* leave it to me." And so the pantomime proceeded, with the old man protesting vigorously against youthful courtesy. Courtesy won.

When the young man got back indoors he was grinning from ear to ear. " No wonder the old boy didn't want me to go out to the car. Gosh! You ought to have seen that boot; bung full; like a mobile larder. I couldn't remember *everything*, but he certainly had a couple of chickens and a goose, and a brace of pheasants; there were loads of apples, and a ham, and quite a few bottles! More than enough to keep him going for a twelve-month if he's got a deep freeze."

*   *   *   *   *

That parochial largess is something legendary most priests would readily agree, but one of John's brethren in another diocese had the surprise of his life in this context. He had made several unsuccessful applications for an account to be rendered—he owed a farmer for a load of stable manure for his roses. When, after six months, the bill was still not sent in he tried once more. " *Do* please let me have my account; I really don't like to let these little debts run on and on, so will you attend to it? " To which his parishioner replied: " Account? Ah, yes! I remember now—for the *manure*. Well, you'd better have it for your Easter offering! " Telling the story to John, he had chuckled gleefully at the recollection: " Ha, ha! Jolly good idea, really; that was *one* Easter offering the Inland Revenue couldn't filch."

*　　*　　*　　*　　*

It seemed that with their splendid generosity went an equally splendid thriftiness; they seemed commendably careful and canny in money values. We, at any rate, saw no evidence of wild-cat extravagance or ostentation—except, possibly, in the Job Middleditch affair; but he, poor man, confronted as he was with a sordid ultimatum, hadn't much choice in the matter.

Job—sixtyish and an alleged woman-hater—had proved himself an adroit evader of the matrimonial yoke, until he fell under the bewitching spell of a purposeful middle-aged widow with a sizeable young brood—a Mrs. Binder, a newcomer to the parish. To everyone's surprise (and probably to his own) he then fell like a sitting duck and, in the circumstances, became understandably bemused. Job, now foreseeing the infinite advantages of a wholly transformed life with Mrs. Binder as an efficient partner, offered to make her Mrs. Middleditch. She was anything but averse to the proposition, but *only on her own terms*, and here she outlined the conditions for connubial surrender. (It was the case all over again of the fairy-story suitor being set a series of impossible tests before the princess's old father grudgingly released her—only in this case it was the lady herself who did the bargaining.)

Her terms, it leaked out eventually, specified a sheepskin jacket, a harmonium, an interior-sprung mattress *and* a " telly "; and this was regarded by some as an intolerably heavy ransom for her hand. It certainly involved the amorous Job not only in an awful lot of reckless spending but also in a good deal of deep delving into dark corners and odd recesses to bring to light the hidden fortune of his sixty-odd years of bachelor hoarding—all stuffed away in old tobacco tins!

The days of parsimony were over for him!

* * * * *

Looking back on the stream of constant comings and goings at the vicarage—on matters official and otherwise—and on our happy rôle as hosts to so many interesting and differing types, it does seem a pity that from the outset we omitted to keep a visitors' book. In later years it would have been tremendously fascinating to scan all the autographs and recall the occasions; and it would have been quite invaluable as a memory-tickler in compiling the present reminiscences—although, of course, for sheer sensationalism it could never have competed with the visitors' book in church, which audaciously recorded, in a scrubby, schoolboy fist, visits from both Julius Cæsar *and* William the Conqueror, both claiming residence in the next parish and, even more incredible, both popping in on the same day! A remarkable confrontation, one would think.

CHAPTER 6

Plague, pestilence, fire and flood—not to mention a sandstorm

IF ever there were false prophets they were our pessimistic friends who, on hearing that we were about to go to a country living, forecast for us the most dismal and unpromising future. If we did not actually die an early death from stagnation and sheer boredom we were, according to their prediction, certainly condemning ourselves to a long sentence of awful depression and primitive discomforts through the very conditions of pastoral exile.

" *You*, of all people," they exclaimed. " You've always been used to an active town life; what on earth will you do with yourselves buried alive in the heart of the country? You'll simply *hate* it! "—thus confirming their double fallibility as seers, because from the word " go " we absolutely adored country life and all that went with it, and an ever-vigilant providence saw to it that we were *never* threatened with stagnation.

On the contrary, we have sometimes wondered, on looking back on the almost unbroken sequence of exciting (though not always *pleasantly* exciting) incidents which highlighted our days there, whether we could have dreamt it all.

Stagnation my foot! Boredom? *Never!*

Our forward-gazing friends, had they been more practical than pessimistic, could have served us better by recommending an intensive course of study in natural history as preparation for our journey to the wilderness, for I do admit that country life embodied for us all the countless hazards of an uncharted sea, and a little bit of advance tutoring would have been an immense help in one or two of our initial dilemmas.

For example, there was the incident of the hornets. Before going to the country we had never met a hornet, but very soon afterwards we were to come into uncomfortably close contact with a determined colony of them; one or two of the most daring members actually took possession of our bedroom one night. We didn't remain to contest their right.

The first intimation came from some workmen who were perched giddily at the top of high ladders painting the eaves (we were in the throes of the periodic disturbance known as "quinquennial dilapidations ").

These men appeared to be alternately painting and swatting, and at one point it looked as if they were practising semaphore. These wild gestures manifestly added to the dangers of their job at such a height.

Then their spokesman descended and issued an ultimatum: " Unless you do something about them flippin' buzzers, we're goin' to pack up and 'op it; we're not riskin' our flippin' necks any longer! "

Invited to be more explicit, he said " Cor, don't tell me yer don't know they're there. There's flippin' millions of 'em; gnats is bad enough, but them flippin' 'ornets—cor! "

So that was his grievance—hornets. He was clearly in explosive mood; he shuffled off in disgust.

And that's how, without tuition in natural history, we learnt that our garden was swarming with hornets. At close range I could easily have mistaken them for king-size wasps, but their buzz was infinitely more selective and ominous. As I listened it sounded like a flight of Spitfires going into action.

Well, what was the next step? Even *we*, raw beginners that we were, were not so naïve as to imagine that indiscriminate fly-spraying out in the open would get us anywhere; it might even stimulate the enemy. Was there an appropriate pesticide for hornets? Was there a legal obligation to report a plague of this sort to some official body? If so, to whom?

The mutinous painters had no practical suggestions to offer; in fact, after that first abrasive encounter they seemed rather hostile towards us. So I tore off in search of Uncle, the gardener, who was patiently pricking out lettuce seedlings and didn't seem to appreciate being disturbed. We had a certain deep respect for Uncle's native wisdom and common sense; when it came to country lore he had a rich fund of knowledge which more than made up for his abbreviated schooling (he had once confided to me that he had left school at the age of eleven because " I'd allus bin very sharp and by then I knowed as much as teacher an' they couldn't learn me nothin' more ").

But this, clearly, wasn't his day; far from bristling with bright ideas, he only added to our rising alarm by confirming that " they flipping things " could do a power of harm; in fact, if they made up their minds they could be lethal. He actually knew of a horse that had been stung by " an 'orrible 'ornet on its left flank " and had died within twenty brief minutes. " You simply can't be too careful wi' *they*! "

He stooped down again with a grunt and became wholly pre-occupied once more with his lettuce seedlings.

The further we pursued our inquiries the more sinister became the fearful possibilities—and results!—of getting stung. Nobody seemed to be particularly helpful, and a few were miserably depress-ing; for instance, they warned us that if anyone got stung by *our* hornets—say the painters or passers-by in the lane—*we* would be held responsible and liable for compensation. (In passing, I should have thought that, in law, the actual ownership of a swarm of hornets, as opposed to a swarm of bees, was far from easy to deter-mine.) However, if they were popularly regarded as *our* hornets we obviously couldn't afford to dodge the issue any longer.

Then we ran into the sexton and he was gloriously reassuring, in one sense: " *You* don't want to worry about them things; just leave 'em to me. *I'll* find the nest, and when I've done that *you* just send for the pest control officer [mentioning the nearest one] and he'll come an' put paid to 'em in no time—with cyanide."

Everything went according to schedule. The nest was located in a huge cavity in one of our old elm trees (which could, possibly, have established *our* ownership); the horde of pests in residence appeared to be literally countless.

The pest man came with commendable promptitude, in a plain van, with his supply of cyanide.

The extermination was a matter of seconds. We thanked him effusively. " Not at all; not at all. It's a pleasure " he bleated. " Hornets are ugly things, I grant you, *but not really dangerous, you know*. They never *sting* unless you annoy them. Cheerio! "

In due course we received a bill from the pest control officer for £1—" in respect of services rendered on your premises."

So we *were* stung after all, only not by the hornets.

*   *   *   *   *

Then take the bats!

They caused, initially, terrific alarm, although we did not

H

immediately associate them with the apparent domestic tragedy that sent John and me racing pell-mell around the house, yelling distractedly " Where are you? Where *are* you? Are you *ill?*" to a visitor who had mysteriously vanished from her bed overnight.

She was eventually run to earth, sleeping peacefully, on the Chesterfield in the drawing-room, with a few hastily snatched bed-clothes draped over her and her rolled-up corsets still clutched firmly in her right hand, truncheonwise, as if she had been using this garment as a weapon of defence—which, in fact, she had.

Emerging slowly from slumber, *she* wanted to know what all the fuss was about. Then she remembered what had happened and wanted to know how on earth we—brought up in civilized sur-roundings and to appreciate decent standards—could tolerate living in this wild jungle of a place, infested first with hornets and now with *colossal* (her word!) bats. It was just beyond her compre-hension! " It's nothing short of a miracle," she went on severely, " that I didn't go stark, raving mad during the night, with things like that fluttering blindly about the room. I turned on the light," she continued, " and there it was, coming straight at me—a *bat!* I grabbed my corsets and tried to swipe it, but I missed it every time. The only thing I could think of was to tie up my head in my vest, grab the bedclothes, and *scram*. Give me town and civilization every time!"

When this tirade ended we went upstairs, and there was the poor hunted little creature hanging drowsily upside down on the curtain, no doubt making the most of its quiet spell while its would-be killer was out of the way.

Uncle's versatile services were finally enlisted. His method of handling may well have been unconventional for all I know, but it was effectual. He approached it confidently with a dustpan, a brush and a duster. The bat allowed itself to be swept gently into the pan, covered with the duster, and then taken down to the orchard and released.

On reflection this seemed a bit silly. Surely it would only encourage the poor thing to try again.

After that bats were accepted by John and me as a normal hazard. If they liked sleeping upside down in our bedroom, clinging to the pelmet, that was their affair; we just ignored them until morning and then emulated Uncle. with dustpan and brush.

In course of time we, too, qualified as reasonably competent bat-catchers.

* * * * *

The invasion by swifts was another cup of tea altogether. We had to acknowledge defeat in this department and vacate our bedroom for one of the spares.

I had gone upstairs at dusk one evening to turn down beds and draw curtains, and my surprise and indignation knew no bounds to find that our chamber was a virtual aviary, with a full circus of swifts performing mad aerobatics—wheeling, diving, swooping, whirring and gyrating as they sought vainly to escape out of the window.

My unwelcome appearance evidently added panic to their movements. They seemed to fly at the speed of light. I tried to count them but, as they never slowed down and never alighted, I could only make a wild guess. " There's a good dozen, at least " I said. John thought it was less.

Here and there the bedspreads already bore evidence of their passage. We flung up the windows and found ourselves calling fatuously to the intruders " Come on, come on; out you go! " They had other ideas, or else our language didn't register with them. They seemed to redouble their efforts, as if maddened by frustration. Then a few of their number whizzed out on to the landing and threatened to invade the whole house.

It was at this point that we hoisted the white flag; we slammed our bedroom door on the invaders and took ourselves off to the guest room.

Next morning all the swifts had disappeared. The many blemishes on the furniture and fabrics fostered the idea that it had been a rather protracted visit. We thankfully repossessed our own bedroom.

Occasionally, after that mass entry, we were honoured by a solitary bird who had missed its way. The graceful diving and jiving of a single bird worried us not at all; but a whole circus of them was another matter altogether.

* * * * *

I had always imagined myself to be a bird lover, in fact a lover of all dumb creatures, but on growing acquaintance I formed a very poor opinion of wood-pigeons. Their plumage is attractive enough, I grant you; and even their monotonous crooning is bearable; but their viciously marauding habits alienated my affection towards them for all time. To watch them swoop with impudent defiance and deadly intention on the freshly sown vegetable garden, purloining seeds wholesale as fast as poor patient Uncle planted them; and even worse, waiting for crops to mature and *then* moving in and systematically raiding row after row just as the end product was ready for harvesting—all this forced me reluctantly to agree that the farmers had good cause to moan over the common enemy and more than a little justification to organize periodic pigeon shoots.

*   *   *   *   *

Reflecting on the more mildly tantalizing aspects of wild life, I recall an amusing story that circulated around the village one sweltering summer when mosquitoes, rather than hornets, were the prevailing plague.

Poor old Jim Grant was getting ready for bed one night when he felt a strange tickle in his ear, at a depth slightly beyond his reach.

He called in alarm for his wife to come and have a look. She couldn't be quite sure, but it seemed to be a gnat, painstakingly exploring the dark recesses of the inner ear.

Old Jim became terribly frightened and fiddled fiercely with his little finger, then with a match-stick, but this only agitated the gnat and induced it to retreat to still deeper and safer levels—and to step up its tickling.

It was getting very late, too late for the bus, and in any case it would surely seem pretty silly to go to the surgery on such a pretext. All the same, the combined effect of fear and the gnat's tireless activities was driving Jim nearly crazy.

Then Mrs. Grant had one of her inspirations. She thought it would be a good idea to introduce a few drops of whisky into the ear cavity, in the witless belief that this would render the insect blind drunk and quiescent!

The whisky bottle was brought out; she lowered three or four generous drops into her husband's ear, then gave him a tot for himself, and finally they bedded down.

Unfortunately the potent spirit had anything but the desired effect. Instead of sinking into a drunken stupour, that gnat became uncontrollably, hopping mad—the gnat's equivalent, one would imagine, of becoming punch-drunk—and it continued and intensified its frenzied tarantella without remission throughout the night.

By morning it was difficult to determine which showed the more obvious symptoms of insanity—Jim or the gnat. Anyway, they journeyed together—reluctant inseparables that they were—to the doctor's surgery.

He favoured more conventional treatment—no alcohol for either until the blood pressure was down; just a drip or two of warm oil.

Everyone was soon satisfied—not least the gnat.

* * * * *

The even more sensational affair of old Bob Stickleton put a heavy strain on the credulity of us all; fair enough, for it could well have been a case unique in human history, but, after a good deal of discreet questioning, John and I were left with no doubt at all as to its veracity.

Bob had retired some years ago from work on the land, but he still occupied a tied cottage on an outlying farm and he took a lively interest in all the local goings on and was regarded, by and large, as a " character " and something of an authority on pre-mechanized farming. At all events, he possessed an inexhaustible fund of nostalgic memories, with which he was never unwilling to entertain newcomers in his own inimitable style—that is, in volume *fortissimo*, in rhythm slow and measured, in general effect *very* impressive.

One mellow September afternoon old Bob came rushing wildly out of his cottage, simply *bellowing* for his next-door neighbour (with whom he was known to be on anything but good-neighbourly terms!): " Mrs. Miller, Mrs. *Miller*, Mrs. *M-i-l-l-e-r*! Come *quick*; I want ye!"

Mrs. Miller, rather taken aback at this apparent sign of hatchet-burying, trotted up affably. " All right; I'm coming. What's the matter wi' yew, Bob? "

" Matter? " he bawled " Why, I've got a hay seed a-growin' in me navel! " As an afterthought he added " What shall I do? "

What, in fact, they actually did in the embarrassing circumstances was essentially their affair; but the disappointing feature of the episode, we felt, was that his impulsive rapprochment was not motivated by a genuine desire for improved relations with Mrs. Miller; it was purely a matter of expediency. He just didn't know where else to turn in his unique dilemma, because his own Mrs. Stickleton—a merry old soul in any circumstances, full of harmless fun—was in the present crisis absolutely convulsed with laughter, which rendered her helpless and inept in her man's hour of need. All the same, most of us felt that this tremendous moment of self-revelation and appeal for aid must surely have done *something* towards restoring a better understanding—if not a lasting peace—between old Bob and his estranged neighbour.

One thing was certain, a local wag commented drily: poor old Bob would never have allowed " one o' they new-fangled owd combine-harvesters " to gather *his* crop!

*   *   *   *   *

As I was on little more than nodding terms with the countless species of wild life occupying our garden, it seemed only common sense to exchange my next book token for a reliable and copiously illustrated standard work on the countryside and its inhabitants. This acquisition opened up a new world for me and I was soon able to identify the majority of our tenants.

In addition to the ubiquitous sparrows, blackbirds, starlings and rooks, we were patronized by beautiful, sleek water-wagtails, brightly coloured chaffinches and blue-tits, wrens and mistle-thrushes, and those three madcap fliers swallows, swifts and house martins, which enjoyed a wide selection of facilities under our protruding eaves—as well as just inside some of the outhouses—to build their cup-shaped mud nests. Also, of course, there were the companionable little robins, one of whom became a regular morning visitor on the lawn outside the scullery window when I was washing up. It would hop into a prominent position as I opened the window, and after a few preliminary skirmishes it would perch on the low stone sundial and wither me with oblique glances until I cast out the daily quota of crumbs. I used to chat away to it, flattering myself that it was civil enough to enjoy these exchanges with me and could understand every word and inflection. Perhaps it could; who knows?

There was another little issue on which I flattered myself; here, however, without a shred of justification. I kidded myself that I knew how to help a robin in distress: its little life was in jeopardy,

I imagined, through enforced exposure to the cruel elements; *something* had to be done; *I* must do it. Alas, my well-meant intervention misfired completely and it all ended in stark tragedy. It happened thus.

A pair of robins had elected to build a nest in our front garden, by the hedge, but actually on the ground, well concealed in the grass-root jungle of neglected undergrowth. It struck me as an odd site to choose in preference to the hedge itself, or the infinite variety of more usual sites—shelves, boxes, assorted flower-pots and cans which littered the potting shed. It was only when this weedy patch was being scythed in preparation for the fête that the nest was discovered, with mum sitting tight on her prospective family—four grey-white freckly eggs. She sat motionless, a perfect example of the parent's instinctive courage and devotion.

The men who found her arranged a few protective twigs over the nest—like a perforated dome—to allow Mrs. Robin easy access to and from her home, and also to ensure that *we* would not tread unsuspectingly on it.

I was deeply fascinated by this first experience of bird-watching at close range and paid countless hurried visits, always tip-toeing, peeping respectfully from what seemed to be a safe distance, and scarcely daring to breathe.

Then the rains came, and what rain! It continued relentlessly, as if buckets were being emptied, until there were puddles everywhere and the nesting-ground was becoming waterlogged. Mrs. Robin, in her demanding rôle, never flinched. At last I ran and fetched John's umbrella and fixed it protectingly over the nest.

By nightfall the rain had ceased and I removed the umbrella; but in the early hours of the morning a real storm broke. It wasn't just rain now; it was a *deluge*—probably a cloudburst.

Lying awake, I thought of the parlous plight of poor Mrs. Robin, surely catching her death of cold out there; so I nipped out of bed, popped on my dressing gown and mac, and scuttled downstairs to get the umbrella again.

It wasn't a very inviting mission I'll admit, and I got pretty wet myself; but, having firmly re-erected her shelter, I returned to bed feeling smugly virtuous.

Next morning, at the first inspection, she was absent, but huddled in a cramped bunch were the four gaping yellow beaks of her new babies. I assumed that there must be some tiny bodies attached to the gaping beaks, but it was just the wide-open, hopefully upraised mouths that dominated the scene.

After a while mother returned and continued her vigil for a short period; then, sad to relate, she deserted them altogether—and how bitterly I grieved to see the four little lifeless creatures! But I grieved even more when someone told me that undoubtedly *my* well-intentioned interference in planting the umbrella had largely—if not entirely—accounted for the tragedy; that robins are jealous of their territorial rights, and that my attentions would be resented and highly suspect. I was also told that, as robins are supposedly cautious birds and accredited weather prophets, our Mrs. Robin was no doubt well qualified, thank you, to take care of herself and her nestful when the rains came.

It taught me a lasting lesson—always to allow nature to know best!

*   *   *   *   *

Pheasants were a familiar sight and my ear soon became attuned to their peculiar cough. A corner of our wild garden used to be regularly annexed by them for nesting, and as we sat by the open window in summer having tea it delighted us to watch these handsome, colourful birds strut home across the lawn, always following the one fixed route—hugging the churchyard hedge up to an agreed point, then turning sharply left and into the thick undergrowth where they resided.

Frequently, too, I would surprise a pheasant relaxing amid the raspberry canes or in the blackcurrant bushes, or half-hidden in the asparagus bed. Sometimes it was they who surprised me, with a sudden flutter of wings at close quarters causing me instinctively to duck—to come up again laughing as I realized it was only a gorgeous pheasant taking off with easy grace and showing its ravishing plumage to full effect.

In choosing our garden to settle in they were no doubt right off the beam, but one can only suppose that they enjoyed there relative peace and tranquillity, and perhaps regarded it as a sanctuary free from violation.

*   *   *   *   *

On closer acquaintance with the wild life of the countryside my early timidity was almost entirely overcome. Spiders, wasps, stag-beetles, bats, squirrels, the odd hedgehog, worms, and even the audacious field mouse, which would dart through the open yard door into the kitchen, where it would scamper round and round with puss in angry pursuit—all were accepted now on the " live and let live " principle, as fellow inhabitants of the rural scene. But I never managed to come to terms with rats, which, with so little effort but invincible determination, forced an entry night after night into the garage or current storage shed where our winter supply of potatoes was packed. Overnight our stock would be ravaged with exasperating thoroughness.

Nor did I ever become reconciled to one particular branch of the crane-fly family, with its vicious-looking red tailpiece. These tormentors had a positive mania for forcing their unwelcome attentions on us just as we were settling comfortably for the night. For all I know they may have been as harmless as the proverbial kitten; but for me, with a lingering hangover from a childhood psychotic fear, they possessed some horrible, sinister quality that could soon send me into a mad frenzy. There would be no peace in our room until John had chased, captured and ejected the invaders, neck and crop, out of the window. And how maddeningly elusive they could be!

Also, during sleepless hours, when the night air became vibrant with the melancholy hoot of the brown owl, or pierced by the screech of the barn or white owl (so difficult, by the way, to mimic), something always seemed to turn to ice within me and an involuntary cold shiver would travel right down my spine.

*   *   *   *   *

It was after hearing through the local grapevine about Jim Grant's inebriated gnat that John, seeing in the incident the wide range of domestic crises that could strike any household without warning and catch them quite unprepared, said to me: " Sally, do you realize that we haven't a drop of stimulant in the place? In an emergency we would be absolutely sunk. Don't you think we ought to get in, say, a half-bottle of brandy—*just to keep in the medicine cupboard*? "

I wholly agreed that it seemed a very wise and necessary precaution—just how necessary I was soon to prove. In fact, the brandy had hardly got used to its place in the cupboard, beside the gargles and embrocations, the cough mixtures and hair lotions, than it had to be brought out and hurriedly uncorked.

It was a genuine crisis, too!

Something had gone wrong once more with our electric kettle, and the schoolmaster had offered us the benefit of his amateur assistance. (We ourselves were still too inexperienced and timid in this field to " have a go.")

He returned it with a reassuring " There you are! You'll find it's quite all right now. You'll be able to have your tea today. Ta-ta! " And he vanished.

Without delay we filled it and switched on, but we *couldn't* have our tea, because the tiresome thing stalled again and we were back in square one.

John commented—a trifle ungratefully, I thought—" Well, so much for his know-how; *some* electrician! Why, I reckon *I* could do as well as that."

Whereupon he seized a screwdriver, and with the kettle in one hand and the tool in the other he got to work—only he didn't get far.

There was a blood-curdling yell; he dropped the kettle and was flung across the kitchen and landed, shaken and much subdued, flat against the dresser.

I, assuming that he had punctured his hand from palm to knuckle with the screwdriver, shrieked in sympathy and began to crumple up. It's a silly habit I have, to shock easily.

At last John reached out mechanically for the brandy bottle. He dosed me liberally, and then moved thoughtfully across the room, switched off the current *and* unplugged the flex. There's nothing like making assurance doubly sure!

Neither we nor anyone else ever understood how John managed to escape so lightly; by all the rules, they said, he ought to have been a serious casualty.

His reflective comment was: " Well, that's funny; *I* had the shock, but *you* had the brandy! "

*   *   *   *   *

A few weeks after that I was struggling, in a great hurry, to open an obstinate tin of corned beef for some visitors who had come to tea and stayed for supper.

In a trice disaster struck again. In my careless agitation the tin slipped, and before I knew where I was the tip of my left forefinger was on the floor and a section of its neighbour gaping open and bleeding copiously. At the sight of blood I usually make a point of fainting, so I was once more a candidate for the brandy award.

John administered it and, as he replaced the cap, I heard him mutter " Perhaps after all I ought to have got a full bottle."

In the events that followed it would have been as well; but who could have foreseen the series of calamities in store for us?

Within a couple of months we had the first of three fire scares at the vicarage. My fire phobia was by no means allayed by the knowledge that the nearest fire station was several miles away.

One night we had got to bed later than usual and I was tossing about, finding sleep difficult to woo. Suddenly I smelt something burning and awakened John. " Can you smell what I can smell? "

" No [without inquiring *what* I could smell!], you go to sleep."

Soon the pungent warning penetrated even John's subsconscious. He sat bolt upright. " My hat! You're right; we're on fire."

There seemed no doubt about it as we opened the bedroom door and the whole place reeked of burning wood.

" Jump to it, Sally! Action stations! " commanded John.

We charged pell-mell downstairs, not even waiting for slippers. As we opened the kitchen door a thick wall of smoke met us. We choked and fumbled for the light switch.

Providentially, the " fire " had burnt itself out already and we came in only for the shock and the eye-smarting aftermath.

We had nobody but ourselves to blame. We had left a bundle of kindling on the top of the closed stove to dry for the morning—a reasonably safe practice, we had imagined. We had often done it before, but this time we had omitted to close up the draught wheel. The fire, packed up for the night with a fierce-burning nut, had quickly attained tremendous heat—sufficient, in fact, to ignite the sticks and reduce them to ashes.

It was a mercy that before going to bed I had removed to a safe distance a loaded clothes-horse and a line of " smalls " airing above the stove.

That was an occasion when John also felt the need for a little stimulant.

*   *   *   *   *

The second vicarage fire occurred one Sunday morning, while we were at matins. We came home to find the place full of smoke which seemed to become denser every second.

We ran from room to room to find the seat of the trouble; everything seemed in order and our fires were properly guarded, so we knew that the outbreak must be up in the flat at the top of the house. At the time I am speaking of the top-floor rooms were occupied by a queer, rather garrulous old man—semi-hermit and semi-invalid— who was a legacy from wartime evacuation, since when he had been handed down from incumbent to incumbent. The bishop jocularly referred to him as our " sitting tenant "; but, as an inheritance, he wasn't all that funny. In fact, we hadn't even known of his existence, let alone that *we* had now inherited him, until after John had accepted the living, and it was the P.O.G. who gave us the first inkling when he made a casual remark about " the old boy upstairs "! We blinked and sought enlightenment.

" Well, he's a widower, a bit eccentric, and he lives like a recluse. He's suffering from disseminated sclerosis and he's jolly unsafe on his legs." This did nothing to reassure us. Further investigation revealed that he didn't feed himself properly and spent a great deal of his time in bed, wearing a grimy old felt hat and smoking evil-smelling tobacco. Hygienically speaking, we viewed our bequeathed tenant with misgivings. He had his own stairway and a separate entrance, but, although John and I did not have occasion to see much of him, we both felt an uncomfortable degree of responsibility for him. He went out only to pay periodic visits to the little village store, and then, because of memory lapses or possible black-outs, he had his key round his neck and a label with his address tied to the lapel of his coat. He was a distinctly pathetic figure, and anything but a welcome tenant.

Easily the most disturbing feature of his occupation of the flat was, to my mind, his reckless use of paraffin—particularly in view of his physical infirmity, which rendered him incapable of coping with any crisis that might arise. His cooking arrangements consisted of a paraffin stove, a kettle and a frying-pan. We had it on the solemn authority of the P.O.G. that the old chap had evolved a Heath-Robinson method of frying, whereby he fixed a wooden plank over his bed, wedging one end in the partially open drawer of a dressing chest; on this plank he balanced his oil stove, surmounted by the frying-pan, serving food direct from pan to plate. It was an operation that we never witnessed; nor would I have dared to do so had he invited us.

I had never had any real peace of mind with this potential danger overhead. The P.O.G. had told us, in the first instance, that the old man was in hospital and was not expected ever to come out again; but, by some perverse effort, he had managed to confound the prophets and return to his flat.

So, with all this in mind, John and I couldn't get upstairs quickly enough on the Sunday morning of the fire.

We took advantage of a short cut by way of a connecting door on our first-floor landing.

I have never mounted stairs at such speed or with such sickening fear.

The wooden surround of the fireplace and the adjacent floor-boards in the old man's living room were blazing merrily, while he was pottering in another room—oblivious, apparently, to the danger threatening him. The grate was unguarded and lacked even a fender to catch any falling cinders.

John, having dealt with the blaze, then read the riot act over the old man, emphasizing that he was no longer fit to be living on his own, and that had this flare-up occurred at night there would almost assuredly have been a real tragedy, for he was virtually isolated up there at the top of his narrow wooden stairs.

He was bitterly resentful of this criticism, but shortly afterwards alternative accommodation was found for him near his son, and the relief to our minds was immeasurable.

*　　*　　*　　*　　*

In the third trial by fire we had a really miraculous escape. The incident left us badly shaken.

John and I were reading in bed late one Sunday night when a very remarkable storm broke over the area. It was remarkable in that it was so sudden and unexpected, and of such short duration that it was all over in a matter of five or six minutes. No preliminary rumblings, no lingering echoes as it died away, but while it lasted it was extremely violent and the lightning quite terrifying.

One bright bluish flash, which seemed to illumine the whole sky, was followed by a positively stupefying crack of thunder. For a second I felt that the top of my head had split. The electric lights flickered violently, nearly went out, and then resumed normal brilliance.

John, convinced that we had been struck, leapt out of bed and carried out a hasty inspection. It was an immense relief to find that everything seemed to be all right; we had obviously had a narrow escape. We settled down to sleep.

The following morning, as I was clearing away the breakfast things, my eye was drawn to a red flicker round the frame of a cupboard door in the kitchen.

I opened it. The entire contents were blazing fiercely—fairly inflammable things, too: cooking fats, sugars, a stock of candles and matches, packaged groceries, and bundles of old papers.

Fortunately for us, at the time we were having a new roof put on the vicarage and I yelled to the workmen up there to come to our aid. They were truly wonderful, shinning down their ladders like professional firefighters, grabbing buckets of sand and cans of water and concentrating every effort on getting our blaze under control. It left a blackened, oily mess to clear up (and a foul smell of burnt fat), but that was of small account.

Meanwhile, John had turned off the master switch in the meter room and had telephoned the electricity board. It was discovered that our immersion heater had been struck and slow smouldering had begun under some boards in the room above the kitchen. This had gone on all night, as we slept blissfully; then suddenly a falling spark had ignited the contents of the cupboard.

But for the blessed vigilance of our guardian angels our predicament must have been tragic.

*   *   *   *   *

Fate allowed us a welcome respite of about six months before the next alarm—one which, in the space of a second, reduced our orderly dining room to a shambles.

At this time we had a young couple occupying the flat, and the wife helped me in the house. On this particular morning she was doing the dining room grate. John and I were in the kitchen. There was a sudden deafening bang, which could only be accounted for by an explosion.

We rushed instinctively towards the dining room, which we judged to be the trouble spot. We collided in the hall with the girl, Mary, rushing out to us, screaming at the top of her voice. " There's been an explosion; there was a big *bang* [almost too obvious to be alluded to, one was tempted to say, only this was no time for facetious comment]. My hair's all on fire "—and she was frantically running her fingers through her locks.

The first assertion was beyond contradiction; there *had* certainly been an explosion and the dining room appeared to have been blitzed; but the second one—that her hair was on fire—was mercifully unfounded. All the same, it looked more than a little dishevelled and was thick with coal dust and bedecked with a few dead cinders. Her face was grimed and she was shaking with fright, but otherwise she appeared to have escaped injury.

Before attempting any fact-finding we all three wended our way back to the kitchen; John went to the medicine cupboard and we sat down to sip our brandy and regain our breath and equilibrium.

Mary then tried to recall the order in which things had happened. She was just clearing the grate, and transferring the residue of last night's still hot cinders to the ash bucket; then there was a sudden flash and a " big bang," and the contents of the bucket were distributed indiscriminately all over the room—even the ceiling was badly scarred. She had felt temporarily blinded by dirt; in short, she thought she had been killed!

The mess it created was no over-statement. I had seen nothing to equal it since the days of the bombing in London. Where to begin clearing up I just didn't know.

Mary, once she was able to talk coherently, telephoned her mother down in the village, assuring her that, despite possible rumours to the contrary, the vicarage was still standing and she herself was unharmed.

Mother responded in person, rolled up her sleeves and asked where she should start.

Then we looked at each other and asked simultaneously the obvious question: " I wonder what caused *that*."

Gelignite in the coal, we concluded, was the only reasonable explanation; so John, after helping us out with the huge carpet on to the front lawn, made off at maximum speed to the coal merchant's office—four miles away. It was urgent that he should warn his other customers!

The coal merchant took a very serious view of it all. " What makes you think it must be gelignite in my coal? " he wanted to know. " Well," parried John, somewhat lamely, " what else could it be? " The man ordered an immediate and thorough inspection of all stocks in his yard.

We three women worked all day like slaves, and our endeavours were not helped by the intrusion of a distant incumbent who had come to solicit John's support for his election to Convocation. With the dining room in utter turmoil, and everywhere else choked with furniture temporarily removed from the battlefield, we could only poke him into an odd corner of the kitchen, where, despite our fatuous repetition of the fact that we'd had an explosion and were in a hideous muddle, he stolidly held his ground until John had pledged his vote and I had served some refreshment; nothing less seemed likely to dislodge him.

By nightfall we were all desperately tired after the day's alarms and exertions—but so profoundly thankful that Mary had escaped unhurt. I crept into bed with just enough strength left to murmur " Thank God for a lovely warm bed and oblivion."

But I was a shade previous: the hot-water bottle had leaked, the bedclothes were soaked, and I had the comfortless job of removing everything, remaking the bed, and trekking downstairs to heat the water for another bottle—the good old stone variety this time.

And the cause of the explosion? It was days before we got that one sorted out. I had been turning out some kitchen drawers and disposing of the usual accumulation of junk, among which were three or four soda-water bullets. These I had deposited in the dust-bin—or, to be very accurate, on the top of the pile of stuff already in the bin—such a pile that the lid wouldn't sit on properly. One of the bullets must have rolled off and into the old ash bucket beside the bin. Then, when the unsuspecting Mary had shovelled hot cinders into the bucket—*whizz*! And the rest is known. We would never have solved it but for the fact that a small jagged piece of metal was found among the debris cleared from the room; on close examination it was unmistakably identified with the discarded bullets.

John telephoned the coal merchant and said he could now call off the gelignite search.

*   *   *   *   *

The next disruption was in a different category altogether; it brought part of the house crashing down with a deafening roar; it left the front drive cluttered with lumps of coping stone by the hundredweight, bricks galore, and an avalanche of tiles and guttering. My first impression, as I surveyed the devastation, was of the film set for *The Last Days of Pompeii.*

It happened one winter afternoon when I was convalescing after flu and officially out of circulation. For this reason we had been obliged to postpone the visit of some relatives. It was an extremely lucky postponement for them, as this load of trouble would have concertinaed any car parked in the drive.

John was out sick-visiting and I was hugging the fire, wrapped in a rug and feeling slightly sorry for myself.

My fireside reverie was rudely shattered by a whole series of ear-splitting, foundation-shaking *thuds.* These awful sounds went on and on, like a succession of bombs released on the one target. Good heavens! What on earth—an earthquake, heavy artillery, or a freak storm?

I was momentarily transfixed, but as soon as I could move I cast an anxious eye round for fallen ceilings. All our ceilings were intact.

My next, and very petrifying, thought was that Mary must have fallen from top to bottom of the long, steep, uncarpeted stairs leading to her flat—carrying, I imagined, some very heavy weight, say a couple of buckets of coal, or stepladders.

With considerable apprehension I ran to the foot of her stairs There was no crumpled body.

Becoming increasingly baffled, I then sped to the front door, intending to call for help, as I was frankly scared and trembling.

There I beheld the mountain of rubble: masses of fallen parapet and bricks. Clouds of brickdust were swirling around outside and beginning to seep into the hall.

For a few seconds I was too scared to move; rooted to the spot, I had a horrible feeling that the slightest movement on my part would probably bring the rest of the house down on top of me.

Then John came running back; he had heard distant rumblings and repercussions, and a passing postman had told him that something serious had happened at the vicarage.

This was one disaster that could have been prevented had professional advice been treated with respect. A few weeks earlier the diocesan architect, on his quinquennial survey, had instantly spotted the potentially dangerous condition of the parapet over the front of the house and had issued a serious warning: " That gable is likely to fall at any moment! " He instructed John, as a matter

I

of urgency, to have it attended to immediately, without even waiting for estimates; and when John had passed the information to the builder responsible for parsonage dilapidations in our deanery he had pooh-poohed the very idea of *urgency.* "The man's an alarmist," the builder grunted. "You can take it from me, it's as safe as houses—you don't need to have any sleepless nights over *that!*"

*   *   *   *   *

By now there was very little brandy left to help us over these testing occasions, yet there still seemed to be a malevolent influence hovering around. We suffered a long and wearying series of trials by water, but these were more aggravating than frightening.

To understand the frequency of the " bursts " which from time to time flooded our home and encouraged the vigorous growth of fungus—and occasionally threatened us with the prospect of evacuation—you would need only to take one glance at the crazy plumbing system—if such a strange assortment of ill-conceived features could be called a " system." Apart from inaccessible stop-cocks and the most unusual siting of tanks, there were miles of exposed pipes running close by northerly windows and beneath draughty eaves, not to mention the long section of pipe which spanned the yard (eastern aspect, of course) to the outside toilet. When arctic winds prevailed no amount of lagging or interior heating had the slightest effect—any more than trying to melt an iceberg with a lighted taper—so we just had to resign ourselves annually to the familiar pattern of freeze-up and burst, always hoping that at the crucial moment we would be on the spot to cope.

It was a particularly cold winter when I was called away to nurse some relatives in London, and John had to battle alone and unaided with these torments. One Sunday, between Sunday school and evensong, there were *ten* bursts (actually this was our record!) and the place was inundated—everything saturated, including our perishable food bank stored in the cellar. To crown the ordeal, John slipped heavily in the dark on some ice-bound steps, and the contact raised a bump on his head the size of a golf ball. But this painful mishap *did* furnish me with a sound excuse to pack my bags and return home without delay.

Once we got used to the set programme it was easy to understand why the house *never* seemed really dry, and we accepted it as axiomatic that freshly papered walls would show signs of mildew in a matter of weeks.

By now we were almost shock-proof, and it was agreed that the little bottle in the medicine cupboard needn't be replenished. We dispensed with it altogether.

*   *   *   *   *

Finally there was the sandstorm that struck the vicarage on an unforgettable Friday morning. It was *not* a natural phenomenon; no " act of God " this, but incontestably the " act of man " (in the plural—two of them, to be precise, and half-wits at that!).

We had gone off early to market, leaving a couple of workmen putting the finishing touches to the newly laid wood-block floor in the hall. The whole disrupting job had dragged on and on for weeks, but now, the foreman explained encouragingly, " these chaps have only got to sandpaper the surface; they'll finish it this morning."

We returned around midday to find the entire premises, and all its furnishings, fittings, ornaments, and even food, lying under a thick shroud of what looked like grubby talc powder; it gave the impression that cartloads of the stuff had been tipped impartially and with reckless prodigality over, under, around and inside *everything*—floors, walls, curtains, carpets, cushions, cupboards, drawers, the oven, the bath, the *lot*.

We gazed with acute distaste at the anæmic, off-white colour that had so suddenly replaced the warm rust tones of our stair-carpet; in fact, we gazed with utter dejection at the entire scene. We were momentarily stunned.

Then we found a scrawled note pinned to a door frame: " There's been a fuse, but the floor's finished "; and it dawned on us that this pair of imbeciles had got to work with an electric floor sander without bothering to seal (or even to close) the communicating doors and apply dust sheets.

After mending the fuse it took four of us and two vacuum cleaners the whole weekend to remove surface traces; and the more inaccessible deposits must occupy odd cracks and crannies to this day.

*   *   *   *   *

I suppose such a persistent chain of untoward happenings " down at the vicarage " could have been interpreted as a broad hint from providence for us to move on in search of a more benevolent climate, but if so it was one hint we preferred to ignore. They were quite different, and totally unavoidable, circumstances that in the end led to John's very reluctant retirement.

CHAPTER 7

It is reported . . .

IT was singularly unfortunate that the bride who was reported
in the local press as having " spent her honeymoon on the
village war memorial after placing her bouquet at Bourne-
mouth " had no sense of humour.

Nothing could convince her that what was obviously a printer's
error was not, in fact, a piece of malicious misreporting designed
specifically to take the glamorous edge off her nuptial joy and
sabotage her social prestige. Mischievous entities in the composing
room had no place in her reckoning. She entertained no doubts that
this diverting little mistake was an act of calculated spite. " I've
been publicly humiliated," she protested, and, of course, in that
state of emotional aberration she could see *nothing* in proper perspective—which was tough on the reporter.

All this, I am thankful to say, happened long before my own
appointment as local correspondent to the regional press, but the
perpetuation of the legend served as a stern warning to me (if I
needed one) to make accuracy in reporting a fetish; to check and
recheck every minute detail, no matter how supposedly reliable
its source of origin. I meant to see to it that, after allowing for
human fallibility, *I* would never never be found guilty of reckless
inaccuracies.

I was destined soon to discover just how difficult it is to guarantee
total accuracy in reportage and that the margin of error is likely to
cover contingencies quite beyond the correspondent's control.

By any standard, a correspondent's lot, as such, is not likely to
be a particularly happy one, and a stout hide is probably more
desirable than protective clothing in any other job. It entails, in
addition to one's ubiquitous presence at all parish functions, a
degree of tireless sleuth work, undertaken in circumstances that are
often far from glamorous. Usually one has to work against the
clock at crippling speed, and frequently the business of eliciting the

simplest facts relating to the most trivial event is as difficult and frustrating—perhaps as abortive—as (I imagine) trying to extract a deeply entrenched tooth from an unwilling patient—preliminary exploration, patient probing, gradual loosening and levering before the final wrench. The satisfactory extraction of clear, lucid, essential facts can be a protracted operation, and after all those delicate tactics, plus the time taken in drafting, typing and running to the post, the editor may have space that week for only a couple of lines with the caption, or possibly for nothing at all, and the people who have just submitted to your third-dregree interrogation, and are consequently ridiculously confident of becoming headline news in the next issue, will then take a lot of convincing that *you* haven't slighted them by foul omission.

Scrupulous impartiality must be your watchword. But will they ever believe you if it comes to an issue?

Now I felt that this weighty assessment of a correspondent's responsibilities was, in my own case, substantially increased by the fact that I was the vicar's wife. The paramount consideration in *all* our actions and public utterances was the likely repercussion on the Church, so in my local reporting I couldn't be too circumspect and discreet, and strict impartiality must be impeccably dispensed.

Nevertheless, experience forced me sometimes to the reluctant conclusion that when the human ego imagines itself to have been affronted sweet reasonableness takes ready flight—as an arrow from its bow—and then, within certain defined limits, the Church can suffer swift, but entirely unmerited, retaliation.

For example, a child could be removed from Sunday school without explanation. Why? There seemed to be no obvious reason; precious time could be wasted in fruitless pondering. It was quicker for John to inquire directly at the home. His patient questioning of the parents would probably meet first with a few fencing gestures and a touch of mild prevarication (oh, no, there was nothing *wrong*; when the weather improved or the measles epidemic subsided *perhaps* Billy or Mary would come again), and then in an unguarded moment the idiotic fact would emerge that their little boy's scholarship success hadn't even been mentioned in the press, whereas the next-door child's trivial painting award was given plenty of prominence—and if that wasn't favouritism what *was*, they wanted to ow! At last a shaft of daylight on a dark subject.

as to discover that serious umbrage could be taken on a pretext that was even more ludicrous and flimsy; for instance, the inadvertent omission of a few names from the list of mourners and senders of "beautiful floral tributes" could bring resounding opprobrium on me, and in fainter measure on the Church. Even the subsequent production of a typed duplicate of the original report, as evidence of integrity, would sometimes fail to appease the slighted ones: somehow, in their opinion, one had failed in one's duty to exercise reasonable care and accuracy. For the next few Sundays there could well be some additional vacant pews.

I recall on one occasion making a personal call on the sub-editor to explain the incredible lengths to which these delicate issues could recoil against the Church and to implore him, therefore, to do his utmost to try to find space in next week's issue for a particular item—concerning a young man's final examination success—which hadn't been given a solitary line in the current edition. Faint rumblings had reached me of his family's freely expressed dissatisfaction; it was soon circulating (with distortions) throughout the village: "Why should she leave him out? Surely his success deserved a mention. Besides, we've always supported the Church, haven't we?" This piece of insanity was reaching threatening proportions, so, rather than jeopardize their parochial allegiance, I had my little heart-to-heart talk with the sub-editor. Fortunately, the report that I had submitted had not been destroyed, but merely squeezed out by a glut of sports items; he hoped to work it in next week.

It duly appeared. The affronted family was placated, my honour was vindicated, and the situation vis-à-vis the Church was unimpaired.

It was in the field of politics that I had to tread most warily, for here temperatures seemed to be constantly maintained at blistering level. I had never before encountered anything to equal the intensity of factional hostility within a local electorate—especially during general election campaigns, when the whole place seemed blanketed by an atmosphere of civil war. To avoid the possible charge of partisanship, I was almost driven to counting out the exact number of syllables—let alone the number of words and lines—apportioned to each report of party political meetings, and our own policy was one of invariable colour-blindness. If we (and by common implication that meant the Church) were not to become embroiled in the prevailing tenseness and ill-feeling it was not enough for scrupulous impartiality to be maintained; it had to be *seen* to be maintained.

While the campaign lasted my headaches were numerous and violent. For John it was a time he dreaded more than any other. As spiritual " public relations officer " of the village, he found his patience, tact and diplomacy strained to the limit by displays of childish animosity that daily threatened the total dissolution of every vestige of community spirit—not to mention Christian spirit!—that it was the object of his life to foster. Some parishioners frankly protested that they couldn't be expected—simply *couldn't* be expected—to come and worship in such tempestuous times; how could they possibly sit next to their *enemies* in church? (For " enemies " translate political adversaries.)

John's entreaties to reason achieved little or nothing. All he hoped for was that with the passage of time tempers would cool and sanity return, and eventually that was the happy outcome.

An illustration—crazy but true—of the acute sensitiveness to published inaccuracies was met in my first few weeks. An old couple had suffered bereavement by the death of their elder son in a road accident in Scotland. The family was well known locally, the boy was born at Upper Bellpull and had lived there until his marriage. Although the funeral was not to take place in the parish, the parents expressed their desire for the event to be reported.

Both parents—but particularly the mother—were too distressed to be interrogated personally for the basic facts. When John called to condole, he found them tearful and quite incoherent. It was not my intention to add to their suffering by even the briefest questioning, yet they wished for a report. How was I to elicit the details?

Their next-door neighbour was a friend of long standing, and their respective sons were old schoolmates, so here was the most likely source.

After a careful interview with the neighbour, I duly reported that Mr. A. B——, aged forty-one years, elder son of Mr. and Mrs. B——, had met with a fatal accident, etc.

The next week I heard that Mrs. B—— was deeply annoyed with me, and I wondered why. As I hadn't a clue, the obvious thing was to go straight to the fountain head and find out.

Coming immediately to the point, I said that I had heard of her displeasure. " Please tell me how I have upset you. Is it something I can rectify? "

Controlling her emotion with great effort, she gulped " He was forty, not forty-one, as you said. It's *very* hurtful."

For the life of me I couldn't see the force of this, but I hastened to express regret if I had unwittingly caused her a moment's distress. " Would you like me to try to get a correction inserted next week ? "

After sober reflection (she might have been considering some tremendously weighty world issue!) she said " No; it doesn't matter *now;* but it's most hurtful."

There the matter was left, and I could only conclude that this minor inaccuracy could have implied that her son was born out of wedlock.

This trivial incident heightened our sense of cautious approach to every breeze of rumour wafted in our direction; henceforth the most cast-iron story would have to be factually substantiated (with affidavit if need be!) before proceeding.

This proved a sound rule on many an occasion, but notably in the affair of young Ginger Merrick.

Someone called at the vicarage one day and asked whether I had heard the *awful* news about young Ginger. My anxious " No; what's happened? " provided just the opportunity she sought to pour out the melancholy story currently circulating. " Why, Ginger's dead! I don't know the actual details, but isn't it too tragic? Only called up for his national service a few weeks ago—and such a bonny lad; an only son, too; oh dear . . .! " She drifted on in morbid reflection.

I seized a momentary pause to ask " Are you quite *sure* about all this? The vicar and I were talking to Ginger only yesterday; we met him at the bus stop on his way back to the depot after short leave; he seemed all right then."

" Oh, I'm *quite* sure," she went on; " it's all round the parish." She was satisfied that her informant was absolutely reliable, although he had admitted that he didn't know the cause of death. " Oh yes, it's true enough, poor boy," she ended up.

After she had gone I began a preliminary draft for the press report. When John returned at teatime I broke the news to him and suggested holding back our meal if he wanted to see Ginger's parents at once. " And while you're there, will you verify Ginger's age, regiment and second Christian name? "

John looked profoundly disturbed and thoughtful; then he said: " Before going to the Merricks about Ginger I want a lot more facts. I can hardly believe it's true. If it *isn't* true, and I go there offering condolences, they'll have a pretty nasty shock, won't they? "

So off he went on a fact-finding tour and was gone a long while, but his reassuring smile as he came back told me all I needed to know. I began mechanically to tear up the half-typed report.

John's little bit of detective work had involved him in some searching inquiries and a long-distance 'phone call.

Ginger was alive and very well, thank you! The explanation of his alleged demise was absurdly simple: the boy had been due for his call-up some months earlier, as we all knew; but for some reason it had been deferred and again deferred. Finally his papers came and he had slipped away unobtrusively from civilian life. Then came this short leave and he was seen in the village wearing the Queen's uniform. This very prosaic piece of news travelled rapidly along the grapevine after this fashion: " Ginger's been called up "; " Ginger's started his national service at last "; then the ambiguous version, " Poor old Ginger's *gone*," which was loosely translated " Did you know Ginger's d-e-a-d? "—and verification hadn't been deemed necessary.

*   *   *   *   *

Some of the items that trickled in to me were totally unacceptable —at least, in their original form, sometimes grossly biased, indiscreet, or even faintly libellous; occasionally a salacious tang would be detected, enough to disqualify out of hand. To meet these contingencies the waste-paper basket was always handy and I exercised my discretionary right.

The waste-paper basket was also useful for the odd anonymous letter.

*   *   *   *   *

I judged the wedding reports to be the most avidly read of all the local news, and to satisfy this romantic demand I took infinite pains to prepare readable, detailed accounts. The press supplied printed questionnaires, and I saw to it that the prospective bride had her form well in advance of the event, emphasizing the need to write plainly and to get some reliable person—usually her mother or the chief bridesmaid—to return the completed form to me with the least possible delay after the wedding. This, one hoped, would eliminate the likelihood of error; but it didn't, because (a) the mutilated condition of the returned questionnaire would sometimes render the whole story indecipherable; (b) legible writing and conventional spelling seemed rare accomplishments; and (c) all too frequently the press correspondent was credited with the ability to thought-read and consequently the vital facts were presented in fragmentary crumbs and masses of meaningless abbreviations. Once or twice the completed form did not come back to me at all; these, no doubt, would have been the ones most informatively packed with precise and interesting details, and when one tried to trace their mysterious non-arrival it would usually transpire that everyone had left it to everyone else: the bride's mother had delegated the job to the chief bridesmaid, whose spelling was a bit shaky, so she had sought the literary assistance of the bride's aunt, who, in all the excitement, must have got it mixed up with the laundry list and sent it away with the washing. And not a few brides actually imagined that " with the least possible delay after your wedding " meant anything up to four or five weeks, by which time the story of her great day had manifestly lost its topical value and nobody paid much attention.

These more or less stereotyped wedding reports (and, to some extent, the funeral reports also) ought to have constituted the easiest form of reporting; in fact, they caused me more headaches than all the rest put together, because I became obsessed by a fatuous desire to make every bride's " story " sound a bit different; knowing these young girls so well, one tried to impart a personal touch each time—to avoid repetitive phrasing, to present the run-of-the-mill details in the least hackneyed terms, in short, to give the convincing impression that each one was *the* social event of the season.

The majority of the couples who came shyly to the vicarage to see John about banns were youngsters for whom we had a genuine regard; usually they had been through the Sunday school, the youth fellowship, and the confirmation class; and now, after having watched their romance ripen, we felt that we were playing a personal part in the sealing of their partnership, and we entertained more than a casual interest in their happiness.

They were nearly always overcome with dumb shyness when they stood self-consciously on the doorstep, so I would try to help them out by " guessing " the object of their visit. " I expect you want to see the vicar about banns; am I right? "—and that usually broke the ice sufficiently to evoke a somewhat sheepish grin. Invariably the girls were less shy and dumb than the young men; and that applied equally on the wedding day when, in full regalia and attended by an impressive retinue (usually including a page boy, whether there was a train to hold up or not!), they became the natural cynosure of all eyes and generally managed to carry off their bridal rôle with masterly composure. (There were exceptions!)

Our village brides had firm ideas about contemporary styles. Gone were the days and the services of the little dressmaker down the lane; no ingenuously simple " country-maiden " outfits for these fashionwise young ladies, who bestowed their patronage on the smart gown shop of their choice in the nearest town, well primed in the latest trends in *haute couture*. And what dazzling pictures they presented on the wedding day, in frocks long and sweeping; or figure-clinging and swathed; or bouffant, shimmering, embroidered, bedizened; or perhaps a captivating period creation, developing into an elegant train! It was always something wondrously transforming, so that, for one unforgettable day at least, these pretty young things became starlets in their own right, and for a delirious moment Hollywood had nothing over them.

The boys, however, showed no inclination to appear on terms of parity for the great event; sartorially they lagged miles behind, their only concessions to wedding livery being, as far as I could see, a new pair of winkle-pickers, extra-flamboyant socks and ties, possibly a barbarous cardigan, the inevitable white carnation, and an unduly generous application of brilliantine.

I found myself once speculating on the remote possibility of these village boys ever plucking up the courage to set sail in full rig—pinstripes, tails, topper and cravat, plus, of course, an air of dashing nonchalance! Such fashion-conscious brides, I felt, were entitled to the support of equally impeccably attired grooms. Had they never heard of the hired outfit?

I realized eventually that in seeking to infuse a *personal* note into these reports I was striving for the impossible. The most monumental efforts on my part seldom produced any striking variation on the old theme: " the bride, charmingly attired . . . given away by her father . . . the hymns, " The voice that breathed o'er Eden," " O perfect Love " and " Love Divine, all loves excelling " . . . Psalm 67 . . . with Mr. ——, F.R.C.O., at the organ."

(And in the mournful field of funerals, in the whole of my reporting career, I racked my brain in vain for an acceptable alternative to " beautiful floral tributes.")

Sometimes, in my obsessional longing to submit less mechanically churned copy on local weddings, I was sorely tempted to insert the occasional amusing asides heard above the excited chatter of the milling guests. There was the time, for example, when a pert little miss in the congregation stubbornly refused to leave as the rest of the guests filed out. Her parents' impatient " Come along, Susan! " was totally ignored; attempts to drag the child out by force served to heap embarrassment on them, for the little so-and-so bellowed like mad and clung limpetwise to a pew-end. Then, in a stage whisper, they asked " Susan, what do you think you're waiting for? "—which brought the prompt, and rather stunning, explanation " I want to wait and see the baby "!

An excited little mite at another wedding inquired loudly of her mother—during that period of awkward silence while the register is being signed—" Mummy, when do we begin to throw the spaghetti? "

A completely unconventional note was struck at one wedding when a number of Teddy boys infiltrated among the guests and raised a tremendous cheer—accompanied by violent hand-waving —just as the newlyweds emerged from the vestry to make their triumphal way down the aisle—the sort of boisterous demonstration one might expect in support of the home team at a football final! Nor had the Teddies any inhibitions about puffing at their cigarettes while they waited; in fact, they had entered the church prepared for the contingency, with unfinished cigarettes parked behind their ears. I sensed the " news " element here, but I didn't suppose that the bride would thank me to make any reference to this episode in her wedding report!

There was one memorable occasion when John had actually to suspend the service for a few minutes to give the agonizingly nervous bride a chance to stop her teeth chattering; he even had a momentary doubt as to whether it would be possible to continue; however, the poor girl—propped up on the one side by her father and on the other by the bridegroom, and nearly paralysed with the ordeal— managed to see it out. Once the service was over her lost composure was restored as quickly as if a fuse wire had been replaced; she went through the photographic ritual outside with the perfect serenity and poise of a practised model.

She apologized later to John for the near-calamity caused by her nerves, and he consoled her by confessing the fact of his own unmanageable nervous agitation at the very first wedding he ever took, when *his* knees shook so violently that he felt convinced the whole congregation could hear his bones rattling; and his hands trembled so dreadfully that his service book was completely blurred, and the organist told him afterwards that the contracting parties were not legally married because he had omitted to pronounce " Those whom God hath joined together let no man put asunder "! Fortunately, *they* made no complaint of not having been given " full measure " (if they even noticed it, which is doubtful), and John was satisfied that it did not invalidate the marriage; and *our* nervous little bride seemed comforted to hear that priests as well as parishioners can be overcome by nerves.

But it was just as well that John had fully mastered his initial nervousness by the time he was required to officiate at a multiple wedding in his first East End parish during the war, otherwise it could have ended in a major mêlée. In the special circumstances of forty-eight-hour forces leave, an impossible number of weddings had sometimes to be sandwiched into the one day, for the manpower shortage in the priesthood was becoming acute. Quite often the only solution in a thickly populated parish was to conduct two or even three weddings simultaneously.

This was once John's experience. He had previously gone over the service with each individual couple, instructing them carefully when to respond, when to kneel, when to clasp hands, etc., and he felt tolerably satisfied that his directions had been properly understood. On the day, however, with the three couples—plus giversaway and best men—ranged in a long line before him, he found that they still needed plenty of prompting, and, to help them out, he quietly whispered or mouthed the responses where necessary. When the moment came to exchange vows they remained motionless, and John, in a stage whisper, ordered them to *hold hands*; when they failed to react promptly he directed them in dumb show —crossing his own arms—and, to his horror, all of them obeyed heartily but too literally! They *all* crossed arms and grasped their neighbours' hands—in one unbroken unit! For one awful moment John thought they were about to break forth into " Auld Lang Syne." His anguish must have communicated itself to them, for

they suddenly came to their senses, broke up into three separate
units, and the ceremony proceeded uneventfully to the end.

*   *   *   *   *

John and I were invariably invited to join the guests at the local
receptions, and these joyous occasions are among our most cherished
parochial memories. We were able to mingle informally among the
throng of relatives and friends, and we usually found ourselves
allotted a place at the top table. We felt that this was the nicest
compliment they could pay us and we were conscious of a glow of
deep satisfaction as we shared in the family rejoicing. Once or twice
the press photographers got us too prominently sited in the family
groups and a hurried reshuffle ensued.

Few churches could have provided a more attractive background
for wedding groups than ours at Upper Bellpull, with its row of low
Victorian-Gothic windows to break up the monotony of the red-
brick south wall; its broad, half-timbered porch, red-tiled and
approached under an avenue of limes; its mellowed clock tower;
and its delightful garden, featuring neatly trimmed lawns, well-
tended flower beds and meticulously tidy paths. To complete this
captivating back-cloth there were a few fine old elms and two or
three slender firs—like tall sentinels on guard. (It was the natural
charm and immaculate tidiness of our churchyard, we were told,
that earned us first place in the best-kept-village contest one year.)
The landscape hadn't always been so pleasing and orderly, but a
surprise gift from an old parishioner had made it possible to implement an ambitious plan that the P.C.C. had been toying with for
some time.

Actually, if a digression is permissible, this was the " legacy "
which John and I always said *we* missed by a hair's breadth, and it
still evokes a reminiscent chuckle. We received a telephone call one
day from an elderly couple—former parishioners who now lived
some miles away. Their unmarried daughter had recently died and
was buried in our churchyard. She had always maintained a tenuous
sentimental link with Upper Bellpull and seemed grateful to John
for his pastoral help in her occasional problems. Now the old
gentleman was asking us to call on him and his wife, and he ended
the conversation somewhat mysteriously: " And please, Mrs.
Green, tell your husband that when you come he will hear some-

thing to his advantage." Down went the receiver. Could there, I pondered, be more than one interpretation of that significant observation? When we arrived it was the old lady who at once took the initiative; she began explaining to me, with great emphasis, that had their Edith lived another fortnight she would have reached her fiftieth birthday. They had planned their gift—*cash*—and had already withdrawn it from the bank. With that she moved to the bureau and took out a thick wad of notes. Thumbing them mechanically, like a new pack of cards, she said slowly, but still with tremendous emphasis, " Now, as our Edith is no longer with us, we have had to decide what to do with this money, and as she thought so very highly of *you* [with a prolonged, direct gaze at John] we feel sure that it would have been her wish that *you* should have the gift we had planned for her; as it would have been *her* wish, it is naturally *our* wish, also, that you, Vicar, should accept this sum of money, if you will [here followed a very long pause!], towards the upkeep of the churchyard. You will find £50 there," and she handed over the notes.

I heard myself faintly murmuring " What a *beautiful* way to perpetuate your daughter's memory! " We managed to preserve a solemn dignity till we got outside, then solemnity gave way to levity and we giggled a good deal on the way home. Clearly that significant phrase " to your advantage " *was* capable of more than one interpretation.

Their munificence was to the immense advantage of the churchyard; its transformation was almost magical. To clear away masses of overgrown laurels and holly bushes and to undertake prodigious levelling and turfing was a bold and arduous task. It entailed the razing of some ancient (and totally neglected) graves and the removal of headstones to a place of permanent preservation against the north wall of the church. The project involved, therefore, a good deal of legal formality; it had also to overcome a massive weight of local prejudice. Opposing camps quickly moved to action stations and words like " vandalism," " desecration," " wanton destruction " and " disrespect " were freely bandied about until a final vote had settled the issue in the democratic tradition.

Actually, the clearance of the jungle undergrowth and the headstones was to prove a great boon in more ways than one, and thereby hangs a distinctly ghoulish story. Beyond a doubt the strongest supporters of the clearance project—particularly in relation to headstones—were three ill-starred parishioners who had constituted the unwilling audience one dark and eerie November night for a terrifying Grand Guignol performance in that part of the churchyard which skirts the footpath along Willow Lane; and in this corner, leaning at all sorts of crazy angles, were some of the oldest memorial stones.

Towards this lugubrious spot old Mrs. Skinner came stumping along on her way home. Suddenly the horrifying forms of two disembodied spirits—white-shrouded—rose up slowly from the nearest graves with trembling, outstretched arms. This chilling manifestation was accompanied by a series of unearthly sounds—first a low, tremulous moan, swelling in powerful crescendo to a despairing wail. Then, with equal suddenness, which the poor old woman found totally unnerving, the fearful apparitions vanished from sight, obviously crouching again behind the headstones.

Mrs. Skinner, of course, was petrified. After a few piercing screams she had remained frozen to the spot, where, some minutes later, Brownlow's stockman and his son—on their way to the local —had found the poor old soul clinging to the fence for support, drooling and gibbering to herself.

As they went to her assistance the phantom figures gave a repeat performance, which sent *them* all but crazy too. However, surviving the impact of shock, the two men got a grip on themselves and began to clamber over the fence to give chase and unmask the culprits if possible; but they were much too quick for their pursuers. These malicious entities, with their shrouds whipped off and thrust hastily under their arms, made off at athletic speed. Their identity was never established, but they were *not* small boys out on and ill-chosen spree; they were convincing adults, and ought to have known better than to scare the wits out of a poor old woman.

But now, of course, there was general relief that, with the removal of the natural churchyard " props," the curtain had been finally rung down on nocturnal apparitions; and the transformed scene received ungrudging approval from everyone—even from the scheme's original critics and opponents. It certainly afforded ideal facilities for the wedding photographers (plenty of space for grouping) and ample manœuvrability for cine-camera enthusiasts eager to secure animated *on-the-spot* records. (Not like the members of one wedding contingent who, after availing themselves of the *register office* for the marriage, slipped coolly across to the cathedral pre-

cincts opposite to pose for the cameramen! But a lynx-eyed verger
had spotted the ruse and the proceedings broke up in confusion.)

Weddings, I confess, have always held a magnetic fascination for
me, so I positively revelled in the spate of them which kept me busy
with notebook and pencil in the parish.

* * * * *

But it wasn't always the reporter's rôle! I recall the rapturous
anticipation with which John and I looked forward to a very " big "
wedding at the cathedral—as guests, free of all responsibility. On
our shoe-string income we contrived (and *contrived* is the word for
it!) an impressively smart turn-out, happy at the prospect of meeting
many old friends there. Ours were not exactly *borrowed* plumes, but
almost entirely *inherited* ones. Going along in the bus (yes, bus it was,
despite the elegant finery), we tried to calculate the number of garments we were wearing, between us, that had miraculously come to
us just in time for this great occasion, although their original owners
could not possibly have known of our current wardrobe dilemma.
I don't think we arrived at an agreed figure, but it was a staggering
count, and we were profoundly conscious of the unfailing bounty
of providence in meeting one's needs in crises great or small—even
such mundane needs as adequate wedding finery!

This was essentially a *clergy* occasion: the bridegroom, the best
man and the groomsmen were all " in the cloth." The bride was
the daughter of a church dignitary, and nearly every male guest in
the packed cathedral wore his collar back to front. The red carpet
was out literally and figuratively, but with all the elaborate cere-
monial it was a very homely little incident that probably left the
most indelible impression. As the guests streamed in there was the
usual atmosphere of suppressed excitement, fed by the eye-catching
display of smart gowns and new spring bonnets. With barely a
minute to spare, in trotted the Archdeacon of X, accompanied by
a small party of friends and—an overpowering aroma of embrocation! At least *I* judged it to be embrocation and assumed that the
poor man was a martyr to lumbago and probably ought to have
stayed at home.

I caught a *sotto voce* whisper from the next pew: " He's used too
much blacking on his shoes; what a smell! "; and someone next to
me thought it was a potent new moth-deterrent. In all directions

there were quivering nostrils and ill-concealed sniffs, and perfumed handkerchiefs were being surreptitiously applied. Whatever the nature of the odour, it was all-pervading and utterly nauseating. As soon as the service was over we almost charged the doors in our eagerness to escape from the intolerable smell and take in a few deep breaths of fresh air.

A week later the mystery was revealed and the poor archdeacon was completely exonerated. I ran into a friend who was a member of the archdeacon's party that day. " I saw you at the wedding," she began; " I do hope my daughter didn't spoil your pleasure. Wasn't it perfectly *awful*? "

" Spoil my pleasure? How? " I asked, quite baffled.

" Well, the *smell*. You see, just as Ann and I were getting out of the car a terrific gust of wind caught her very full skirt and slapped it against a freshly painted pillar-box. Just imagine it . . . a huge scarlet blob on a delicate pastel frock! She nearly wept. There wasn't time to go home and change, and she simply couldn't go into the cathedral like *that*; but for my brainwave I really don't know what we would have done! "

On mother's inspiration they had dived into a nearby chemist's shop and got him to treat the eyesore with turpentine, and it had required a really copious application!

* * * * *

Local news reporting settled down to a rather dreary, humdrum routine—whist drives, fêtes, council meetings, dances, parties and outings, flower shows and harvest thanksgivings, with weddings and funerals the predominating features. Very rarely indeed did the familiar pattern deviate to the point of sensationalism.

Stack blazes, chimney fires, the odd break-in and the occasional road accident caused scarcely a ripple on the calm surface of village life, but the evil genius of juvenile delinquents sometimes created a stir; as, for example, when a couple of mischievous ten-year-olds sought relief from boredom by entering the village hall—by a rather ingenious method—and then going berserk in the canteen store, scattering sugar, flour and the contents of dozens of jars of preserved fruit over the floor, the furniture, and the platform, and tipping the residue inside the piano. This really proved their undoing, for having opened the lid they couldn't resist a four-handed recital. It was this unholy din that attracted passing attention, and then the game was up. Not to be outdone, a few of their older cronies broke into some farm premises and engaged in a lively egg battle, vigorously pelting each other (and the surroundings) with the entire consignment waiting to go to the packing station. It was a merciless bombardment while the ammunition lasted. As hostilities ended, the enraged farmer appeared on the scene and lunged at one of the egg-coated combatants; the others got away.

The " heroes " of these two escapades may have gloried in the headlines given to them, but it is doubtful whether brief notoriety compensated for the tanning meted out by their irate parents, who had to foot the bill for damage.

I recall two other colourful incidents that perhaps qualified for press comment, though it may well be that my personal involvement in both cases tended to invest each with a significance it hardly warranted.

The first concerned a strange phenomenon encountered on my way to the post one morning. Everybody I met appeared to be travelling at the speed of light, regardless of appalling risk to life and limb.

I had strolled casually down our drive, clutching my handful of letters. As I reached the gate, somebody shot past me on a bicycle at such meteoric pace that I was convinced he had lost control of his machine—and he was heading straight for the main road, and almost certain disaster if he met oncoming traffic. I noted, although he was crouched almost double over the handlebars, a look of mad terror in his eyes; he pedalled just as if possessed, and his jacket flapped in rhythmic accord. Clearly nothing short of death—or the threatened crash—was going to deter him from reaching wherever he was making for.

I stood staring in plain wonderment as he vanished out of sight. Then there appeared a running figure on the far side of the green, although *running* is an understatement. I watched the woman, tearing along like a maniac, rather cleverly taking periodic backward glances, but without for a second slackening her speed. In fact every movement indicated a determined policy of acceleration. Here was a panic-stricken parishioner if ever there was one, running away for dear life—but from what?

There was no sign of a pursuer. I did not immediately associate her with the frenzied cyclist.

A few yards farther on another pedal cyclist, proceeding from the same direction as the first one, whizzed by me like an arrow, nearly depositing me in the ditch with the wind force her passage generated. She neither stopped to see if I was all right nor even glanced my way. (On reflection, I don't suppose she even saw me.)

Even more incredible, there was lame Miss Tubbs, padding along at an almost brisk trot, despite the double handicap of her ninety-odd years and chronic arthritis. I couldn't believe my eyes.

In short, this reckless pattern of locomotion seemed to have infected *everybody* that morning. They were all either careering madly towards some distant, unidentifiable goal or else diving purposefully into the nearest bolthole.

Why was *I* dawdling? I wondered.

At last I managed to make my voice heard above the prevailing hum of excitement, yelling out to one of the cyclists as she hurtled by " I say, what's all this in aid of? "

Without slowing down for an instant, this woman screamed over her shoulder " Brownlow's bull's got out; it's gone mad! "—and with that she was out of sight.

Without further hesitation I joined the also-rans.

*   *   *   *   *

The other little news item in which I was unconsciously embroiled was the outcome of an attempt to establish within the parish a centralized control of all the charitable projects undertaken on behalf of the recognized good causes. It could have earned me a severe official reprimand.

My name had appeared in the press as honorary secretary of the local charitable appeals committee, which was designed largely to prevent overlapping in door-to-door collections. We calculated that our small community could stand only a limited number of appeals each year—and well spaced at that. Area organizers of the big charities were invited to make application to me for approved dates.

All this seemed to work smoothly and satisfactorily until a parishioner telephoned me one day to ask whether I had authorized some small boys in the village—naming the usual handful of scally-wags—to go round collecting for a children's playing field.

I assured her that I knew absolutely nothing about it; in any event, it was illegal to appoint collectors under sixteen years of age.

" Please tell me the worst," I begged her. " How long have they been at it? Have they covered the whole village?"

Then it was revealed that these little toads—dishevelled, dirty, and at a loose end—were coolly going round from door to door, rattling an old rusty saucepan in the face of whoever answered the door, saying that they were collecting *on behalf of Mrs. Green* for a playing field for local children!

I swayed at the thought of the possible consequences of this campaign. My informant had surrendered her tribute without question, but her sister had had misgivings, so they thought it better to consult me before the fund should be further augmented.

What was the next move? My first step seemed to be to round up the collecting squad; but before I could even set out on the warpath there was a bang at the vicarage door and, behold, I was confronted by the boys themselves—armed with their saucepans and expressions of beatific innocence.

I was just in the mood to devour them, and the miracle is that they escaped assault and battery.

" How *dare* you go round saying that *I've* sent you, you little horrors? Don't think I don't know what you've been doing; people tell me all that goes on here, and you are *very* wicked boys to tell untruths. Don't you know that *I* could be had up for sending children under sixteen round collecting? Tell me, how many houses have you been to? At least *twenty*? And did they all give you something? Well, you can just go straight back to every one of them and return their money—and say how sorry you are, and also say that *I* had nothing to do with it. By the way, why have you called here now?"

The ringleader, seeming to interpret the glint in my eye, looked a trifle subdued and shaken. He moistened his lips to explain: " We've come to get proper collecting boxes from *you*, because someone told us that a saucepan was no good and we must have a sealed box to make it proper."

His tone was suggestive of offended innocence rather than calculated naughtiness.

I began to relent a little as I saw that for once, perhaps, they were actually more naïve than wicked. No doubt they had heard a good deal about the appeals committee and my connection with it, and they probably thought that a spot of initiative on their part would pay rich dividends.

To their credit, they *did* go back and refund the money collected. Nevertheless, I was compelled to make some reference to the episode in the press to cover myself, as the rumour had already spread like a prairie fire that the children were using my name to raise funds for a field.

* * * * *

It was an immense relief to me that the reporting of cases at the magistrates' court—even when involving local people—was quite outside my province. Nevertheless, in the course of my parochial duties I was to come into unpleasantly close contact with court procedure, and it was an unforgettable experience.

A parishioner had to face a charge of annoying her neighbour—not for the first time either. From every angle it was a pathetically sad affair, for the defendant was an elderly spinster, for whom life was a prolonged battle against natural handicaps. She was eccentric, lonely and shunned because she was undeniably awkward. She was extremely hard of hearing and afflicted with a severe impediment in her speech. Temperamentally, she was bound to meet storm and tempest at every turn. It was regrettable that at the hands of a few in the village—notably the less-disciplined teenage boys—she suffered near-persecution.

It was a singular misfortune that her next-door neighbour (they occupied semi-detached cottages) was an elderly retired gentleman who, to say the least, was peppery and pernickety. It would be difficult to imagine two more ill-matched neighbours.

No doubt she tried him to a point of exasperation, taunting him whenever they met and, without provocation, throwing things over the hedge at him—vegetable waste, eggshells, apple cores, and so on; once she caught him in the eye with a snail! He, by his very aloof manner and unyielding insistence on his " rights as a rate-payer," was a constant irritation to her. Everything conspired to incite her to outbursts of ungovernable rage.

When it came to this court case, she, poor dear, was in a real spot. She sought our advice. John recommended her to employ a solicitor to defend her; at the eleventh hour he contracted out (so she said) and she simply didn't know what she was going to do in court.

Neither did we, in view of her physical handicaps.

As John had an important engagement, I volunteered to accompany Miss X to the magistrates' court, and seek permission to act as interpreter, for it was obvious that, unaided, she could neither hear what would be said against her nor articulate understandably a word in her own defence; and in any event her tempestuous nature, under the strain of the frustrating circumstances, could be counted on to damage her case hopelessly.

The chairman gave me permission and explained my duties: I must stand close beside her and repeat verbatim and fortissimo, direct into her ear, everything given in evidence by her accuser.

Little did I guess the sort of pantomime this would develop into!

I stood close enough and shouted with the stridency of a ship's siren right into her ear word after word of his protracted story, but with little effect. At the first attempt it *never* registered; at the second go (uttered at screaming pitch) she would show a faint sign of puzzled awareness; but with luck the third effort—at absolutely full throttle, mouthed slowly, syllable by syllable, as if making an announcement over a loud-hailer to someone on Mars—usually got through; and it usually sent her into an awful frenzy, for she contested every point.

This turned out to be not only a long and very exhausting assignment but a somewhat embarrassing one, for, as it reached the point of climax in their domestic warfare, torrents of unsavoury language were alleged to have been exchanged; and this all had to be recounted in specific detail! Thus I found myself, in public court, screaming out, " He says that you called him a ***** *** *** ******" (for the first time of asking); then again (in response to her " Eh? ") " He says that you called him a ***** *** *** ****** " (and by now a faint titter began to disturb the solemn atmosphere of the court room); and then, in near despair, I would *bawl* it out for the third time—and so on until it actually registered.

When the alleged obscenity finally sank in, she fairly exploded with wrathful indignation, and I was at a loss to know how to soothe her.

To this day I blush at the recollection of the fluent, uncensored recital of foul language required of me that day in open court—and at full volume!

In my wildest dreams I had never imagined that such an unbecoming assignment would fall to me. The reward for this un-sought notoriety was a congratulatory word from the chairman on " the discharge of a somewhat onerous duty."

Sporadic warfare continued to engage these two neighbours over the years, her £3 fine proving no deterrent; between two such in-compatible natures conciliation was an utterly forlorn hope. But eventually *he* moved away, and a delightful young couple took possession. They seemed to understand from the outset the sad and difficult personality—and handicaps—of the woman next door. They were kind, tolerant and neighbourly; and because they treated her with understanding she gave them no trouble at all.

It was they who found her lying dead on the kitchen floor one Sunday morning, after seeing her newspapers and milk bottles on the step for a couple of days. She had suffered a cerebral thrombosis and had probably been ill for several days without anyone knowing.

When she was laid to rest only John and I and the young neigh-bours who had brought a gleam of warm sunshine into her drab existence were there to represent the village; and none of us, I felt sure, was disposed to mourn her passing—from the torments of a world that had treated her rather shabbily—at last into a haven of unparalleled peace.

*   *   *   *   *

I was not astute enough to foresee that once the identity of the local press correspondent became known it could involve me in a good deal of additional, unsought writing in and for the parish. Reckoned singly, these were small services, willingly rendered; *in toto* they assumed alarming proportions and were cruelly time-absorbing.

Once or twice I was persuaded to act as private secretary in a protracted family exchange, and found it impossibly hard to main-tain a detached view. Of course, the drafting and typing of the odd circular for this or that organization was almost taken for granted. Then there was an aspiring fiction writer (and what fiction!) who regularly and gratuitously sought my humble opinion of her prolific literary creations (as far as I know she is still *aspiring*). A more sur-prising request was to type an old lady's will; and later came repeated requests to act as ghost writer for the reluctant orators—those well-intentioned parishioners who had impulsively under-taken to fill the star rôle at some public function, only to be seized by sheer panic when it dawned on them that " opening the bazaar " or " presenting the school prizes " normally calls for a suitable speech. Petrified at the prospect to which they were now committed, they implored my poor help, in terms not easy to refuse: " I'm in an *awful* jam; will *you*, oh *please* will you write a few words for me to memorize? "—as if brevity were the sole key to the situation.

I never found it easy to insinuate myself into the others' minds, and their over-confident heart-cry, " Oh, *you* know what I want to say," served rather to accentuate my mental vacuum than to inspire the flow of eloquence they seemed to think was available on tap. Especially was this so in the case of the " speaker " who, when invited to go back to her native town for some jubilee celebrations, was obsessed with nostalgic longings and wanted to reconstruct in her speech the scenes and events of her distant childhood. How could *I* be expected to strike an authentic note?

*   *   *   *   *

A more ambitious undertaking to which I committed myself in a moment of incredible weakness (or incredible vanity?) was the production of a village history. The pressure group appointed to wait on me certainly knew how to turn on the pressure full kick, and their patience was monumental.

Apart from the obvious topographical details and the material available in the parish registers, I envisaged two main sources of information: (a) the local archives in the county record office and (b) the pooled testimonies of " ye olde inhabitants," whose tender reminiscences I planned to string together on a fragile thread of narrative.

A smallish committee was formed: its terms of reference " to collect, verify and approve relevant facts." I urged its members to try to recall any sensational happenings within living memory. Once we had the essential data I would soon get the job on the assembly line, I kidded myself! Why, the finished article might even be on sale in time for the coming fête.

This optimism, however, made no allowance for the relentless tenacity and vigour with which *every* single detail of *every* single incident—no matter how trivial—would be contested by the members of that dedicated committee. The likelihood of ever reaching agreement, or even a compromise, on any " sensational happening " became increasingly remote with every minute spent in session, and I soon realized that *memory* is a singularly dubious instrument for factual measuring.

One whole session was wasted in spirited argument as to the actual spot where a foundering balloon was alleged to have come down in the year of Queen Victoria's jubilee. Mrs. Jones said emphatically that it was on the far side of Woodman's meadow; this she knew for certain because the men in the basket had actually asked her grandfather where they were, and he had set them on their course. Mrs. Pymm rejected this version—with uncalled-for contempt, I thought—as " pure rubbish "; *everybody*, she said, knew that it was right by the main road, actually on Stock Hill; after all, her aunt had watched it come down, and how could she possibly have seen three miles to Woodman's meadow, with all those cottages in between? Mr. Groom showed signs of gathering impatience; that balloon, he insisted, had *definitely* landed in the second field from the copse, and if we were not going to be accurate in our history we had better say so now and not go on with it. Accuracy with him, he reminded us menacingly, was " a matter of principle." He threatened resignation, and the next minute retracted it, to everyone's secret disappointment, for Sam Groom, with his built-in pomposity and his irritating habit of clinching every argument with a fierce flip of his wayward forelock, was never really popular. (I was told that they tolerated him on committees only because of his unconscious genius for spoonerisms, which added light relief on dull occasions. Once, when he had been challenged about the village hall estimates, he had roared in defence: " *I* know what I'm talking about; *you* ought to make sure of your ficts and fagures "; and on another occasion, when the temperature of the P.C.C. was nearing fever heat on a point of vestments, Sam— an incorrigible " low "—wanted to know " What do the bishops look like, all dressed up in their kites and mopers?)

But to revert to the balloon episode, little Miss Court—the very able leader of a splinter group—presented a totally different version from all the others and thus added her quota to the general confusion. According to her old grandmother, the balloon hadn't come down at all, but had been seen drifting helplessly towards the church tower; then somebody in the basket had thoughtfully hurled ballast overboard just in time to miss the weathervane, and they had gained height and sailed off happily.

The discussion seemed likely to continue all night. I, as a mere foreigner and only the official compiler, felt tempted to suggest tossing for it, but instead I proposed as tactfully as I could to omit the incident altogether, assuring them that the subsequent history would be just as convincing (or as unconvincing!) without it.

Thereafter I kept a sharp look-out for potentially controversial issues, and generally managed to side-step them.

The history appeared in due course and was soon over-sold; but I never heard of anybody reading it.

*   *   *   *   *

I had a sneaking fear that these numerous little " literary " demands within the parish might begin to put ideas into John's head; but, to his lasting credit, he never sought to burden me with any responsibility for the " monthly nightmare," as most clergy irreverently call their parish magazines. That was essentially *his* pigeon, and such it remained until he relinquished the editorship on his retirement.

*   *   *   *   *

As a counter-gesture, I, for my part, resisted the sore temptation to report John's encounter with the phantom marauder—despite its sensation value!

For years we had been vaguely conscious of an incurable creak on the fifth stair of the vicarage, but it hadn't bothered us unduly until the night of the visitation, when we were wakened simultaneously by the tell-tale creak, followed by stealthy footsteps on the landing (or so we thought!).

John, moved to heights of unspeakable gallantry, leapt from bed like a zealous fireman at practice drill and, unarmed except for a bedroom slipper grasped truncheonwise, began a search of the upstairs rooms. (As a self-confessed coward, nothing much was expected of me.)

There was no lurking burglar on that floor, so John rushed downstairs after his supposed quarry, hoping to prevent a clean getaway, but there was not a sign or sound of disturbance.

Manifestly relieved that everything was safe and intact—and

even more relieved that there had been no hulking thug to overpower!—John trudged thankfully upstairs again, only to come face to face on the landing with the figure of a man, pin-pointed by a shaft of moonlight streaming through the mezzanine window.

Poor John, suddenly petrified and incapable even of yelling, lifted his hand shakily to his brow. So, with mocking precision, did the " man "—and John recognized his own reflection in our full-length landing mirror!

That original creak? We dismissed that as " just one of those things."

Throughout the entire episode *my* cowardice was despicable.

CHAPTER 8

Visiting

OF all the irresponsible charges brought with sweeping imprecision against the clergy the commonest, I suppose, is that of their alleged failure to visit. Of course, there are undoubtedly *some* who don't visit if they can possibly avoid it, just as there are *some* who don't play the guitar, or don't go prematurely bald, or don't like Debussy; but this is no argument for branding them collectively. In my experience the non-visiting parson represents a very small minority, and whenever I hear this particular criticism levelled against the Establishment I am sorely tempted to retaliate " And how often, may I ask, do *you* call on the Church? "

Most of the parsons I know, however, are far more charitable than I am, and instead of retaliating they just turn a deaf ear—or the other cheek?--to their tormentors and continue patiently on their parochial rounds, hoping always that one day the people at No. 7 or at The Limes will stop peeping furtively from behind the curtains and come out and open the door as eagerly as if they had spied the postman, rather than the vicar, trudging up the garden path.

I hold no brief for the non-visiting parson, but in extenuation it should be borne in mind that even among the clergy there are painfully shy temperaments: possibly good, conscientious men—often of the more scholarly type—but so inherently reserved that parochial visiting (or indeed any other social obligation) is for them a major ordeal, enough to render them clumsy, awkward, almost dumb— even boorish. Not for all are the social graces! Maybe these deserve special dispensation.

Then there are those saddled with such immense and thickly populated parishes that even if they made an average of ten calls every afternoon throughout the year (and that would certainly be a superhuman achievement over and above their other multifarious

duties!) they would still probably not cover more than a third of
the homes in their parish in a couple of years. In these circumstances
the harassed and overburdened incumbent is obliged to devise
some system of priorities: the bereaved, the sick, the aged and
lonely, those known to be in specific trouble, any newcomers, in
roughly that order; and he has to put up with stray jibes from the
rest about what they sometimes term " neglect of duty." With no
more than the allotted twenty-four hours in his day, the poor man's
actual *working* hours are disproportionately long; a fourteen-hour
day is not unusual—flat out all the way!

There may well be other valid reasons for infrequent visits, but
very rarely is it from studied unwillingness or bone laziness that the
parson fails to call often enough to satisfy his flock, for he is
reminded in season and out of season that " a visiting parson means
a flourishing church." Actually it does not necessarily follow that
this is the case, for where attendance has lapsed over a long period
it is not easily—if ever—fully restored however assiduous a visitor
the new man at the vicarage may be. The absentees may become
well disposed towards him as a man—indeed, accept him as a friend
—and yet still prefer to remain absentees, satisfied to render financial
support by stealth and " keep out of it all." He will seldom succeed
in probing the real reason underlying their obduracy, though it can
usually be assumed to stem from past feuds—irreconcilable hang-
overs from bitter hostilities in years gone by; sometimes, alas, old
family feuds perpetuated for no known reason at all. (A young man
once confessed to John: " I know I mustn't speak to my cousins,
but I don't know why "!)

One particular instance of lapsed attendance, which John tackled
with dogged persistence, had a singularly unprofitable ending. It
was the case of a bluff old farrier, heading for the eighties, a man
of massive frame and very lame in the right leg. His rugged features
were dominated by an unbecoming black patch over the socket of
his missing right eye, a handicap that seemed to impart a glint of
intense severity in his one sighted eye. He was known—with affection rather than disrespect—as Blinker Prentice, and was reputed
to be a man of considerable substance. *He* was one who supported
the church with spasmodic generosity (spasms that were exceptionally handsome and welcome!), but he never put in a personal
appearance. John plugged away with monumental patience and
tenacity, but to no avail—until the old man lost his wife, whom

John had regularly visited during her long and painful illness. Offering graveside consolation to the bereaved Blinker, John had used the words " She's better off now! " and was rewarded with a sharp, suspicious glare and the brusque rejoinder " D'you think so? "—seeming to imply that he took it as a very dubious compliment to himself. John regretted his choice of phrase. The next Sunday morning, in accordance with country custom, all the family mourners assembled in church for matins, including, to John's gratification, even the confirmed absentee, Blinker. The second lesson, from the appointed lectionary, was St. Mark chapter 9, and when John came to the exhortation " . . . if thine eye cause thee to stumble, cast it out; it is good for thee to enter into the kingdom of God with *one* eye, rather than having two eyes and be cast into hell . . . " poor old Mr. Prentice, emerging from a reverie, sat bolt upright, turned an apopletic purple, and glared scorchingly at John, who was innocently pursuing St. Mark, unaware of the wrath brewing in Blinker. Apparently he thought that the vicar was being offensively personal, and he resented it. Maybe he feared that next time (if there was a next time!) his other infirmity might attract the comment " . . . then shall the lame man leap as an hart . . . " —a wildly exaggerated promise, if ever there was one, to a man of his ponderous stature; safer not to risk a second public allusion! He never came again, and it did seem hard that it was probably adherence to the lectionary that cost John the old man's favour!

It also cost the church those spasmodic donations.

*   *   *   *   *

The visiting parson—even allowing for fanatical zeal—finds plenty of obstacles to overcome before fruitful contacts can be established, including the specific hazards of the new social order, which calls for an entirely new technique in village evangelism— for instance, the fact of everybody being out at work all day, with the domestic chores crowded into the all-too-short evenings and the week's wash reserved for Sunday morning. Then there is that monopolizing monster the telly, which can make the ill-timed arrival of a chance caller—parsonical or otherwise—anything but a welcome interruption. From the clergy standpoint this can safely be counted upon to nullify the whole purpose of a visit: the programme may be grudgingly switched off, causing the younger folk, with whom he would have welcomed a chat, to drift off a trifle sullenly to another room; or perhaps, for their benefit, the parents may leave it on at full kick, making conversation a test of lung-power and sustained concentration a sheer impossibility.

In these circumstances the best the poor vicar can do is to try to avoid intruding on the popular serial nights, or during the sports reviews, or the international boxing contests, or the favourite quiz sessions, or the celebrity concerts, or " Panorama," or ballroom dancing, or, of course, the news! This leaves only the weather reports, which don't last long enough anyway for the normal visit; and even weather reports, in a farming community, can have an almost sacred significance! Poor parson!

Fortunately, John suffered few inhibitions about visiting. He is naturally friendly and prefers chatting informally in the kitchen to being ushered in state into the seldom-used parlour, which may well be unheated in winter and unventilated in summer, and a trifle musty in either event; conversation here was more likely to be stiff and stilted than relaxed and free-flowing. He had also schooled himself, through the medium of squalling infants at baptisms, to compete successfully against the background noises, so the radio and television did not worry him unduly.

John regarded visiting as one of the most—if not *the* most—important features of his ministry and from the outset he made no distinction between the committed and the uncommitted; Anglican or free church. There was a small Congregational chapel in the village, but no resident minister. That faithful little flock was served Sunday by Sunday by a visiting preacher—usually a layman—from the nearest town, so John was only too happy to take them all under his pastoral wing, and it became a source of immense satisfaction to us both that eventually we numbered the " brothers across the way " among our best friends. John's aim from the outset was to achieve a happy relationship with them; on occasions he would take part in their special services, and at times their members would be seen worshipping at the parish church, signifying a welcome degree of mutual respect and tolerance many years in advance of the now widely accepted ecumenical trend. And, of course, he had the privilege of marrying their young couples.

Having something of a flair for hospital visiting, John regularly toured the wards, although our nearest hospitals were eight to ten miles away; and it often astonished us that from so small a com-

L

munity as ours at Upper Bellpull hardly a week passed without at least two or three of our parishioners becoming in-patients.

*　　*　　*　　*　　*

To a lesser extent, I too joined in the general visiting campaign. If I could find some pretext for calling (and this was not insuperably hard, as there were always the garden cuttings to exchange, or the windfalls to offer) it gave me the opportunity of meeting the women of the village on their own ground and getting to know the family set-up and the sort of interest that would be most likely to win their support. The pretext with the newcomers to the parish was simply to take a typed list of the women's meetings and organizations, inviting them to come first as my guests, with a view to membership later on if it appealed to them. Having broken the ice, the rest seemed easy; as a recruiting dodge it brought results.

There was one difficulty, however, which both John and I thought we would never master—the country dialect and voice inflection. No matter how attentively we listened, much of their speech in the early days left us completely bewildered. In fact, even after our fifteen years among them there were still a few parishioners to whose remarks we could only respond with a non-committal " Um! " or " Ah! "—or possibly with a movement of the head calculated to signify either a knowing " Yes " or an equally knowing " No " as the case demanded; for we hadn't an inkling as to what they were trying to convey and we hesitated to embarrass them interminably with " beg pardons " and " ehs." I haven't a doubt that our nods and grunts frequently misfired; nor had we any doubt that our country-bred flock must have experienced a similar problem in us. Many a time I intercepted a frankly puzzled expression, and there were occasions when I gave up trying to extricate myself from a verbal deadlock.

*　　*　　*　　*　　*

In the course of our visitations we crossed every type of threshold —architecturally and socially. During our first month in the parish John and I presented ourselves one evening *in error* as dinner guests at the home of a reputed millionaire shipping magnate! Mercifully, the owners were away at the time; a sophisticated uniformed maid answered the door, and when we asked for Mrs. J—— she quickly redirected us, almost as if we were itinerant junk dealers, to " that *small* house at the end of the lane, with the green tiles." Later on, however, John made a pastoral contact with the tycoon, and there were no more *embarrassing* encounters; a friendly reception was reserved for us.

At the other end of the scale was the tiniest and most tumbledown cottage imaginable, on a weekly rental of one shilling and sixpence —and the tenant thought the landlord unduly neglectful and inconsiderate in not carrying out routine repairs! (Heaven knows, they were badly needed.)

Between these two extremes there was a varied range—cosy farmhouses, the odd few fine Georgian mansions, the clever pseudo-Tudor conversions, the usual quota of primly utilitarian council houses, sun-catching little bungalows, and a sprinkling of caravans.

The oldest thatched cottage in the village was said to be at least 400 years old—gauged, presumably, by the way the laths were fixed. It was an interesting example of the characteristic methods of the age, with its lath-and-plaster walls on an oak-beam framework, the laths interlocked into grooves. A more recent survey of the walls revealed the osier peelings binding laths together (osier beds had formerly been a special local feature and basket-making was at one time a flourishing little village industry). This quaint little cottage, with its uneven floors and crudely asymmetrical walls, had passed through its many phases of modernization, ending with all mod. cons., electricity and central heating, and its market value had rocketed accordingly from £300 to over £4,000 even in our short time.

In due course we mastered the approved local custom of dropping in informally at the *back* door in most cases, while making a careful mental note of the exceptions where approach by frontal assault was expected.

But easily the most informal and unconventional of all John's pastoral visits were to the local hermit, old Jock MacPhee, who occupied, in unchallenged independence, a derelict wartime blockhouse set up during the invasion threat in a field by the river bank. John had stumbled on him quite by accident and in fantastic circumstances.

Not having a car, and being unable to ride a bicycle because of dangerous imbalance resulting from an operation on the middle ear (his last brave attempt had notched up a score of one sprained ankle, two deeply lacerated knees, a gaping rent in a trouser leg and a buckled front wheel!), John was obliged to foot-slog his way around his extensive, straggling parish—trailing along dusty lanes and diving nimbly into ditches and hedges with every passing car; taking fields, fences, stiles and streams in his stride; now weaving a fastidious way along muddy bridle paths, now plunging through overgrown copses; and occasionally trespassing on the lush preserves of grazing cattle and finding sometimes the hostile stares and threatening advances of a resentful herd anything but reassuring. It all added up to a vocational aspect that was originally undreamt-of. (The one obvious advantage, of course, that the priest circulating on foot has over his car-owning brethren is that he is bound to *meet* his people and it is a great aid in establishing contact.)

It was on one of these pastoral jaunts that John came across our hermit.

Returning one afternoon from a remote farmhouse, zigzagging his way across a meadow to dodge some sludgy puddles, John noticed clouds of thick smoke belching from the old pillbox. Assuming that children were on a camping spree, and foreseeing possible danger if they were playing with fire, he strolled over and peeped inside the fug-hole; but there were no mischievous children there. Instead—and to John's utter amazement—there was a wizened little man, rising seventy, he guessed, rather like a faded gnome, squatting on an old orange box and watching over a stew-pot. This rested on a few bricks, and the red embers glowed cosily through the smoke. What he was using as fuel was anybody's guess, but it created this almost impenetrable smoke-screen and a slightly strange smell. The old man was alternately thumping his chest as he coughed and stirring the stew with a piece of stick. Far from resenting John's surprise intrusion, the old chap was quite welcoming, engaging him at once in a torrent of conversation, which John could only partially understand because of the fabulous speed at which he spoke and his incommunicable Scottish accent. With difficulty John pieced together the main details: the hermit's name was Jock MacPhee; he hailed from a "wee toun" on the outskirts of Lossiemouth; he had spent most of his life at sea, but had now settled permanently for the free-and-easy life and had no regrets about contracting out of the modern rat race. He was in the throes of cooking a local rabbit for supper and was anxious to share it with John.

Over the smoky repast a few remarkable facts emerged: Jock was obviously a man of considerable learning, with a profound knowledge of history in general and of the Restoration period in particular. He claimed to have had university connections (!) and to have received the most exhaustive Biblical grounding from his mother.

Jock thoroughly appreciated his unchallenged possession of the pillbox, and the farmer on whose land it was situated turned a conveniently blind eye to this unauthorized tenancy. In fact he provided Jock with enough casual work at the standard rate to keep his modest needs supplied. His material possessions seemed to consist of the orange box and stew-pot, a lumpy old mattress, a tin kettle, a couple of enamel mugs and a plate; possibly he had other treasures stowed away, but he boasted proudly of having no worries or responsibilities. He had a little grizzly beard, but his head was nearly bald. He appeared entirely unembarrassed by the rags he wore.

John had some difficulty in disengaging himself from his talkative host (and new parishioner!), but he promised to look him up again. Old Jock, for his part, promised to come to kirk next Sunday. Strangely enough, this was one of the unsought church-coming promises made to John that was duly honoured—to the amazement of the congregation and the mild consternation of the sidesman on duty. The consternation was accounted for (a) by Jock's late and noisy entry, about halfway through matins (having no clock, he was obliged to estimate time by the sun), and (b) by his tardy recognition of the collection bag! There stood old Mr. Biggs, patient and respectful as always, thrusting the bag pointedly towards Jock, but it seemed minutes before its significance registered; and when it did he took an unconscionably long time to unbutton his rags (the top layer was tied round the middle with string), dive down into his trouser pocket and fish out the large leather purse that held his wealth. Slowly, deliberately and with deep calculation Jock extracted his offering, and Mr. Biggs made his belated journey up the aisle with the alms bag.

For a while Jock came more or less regularly to matins, but after that initial hitch Mr. Biggs took the wise precaution of putting on an extra sidesman, whose duty was mainly to wait on Jock.

Then one Sunday morning he was missing and we thought that he must have vacated his pillbox and moved on in search of more commodious premises in pastures new. But not a bit of it; the following afternoon I ran into him outside the little village shop, and he was effusive in his apologies to " His Riverence "—as he invariably called John—for yesterday's absence. With engaging frankness he offered his explanation—a very intimate one! " Mrs. Green, will ye please tell His Riverence that I would ha' come to the kirk yesterday, only I had had a wee bitty accident—sour fruit it was that caused it—and I had to go down to the river to wash ma pants. I spread them over a bush to dry, but they were na' dry in time. I'll be there next Sunday, tell His Riverence."

On Christmas morning old Jock was in his place in kirk and, conscious of an upsurge of seasonable spirit, we invited him back to the vicarage for a drink and a mince pie. I confess to certain misgivings as his grimy, smoke-laden rags settled comfortably against the smart new cushion covers on our settee—but, there, it was Christmas; why worry? Warmed by the sherry and the cheerful fire, Jock's conversation flowed ceaselessly; indeed, we had considerable difficulty in dismissing him gracefully in time to keep our own Christmas rendezvous at our friends' delightful seventeenth-century timber-framed house, where the traditional welcome of a colossal open hearth, piled high with blazing logs, and the seductive aroma of superb cooking awaited us as we stepped into the candle-lit oak-panelled hall.

Later on in our association with poor old Jock I began to find it advisable, if not imperative, to try to dodge him when I saw him coming up our lane; he was such an inextinguishable talker, usually on the most abstruse topics, that I never knew how to get away—and my time was precious. He also had a revolting habit of punctuating every other sentence with a routine expectoration—and the wind could be in the wrong direction!

But the first sign of impatience on the part of his audience could quickly inflame the old man's temper. Once when I had popped out to the post, leaving John ill in bed and the kettle plugged in, it was with a sinking heart that I spotted old Jock making straight for me. I pretended to be deeply lost in thought and singularly unobservant. But Jock took a lot of dodging! This time he tapped my arm and asked after " His Riverence," and then launched out on a maddening dissertation on the political implications of Charles II's marriage to Katherine of Portugal and the economic advantages of the possessions he received with her.

When I cut in with a firm " Really Jock, you'll *have* to excuse me today; His Riverence is ill and my kettle will have boiled dry " he rewarded me with a withering glare and the crushing observation: " Ye're always in a hurry when I'm trying to tell ye things; if ye were paying fees for this information, in a lecture room, maybe ye'd not be in such a hurry after all; ye'd stay and learn a bitty "!

I felt thoroughly rebuked.

One day Jock didn't turn up with the others in the beet field. The farmer had a hunch that something was wrong, so he and his stockman trundled over the fields to the pillbox.

Jock was lying dead in the entrance, as if in his last human effort he had struggled to get out to summon help.

* * * * *

The amount of walking involved in John's visitations was acceptable enough in good weather, but it had its peculiar drawbacks in our line of country when conditions were foul; and until he had had a chance to become familiar with the terrain there were not a few lurking dangers. For instance, one evening, in a swirling fog, he emerged from a farmhouse and tried to grope his way clear of the yard on to the main road—and he missed a reed-infested pond by a hair's breadth; and, for the unwary, the apparently obvious bridle path sometimes led into a no-man's-land of squelching mud, ankle deep and treacherously engulfing.

On one unforgettable occasion, as John was making tracks home in the gathering dusk he was just on the point of crossing a bridge that wasn't there. He came right up to the disused watermill by the river bank, and suffered a queer jolt when he found the ancient stone bridge had disappeared into the river and only a flimsy piece of rope was stretched across the path to prevent a headlong fall into the water—in spate! The bridge, he learnt afterwards, had spectacularly collapsed that morning as the village postman was about to cycle over it with his daily load.

And then there were dogs! Few farms were without their splendid guards, adequately trained for the job. John and I eventually felt justified in deleting one or two names from our visiting list solely because of the canine ferocity with which anyone setting foot on their masters' territory was certain to be greeted. This was a reluctant decision—you may think a cowardly one—reached only after

John had suffered two bites, one torn trouser leg and countless bad scares. Frankly, I used to be terrified by the wild barking and bared fangs, and the owner's calm assurance that " Rover wouldn't really hurt you; it's only his welcome " did nothing to restore my confidence in parochial pets. I was far from convinced that Rover interpreted his hostile gestures in the same terms.

*   *   *   *   *

One dark night when John had failed to return for tea and was still missing at eight o'clock I began to feel genuine alarm. Eventually he staggered in, looking obviously shaken, dishevelled, and indescribably muddy. There was a jagged tear in his coat sleeve. This time he had called on a sick parishioner in some outlying cottage beyond the river, and her well-intentioned husband had recommended a short cut back to the vicarage. " You don't want to waste time tramping through those *three* fields," he said, knowledgeably; " just take that little lane sharp left past the spinney, then veer right and you'll save yourself a good mile; it will bring you right out by the farmyard gate, in your lane. You can't miss it "!

But can't you?

Against his own better judgment, John took the " short " cut, which, like most other short cuts, soon involved him in a veritable maze of unsuspected twists and turns, overgrown paths, unyielding gates, and partially concealed ditches and puddles. Every step seemed to be leading directly away from his goal. Darkness descended and a sinister, enveloping mist rolled up from the river. John—like his feline counterpart, Felix—kept on walking, accepting as philosophically as possible the fact that he was completely lost and stood a very good chance of ending up, unwittingly, in the river. But fate had other plans for him, no less distasteful: the " little lane, sharp left, then veering right," etc., brought him at long last up to Bolton's hedge and what looked—through the gloom —like a nice, friendly gap into the farmyard. Instead it was a businesslike barricade of barbed wire. After hesitating for a moment, poor John decided that the only way to get home now was to negotiate the barbed wire; but having wriggled and wrenched and insinuated his partial way through he found himself face to face with a very irate black sow, which challenged his right of entry in no uncertain terms. Discretion inclined him to defer to her wishes without further argument, and he retreated shakily and a trifle painfully. Then, edging his way gingerly to the right, he stumbled with a thankful heart against the farmyard gate and into our lane. In his immeasurable relief he nearly sang the *Te Deum*.

* * * * *

By gradual stages John succeeded in breaking down the barriers of shyness and reticence in his parishioners—at least in most of them. They began to show signs of accepting him as a friend; initial dumbness gave way to breezy exchanges, to sharing confidences and to the odd joke. But there remained the few exceptions who preferred, apparently, to stay in deep freeze—the incorrigibly withdrawn and inarticulate souls resisting, consciously or unconsciously, every attempt to establish the communication that John sought so earnestly.

The poor defeated parson, driven almost to distraction in a sterile situation (and denied the conventional tongue-looseners and aids to conviviality!), will clutch at any likely straw to achieve the desired break-through, though it may well involve him in the most inane observations. He will cast a furtive eye around the room, searching desperately for some prized picture, or ornament, or family group—*anything*, in fact, that could provide a possible opening: " Oh, that's a picture of Brighton [or Blackpool, or Yarmouth!], isn't it? Do you know that part well? Wonderful air there . . . "; and if this brings no more than a monosyllable he must switch quickly to the family group, opening fire with an encouraging " What a *delightful* photo—your grandparents, I imagine. There's a strong family likeness, especially about the eyes . . . "; and that may serve to induce a few fitful sparks of conversation—unless, of course, his amiable guess was entirely off the beam and brings only an abrupt disclaimer: " No relation, only my first husband's father and stepmother."

And if all that fails there's only one thing left—illness and all its melancholy symptoms, with operations held as a trump card.

There was one such human hurdle—in the person of Mrs. X—that John never surmounted, although he plugged away with regular visits to her little bungalow. In the end his patient endeavours succeeded only in covering himself with confusion and plunging Mrs. X into depths of pained embarrassment. It should be explained that she was elderly, frighteningly prim and unbending; she suffered perpetual bad health and spent most of her days in bed, in an overcrowded bed-sitting room, waited on with unfaltering solicitude by her unmarried daughter. Mrs. X received the vicar only on her *good* days, i.e. when she chose to sit *out* of bed, in a smothering collection of shawls and wrappers and the smelling salts always to hand. On the day when John disgraced himself he had looked around in vain for any fresh prints of Brighton or wedding groups, but his eye lighted in triumph on a fine Chippendale-style chair, and he hopefully seized on this item as a possible topic. " Forgive me for remarking on your *lovely* Chippendale chair; you've got a gem there; it's a period that I admire so much; in fact, we have four chairs *exactly* like yours in our dining-room at the vicarage."

Alas, this gambit evoked no reciprocal comment, only a tight-lipped blush, which was hardly surprising, for, just a second too late, John realized that Mrs. X's Chippendale piece was no ordinary chair. As a throne it was specifically and intimately functional. Oh, fool, fool, *fool*! Why had he selected that, of all things, as conversational bait? And he had even asked her to believe that we kept *ours* —all four of them!—in the vicarage dining-room!

*   *   *   *   *

Inevitably we had our local Mrs. Malaprop, who kept us constantly amused with her innocent blunders. John would come home after visiting her in a state of boisterous hilarity, to tell me the latest.

Once, when Mrs. Malaprop's better half was in hospital (with his stummick!), John had popped over to ask for the latest news. " Proper poorly, Vicar; when I saw 'im yesterday 'e was that exhausted 'e could hardly speak; ever so weak. But what could you expect? They'd given 'im four *anemones* "!

Well, what *could* you expect?

When I inquired one day about her hacking cough, which seemed even more hacking than usual, she gasped, between her spasms, " It's me artilleries; there's something always a'tickling me artilleries," and I pondered that one, unsuccessfully, for a long while. That was the occasion, by the way, when her loving husband, showing sympathetic concern, had *bawled* at her " Wot's up wi' ye? Got summat stuck in yer hatch, woman? "

The classic example of Mrs. Malaprop's genius for misapplied words puzzled John deeply; he came in shaking with laughter. Mrs. Malaprop and her immediate neighbour were known to be not on the best of terms. John, anxious always to promote improved relations where things were a bit strained, had tactfully asked Mrs. M if she had seen Mrs. Flint recently, adding " I don't think she was in church yesterday."

In tones of dark insinuation Mrs. M responded: " No, she wasn't there, and I don't mind telling you that she's being proper disloyal to her own parish; yesterday she went over to *Lower* Bellpull church; and what's she up to, I want to know, *fornicating* with Mr. Earl? " (naming John's friend and rector of the adjoining parish).

What indeed? Surely one of the great imponderables. After much speculation our nearest guess was that she intended *fraternizing*!

Our Mrs. Malaprop was the very last one who ought ever to have been entrusted to move a vote of thanks at the W.I., but this was a simple little formality which we were invited in turn to undertake. The majority, subject to paralysing nervousness, firmly declined, but not so Mrs. Malaprop; she had no noticeable inhibitions.

She was briefed by the president, who felt reasonably confident that in half a dozen rehearsed words she couldn't go far wrong. But you bet she did!

" On behalf of the members of the Upper Bellpull Women's Institute, I wish to express our most grateful thanks and appreciation to you, Mrs. *Mangle*! " The speaker glared at her like a wounded tigress and hissed " Ringer, you mean; it's Mrs. *Ringer*."

*   *   *   *   *

I used thoroughly to enjoy my little homely chats with these country women—particularly the elderly ones, from whom I was able to glean much valuable knowledge. They seemed to have an inexhaustible fund of country lore to pass on. From one I culled dozens of unusual cookery recipes and household wrinkles; and from another—the recognized layer-out—I gained quite a wide knowledge of local legends, superstitions and ancient simples. Many of them I have since forgotten, but I recall that her unorthodox treatment for a whitlow on the finger was to roll up a piece of dark brown paper and light it so that it smoked. The affected finger must then be plunged into the smouldering paper cylinder, and this routine had to be repeated four times a day. The whitlow, she claimed, would entirely disappear in six days. For ringworm she recommended one and a half ounces of flowers of sulphur mixed with once ounce of pure lard (not shop lard, she stipulated!); this, rubbed into the affected parts, was supposed to have almost magical results.

Another of her beliefs, I remember, was that a white juice exuded by the stalk of fig leaves was a sure cure for warts—a drop to a wart, lightly dabbed on. But as a second string to this particular bow she also favoured the mysterious powers of the wart charmer.

She also insisted that the bruised leaves of the foxglove provided a reliable healing agent for open wounds and king's evil; and for a sty she advocated simply rubbing the eye gently several times with a plain gold ring.

It is not difficult to imagine what orthodoxy would have to say about these old wives' remedies! Anyway, my curiosity to learn more of these quaint customs furnished me with a ready-made excuse for calling on old Mrs. Nettlefold, and I always found it a rewarding session. As a local *character* she enjoyed considerable popularity; and in any event, having no doctor within six miles and no resident district nurse, there was some comfort in the knowledge that Mrs. N's private pharmacopœia was readily available in a simple emergency.

*   *   *   *   *

There was one enchanting little cottage where both John and I loved to call. The low thatch and diamond-pane windows were in perfect harmony with the old-world charm of the people who lived there. The occupants were a sweet, gentle old couple, who seemed to reflect an aura of all that was lovable, brave and tranquil in old age accepted with grace. *She* was so patient with his increasing deafness, and *he* displayed for her all the affection and gallantry of romantic youth. To watch these two wonderful old people—both well over eighty, and known to all and sundry as Darby and Joan—sitting on either side of their tiny fireplace, so obviously enjoying each other's company, was an enriching and unforgettable experience. They both loved flowers and possessed an uncanny skill in plant culture. Often the old gentleman would send home to me by John one of his choicest blooms—a specimen rose or a flawless carnation—or perhaps a magnificent primula in full bloom. The old lady, despite her years, was always one of the most zealous and successful exhibitors at the local garden show, and this floral skill, combined with her superb cookery entries, secured for her on more than one occasion the ladies' silver challenge cup for the highest number of points.

My last call there was on the occasion of their golden wedding, when I, on behalf of the Women's Church Guild, was the bearer of felicitations and an armful of golden blossoms—daffodils, tulips, yellow narcissi and forsythia—tied with a gold satin ribbon bow.

It was a soft, sunny April morning and the whole countryside was flooded with the light of spring. As I approached their little cottage—nestling comfortably in its picture-postcard setting—I saw them first through the open window of their small living room; their heads were close together as they bent over the table laden with gifts and cards. They were still opening the last of their wonderful pile of greetings, smiling happily at each other, and almost trembling with excitement.

It was a vision of utter joy and contentment that I shall never forget. I saw in that dear old couple the personification of human bliss. At such a moment it seemed almost an impertinence to intrude on their private paradise.

There was only one disenchanting feature for me! Dear old Darby had always longed to possess a violin, and his son had managed to buy him a secondhand one to mark this golden anniversary. He was quivering with pride and irrepressible excitement in his new possession. He had received it only the previous night, but he had already spent several delirious hours struggling to pick out—without, of course, even the most rudimentary instruction—his favourite hymn tunes, and he was clearly longing to entertain me with an impromptu recital of " Praise, my soul, the King of heaven " and " Onward, Christian soldiers."

Instead of holding the fiddle under his chin he placed it unconventionally across his knees, bowing in cello style; and he seemed happily convinced that the torturing, scraping, discordant sounds that he produced faithfully represented the tunes he named. No Menuhin he! It was more painful than the worst toothache I ever had.

His smiling Joan appeared to be awe-struck by his swift mastery (!) of so complicated an instrument. Having run through his—as yet—limited repertoire, he was emboldened to invite me to name my requests—and he would oblige. Having congratulated him on a performance which the composer himself could never have recognized, the poor old man went on interminably, scraping, bowing, pinging totally unidentifiable tunes, and appealing to me each time " You know what that one is, don't you? " and I, rather than wound his feelings or dim his wedding rapture, prevaricated outrageously: " Oh yes, of *course;* why that's—oh dear, I know it so well; it's right on the tip of my tongue; h'm, h'm, actually it's one of my favourites " !

For once I felt satisfied that Christian charity justified (nay, *demanded*) shameless hypocrisy. Anyway, his beaming satisfaction afforded me ample dispensation.

*   *   *   *   *

There came a point when John and I had cause to wonder whether his growing reputation as a tireless visitor was not seen as an invitation to take advantage of good nature. We were constantly being telephoned to deliver local messages—and I don't mean urgent ones—and on several occasions young parishioners who had contrived to miss their last bus home at night had tinkled us to ask the vicar to " let mum know I shan't be home tonight." This happened once when we were actually in bed and comfortab y drowsy; the telephone bell brought us to with a start: it was the now-famil ar request, and we began to see it for the racket it was. However, John, in an excess of pastoral solicitude, relented. " Oh, all right; I'll go and let your people know, but I don't mind telling you that we're already in bed, and I don't relish getting up and going out." (There was a faint " Oh! " at the other end of the line; not a word of apology.)

Having dressed and walked the half-mile to that young lady's home, John's reward was a scowling reception from an enraged parent, who had been saving it all up for his wayward child. There he stood, waiting at the gate, with his little piece fully rehearsed.

John got the lot—and no thanks.

*   *   *   *   *

By now we had received so many strange telephone calls and queer requests that we ought not to have been surprised at anything—or shocked! But we were on the night when Mrs. Gimlett called John to the telephone in a state of threatened hysteria.

The conversation proceeded pleasantly along these lines:

" Is that you, Vicar? "

" Yes, it is."

" Well, can I have the bed-pan? "

" I *beg* your pardon; did you say the *bed-pan*? "

" That's right; Mrs. Pettit [naming her sister-in-law] wants it urgent."

" I don't think I quite get you. *Whose* bed-pan, and why ask *me* for it? "

" Well, haven't you got it? I thought you had all the stuff down at the vicarage."

At this point a little explanation seemed desirable, and Mrs. Gimlett was invited to make her case clearer.

Apparently, at some remote date long before we came, Upper Bellpull had been farsighted enough—and public-spirited enough— to try to inaugurate its own modest health service and social welfare scheme. The first step had been to hold a weekly surgery—in the vicarage, of course!—each Wednesday. There was no bus service in those days, and the prospect of having Dr. Stiller drive over in his phaeton from Lower Bellpull promised to be an undoubted boon—at least to those who could contrive to have their accidents or develop their symptoms on the right day; but an exasperating prospect for those who timed things less successfully.

The second step had been to provide a parish layette to meet the contingency of improvident or unexpected arrivals. (The design and coarseness of these garments stamped them as authentic museum pieces, and after being scorned by several generations of more enlightened mothers they found their way ultimately to some earthquake-stricken area in a refugee parcel.)

The third and most practical step had been to acquire a collection of sick-room requisites, to be stored—like most other parish clobber —" down at the vicarage." But as the items had entered into circulation they had become planted indiscriminately all over the village; there were bed rests, hot-water bottles, feeding cups, thermometers, rubber sheets and all the more intimate odds and ends of sick nursing dotted around like vague clues in an inconclusive mystery plot, because no one had thought to record the details of their issue.

John, now appealed to in this delicate dilemma of Mrs. Pettit, proved himself resourceful, co-operative and nimble—as well as soft-hearted. He set to work without a moment's delay to track down the parish bed-pan for the distressed patient.

It cost him five telephone calls and three personal visits, mostly abortive. " No, Vicar; we *did* have it, but we passed it on to the Bettertons, didn't we, dad? Or was it to the Dunnetts?" "No, really, Vicar; we haven't got it; I was under the impression that the Slessors had it after us; if not, you *could* try the Mortons "; and so on.

I felt that it said much for his sleuth work that an hour and three miles later he had run it to earth and obligingly trotted up to the Pettits' home with the elusive article tucked under his arm—a homely little service for which he was profusely thanked by Mr. P.

After that incident we decided that the sick-room equipment must be handled more methodically, so all the items were—with considerable difficulty—reassembled and carefully listed, and future borrowers were required to sign for the things they took away; and we noted the date.

Also, let it be added, future borrowers were required to call and collect their requisites. John, I felt, had done more than his share of portering.

♦   *   *   *   *

John's soft heart let him down time and again. He seemed to have an uncanny knack of dropping in on parishioners at the crucial moment when they were engaged single-handed in some stupendous struggle against overwhelming odds; when, in fact, it was virtually impossible for him honourably—and with dignity—to dodge involvement. On one occasion a poor frail soul was trying to uproot some obstinate old evergreens, and under the tremendous strain of levering and tugging was visibly wilting. John offered to help, and when the massive roots eventually yielded he had bowled over backwards on to some prize begonias, unintentionally hurling a spadeful of dirt at his astonished parishioner as he fell.

Another time it was a jammed window that was defying its owner's pathetic efforts to open it; and it was John who, in his eagerness to be helpful, thrust a hammer slap through the lower pane.

But it was the chimney-sweeping episode that called finally for a complete change of policy; thereafter John assisted only in an advisory capacity. He had gone to ask Mrs. Cathcart—eighty-plus and nearly blind—how her bronchitis was. He found her waging all-out war on her flues; her fire just *wouldn't* burn up, she sighed; she got smoked out every time she tried to light it. There she was, on her poor old rheumaticky knees, begrimed and despairing, prodding away with a silly little short-handled flue brush. There was a thick film of soot over everything and an obvious blockage in the chimney. John volunteered to go and collect the bundle of village chimney brushes and have a go!

He screwed together several lengths and began to push. He soon shifted the blockage, a shower of bricks and a ton of soot—mostly over himself. This lot fell with the appalling suddenness of an avalanche. Ah, well, in for a penny, in for a pound! He thought he had better finish the job properly while he was about it. He lengthened the sticks and shoved higher and harder, but when he tried to withdraw the brush it didn't respond; in fact, it was tightly wedged and resisted his most frenzied efforts. It was a queer, old-fashioned cottage chimney, and all the tugging in the world was to no effect.

It was poor John who had then to get a builder to come and demolish the best part of the chimney stack, release the brush, and rebuild; and it was he, also, who was privileged to settle the account.

Before leaving, John advised old Mrs. Cathcart, in any event, to invest in a patent fire-lighter; she looked puzzled, so he explained —one of those cute little chunks of fire-brick with a strong wire handle; it would save her no end of time and kindling, he assured her. But a week or two later when John called to see her she still had problems: the patent fire-lighter wouldn't light, she moaned. "That's very funny," mused John, "perhaps you didn't leave it long enough in the paraffin."

"Leave it *long* enough; you didn't tell me to put it in paraffin at all!"

So there she had been, poor dear, waiting patiently for the miracle to happen, never dreaming that a *patent* lighter wasn't altogether patent and self-sufficient.

M

CHAPTER 9

Merry-making

FROM the early Middle Ages until the coming of the combustion engine rural life in this country had altered very little; the small country communities were virtually isolated from the broad mainstream of social activity, depending inevitably upon their own home-brewed amusements to appease the pangs of boredom. Communication with the outside world as we know it—through the media of easy travel, telephone, radio and television—was denied them, so local fêtes, pageants and parties, whist drives and day excursions (shades of the old horse-drawn brakes!) were naturally measured in terms of quite fictitious importance. These homely diversions became immensely popular features of parochial life, approached with a zestful enthusiasm that would compare strangely with our current tendency to pleasure-surfeited apathy.

John and I witnessed the declining phases of this rural phenomenon at Upper Bellpull. It had survived the war and was still flourishing in our early days there, with competition for places in the coaches and tickets for the whist drives still keenly maintained; but it all began to slacken perceptibly as post-war conditions took shape and a changed pattern was emerging. In the last few years, under the powerful influence of the new trends—the ubiquitous radio and television, cheap cars, air travel for the masses and, above all, the revolutionary benefit of paid holidays for all workers—we saw a rapidly shrinking demand for parish outings and all the other innocuous revels. In the end it was difficult to fill a single coach where formerly a string of them had been needed to accommodate all who clamoured for seats. Whereas a day's outing to Clacton or Ramsgate used to constitute th· family's summer holiday, saved for for weeks in advance, now, in the new welfare state age, that odd coach fare and the hoarded spending money were more likely to be put towards the cost of a really ambitious journey—probably by air or private car to the Continent or the Channel Isles, or for a whole fortnight's sun-tanning in exotic surround ngs on the Costa Brava.

We saw the old order change with a vengeance, giving place to new; and we were not always convinced that the " new " compared very favourably with the old.

* * * * *

Most of the parish events, we noted, had a pleasant way of being co-operative in their scope and appeal. For ins ance, outings classified ostensibly as choir or Church Guild were likely to attract as many non-members as those affiliated. The Sunday school excursion became, in effect, a family beano, and the British Legion children's treat might well consist of as many old-age pensioners as youngsters.

This practice of tagging on to take advantage of a cheap day by the sea was a sensible, integrating arrangement; it not only spread the costs but, as far as the Sunday school outing was concerned, relieved the vicar and the teachers of undue personal responsibility for the scholars' safety. After all, what were parents for? Besides, in the event of glaring you hful misdemeanours, having the parents at hand served to divert embarrassment from the vicar and his staff and fasten it squarely on the parental shoulders; though, in all fairness, it must be admitted that the Bellpull children usually acquitted themselves remarkably well when on parade, and John's mild apprehension s'emmed mainly from memories of his first East End Sunday school outing—by train to Southend on the old L.N.E.R. Unfortunately, on that occasion there were no reserved compartments for the children; they just bundled in with the rest of the travelling public, so exemplary behaviour was something he fervently hoped for but didn't get! For instance, there was the fidgety little elf from the primary class (under seven), to whom everything was new and frightening; for the first quarter of an hour she snuggled close to her teacher and gazed with flattering curiosity at a donnish old gentleman in the corner busy with notebook, pencil and masses of calculations. Presently she wondered aloud (and how loud!) why that funny old man with hardly any hair was doing his sums here instead of at school. Teacher feigned deafness, but the incorrigible child persisted, in shrill *fortissimo*, until the train suddenly plunged into smoky, inky blackness, which simply petrified her. She clutched teacher's hand and let out an agonized " Oooooh! " They had scarcely emerged again into daylight than the train dived a second time into total darkness. As they came out his time the terrified child clung like a limpet to her neighbour, *screaming* " We ain't going through any more b***** tunnels, are we? "

Well, that was safely in the past. Here it took time for us to get the hang of the accepted local pattern. I recall being frankly puzzled in our first experience when the coaches for the choir outing began rapidly to fill up with nearly all the over-sixties, although the bona fide choristers numbered less than twenty, of average middle age.

That, by the way, was the memorable occasion when old Dan Skinner's anticipated enjoyment was potentially threatened by a serious oversight in his preparations but eleventh-hour awareness saved the situation. Everybody had assembled on time (the rendezvous was always the church gate); names had been checked and coach seats taken; the driver had climbed in and closed the sliding door—then Dan's hand shot up jerkily to his mouth and he bellowed in panic " Hi! Hold on! you'll have to wait a bit; I've left me teeth at 'ome. I must go back and get 'em."

He lived conveniently near, and off he stumped while the rest tried to exercise patience. After a prolonged absence *Mrs.* Skinner thought that she had better get out too, and join in the search for Dan's dentures. " He'll never find em; 'e can never remember where 'e's put *anything*—specially them teeth " she explained with a touch of resigned fatalism, born no doubt of fifty years' attendance on Mr. S.

Away trundled his dutiful wife, and everybody groaned, for she was never a brisk walker.

After a seemingly interminable wait they reappeared—*he* stepping out independently, his usual dozen yards ahead of his spouse; *she* rolling along contentedly in his massive wake, like a saucy little frigate trying vainly to keep up with a battleship.

Back in the coach, Dan became the target for a whole fusillade of good-humoured quips, which he accepted with lofty disdain and a triumphant display of china. " Well, I don't reckon I'd 'ave bin much good without *they*!"—and off they bowled to Hastings.

Nor would he have been much good without " they," for there was an approved ritual about these trips, and feasting played a prominent part in it: a sumptuous three-course dinner, a fish-and-chip-cum-fruit-salad-and-cream tea, and a final snack (albeit a mighty substantial " snack ") at an agreed port of call on the homeward journey, when the organizer was suitably toasted. All these were incontestable features of the " day out," and provided an inexhaustible talking-point most of the way.

(Dan, by the way, was curiously accident-prone with his dentures. He had sneezed them into a trough of bran mash; he had coughed them into the hearth among the cinders; and once, having removed them to facilitate the disposal of raspberry pips, he had absentmindedly left the top set on the draining board and the dog had jumped up and run off with them, the chewed remains being later retrieved from the kennel.)

*   *   *   *   *

Admittedly these village jollifications were more or less stereotyped affairs and noteworthy episodes were rare, but when they did occur it was not singly; nor were they equitably spread! I felt almost personally responsible for the sequence of calamities that befell Mrs. Hinchliffe, a tired, frail and sad little widow. I felt she needed a break, but the suggestion raised little response, so I talked her into joining the Church Guild outing to the sea. " It's just what you need—a complete change of scene. It will do you the world of good to get right away from it all, even if it's only for a day. Now *do* come! "

She did, and this was her reward: while her little coterie of friends went off to paddle she waited alone on a promenade seat. She was promptly accosted by a slightly inebriated stranger—with walrus moustache—who, with disarming swiftness, began to make amorous advances. He was not easily shaken off and his final dismissal was effected only by vicious kicks on the shin and threats to call the police. Mrs. Hinchliffe had scarcely time to compose herself when a savage little mongrel terrier bounded up, snarling and snapping angrily at her ankles. She was quite badly scared—too scared, in fact, to move until someone came to her rescue and the dog was secured, having drawn blood. And it was possibly the nerve-racking effect of these ordeals, coupled with over-indulgence in ice-cream blocks, that accounted for poor Mrs. H's subsequent tummy upset, which delayed considerably the party's departure for home. Everyone was sympathetic and willing enough to wait, but nobody—

least of all Mrs. Hinchliffe herself—was prepared for the stupid fact that, until a specified future date when the season officially " began," not *all* the essential amenities of this delectable resort were fully laid on, and she found with dismay that the turnstile was unyielding and unattended! In her humiliating dilemma she wriggled her way through and back, while her two boon companions stood in fits of laughter. Shyly modest though she was, Mrs. Hinchliffe was not wi hout a nice sense of humour, which encouraged her to confide to the vicar the intimate facts that had caused the delay (a slightly expurgated account, maybe), and by now the whole coachload was in convulsions.

Actually she arrived home in pretty poor shape, permanently disillusioned about the vaunted benefits of " a change of scene, even it it's only for a day "!

*   *   *   *   *

Parish parties—under the auspices of no matter which organization—were always popularly acclaimed. Naturally they entailed plenty of hard work, particularly on the catering side, but there was no shortage of helpers. The major problem, John and I found, was providing the entertainment; we were everlastingly on the look-out for novel ideas and trying to devise workable competitions. Fresh ideas seemed perversely elusive.

The warming-up process, I noted, was always tediously slow. Every party, it seemed, had a way of beginning in a frigid, self-conscious hush which, for the first half of the evening, defied every known means of thawing out; the traditional parlour games—a ritual feature with them—proved about as relaxing as routine pack drill. It worried us a lot and sapped much of our vitality as we struggled to make things hum. Then, with bewitching suddenness, the miracle would happen: that deathly tense atmosphere would dissolve and the rafters would begin to ring with shrieks of merriment; a steadily increasing buzz of chatter was evidence that *at last* the shy reserve was overcome and the party was really under way. From then onwards it would gather hilarious momentum right up to its sentimental climax, when strains of " Auld Lang Syne " would probably echo a couple of parishes away.

What was the ignition key to the welcome transformation?

From close observation we noted that it was the introduction of some form of dressing-up game. It seemed as if the very sight of each other as real figures of fun in all sorts of grotesque disguises— the more preposterous the better—released some inner tension; the inhibiting self-consciousness evaporated entirely. False noses, wigs, Robey eyebrows and silly little hats seemed to constitute the last word in side-splitting amusement. With the habitual mask of staid decorum lifted, we saw our parishioners as the happy revellers that they were at heart—possessing, in fact, a tremendous capacity for fun and laughter.

That *we*—John and I—should be more than ready to join in and match our mood with theirs seemed at first to surprise them beyond belief—but not for long! We soon convinced our flock that we had an equal capacity for frivolity. John usually played the piano for the dancing, and he missed none of the round games if he could help it.

Parochial tastes, we learnt, were as conservative in merry-making as in everything else, so we needn't have worried initially about lack of *new* ideas. Their favourite party game—in perennial demand— was " rummage," always a source of uproarious fun to the point of hysterical exhaustion. John and I, in our ignorance, needed to be initiated.

Its simple elements may be worth passing on. The players sat in a wide circle round the room, waiting for the old clothes dealer to enter dragging a colossal sack crammed with a fabulous assortment of shabby garments—anything from underwear to hat-trimmings, mostly vintage specimens. As the music began, the dealer started to trudge round with her load; as it stopped she halted and the player nearest to her had to pick a garment blindly from the sack and put it on! This went on and on till we were all positively weighed down with the weird, ill-fitting accretions that encumbered us. Of course, every dip into the bag was a signal for fresh peals of laughter, and after we had each had four or five dips the whole company looked hopelessly and unbelievably mad. It made me think of Mrs. Jarley's waxworks on a grand scale—only we were far too boisterous and animated for waxworks.

When the sack was empty we all lined up to parade round the room, amid renewed paroxysms of mirth. I shall never forget the incongruous spectacle of John wearing—over and above his sedate clericals—a chartreuse-green blouse that wouldn't button up; a pair of frayed pink corsets; a tired black bonnet (*circa* 1875) decorated with wilted ostrich feathers, jet ornaments and bow strings under the chin; and, as an impressive finish, a black bearskin muff! This get-up evoked a sensational gasp—but not of horror; it was manifestly of incredulity and warm approval. He was awarded three rousing cheers.

Another perennial caper was the men's miming contest—a guyed act to demonstrate their nursery know-how: bathing, topping-and-tailing and then dressing an imaginary baby. Sitting in a row across the platform to give everyone an uninterrupted view, they had to don long, bustly skirts, workmanlike aprons and caps, then set to work in earnest gesture. It was not only the ludicrous get-up but also the exaggeratedly purposeful manipulation of intractable safety pins, powder puffs and talcum tins in the nappy drill that always brought the house down; and eruptive titters were likely to go on and on for ever, like recurring decimals.

All this harmless nonsense supplied the obvious pointer for hotting up the next party from the word " go "; we must make it a fancy dress bonanza, with prizes for originality.

The suggestion was not received with immediate enthusiasm, but the propaganda machine was turned on at full kick and soon there were signs of growing keenness. Having worked up the parishioners to fever pitch, John and I realized guiltily, only an hour before the event, that *we* hadn't done anything about fancy costumes for ourselves; we had visions of mild barracking if we dared to turn up in ordinary attire after bullying everyone else to " enter into the spirit of the thing." It wasn't unwillingness or apathy on our part either, but simply that life was geared to such a furious speed with its innumerable demands, and time wasn't elastic enough by half.

However, with only sixty minutes to go I plumped for a gipsy effect, because it seemed the simplest to improvise; so down came the spare-room curtains—gay cretonne, full, flouncy things—and these provided my skirt, held up with pyjama cord threaded hastily through the little brass rings; a paisley shawl amply concealed the workaday blouse that I hadn't time to change; brass curtain rings dangled from my ears; and a bandana handkerchief hid the un-achieved hair-do. For a final authentic touch I grabbed the wooden peg basket as I rushed out.

Meanwhile John had effected a staggering transformation into a tolerably convincing French artist—straight from Montmartre!—

in dark corduroy trousers, a rather blousy open-neck shirt offset by a colossal black bow, the inevitable Basque beret, and a trim little steel-wool goatee beard.

If we lacked originality we at least showed willing, and I must say there was no absence of warmth in the opening stages of *that* party, with its milling crowd of familiar faces in wildly unfamiliar rôles. Here was a truly cosmopolitan bunch, in bold, ingenious creations, with enough originality to set the judges a teasing problem.

*   *   *   *   *

The children's parish festivities were much easier to run—mainly, I suppose, because young revellers have a slap-happy way of running their own mad orgies. In any event, as official organizers of jollifications for this age group John and I still had our " L " plates up. Having no children on either side of the family from whom to take our cue, we had to rely on faded memories of our own Sunday school days, and we quickly learnt that the current pattern bears no resemblance whatsoever to the accepted tradition of the early 1900s.

Our scholars at Upper Bellpull had preconceived ideas as to what constituted a party worthy of the name, and we really needn't have bothered to make elaborate provision for entertainment, for they manifested far less interest in *our* carefully devised programme than in the rackety, harum-scarum rampaging which they devised for themselves. We could waste precious hours and vast energy drawing up an impressive list of organized games and suitable competitions (suitable, that is, to *our* way of thinking!), but invariably the proceedings developed into a boisterous free-for-all, with struggling masses of juvenile humanity pushing, shoving, pummelling, heedlessly tipping over chairs or any other solid obstacles that happened to be in the way—all amid a deafening volume of yells, screams and cat-calls. In the interests of safety we would try to quell the mob; we were afraid that some of the tiny ones—particularly the little girls—would get pulverized, but frequently it turned out that they were the ringleaders. We would try also to rescue the furniture before it got beyond repair, but on a final count the casualties—either to children or chairs—were remarkably slight. Shades of St. Trinian's! I think we worried unnecessarily, and we seldom had need of the mild tranquillizers we slipped into our pockets.

An acceptable alternative to our dull programme, the children made quite clear, was a professional entertainer—Punch and Judy, ventriloquist or conjurer—provided he was in the top flight of show-biz (as television addicts they were discerning critics); but that cost money, and Sunday school funds were usually at hoe-string level. So we settled for a compromise and let the children do the entertaining—for prizes. On the pretext of talent-spotting, we invited them to come up on the platform and show their mettle. Those same little hooligans who five minutes before had been engaged in gang warfare—with no quarter shown to any who blocked their path—would now trot up agreeably and give a confident, if giggling, rendering of " Little Lamb, who made thee? " or " Away in a manger " (or possibly " The Lambeth Walk " or " Coming round the mountain "!), with a touch of subdued reverence (or a dash of professional raciness, as the choice demanded), in exchange for a slab of chocolate, a bag of toffees or a mouth-organ. We hoped this wasn't a permanently corrupting form of bribery.

The main thing, of course, was to provide plenty of food of the right sort. Here again, with our scanty knowledge of juvenile tastes, we were prone to error; in any event, it would have been well-nigh impossible to keep pace with their changing crazes: one year everything had to be sweet, sticky and creamy; the nex time only savouries were in vogue and our liberal provision of éclairs, doughnuts, chocolate ateaux and cream trifle would go begging. The only solution was a yearly opinion poll of parents.

I suppose there has never yet been a children's party without its quota of embarrassing moments. We certainly had our hare, but only two left a really indelible impression on me, and both involved the same family.

Halfway through tea six-year-old Jennifer was sick. There's nothing very unusual about a child being bilious at a party; everything conspires towards it; but Jennifer's was an entirely original act because she neither gave the customary warning of her intention nor betrayed the mildest embarrassment or loss of poise in the event; nor, after being cleaned up, did she suffer the slightest impairment of appetite. One minute she had been industriously putting away piles of paste sandwiches, chocolate biscuits and meringues, and had just made the first tentative inroads on her jelly trifle; then, in the twinkling of an eye, all this was back again—neatly deposited on the tablecloth—without a sound or a whimper or the batting of an eyelid. Her neighbours, not unnaturally, reacted a bit squeamishly, and we rushed to remove the child from the table. Her fat little cheeks showed no sign of pallor and she trotted out with magnificent composure. The minute we had got her spruced up again she was back at work on he jelly-trifle course as if nothing had happened—happy, unruffled, and quite ready to advance to the coconut pyramids.

I regarded this performance as a remarkable phenomenon, for which I suppose there must have been a pathological explanation. But how I envied that child her superb coolness in a moment of unheralded crisis!

Her small brother—only three and a half—got plainly over-excited, with rather uncomfortable results. That dilemma, too, was not uncommon, and it was solved by sending a messenger to his home for some fresh d y pants, while we whisked him temporarily behind the scenes. But, like Jennifer, he was totally undismayed, and while waiting for the dry pants he could see no earthly reason why he should be forcibly restrained from joining in musical chairs in the semi-nude.

I couldn't help feeling that there was some fine stoic quality about tho e two children (possibly a family trait) which the fussy, over-anxious majority of us might profitably ponder and emulate.

* * * * *

Looking back, it must be confessed that John and I were not born disciplinarians. Our attempts to tame the spirits of the rebellious youngsters made little or no impression, although we *did* run with some m asure of success a youth club for a matter of seven or eight years. Here, however, we had to deal with over-fifteens and the p ob ems were different.

One night the club meeting nearly ended in catastrophe when two Romeos began fighting to the death—with chairs—over the same Juliet. John, in the rôle of mediator, was peremptorily ordered to " keep out of this; it is a private and personal matter "! They were both powerfully built lads, inches taller and pounds heavier than John. As he tried to get between them, one of the chairs came down with a murderous crash; it obviously wasn't intended for John's innocent head, but it missed him only by a hair's breadth. It served to bring them to their senses; they abandoned their cumbersome weapons and retreated to the roadway to settle their romantic differences with bare fists.

If we had any recriminations about our failure to discipline the young, it was at least consoling to note that we were not the only ones who failed. The scout leader, too, suffered insolence and persistent insubordination. When he left the district his place was taken by two local ex-Army sergeants. From the outset they were familiarly addressed as " Tom " and " Dick " by the cheeky little blighters, and after a fortnight in office they abdicated on the grounds that " it's no good wasting our time on kids who won't do a blind thing they're told "!

For their vicar, by the way, the same little blighters reserved the endearing nickname " Govvy "!

" Govvy," however, ignored the cheek and sailed doggedly on in the teeth of perverse winds and occasional storms—always hoping that somewhere beneath the enigmatic surface of their seeming indifference there lurked the vital spark of grace and sensitivity which, with persistent fanning, might one day burst into a steady flame of faith and reverence. When I felt that they were sapping his vitality to no useful purpose he would remind me: " You can never tell with these youngsters whether you've made any impression or not, so you always *hope* and push on regardless; sometimes the biggest surprises come when they're least expected and from the unlikeliest toughs "!

*   *   *   *   *

The annual garden show was always an irresistible attraction. It had even been known to lure cricket " fans " from a home match!

To John and me it had a very special significance. It was not *merely* an efficiently mounted display of superlative entries—a dazzling exhibition of fruit and vegetables cultivated to perfection, of exquisite floral arrangements and flawless pot plants, and of culinary masterpieces ranking easily for *cordon bleu* honours. It was, of course, all this; but much more besides. As *we* saw it, the garden show was the outstanding occasion for parish integration; an atmosphere of unifying good will prevailed. It was the one day of the year when everyone dispensed with labels—political and denominational—and forgot the current feuds and really got together in the common interest of gardening. Even the razor-keen competitive rivalry seemed to generate no obvious symptoms of bad feeling.

Looking back over the years, if there is one scene imprinted more clearly than any other on the tablets of my memory—like a sharply defined etching—it is of the whole village, on garden show morning, converging on the judging marquees carrying their precious load of entries with infinite care, all grimly set on getting them in before ten o'clock, when judging began. I can see them now, making their way from all directions—singly, in twos and threes, and in family units—like a stream of devout pilgrims intent on Mecca, only pilgrims wouldn't be bearing trayfuls of iced cakes, baskets of fragile flowers or meticulously arranged bowls and vases, or pushing wheelbarrows loaded with choice collections of mammoth vegetables and unblemished fruit. Some of the produce, of course, was simply and easily unloaded from the family car or van, and these fortunate competitors were spared the hazards of sudden disarray and possible damage in the event of high winds or squalls; but mostly it was a cavalcade on foot and we all prayed for " show weather."

The night before the show the whole village seemed deadly quiet and almost deserted, because everyone would be at home, sedulously preparing their entries: picking, selecting, grading; cleaning vegetables and measuring and weighing for uniform size; ear-marking the right blooms to be cut with the dew on them next morning; getting vases and bowls ready to receive them; and, on the cookery side, assembling the full range of entries—jams, pickles, bottled fruits (jars given a final rub with methylated spirit to remove the slightest suspicion of a smear, and handled thereafter only with gloved hands!); setting out in symmetrical order the cakes, gingerbreads, pies and tartlets, and checking entry cards; and then standing back with a sigh of satisfaction to admire the results of one's labour, wondering inevitably whether anybody could *possibly* submit superior items. And, of course, they usually did.

On that spell-binding pre-show evening it was only the children who were out in the fields and byways, gathering material for their special class: " wild flowers in a jam-jar "—and what enchanting effects they achieved by simplicity and effortless art!

Then we would all be up with the lark next morning, to add the last anxious touches here and there, then off on that familiar pilgrimage.

The entire ritual was a predominant motif in the set local pattern.

Here was a new experience which John and I simply could not resist; indeed, I think it would have been counted permanently against us if we had attempted to do so. Competition fever was the annual epidemic; it soon gripped us. I baked tirelessly in preparation for the contest, though I still had much to learn from the old hands; and we put in the best that the vicarage garden could produce in potatoes, onions, scarlet runners and carrots; apples, currants, gooseberries, and lovely raspberries. Our Early Rivers usually won a prize in the plum class—that is after our initial howler, when we carefully *polished off* all the soft bloom! John had a sneaking feeling that he had been guilty of a tactical error—albeit unwittingly— in winning a first for potatoes and onions one year, an acknowledged learner romping home against veterans who really knew their stuff; but he talked a lot about " beginner's luck " and passed on the prize to Uncle, who had really wrought the miracle anyway.

Although it earned me no award, I always had a smug conviction that my floral *pièce de résistance* was a miniature lily pond effect in the " bowl of floating flowers " class; it was very simple—just a few unfolding buds of *anemone japonica* resting on a handful of nasturtium leaves (punctured here and there with a knitting needle, to allow the abbreviated anemone stalks to be poked through). With the absolute minimum of persuasion the floating leaves provided an ideal (and almost " life-like ") base for the lily-like flowers sitting on them.

On the other hand, the most severely testing of all the classes in which we " had a go " was, to my mind, " flowers arranged in a thimble "—a feat demanding far more patient ingenuity to make the thimble stand upright than artistic skill to fill it with flowers. It took me the best part of a day, in fact, to construct a miniature tripod of split cane, holding the thimble sunk in a cunning little b d of sealing wax; but less than a couple of minutes were needed to arrange in it a few true miniature rosebuds with two or three microscopic wisps of fern and a solitary forget-me-not.

Personal enthusiasm apart, we felt that unreserved support for the show was sound policy, so we submitted an increasingly large number of entries; but the entrance fees totted up, and we calculated that between us we must pull off at least two or three prizes to break even! The memorable year that brought me a first for mixed sweet-peas (and the biggest surprise in all my horticultural adventures) showed an actual profit.

But our involvement in the garden show wasn't only at competition level; John was a vice-president (an expensive honour!) and a press-ganged steward on show day. *My* official rôle was a shade more impressive and something of an ordeal—at least until I had grown accustomed to the pattern of events and had acquired a little more self-confidence in public. I was, in fact, invited to present the prizes!

" Willingly " I had responded, not realizing all that it entailed. The distribution took place on the village green and the rigged-up platform was a hay-wagon, which I mounted with considerable misgivings. The ascent was no easy feat; it involved a good deal of human haulage to land me safely.

This being my début in the distributor's field, I was assailed by nagging doubts as to appropriate attire: garden-party frock and best Leghorn model? Summer suit, hat and gloves? Or just the informal cotton frock and no hat? I was fully convinced, the moment I found myself perched on that hay wagon, that I had made the *wrong* choice.

Confronting me was a sea of blurred faces, but the mists gradually cleared as a tiny spark of confidence returned and award after award was safely handed out and the prize list neared exhaustion. I was tempted to giggle as I pocketed my own modest winnings and then handed John his. Then there remained only the silver trophies to distribute; after that I could thankfully escape from my elevated location.

The first was the children's challenge cup; next the onion bowl—and so on. The last to be presented was the ladies' silver challenge cup. A triumphantly smiling Mrs. Appleyard trotted up to receive it—with the usual few flowery remarks from me and a splendid ovation from the whole company.

That's it, I thought! But it *wasn't*; for I was suddenly aware of faint murmuring beside me; a whispered consultation was going on between the secretary and the treasurer. Taking an oblique glance, I could see that they were in a state of dreadful panic. Well, the fact is, there was a serious hitch: someone, *somehow*, had slipped up badly; a rather dry-throated secretary begged " Please don't go yet; there's been a little (!) mistake somewhere; we're just rechecking the points "!

There was an interval of stunned silence while we waited in an atmosphere of time-bomb suspense.

Eventually it was discovered that somebody couldn't do his arithmetic; the ladies' silver challenge cup, instead of being won by Mrs. Appleyard—to whom I had so graciously presented it with those nice felicitations!—had indeed been earned by a Mrs. Bodkin, her own next-door neighbour! So here was a delicate situation if ever there was one.

Now a crestfallen Mrs. Appleyard had humiliatingly to return to the wagon, hand back the elegant cup that she thought was going to adorn her sideboard for the next twelve months, and then efface herself as best she could in the crowd. There was a terrible silence.

Next a somewhat dazed, but beaming, Mrs. Bodkin advanced diffidently (have they added it up correctly now? she seemed to be pondering), and I made the presentation for a second time, but with the same little flowery words!

In the circumstances nobody seemed to know whether to applaud or not, so they compromised with subdued clapping and a *sotto voce* " well done! " here and there. To Mrs. Appleyard's undying credit, I noted that she joined with simulated heartiness in this shy applause for the rightful *victrix ludorum*. It was surely as unfortunate as it was incredible that these two cup contenders should be immediate neighbours.

The only other serious upset that I can recall was caused by the failure of one of the judges to scrutinize *every* entry in the rich fruit cake class; no doubt it was easy enough to miss an odd one among a large number. Anyway, Miss Topliss, who entertained high hopes for her cake, made a beeline for the cookery tent when the show opened and began totting up her points. Somehow the judge had missed her altogether; her card had not even been reversed. This oversight would not have created quite such a stir if Miss T had not been well in the running for the cup with all her jams, preserves and floral exhibits. An emergency committee meeting was convened; what should be done about it? The judge had already left the ground some hours ago; she lived at a distance. The secretary did some hurried telephoning, but the judge could not be contacted. The only possible solution was to try to get another qualified adjudicator to come along post haste and rejudge the whole lot.

At tremendous inconvenience to herself, and unforeseen expense to the organizers, a professional pastrycook turned up; she examined with scrupulous care *all* forty-seven rich fruit cakes, and found Miss Topliss's undeserving of recognition; and the original prize-winners were placed exactly as before.

So we were all back where we began—minus a second judging fee.

*   *   *   *   *

Before we left Upper Bellpull there was to be another innocent little contretemps in the field of presentations—involving John this time.

A teacher at the local school—much loved by the successive generations of villagers whom she had taught—was retiring, and the usual presentation was planned. Money poured in liberally and it was agreed, after tactfully sounding Miss Pring herself, to mark her departure with (a) a fat cheque, (b) a bedside reading lamp and (c) a bouquet.

A vast gathering assembled in the village hall on the day of the farewell; it included, inevitably, all the top brass, school managers, the education officer, past and present scholars, shoals of parents, and as many more as could manage to squeeze in.

The vicar was appointed to make the actual presentation, and I was entrusted to hand Miss Pring the bouquet. For John and me it had been one of those dust-raising mornings—not a second's breathing space from the moment of waking till we found ourselves, flushed and breathless, up on the platform, flanked on either side by V.I.P.s, with an obviously emotional Miss Pring occupying the seat of honour.

Beside the tremendous sheaf of orange gladioli stood the handsome reading lamp. The scene was set and everybody seemed pretty tense. John, who on this occasion looked as strung-up as poor Miss Pring herself, was mechanically folding and unfolding his speech eulogizing Miss Pring's talents and virtues. He signalled to me to offer the flowers; he beckoned forward the distinguished old scholar —on vacation from California—to add her pæan of praise; then he addressed the now trembling Miss Pring: " On behalf of the village and of all your past and present scholars, I ask you to accept this cheque and this bedside lamp, both of which we hope you will find useful in your retirement." (Hear, hear! echoed from all sides.)

N

He picked up the lamp and handed it to her. She grasped it very nervously and stood in patient expectation, obviously uncertain whether to *ask* for that cheque or to begin saying her little piece without it, and trust that one fine day, when turning out his pockets, the absent-minded vicar and chairman of managers would come across it and belatedly implement his presentation speech.

I was thankful to be sitting near enough to pinch John's leg meaningfully, and behind my handkerchief I hissed " *Cheque*! Give her the *m-o-n-e-y*! "

Really it all happened for the best, for that homely little incident served to break the emotional tension, and those on the verge of tears—which included most of us, for we all loved Miss Pring—changed their minds and had a good hearty laugh.

Her farewell ended up on a much gayer note than any of us had dared to expect.

*   *   *   *   *

Looking back on the varied and colourful scenes of village activity, it is undoubtedly the annual garden show that evokes some of the most agreeably vivid memories for me; though perhaps it is invidious to risk any distinction in the light of such an abundance of happy recollections.

CHAPTER 10

All in favour?

THE majority of parish priests, I am inclined to think, would be prepared to challenge Shakespeare's contention " Frailty, thy name is woman," for the parish that hasn't its loyal little band of women workers—be it Women's Fellowship, Mothers' Union, Church Guild, Sunshine Half-hour, Sanctuary Workers, or whatever else it may be called—who can always be relied upon, in season and out of season, to shoulder the lion's share of service in any arising project must be rare indeed, and its incumbent a sorely harassed man.

If there *is* such a parish, it has never really come to life; or, alternatively, through some strange misfortune, it has become moribund.

Upper Bellpull suffered no such handicap. Our Churchwomen's Guild, which had its origin in the Mothers' Union, was a willing little group—happy and harmonious in its enterprises, content to remain for the most part a splendidly active cell behind the scenes, yet providing, in fact, a strong backbone for the whole weight of parochial endeavour.

Its contribution at all levels—financial, in kind, in terms of service and solid hard slogging—was an immeasurable help to John, and he was the first to acknowledge its asset value to the church.

No noticeable " frailty " in the female sector at Upper Bellpull! On the contrary, every indication of robust stamina.

Their only *possible* weakness was in the matter of articulation (or, to be more precise, their *lack* of it!), and even this, I suppose, could be interpreted in certain circumstances as a sign of strength rather than weakness; but for all practical purposes—and in particular the purpose of holding a meeting—the prevailing dumbness was positively immobilizing, like jamming on the brake. Because of this seeming conspiracy of silence, guild meetings were always subject to painful and prolonged pauses, with the constant danger of grinding to an embarrassing halt; but as it was obviously a silence that stemmed from shyness and lack of confidence, rather than from sullen moroseness, one had to accept it.

As their leader, I was soon driven to adopt an administrative technique that was far from democratic in order to get any specific resolution passed, let alone to bring the broad proceedings to a satisfactory conclusion. Clearly there was the danger of my becoming a dictator in a small way—though always a reluctant one.

I would seek vainly to get the feelings of the members on the simplest of issues (maybe so pedestrian a matter as the venue for the next outing, or whether to send the usual two guineas to Moral Welfare or make it three), and after appealing unsuccessfully for the second, third, or even the fourth time for suggestions there remained only the one course open if we were not to sit there through eternity: " Well, if *you* have no proposals to make, how about this [voicing the line I imagined would be most popular]? Hands up if you think that's a good idea."

A holy hush and timid glances at each other usually preceded the eventual self-conscious show of hands—seldom fully and courageously extended, but just tentatively raised to shoulder height, or enough for you to be justified in *thinking* that they were in the affirmative—a classic example of the eloquence of silence carried a shade too far!

" Good! " I would proclaim. " I see you've *all* put your hands up, so that's settled and now we'll get on to the next item."

In this bulldozing, autocratic manner I would hack my way through the agenda, happy in the knowledge that nobody would ever be bold enough to avail herself of the A.O.B. provision at the end.

It may sound strangely ungracious to confess that my personal reaction to the routine monthly meetings of the guild was sorely mixed.

As friends and loyal co-workers, I *loved* the members of this little band; and as an opportunity to serve the parish, in however humble a capacity, I gladly accepted the responsibility; and in our more relaxed moments—over that unfailing " cuppa "—I appreciated enormously the warm friendship and trust with which, I felt sure, they honoured me.

But it was all so unbelievably exhausting. The sheer weight of trying to carry through a meeting against the overwhelming odds of mute shyness seemed to sap all my vitality, leaving me shockingly depleted; a warning palpitation would lead to a throbbing head, and by the time I got back to the vicarage I was utterly limp and trembling. It became a routine drill after meetings for John to place the aspirin bottle beside the pot of strong tea on the trolley, and he would wait solicitously on me.

Ironically enough, I was as inherently nervous as they were, to the extent that presiding at meetings and struggling to find the appropriate terms in which to thank the speaker constituted for me a big ordeal; yet somehow the members nursed the conviction that *I* was blessed with a cast-iron nervous system and positively revelled in officiating! Perhaps it was just as well that they never knew what it really cost me in sedatives to fulfil that rôle.

I tried to comfort myself that it was largely this suppressed nervous tension—rather than sheer imbecility—that, in the earlier days of my parochial initiation, accounted for one of the most unfortunate howlers of my whole career. (Perhaps there was also an element of excusable ignorance about it, as I was, indeed, a *very* new girl at the time.) An experienced executive of the Mothers' Union honoured our branch with a visit and gave an inspiring address on overseas work. Just as she was leaving she asked me, with tremendous earnestness, " Are you praying for George? " And I, incredibly surprised at the reference to a mutual friendship, answered reassuringly " Oh, yes, we are; we've had him on our prayer list for several weeks now." Her mouth opened; she said not a word, but her puzzled look ought to have warned me that we were not both on the same wavelength. Anyway, I was not alert enough to sense that I had blundered hopelessly. But back at the vicarage, over tea, I mentioned to John the remarkable coincidence that Mrs. X knew our sick friend George Hudson.

" How did that come up? " he wanted to know.

" Well, she asked me if we were praying for George, and I told her that we both were."

John groaned. " Not *Hudson*, you dumb-bell! Didn't you know that there is a *diocese* of George in Africa—linked fraternally with our own diocese? "

* * * * *

It was by no means easy to ensure that we always had a speaker. Many who would otherwise willingly have helped us were not prepared, particularly in winter, to journey out to our rather isolated little rural parish to talk to the proverbial handful of people for a mere half-hour or so and then face a wearisome jaunt home involving interminable delays through atrocious connections. Hospitality was the real answer—it usually involved lunch and tea; occasionally also a bed for the night. This, then, usually added up to the best part of a day's domestic preoccupation for me, for a single short meeting; nevertheless, it was seldom that we failed to find a speaker by the appointed day. I was obliged to fish in waters far and wide to land some of these welcome catches, but persistent angling rarely went unrewarded. At times a little diplomatic bait was helpful! We tried to broaden our horizon by encouraging as wide a range of subjects as possible. Travel talks—illustrated, of course, with coloured films or transparencies—were always immensely popular; in fact, almost *anything* offering escape from domestic chores was accepted and appreciated—but never demonstratively so. That would have been out of character.

Attendances were affected, naturally enough, by seasonal field work, and I soon got the hang of these fluctuations; but on one particular occasion, when there was no specific picking campaign in progress and there seemed no valid reason for mass absenteeism, I was a bit piqued. Subsequent investigation revealed a grotesque misunderstanding about the subject; it caused eventually a good deal of amusement. I had approached an old school friend, begging her to help me out. " I'm in a desperate fix; no speaker for next week. *Do* be an angel and come! " She was already heavily committed, but for the sake of the old school tie said " Yes, all right; I'll come if you don't mind a subject that I've already got prepared. I'll talk about brass rubbing, and bring some with me."

Announcing it on the Sunday, John had appealed for " an extra good attendance to hear Mrs. B's talk about brass rubbing."

My friend brought along some fine examples from her late husband's valuable collection (the bulk had already been given to the Ashmolean Museum), and it proved an absorbing topic. The specimens she brought covered a vast survey of churches throughout the country. When I finally discovered why so many of our members had played truant I was flabbergasted: they were under the impression that this was to be a brass *polishing* demonstration (advertising, presumably, some new commercial product!). They had deemed it a boring prospect and may even have suspected a subtle conspiracy to recruit more volunteers for cleaning the church brass.

After that we were at great pains to be more explicit in our announcements.

*   *   *   *   *

My prevailing dread was that the day would arrive when I might find myself at the twelfth hour without a speaker and have to face the emergency straight off the cuff. As stand-in I had no personal ambitions; public speaking I did not regard as my strong point. Being aware of my inadequacy, I wouldn't risk an extempore homily, for an ill-prepared talk, I reasoned (or my defence mechanism reasoned for me!), would be worse than no talk at all. I hoped devoutly that the contingency would not arise.

But it did, actually on two occasions, with the results recorded later in this chapter; and on several other occasions providence offered a merciful solution just as the beads of cold sweat were gathering on an anxious brow. In one instance the appointed speaker telephoned me about twenty-four hours before the meeting and her hoarse whisper indicated severe laryngitis. I thereupon made five abortive calls to possible understudies, and after drawing the fifth blank hope sank to zero and I started to panic. John's exhortation to " stop worrying; the right solution will come, you'll see! " seemed a shade heartless. To " stop worrying " sounded fine, but *he* hadn't got to fill the gap.

At that juncture he went out on a parish call. He was gone less than fifteen minutes and returned to find my haggard countenance transformed by a broad grin.

" It's all right, I've got a speaker; he came to the door for *you*, but I bagged him."

" I don't quite follow you. Who came to the door for me? "

" Dr. Barnardo's."

The brief explanation was that seconds after John went out a car had drawn up and out had jumped an energetic young man asking for the vicar and introducing himself: " I'm the area organizer for Dr. Barnardo's."

" I'm sorry, the vicar's out; will I do? "

" Hardly," smiled the young man. " I want to fix a date with him." What he wanted was to preach and show a propaganda film in the parish church on a Sunday evening.

Seizing the heaven-sent cue, I said " You'll certainly have to see the vicar himself about that; but meanwhile, what about giving a show tomorrow afternoon to my guild—2.30 in the village hall? "

" Fine idea," he said, fishing for his diary. " Yes, that's all right; I'm free; I'll be there. I've got a couple of jolly good new films."

He not only saved my bacon with a splendid programme, but he also won our zealous support, as a group, for the homes; so a double purpose was served by a providential call.

A growing awareness of an unfailing guidance over the day-to-day aspects of our parochial work was having a profoundly sobering and humbling effect on both of us, and in me at least it infused a much-needed spark of confidence. This seemingly uncanny sort of intervention was experienced time and again—in fact whenever a real need arose.

The classic example occurred during one of John's spells of convalescence, when for several weeks he had somehow to find deputies for all his Sunday duties. He had managed with great difficulty to arrange for all but his final convalescent Sunday, which was proving a really knotty problem. We had unsuccessfully approached every retired parson within reasonable distance, and all the neighbouring lay readers. Alas, there are far too few of them! With only three days to the date line, John was toying with the idea of personally struggling into the pulpit, in defiance of doctor's orders. He decided to go to the surgery and try to get signed off, and set out in a state of most uncharacteristic depression. Now, of course, it was my turn to exhort *him* to stop worrying!

He came back looking downcast; doctor wouldn't hear of his putting on harness yet.

But he found me as excited as a dog with two tails. " I've fixed up for someone to take everything off your hands on Sunday! "

" What! Oh, you shouldn't have done that without first consulting me."

" Fiddlesticks! You were in a tight corner, weren't you? Well, then, I've got you out."

" But who is he? Is he someone I know? "

" No! "

" Good heavens! Is he a priest or layman? "

" Priest."

" In this deanery? "

" No! "

" In this diocese? "

" No! "

"I suppose," with a touch of cynical doubt, "he's in this country?"

"Only just!" I beamed. "He arrived from Montreal yesterday. But keep calm; he's *all right;* he's quite *safe;* and he knows your pulpit as well as you do."

And here it seemed kinder to stop teasing and do a bit of explaining. In fact, just after John had gone out there was a telephone call from one of the wardens asking whether we had found anyone to deputize on Sunday.

"No! We're really in the soup this time," I wailed.

"No?" he echoed. "That's *good;* glad I'm in time. The man who was vicar here twenty years ago is over from Canada. He's just 'phoned to ask if we can put him up for the weekend; longing to see the old parish and wants to know if there's any chance of taking a service or two."

Well!

Why had we worried? we asked ourselves. After all, is not our concern only to plod on undeterred to the very shores of the Red Sea—and then to stand expectantly?

*   *   *   *   *

On another occasion *I* was rescued from a guild dilemma in equally uncanny circumstances.

I had written about a year previously to a Mr. G—area organizer for the Geranium Day appeal—inviting him to speak at our Women's Guild. Very surprisingly, I had not received a reply; months elapsed with no word from Mr. G, and I was peeved.

By the skin of my teeth I managed to get a suitable substitute for *tomorrow's* meeting, and, by a strange coincidence, on the very night before that meeting I was drafting the syllabus and typing speakers' invitations for the *following* twelve months. By ten o'clock I was weary and felt tempted to call it a day; but still one date remained to be considered; whom should I ask? Was it worth trying again to get Mr. G? He might be more co-operative this time! I hesitated for several minutes—perhaps a trifle piqued because he had ignored my earlier approach. Finally, I popped the paper in my machine and typed as far as "Dear Mr. G,"; then, for no reason on earth that I could rationally account for, I turned to John and said " I'm pocketing my pride and asking Mr. G once more to come here; I've started his letter—but I've a hunch to 'phone instead. Do you think it's too late to get him tonight? "

" Of course not; go ahead," said John. But the odd fact was this: I had every intention of *writing*, for I detest telephoning if I can possibly send a letter instead.

Well, late as it was, I put through a toll call to Mr. G and I could scarcely believe my ears to be greeted from the other end: " Hello. Is that Mrs. Green speaking? I was waiting for you to ring. When I got home tonight I asked my wife if a Mrs. Green had rung up; she said ' No,' but I felt sure you *would*."

" But, *why*? What made you think I should 'phone you? I don't understand it at all."

" Well, I'm seeing you tomorrow, am I not? "

" I hope *not*. Why should you? What about? " (It dawned rather too late that this was anything but a courteous reply!)

" But I'm due to speak at your Women's Guild tomorrow afternoon; your parish *is* Upper Bellpull, isn't it? "

I was flabbergasted; almost mentally frozen; but, with the awful prospect of a head-on collision the next day between Mr. G and the expected speaker, I managed to gasp " I simply cannot understand this at all. Last year I *invited* you to come, but you didn't reply. Now I have made other arrangements. I am merely 'phoning you tonight to ask whether you would consider a date for *next* year."

Of course, we argued heatedly about the fate of that letter which he vowed he had sent me a year ago; he referred to his postage book and said that was proof enough for him. I referred to my files and assured him that his missive had never reached me and again entreated him *not* to come tomorrow, and eventually wheedled his promise to do so next year.

I don't think he was too enchanted about the mix-up; he had already got the films and equipment loaded on his car, he said. Fortunately, time is a good healer and we found him a delightful visitor when he eventually came along with his films—twelve months later!

But for that compelling hunch I would have been confronted next day with rival speakers.

Honesty requires me to admit that just such a catastrophe did, in fact, happen at one of our later meetings—through a fallible human agency—and I was faced with a singularly delicate diplomatic crisis. How gratefully would I have welcomed a timely intervention by providence that day! However, I was conscious of no intuitive warning, so I philosophically figured it out that some hidden purpose had to be served by the unforeseen collision of two strange satellites in orbit.

We were expecting that afternoon a special speaker on behalf of Oxfam; the title of her talk, with coloured slides, was " Refugee work in the Holy Land." It sounded promising, especially as it would be breaking new ground for us.

Arriving early, with all her equipment to set up (and our hall to black out with the usual ramshackle collection of old tablecloths, blankets, and the odd coat or two!), she asked to begin *very* promptly, as she had another engagement to fit in.

She was all set to start and I was getting to my feet to introduce her when someone tugged my sleeve and whispered " The speaker's come."

" Yes, I know. Ssssh! She's just going to begin."

" No; she's at the *door*; she's asking for *you*."

Utterly pixillated, I felt my way down the darkened room to the outer door. There stood a book-laden little lady who confidently introduced herself: " I'm Mrs. Warwick, the speaker. Is it all right to park my car just over there? "

Merciful heavens! The full implication of her words struck me all of a heap.

" The *speaker*? But haven't you made a mistake? We *have* a speaker and she's just waiting to start. Oh dear, what *can* have happened? *Do* come in "—though what I proposed to do with her when she came in I hadn't the faintest notion.

" But this *is* Upper Bellpull Women's Guild? Then I'm right; you *asked* me to come "—in a challenging tone, as if daring me to accuse her of frivolous gate-crashing. Then, even more severely, " I thought you were rather remiss not to send me a reminder."

" But, please, *please*, a reminder of what? This is the first I've heard about it; I don't *know* a Mrs. Warwick," I retaliated defensively.

She had come all the way from Maldon, she wailed; and, clearly, for all her outward charm, she was extremely put out. Small wonder, for, having prepared her talk and driven over twenty-five miles to deliver it, it must have been rather crushing to find herself forestalled on the dais; not to mention that impressive load of literature which she had planned to distribute for our edification.

In the circumstances, all I could do—apart from perspiring copiously—was to push Mrs. Warwick forcibly into a seat beside me and beg the now agitated Miss Drinkwater to begin without further delay her journey to the Holy Land, hoping that by the time it was over I would have had a chance to collect my wits and devise some tactful formula for placating Mrs. Warwick, the deposed orator!

Whatever organization did she represent? I wondered. Or could she, perhaps, be a free-lance propagandist, with some lunatic bee in her bonnet, trotting around under her own steam in the unflagging hope of eventually winning a few attentive ears?

As Miss Drinkwater developed her theme I sensed that Mrs. Warwick—after an initial patch of restless fidgeting—was simmering down nicely—obviously becoming an absorbed listener, and at one point she betrayed immense excitement. It was where the Holy Land lady made references to the distribution of Bibles among the refugees in Palestine. Here Mrs. Warwick's interest seemed to be bordering on rapture.

There followed the usual brief period for questions (normally no more than a hollow formality at our meetings), and, to everyone's surprise, it was Mrs. Warwick who leapt eagerly to her feet and said that, as a representative of the British and Foreign Bible Society, she was delighted to note her rival's allusion to distribution of the Scriptures to her refugees, and would she care to have the very latest official statistics? Having thus established a point of common interest, these two merged themselves into a forceful propaganda unit, rendering excellent team work—the one putting pertinent leading questions which the other answered with adroit authority. All told, it was a tremendous success; the contending speakers ended up the best of friends, and two topically important birds were expeditiously dispatched with more or less the same stone. *I* was generously forgiven for an error that was not mine anyway, and Mrs. Warwick was civil enough to offer her services for a future occasion.

That mystery took a lot of unravelling, but it finally emerged that the secretary of the Bible Society's local auxiliary had fallen down over her liaison work, having made the fixture with Mrs. Warwick without letting me know about it. Actually, she maintained that

she *had* sent me a letter; if so, it was the second one to get unaccountably lost.

* * * * *

Our Women's Guild was not restricted to Anglicans; the hand
of friendship was extended to all, and our numbers grew encouragingly. In my pious simplicity it hadn't occurred to me that there
could be more than the one obvious reason for joining a basically
religious organization, so it was a trifle shattering when, in the
course of a recruiting campaign, one parishioner towards whom I
had cast my line with patient finesse finally capitulated with a frank
and somewhat grudging "Oh, well . . . all right! *I don't mind
coming*, if you want me to; it's somewhere to go, isn't it?"—and
I wondered just how badly I had presented the *raison d'être* of the
Women's Guild. Well, this new recruit might have come for the
wrong reason, but she stayed, I hope, for the right one.

* * * * *

The two occasions when we were really and truly speakerless
bore sensationally contrasting results.

On the first occasion I had no warning. (A genuinely apologetic
speaker telephoned me the next day about a chaotic transport
mix-up which had landed her miles off the beam, with no earthly
chance of reaching us in time.) So, John having concluded the
opening prayers, I was faced with forty-five long minutes to fill as
best I could. I began by suggesting that we ought not to be
so dependent upon outside talent; we ought to be prepared to fall
back on our own resources, etc. (That took up five minutes, though
it could easily have been said more concisely in five seconds.)

What on earth could we do in the remaining forty minutes?

Could they, I wondered, be prevailed upon for once to overcome
that paralysing shyness and themselves contribute *something*, however trifling to a scratch programme? Remembering the pathetic
failure of the debate I had once tried to launch, I didn't entertain
much hope now. The *debate* had begun and ended in a monologue;
I, as proposer of the motion, had been as provocative as I knew how,

but it had all fizzled out like a damp squib, and, with no apparent backers and no articulate opponents, I had felt faintly ludicrous.

However, now, with forty minutes to fill, something *had* to be done. I fired the opening shot: " As we haven't a speaker today we shall have to entertain ourselves. If we really try, it may surprise us what we can do! I suggest " Books "; it's a subject we must all know something about. Let us, in turn, each name our favourite book and in a very few words say *why*. I'll set the ball rolling, if you will follow on."

Having said my little piece, there was deathly silence.

" Now, Mrs. Fraser, what about you next? There's no need to be shy among friends; just tell us, what is your favourite book? "

" I never read " was her brief contribution to the programme.

This was a handicap I had not foreseen. Surely everyone *read*— occasionally.

" Well, we shall have to let you off, then. Now, how about *your* favourite book, Mrs. Hagger? "

She acquitted herself with equal brevity, " I don't read either."

Well, well! When my third shot was rewarded with " And no more don't I " I began to realize that literature played no vital part in the local culture. A switch to a more likely topic seemed clearly indicated. Oh for an inspiration to fill the remaining thirty minutes!

" Well, as you don't seem to be *avid* readers, let's leave books and try something else. Now, I suppose we all have our pet dislikes. Shall we make a roll-call of the three or four things we dislike most? " (How inane can one be in these dilemmas? I still blush at the remembrance of that fatuous suggestion!)

There was no manifest enthusiasm, but, hoping that my own intimate confessions might act as an incentive, I rattled off a random selection of my private hates: the smells of paraffin, onions and garlic; queue-jumpers; fat, sardines and damsons; finding my newspaper in an unholy muddle; hard-centred chocolates; the maddening little legend " Now turn to page so-and-so."

" Now, will *you* carry on, Mrs. Woodcock? " I wheedled.

Mrs. Woodcock's reluctance was absolute and final. Her sphinx-like expression dashed any slender hope of winkling out *her* inmost secrets.

And so it was with all the others; nothing emerged, save rows of sheepish grins and stolid silence. Whether the mute reaction indicated total satisfaction with all that life offered them—even at its

homeliest levels—or whether, in fact, what grievances they harboured were too intimate to publish there was no means of judging.
Silence prevailed.

On a sudden and blessed inspiration I proposed an early and
prolonged tea break; that was adopted unanimously.

* * * * *

With that barren experience lurking always at the back of my
mind, I was seized with overwheming pessimism when we again
found ourselves, after a couple of years of unusually smooth running, without a speaker one afternoon—just as we were due to
begin.

Faced with a split-second decision, I resolved to give them just
one chance of self-entertainment and if that proved as abortive as
the " books " and the " grievances " an adjournment would be
called and the troops dismissed.

" I am sorry to say that our speaker hasn't arrived; I don't know
why. This means that we must provide our own programme today.
I'm going to suggest that we each tell an amusing child story—a
true story or a genuine school howler. We must all know plenty,
either in our own family circles or from friends. They're much
funnier when we share them, so let's fire away. Who'll begin? "

Secretly, I didn't anticipate any response at all, let alone the
veritable spate that carried us right through the afternoon. This
was my grossest miscalculation ever, but what a gratifying one!

Afterwards, searching for an explanation for their very surprising
volubility, I concluded that it was simply a case of one proud
grandma bristling with a brand-new story she was itching to pass
on, and here were a ready-made audience and a pressing invitation
that amounted almost to a bribe. Drawing on hidden springs of
courage, she made a bold start almost before she had time to realize
that she was actually making her public-speaking début; and all
the others, infected by a sort of mass hypnotism, just followed suit.
Her example, like a pep pill, *did* something to them. It was a strange
phenomenon, nevertheless.

* * * * *

Grandma's anecdote was about seven-year-old Billy, a lonely
little singleton who hankered passionately for a baby brother.

He made it a matter of earnest and confident prayer, but disillusionment awaited him, for he went home one day and said "Mummy, did you know that Jesus makes mistakes?"

"No dear; Jesus doesn't make mistakes—ever."

"Oh yes He *does*; I *know*, because I've just found out."

"Billy, whatever do you mean? You shouldn't say such things."

"But, Mum, I've been asking Jesus for two whole years for a baby brother, and now He's gone and taken it over the road to the Turners; and they couldn't have wanted it, they've got four already. I can see what's happened, Mum; Jesus got the right road, but He's gone and muddled the number. Shall I start all over again?"

Apropos the Turners' new baby, it was further revealed that Billy and the four other little Turners had been in secret conclave over the whole mix-up. Some months earlier Mrs. Turner had been in hospital to have her tonsils removed; so when the phenomenon of the new baby was under review the eldest little Turner had queried "I wonder where she got it from," and the next one had helpfully suggested "I reckon she got it round the tonsil 'ospital."

Grandma, immensely encouraged by the round of applause and laughter that her recital evoked, ventured to relate another of Billy's prayerful disappointments. He had been devoutly asking the Almighty, ever since the gales last March, not to let grandma's chimney pot fall off; and when, in fact, it crashed with a tremendous thud during a recent hurricane Billy's resigned comment was "I suppose God must have clean forgotten what I said and let the wind blow on the wrong pot"!

With only a momentary pause for breath, grandma gave a second encore; it touched on a later stage in Billy's spiritual pilgrimage.

He joined the church choir—a diminutive, tremulous aspirant for solo honours. He was initially a trifle peeved to find himself allotted the inconspicuous place of "last boy in"—far removed from the star soprano. Mum encouraged him: "If you want to get to the top, work hard and don't miss a practice." Within the month he rushed home from matins bursting with jubilation. "I've got it! I've *got* it! I'm going up to the top, Mum!"

"Surely not already. Who said so?"

"The vicar, mum; he gave it out in the lesson this morning; he

said straight out ' The first shall be last, and the last shall be first.'
Isn't that wizard? "
Poor little Billy!

* * * * *

Next a young mum told us about Miranda—only eight and a bit,
but already fashion-conscious.

The parents were going to a gala dance and a smart new gown
was a " must." Miranda was spellbound by this fabulous creation;
on the night she was allowed to stay up and see her mother in full
regalia.

All set for the occasion, Mrs. S sailed triumphantly down the
stairs to receive Miranda's approval. It was unqualified: " Oh,
Mummy, *you'll* be the *belly* of the ball! "

* * * * *

The next anecdote could have implied that poor John was secretly
addicted to corrupt practices; in fact, not above an occasional
bribe! Mrs. Winters had taken her thoughtful little grandson to the
churchyard to tidy up grandpa's grave. The child, casting a critical
eye along the lines of new headstones, mused: " I suppose you have
to be very well in with the vicar to get one of these."

* * * * *

The churchyard, not surprisingly perhaps, provided a natural
background for a good deal of unconscious humour and youthful
speculation.

For instance, Mrs. Braden's younger child had posed a singularly
pertinent question on Christian burial. The old gentleman next
door had just died, and Julie seized the opportunity to clear up once
and for all the mystery that had long puzzled her. " Mummy, do
we really go to Jesus when we die? "

" Yes, dear; that's right."

" Well, then, why have they dug that great big hole to put old Mr.

o

Jessup in? Is Jesus down *there* [casting her eyes earthwards] or is He up *there* [pointing to the sky]? You just tell me that! "

* * * * *

But of all the stories inspired by the melancholy contingency of churchyard burial Sally's was the gem, and it demonstrated, in an under-five, a remarkably mature grasp of the elements of social justice. It happened in a neighbouring parish.

A " big " funeral had taken place and the following day the widow had come to the churchyard to inspect the flowers and list the senders. To her horror, the grave mound was starkly bare except for a handful of wilting tulips; wreaths, crosses, cushions and mutilated sprays were distributed far and wide; there were traces of hastily disarranged bunches and odd, broken blooms dotted around indiscriminately; the entire churchyard was in a state of floral chaos. The poor woman, shockingly distressed, had rushed to the vicarage to deliver a bitter tirade to the hapless vicar: " I demand an explanation and a full apology for this wicked vandalism; my husband's grave has been desecrated; the culprit must be found and punished! "

Discreet inquiries revealed that someone had seen Sally, the vicar's grandchild, playing in the churchyard—but surely *she* would know better. Sally's mother felt less confident. " Sally," she asked, " did you go into the churchyard this morning? "

" Yes, Mummy, I did; and what do you think? They'd gone and put *all* the flowers on one grave and none on the others. That wasn't fair, was it, Mummy? So I took them all round and gave some to everybody! "

* * * * *

As we expected, the schoolmaster's wife had a rich repertoire. She told first of the war-time visit to the school of a professional string quartet to infuse an extra spark of culture into the routine syllabus. After the concert the instrumentalists had dinner in the hall with the children. One small boy, after a prolonged stare at the cellist, whispered to the master sitting next to him: " You can easily tell she's the cellist, can't you, sir, by the way she cuts up her meat."

And from stringed music to the incident of Derek Page and the carol-singing.

Derek, though not blessed with a sparkling wit, was a docile, obedient little lad who at least tried to respond. The headmaster prided himself on the school's musical tradition; choir singing was a great feature. Shortly before Christmas the boys were rehearsing for the end-of-term carol service. The headmaster was a man of immense vigour and consuming zeal. There he stood on the rostrum, getting increasingly purple as he waved his baton like mad. They began " Good King Wenceslas," but at the end of the first verse there were signs of wandering attention and slackening rhythm. The conductor paused, glared fiercely, recharged his lungs and then, with a sharp tap of his baton, roared: " Now then, pay *attention* all of you; ' *Hither*, page, and stand by me.' " Without hesitation little Derek trotted up and planted himself on the dais, with a questioning look on his otherwise vacant little face.

And to this very day—after twenty years or more—Derek is known among his contemporaries as *Hither* Page!

* * * * *

Most of the members with youngsters attending Sunday school had an inexhaustible fund of stories hinging on recent lessons. There was Richard, who had gone home one Sunday strongly doubting the validity of teacher's staggering claim about God's omnipotence.

" Mummy, do you really believe that God can do *anything*? "

" Yes, dear; why? "

" Well, I doubt it. Teacher told us that God is so powerful that there's nothing He can't do; but do you reckon He could swallow a tomato whole? "

And a little girl who had listened enthralled (if not with complete understanding!) to the story of Solomon and his domestic set-up proved an embarrassment to her parents when she went home to tea—where a small party of friends was gathered round—and demanded: " Daddy, is Mummy your wife or your *porcupine*? "

* * * * *

The story that impressed us for its unanswerable logic came from Mrs. G, whose Judith was known to be rather precocious. After some painstaking instruction in the story of the Garden of Eden, Judith had treated her parents to a rehash over tea: " Did you ever hear about the lady and gentleman and the apple they stole? God was awfully angry with them and punished them for being so wicked."

" Yes; you mean Adam and Eve. Of course God was angry, because they disobeyed Him. If *we* disobey Him He is angry with us, too."

" Well, I can't see it, Mummy. You see, the lady blamed the gentleman, and the gentleman blamed the lady; but *I* blame God Himself."

" Blame God? Oh no, dear; what makes you say that? "

" Well, if God didn't want them to eat any apples off *that* tree, why did He plant it in *their* garden? He should have kept that one up in heaven, then they couldn't have got at it."

*   *   *   *   *

In its homely setting, the story of Elizabeth and her encounter with a one-armed whitewasher tickled us immensely.

Elizabeth's parents were having some interior decorating done, and a man with only one arm came to do some whitewashing. His physical handicap was a strange phenomenon to Elizabeth. After a prolonged and puzzled stare she sought an explanation from her father.

" Daddy, that poor man's got only one arm; where's his other arm? "

Daddy answered rather mischievously: " Why don't you go and ask him yourself, Elizabeth? "

So she approached the whitewasher and said shyly " Please excuse me, but where is your other arm? "

" I lost it in the first war."

And Elizabeth gasped, incredulously, " Oh, my goodness gracious me; did *you* really and truly fight the Normans? "

*   *   *   *   *

Having no first-hand child stories of my own, I fell back on some the district nurse had told me. She often dropped into the vicarage for a quick warm by the fire and a cup of coffee; it was a brief relaxation which we both valued, and she was nearly always good for an amusing yarn or two. She vouched for the truth of this one. A young couple started their married life under the parental roof, where there was a lively bunch of younger brothers and sisters.

Nurse was attending the young wife in her first confinement. She was called to the house early one morning, but, deciding that her services were not immediately needed, she parked a black leather case in the little front parlour, saying " I'll be back later on."

One of the young brothers soon spotted the black case, and wanted to know " Mum, is Mary's baby in there? "

" No, dear; the baby isn't in there."

" Oh, well, what *do* you think nurse has got in there? Do you reckon it's a fiddle? "

" No, she wouldn't have a fiddle in there either."

Later in the day, immediately after the baby's arrival, grandma came bustling downstairs to proclaim the glad tidings to these excited new aunts and uncles.

" Mary's got a *lovely* little baby boy."

" Cor! Can we go up and have a look, Mum? "

" Presently; but not just yet, dear. I'll tell you when you can."

" But I want to go *now*! "

" Well, you can't; I said presently; not yet."

" Oh, why can't we go *now*? "

" Because the baby hasn't even been washed yet."

" Washed? *Washed?* Why *washed?* Hasn't Mary got a brand-new one after all? I thought she was going to have a proper new baby "; and, from his tone of disgust, he evidently regarded the affair as a colossal swindle.

*   *   *   *   *

Poor nurse was often the target of unmerited abuse from young critics. Once her prestige suffered near-extinction when she delivered little Lucy's seventh brother after a *sister* had been specifically ordered. Lucy didn't try to hide her contempt for nurse's poor performance—surely she could have done something better than that! The next day Lucy was overheard snorting to her little friend: " Oh, that *stupid* Nurse Wittle! She only brings little *boys*."

Her sweet unreasonableness reminded me of one of my own godsons who, many years ago, had gone into a sweet shop and asked for " a quarter of a pound of jelly babies, please—*all boys* "!

*   *   *   *   *

I told them also about the little chap on the bus; there were crowds of schoolchildren on board, but it was this handsome little fellow who held my attention. He was a picture, in an obviously new blazer, and school cap at rakish angle. His eyes were riveted on an elderly man sitting in front of him. I wondered why the child stared so intently—although " stared " is hardly the word for it; rather it was a concentrated, absorbed study, as if he were at work on a problem. Presently he got up and electrified the man—and, indeed, all of us within earshot—by asking " I say, are you a milk-man? "

The poor man, at first quite nonplussed, evidently decided that this wasn't plain insolence—not with that straight, earnest gaze!

"A milkman? No, sonny, I'm not. But what makes you think that I might be? "

" Well, you've got such big ears! " How right the child was! Those ears were nearly (repeat, *nearly*) the size of a whale's fin, and they stuck right out like a couple of sore thumbs.

Mercifully, the question was accepted as a matter of innocent curiosity, with no facetious undercurrents. The man simply roared with laughter—as we all did. But I pondered on it for a long while. What was the point? Where was the connection?

I sensed a metaphorical link with the milkman who served the little boy's family. I think he must have been a notorious bearer of local news and gossip, and probably the child had often heard his mother say " *He's* got jolly big ears! "

Q.E.D.

*   *   *   *   *

The bus story reminded another member of *her* child's mishap on the way home by bus from her cookery class. The special dish that day was Irish stew, and Beryl was bringing home her precious concoction in a basin—not too securely covered. The child was strap-hanging, with the basin clutched in the crook of her free arm.

Suddenly the bus gave a violent lurch, neatly depositing Beryl's mess of pottage slap in the waiting lap of a lady who was gazing serenely out of the window.

Beryl's mother, when she heard about it, was frightfully per-turbed with thoughts of compensation. " Whatever did you *do*? Was the lady terribly annoyed? Did she create? Did you have to give your name? "

" I don't know if she minded, Mummy; we were just coming to a stop, so I nipped out and left her still looking out of the window."

* * * * *

By now we were running up against time, though far be it from me to clamp down on anyone in this strangely communicative mood. Just then John came in. It was his custom to slip out and make a few pastoral calls while we had our talk, then drift back in time for a cup of tea and a word here and there with individual members. It was all part of a studied policy to make himself accessible.

On this occasion he was clearly taken aback to find not the relatively sedate gathering he had left an hour ago but a bevy of bubbling, hilarious females, reluctant to stop—even for tea.

He manifestly approved of our lighthearted improvisation, reminding them that spontaneous laughter was apt to be a rather neglected feature of the Christian image, and he stressed the merits of a " cheerful countenance "—which encouraged grandma, who had opened our recital, in her bold bid to get John himself to wind up for us. He responded.

" I can't at the moment recall a *child* story; but here's one about my friend the Bishop of —— (John admitted that he couldn't vouch for its truth). The bishop was making a pilgrimage on foot, during a very hot summer, through some of the quiet hamlets in his diocese, calling informally on as many of the cottagers as possible. Regretfully, he found them painfully shy and nervous. One dear old soul, completely overawed by an episcopal invasion, became nearly dumb with fright, and when she tried to answer she could only gibber and stutter. His lordship, sensing her dilemma, soon got up to go, but, feeling parched with the heat and dust of the lanes, he begged a glass of water. With nervous fussiness she handed it to him.

After the first refreshing sip he commented " This is *excellent* water, my good woman; where does it come from? "

" It comes from the Lord, my pump! "

* * * * *

By now their appetite for light entertainment seemed insatiable; they were greedy for encores, so John added the incident of his own uncle, who, being rather near-sighted as well as slightly deaf, always took his own large-type hymn book with him to church. At evensong one Sunday, as he opened his book for the first hymn, he was heard to splutter, in the particularly penetrating " whisper " that sometimes accompanies deafness, " Oh, good Lord, I've brought the dictionary with me! "

And that, of course, reminded him of the episode of his aunt Clara and her false teeth. She, poor dear, had never managed to come to terms with her new-fangled dentures; so, for her greater comfort and peace of mind, she kept them at all *im*material times in the pocket of her black silk apron. That was all right until the day she forgot to take off her apron before going to church. There, in the execution of a deep genuflection, her teeth skidded noisily up the aisle. A self-conscious sidesman retrieved them and handed them back to her with a ridiculously deferential bow. She then had to make a ticklish snap decision: whether to return them to her pocket, and thereby risk a repetition, or to pop them furtively into her mouth and suffer the tortures of hell for the rest of the service.

She opted for comfort and pocketed them again.

*   *   *   *   *

But for John's obligation never to betray pastoral confidences he might have told of the local teenage boy who wanted to be prepared for confirmation. Initial questioning revealed that he had missed baptism in infancy. With his parents' consent, he now sought to make good this omission, and he was duly instructed. He seemed to understand that he would be required to make his own promises; but on the day, when it came to the vital issue " Dost thou renounce the devil and all his works, the vain pomp and glory of the world . . . ? " John was simply staggered to hear his prompt and emphatic " No; I *don't*."

His baptism was adjourned *sine die*.

Nor, of course, could John divulge the little matter of the grocery list that found its way into the alms dish!

A parishioner due at any minute to become a young mum had risked coming to matins one Sunday, then hurried home and produced her first-born before teatime. Grandma, in fitting recognition of God's bounty, came to evensong, armed with the good news, a broad smile of relief, and—ostensibly—an offering commensurate with deep gratitude. But, in all the excitement, instead of popping in the intended treasury note she had inadvertently substituted a neatly folded list made out for the grocer. It began: " Lark's Cottage; ½lb. short back; ¼lb. streaky " and ended with " 2 tins of sardines, 1 metal polish."

*   *   *   *   *

I half expected that the Storker story might have got a mention in our impromptu recital, but it didn't really qualify, for although young Storker was childlike he wasn't a child. Ben Storker, in fact, was a lanky young serviceman, who had so outgrown his strength that he was inevitably nicknamed *Beanstalk*. He suffered from a mild squint and an almost pathological simplicity. He was what is usually termed a " *devout* churchman " when you don't want to use the word " fanatical " or " spiky."

During the war Beanstalk was conscripted to the armed forces and was duly posted to his unit. He had absolutely dumbfounded his fellow recruits by his choice of pin-ups: not the current bunch of undulating blondes, redheads or brunettes, but a couple of rather tatty press photographs of (a) the Archbishop of Canterbury in full regalia and (b) the rural dean, leading a slightly bedraggled band of pilgrims—in torrents of rain—on their way to some hallowed shrine, with the leggy Beanstalk himself, towering head and shoulders above the rest, manfully bringing up the rear.

Rumour had it that the sergeant fixed Beanstalk with a steely eye and curtly ordered him to report next morning to the M.O.

" Yes, sergeant," the amiable Beanstalk was alleged to have said, " but what for? What shall I tell him? "

" Oh, just that you're nuts."

Nothing ruffled Beanstalk and, returning eventually to civvy street, he continued to go his guileless way, happily oblivious to his own oddities and the amused titters they usually evoked.

He bought an Alsatian puppy and in due course went to the post office to get a licence.

Sure enough, when the counter clerk asked " Name? " Beanstalk answered naïvely " Lassie; it's a girl! "

*   *   *   *   *

The long-overdue tea was never more welcome; hilarity seemed to have created an insatiable thirst. Cups were filled and refilled as we lingered in complete relaxation.

In that mood, I wished that I had with me a collection of original drawings by a class of under-sevens for whose religious instruction I was once responsible. These works of art had seemed well worth saving. They depicted simply and realistically the familiar Bible stories on which their lessons were based. To this day I can enjoy each one with the perennial freshness of a masterpiece—particularly the virile impression of a dauntless Daniel fraternizing with a quartet of dejected-looking lions, and the arresting picture of our Lord journeying up to Jerusalem on a drowsy donkey—all in meticulous detail, even to the initials " J.C." inscribed on His little attaché case.

CHAPTER 11

Market gardening

IN case you don't know, " neteeliums " are the bewitching little white flowers that constituted a substantial part of our floral stock-in-trade, but you won't find the plant listed in any reputable seed catalogue, or even—under that name—in any reference book on wild flowers. The plant itself is common enough, but the name is virtually our copyright. We sold vast quantities of it. Obviously we couldn't expect to meet with a wildly hysterical demand for shameless bunches of *white dead-nettle* (known sometimes as " white archangel "). On the other hand, with a large waste corner of our orchard simply abounding in it, it did seem a pity not to turn the thing to good account.

" What's in a name? " you may ask. In our opinion a great deal, and that's why we coined the word " neteelium "

I was constantly experimenting with flowers, both for the house and for market, combining sometimes the most unlikely varieties to produce attractive, saleable little posies. For example, love-in-a-mist, I found, teamed well with pale salmon godetia, honeysuckle and a few white cloves; doronicum and Solomon's seal mixed agreeably with an early lupin or two; and the warm glow of marigolds, geums, montbretia and yellow antirrhinums, with a vivid nasturtium slipped in here and there, seldom failed to please.

In this way, trying out one flower with another, I discovered the immense possibilities of the common dead-nettle. With all the foliage carefully removed (essential for the best effect), these delicate little whorled white blossoms reminded me of tiny orchids, and I could foresee endless permutations with other members of the wild garden to produce some striking results. For instance, our humble " neteeliums," I found, combined exquisitely with early wild arums (these grew prolifically under the shady front hedge), wild white hyacinths, leucojums, two or three sprigs of forsythia, a few fronds of cow parsley, and—with luck!—a late pheasant-eye narcissus or two for fragrance. These, arranged in a simple shallow bowl—say an old glazed ovenware dish—make one wonder why we ever bother to spend fabulous sums on professionally arranged specimen carnations, hot-house roses, exotic lilies and similar aristocrats.

From the moment of discovery it didn't take long to estimate the market value of the neteelium as a liberal basis for the quantities of mixed flowers which we took to market on Friday mornings. It has all the advantages of the hardy, free-flowering perennial; it needs no pruning, no encouraging fertilizers; it is gloriously impervious to freakish weather; it lasts a long time in water (though, admittedly, the angle of the stems tends to deviate as the days pass); and it has the added merit—presumably because it is a weed—that it grows in profusion when all else fails, flowering from April to December. Incidentally, it is rich in honey and attracts the early bees.

The first time we submitted our speciality to the stall—the W.I. open market stall—the supervisor, who checked all incoming produce, appeared frankly puzzled. " That's a pretty little white flower. I don't seem to recognize it. What is it? "

She being deemed an expert gardener and botanist, I answered guardedly " I'm not very well up in botanical names, but it always reminds me of the orchid family. We have quite a lot in the garden."

" Quite a lot " was a gross understatement; just then the orchard was inundated with it.

We were elated at its instant success; it sold right out, and at a fair price. Then it was that we decided it needed an impressive name, but not one that was *too* easily identifiable. From that moment it was plain sailing. The stock appeared to replace itself from week to week without any human assistance or coercion, and there seemed to be a guaranteed outlet. (Plain sailing, that is, until the day when Uncle's successor, in a fit of inexplicable zeal, scythed ruthlessly all that part of the orchard and deprived us of the entire crop at one fell swoop. I suppose its commercial value had escaped him; anyway, he had a " thing " about tidiness.)

In preparation for the market on Friday, John and I were obliged to devote every spare moment on Thursday (not that John had any legitimate *spare* moments on any day) to picking, grading, bunching, weighing and stacking. There was also the invoicing. To me it was

an unmitigated joy to wander out in the garden and gather basket-
fuls of produce—especially the flowers.

Ours was predominantly a spring-flower garden, supplying us
with intoxicating masses of every conceivable variety: snowdrops
carpeting the shady end of the lawn like a liberal top-dressing of
white jewels ; crocuses ringing the tree trunks in colourful circles ;
primroses and violets clustering in the hedges ; daffodils, narcissi
and tulips jostling for position ; vigorous clumps of leucojums in
many unexpected corners ; abundant stylosa (or *iris unguicularis*
as the pedants will have it!), whose delicate, ethereal beauty found
so pleasing a background in the mellow brick wall ; and broad seas
of bluebells shimmering and rippling in the wild garden, in the
flower beds and, most strikingly of all, in the orchard, where,
merging with the pale pink clouds of apple blossom, the sheer
beauty of it all had a spiritual quality that would be hard to capture
in either words or colour. I used to stand entranced in the midst of
nature's wonderland and speculate on the uncharted mysteries and
possibilities of paradise. To my constant joy, there never was a
season when I couldn't wander out and find at least enough flowers
of one sort or another to fill a vase or two. Our gay carpets of
aconites unrolled just when spirits were at a low ebb after a bleak
winter, so profuse in their eagerness that one feared treading on
them—and that would be unbearable; and among our valued
perennials, that strong colonizer *bergenia* grew in bold drifts of lush
purplish pink—a plant of dual merit if ever there was one, first as
an unrivalled weed-suppressor and then, for the sake of its foliage,
as the flower arranger's popular ally. When blooms were hard to
come by there would be the rich assortment of berries and autumnal
leaves, and green cascades were never despised when catkins were
available.

Having completed our Thursday picking campaign, the bunching
of such wholesale quantities was a stupendous task, but a delightful
one—counting out daffodils in dozens, grading them for length,
adding a handful of spikes, whipping on the rubber bands, and then
stacking them in buckets of water overnight. Next we would be
nipping off all the lilac foliage ready for sale, working mock orange
blossom into sizeable bouquets, snicking the tiresome thorns off
the rose stems, or sorting out the sweet williams in piles according
to shade.

John's speciality was Victorian posies, at which he became very deft and nimble-fingered. Between us we managed quite an impressive output; soon we found ourselves calculating everything in wholesale terms—a dozen bunches of this or a couple of dozen of that. We could estimate a twelve-pound chip basket to within an ounce, and for apples, plums and pears we now reckoned in bushels.

In some ways the vegetables constituted a more demanding problem. They had to be cleaned; radishes, spring onions, young carrots and the asparagus had to be bundled; and experience taught us that it takes a vast quantity of spinach to weigh up to ten pounds! Mint and parsley, by comparison, were very accommodating items —we just snatched handfuls recklessly in passing, adjusted rubber bands, and they never fetched less than threepence a bunch (small, medium, or extra O.S.). Lettuce we found to be a doubtful and rather exasperating commercial proposition; ours had a perverse habit of bolting on Thursday, just as we were counting on a record crop for Friday.

The major problem, of course, was getting the stuff to market— especially the flowers—without crushing. It was a situation that posed countless questions. How many trug baskets could possibly be stowed under the stairs of the bus? What if the space was already stacked with folding prams and hand luggage? Sometimes we had to take the load *inside* the bus—and if we had to strap-hang, what then? We couldn't have been very popular with our fellow travellers or with the conductors. During the height of the season, when there might well be a simultaneous glut of fruit, vegetables and salad stuffs, as well as flowers, the only solution was to hire a car; but as it required such an enormous amount of produce to cover the cost this was not always practicable, and never really profitable. Besides, there was always the possibility, during these gluts, of the lot being left on our hands; all the other producers would be equally sur-feited, and the sales assistants at the stall—magnificent, dedicated, voluntary workers that they were—couldn't do the impossible. In these circumstances, quantities of market produce had often to be thrown away. If it was still fresh and usable it was taken to the nearby hospital.

So one way and another we found the greengrocery business a somewhat precarious undertaking.

Then why bother? many friends asked us. Well, being saddled with such a colossal garden there were two alternatives: letting it go to utter rack and ruin, until the garden was one vast jungle, or employing some help to maintain reasonable order and ensure regular supplies for our own table. We chose the latter course, but to pay for help we were obliged to market the surplus. In a sense we were pitchforked into the whole exercise.

Incidentally, we had to acquire new skills. We learnt to climb trees, though an earlier start than at well past middle age would have been a distinct advantage. We consoled ourselves that it was good exercise, though we were rather disposed to change our opinion when John, like an over-venturesome fledgling, plummeted from a tall old apple tree on to some unfriendly rockery and broke a bone in his wrist. But between us we notched up only the one casualty in the whole fourteen years—not too bad for greenhorns.

To be truthful, even I—garden fiend that I was—felt less enraptured with the sales project when in windy, bleak weather I had to forsake the seductive warmth of the fireside, don wellingtons and an old mac and venture forth to gather cartons of sprouts, spinach, kale or purple tops, or whatever was flourishing. And I *never* became entirely reconciled to the fixed policy of selling the bulk of our lovely asparagus; but, as there was always a hungry market for it at an attractive price, we practised self-denial with what grace we could.

When the W.I. stall was regretfully obliged to reject produce because of a glut we had to make a snap decision. Here we were, weighed down on one occasion with forty-eight pounds of gooseberries (two twelve-pound chip baskets apiece). What does one do with unwanted gooseberries? To cart them all home again was unthinkable—besides, I needed the empty baskets for my week's shopping—so, following the instincts of my brief war-time experience as a commercial traveller, I decided to do a deal with the nearest greengrocer. We whooped with joy at our quick success—and also at relief from the numbing weight of our load. There was no haggling; he looked at our samples, agreed to take immediate delivery, paid spot cash, and indicated his willingness to consider any future lines we might have. John and I were quite delirious at this expansionist trend; we felt that for mere beginners in the market garden game we were not doing too badly to be opening a fresh account so soon and on such favourable terms.

(We marked the occasion by dropping into our favourite café, nearby, for well-earned refreshment. As we sat looking out of the window and sipping our coffee and munching oven-hot scones we were unexpectedly entertained to a most novel free performance outside. An obstinate old sow—doubtless a very terrified old sow—had escaped from the market and was being hotly pursued down the High Street, in and out of the traffic, by a couple of distracted drovers. Their chivvying tactics served only to inflame the sow's temper and she led them a merry dance, until she finally took a firm line and stormed into the solicitor's office opposite the café. Here the reception could not have been too cordial, for she quickly stalked out with a touch of lofty disdain, crossed the road—to the utter confusion of both motorists and pedestrians—and marched straight into the undertaker's parlour, next door to our café. Had she wanted to make her will before a last dramatic gesture? We had a wonderful ringside view of the whole performance, but it grieved us to hear later that the poor frightened creature had died as a result of her escapade.)

The outlet we had so unexpectedly found with the greengrocer was amicably maintained and considerably extended over the years. Around Christmas time we disposed of large quantities of holly—liberally dotted with scarlet berries—for his seasonal trade in wreaths and crosses. This transaction was arranged on " ex garden " terms, which gave us further ideas; while he was on the spot for holly, why not the wholesale collection of apples, by the bushel, direct from our store shed to his transport? This plan, which he readily approved, struck me as superior in all respects to our own laborious portering. So we gradually rationalized our methods.

And from this expanding relationship I invited the greengrocer's talented wife to come and give a talk and demonstration on the care and arrangement of flowers to our Women's Guild. She was a notable success.

A profitable outcome, that, from the stall's rejection of a load of gooseberries!

*　　*　　*　　*　　*

In a sense it was tantalizing to have so much available ground and so little time personally to cultivate it. Although I lacked the proverbial green fingers, gardening held an irresistible attraction for me, and I was so eager to learn.

Not so John! Gardening to him was refined torture, and his sporadic obligatory efforts must have been sheer martyrdom. His natural approach to gardening was like that of Shakespeare's " whining schoolboy . . . creeping like snail unwillingly to school," though, to give him his due, John concealed the whine with credit-

Gardening to him was refined torture.

able self-control; nevertheless, it clearly remained a maddening, frustrating drill. In this ill-fitting rôle he always reminded me of the little cockney girl who was trying to face up to institutional life. Occupational training was a feature there; each child was encouraged to choose a hobby and expected to pursue it with diligence. This little girl, unable to make up her own mind, was assigned to gardening. When some V.I.P.s came down for " open day " she was detailed to pilot one of these important gentlemen round the grounds. Coming to an extra barren and arid little patch, boasting a solitary, stunted green shoot, he asked dubiously " And what's *that*, my dear? "

" That's me 'obby, and I 'ates it! " was the prompt answer.

That being virtually John's attitude to gardening, it always filled me with apprehension—as well as pit —when I saw him slinking off armed with secateurs or Dutch hoe. *Now* what will happen? I wondered instinctively.

We invariably made a superhuman effort to get things ship-shape for the fête, and to this end one stiflingly hot June evening John weeded and weeded as if obsessed, until sheer exhaustion and thirst drove him indoors around ten o'clock, dripping with sweat, feet dragging, limbs sagging.

The following morning I noticed Uncle working stolidly and, I thought, a trifle glumly on the bindweed and mint growing in the wrong spots.

Anxious to be encouraging as well as amiable, I called out " Morning! Still at it? The vicar did a *lot* of weeding last night."

" So I see," retorted Uncle with ill-concealed disgust, " and 'e's taken up all they gaillardias! "

(*They* gaillardias, I need scarcely mention, were among the few items showing remarkable promise just then—over which poor Uncle had almost felt constrained to keep an all-night vigil.)

John had also a genius for snicking slap through the main growth of everything at hand once he was let loose with secateurs. He became sort of scissor-happy and nothing was sacrosanct, so it was not only for his own sake that I never *encouraged* him to set out on a gardening foray.

Our gardening sessions, by the way, were not minimized by the use of pampering modern labour-saving equipment; no combined stool-trug devices, autogrip apple pickers, rubber-toothed rakes, fibreglass featherweight wheelbarrows, all-purpose garden sweepers which gather up leaves and wormcasts as they go along, or barrows subtly described as " ideal for elderly people," with a narrow track, longer-than-usual handles and sturdy wheels with solid rubber tyres! None of these—not even a motor mower—found a place in *our* working armoury. We gardened the hard way—blood, sweat, tears, with unlimited toil!

We never ceased to marvel at the prodigious amount of work covered by Uncle in his relatively short hours by simply pursuing his own steady, rhythmical tempo. He was never seen to hurry or to exert himself unduly; in fact he appeared constitutionally incapable of anything beyond a fixed, sluggish pace; but we never saw him waste a single minute, and so he could dig or weed a vast area in the space of a morning.

Incidentally, it was thanks to Uncle's shrewd stratagem that I once received the Women's Institute " spud star " for the " most prolific crop of the year from a single seed potato."

The president had impartially distributed from her official sack one seed potato per member, so that we all started on level pegging.

In complete innocence, I asked Uncle what he regarded as the most favourable aspect for root crops. Disregarding my actual question, he whispered darkly—as if engaging in a cloak-and-dagger intrigue—" Yew wants to *slice* 'un; just yew do as I tells yew "—accompanied by the most prolonged and knowing wink.

" Slice 'un? " I echoed, genuinely puzzled.

" Yes; *slice* 'un [with a pitying look that implied " How green *can* you be? "]; yew just cut 'un in two and plant the bits."

Conciliatory to the core, I bisected my seed potato and proceeded to dibble in the two halves, while Uncle allayed my obvious doubts with an assuring " Yew'll get a deal more spuds from 'un that way."

In due season my original seed potato yielded such a prodigious crop that a second count was necessary; but there was no mistake —thirty-four offspring, giants and pygmies ranking equal for competition purposes. Some of the pygmies, admittedly, were scarcely discernible to the naked eye, but this didn't disqualify them from inclusion on the birth certificate; mammoth or microscopic, they each counted one point.

" What did I tell yew? " asked Uncle drily. " I knows a thing or two."

That he did! And I felt guilty of mild fraud.

When Uncle's rheumatics got too much for him his successor was just such another demon for work, but he was unique in having the strength of ten ordinary men. Like Atlas, his steely muscles and broad shoulders looked equal to the strain of carrying the whole world. I have seen him dig, loosen and toss aside an enormous spadeful of heavily waterlogged clay soil as if it were a weightless pile of thistledown, and go on doing it long after the average manual labourer would have been counted out and well on the way to hospital. Our new man came from the north and had once been a miner, which no doubt accounted for his phenomenal strength. But strength wasn't his only commendation; he was the most willing, cheerful and co-operative man you would meet in a day's march. Alas, he was *not*, even by the meanest standard, a qualified gardener, as he himself was the first to admit; but he seemed touchingly eager to graduate, although heading for the eighties when he came to us.

His admitted lack of know-how—together with his *un*admitted lack of know-what—led occasionally to some confusing exchanges, and a few minor tragedies among the flower beds. For instance, there was the day when he neatly decapitated all my precious lavender just as it was coming into flower, because he thought it was *grass* and looked untidy. (And lavender was such a popular seller at the stall!) Then he once uprooted a healthy-looking row of zinnias, while lavishing attention on a bed of buttercups, to which he pointed with pride when he saw me approaching. " Them zinnias are comin' on fine, aren't they? " he said, indicating the buttercups. " Them zinnias," I said, as unreproachfully as I could, " are buttercups, you know. Where *are* the zinnias, by the way? "

He stood his ground with immovable conviction. " Them's *zinnias*! " Further argument seemed an unprofitable waste of time.

We were often at variance over the actual significance of words: sometimes I wondered whether we spoke the same language. We got once into an inextricable muddle over a sweet-pea trench. I asked him to prepare a trench for autumn sowing, and, because he always displayed such spontaneous willingness, I was puzzled not to find the trench ready, or at least started, the next day or the one after. Nearby was a lengthy mound of earth, like a miniature mountain range, the purpose of which didn't interest me.

The next time I mentioned the trench I thought he murmured " Yes, I've done it." The following day I slipped out and set to work myself, with very moderate success. I saw the old chap eyeing me, and I made the inanely obvious remark " See, *I've* dug the trench " —pointing to it.

His strange rejoinder, " Yes; I'll soon fill that in for you," left me speechless and in some doubt as to his sanity. But someone put me wise afterwards: " trench," it seemed, was a north-country term for building *up* (to *trench* up potatoes, celery, etc.); hence, then, that miniature mountain range! What I should have asked him for was a *ditch*.

In spite of it all, we got on very amicably—even when he denuded our prized hazel-nut tree of all its accessible branches to provide sticks for the sweet peas that eventually went into my trench/ditch and, at a later and more crucial stage, in the cause of his obsessional tidiness, drastically weeded that same sweet-pea bed and in doing so uprooted eighty per cent of the lovely young seedlings, all carefully selected strains, quite expensive, and designed to win a first prize at the coming show.

But one just couldn't be angry with him—he was so obliging and conscientious, a really lovable character.

Under his cultivation our " antrinny-ums " flourished as they had never done before; then I spotted him pushing some little pep pills down into the surrounding soil. As *we* hadn't bought any, I concluded that this was his way of indemnifying me for the sweet pea losses.

He put in countless hours of ungrudging, unpaid overtime during the dry spells to ensure that our flowers had their evening drink; and only a man of his Herculean strength could have carried gallon after gallon of water from the yard to the beds without turning a hair (a garden hose was not included in our armoury, either). And when the tank in the yard ran dry he had still farther to hump the heavy cans.

There was a touch of sentiment about that old tank, because once, soon after we came, we nearly lost it—in shady circumstances!

John had answered a ring at the door one day and found a couple of scruffy scrap-metal dealers standing in the porch—an old chap of seventy or more, who moaned ceaselessly about his lumbago, and his son, who sported a vivid shirt and kept saying " Oh, forget it, Dad! " Together they presented a picturesque partnership—the original prototype of successive Steptoes, beyond a doubt.

And were they astute?

" Steptoe " senior, if one may use the name without offence in either direction, wore a dented bowler hat and an expression of sharp pain when he moved. He took the initiative with " Good day, gov'nor; we'd like to buy yer tank."

Ever polite, John responded " I *beg* your pardon."

" Yer *tank*; we'll buy it off yer."

" My tank? But I haven't got one—except in the roof; you can't have that." For the moment we honestly believed that this was the truth; we had accepted the general set-up of the yard without taking any specific notice of the squat little tank, partly wood-boarded, planted against the outer wall of the stables; we had had no cause so far to use it.

" Yus, gov'nor, you 'ave! Mind you, it's only a rotten old one and you'd be just as well orf wivout it. But I wouldn't mind givin' yer five bob to take it away."

There was something touching about such generosity.

John gave him a pretty steady gaze, while he thought furiously. " Steptoe " seemed to interpret this as a sign of wavering indecision, for he hastened to improve his offer: " Well, gov'nor, I tell yer wot; I'll 'ave it for seven-and-six an' you'll be well rid of it."

(Lack of business acumen in the clergy is too often assumed by the laity.)

" How do you know I've got a tank? " parried John—a reasonable question, especially seeing that we ourselves had not known it until a minute ago.

" I jus' sees it round the back there in the yard "—trying to look as guileless as an unshorn lamb.

So they'd evidently had a jolly good prowl round, for no part of our yard was visible from the lane or the drive.

" No! " said John firmly; " nothing doing. I need that."

" Anything else, then, gov'nor? "

Quickly John had thought of the collection of obsolete brass lamps and fittings languishing in dust up in the church tower ever since paraffin had been supplanted by electricity.

The dealers followed John into the tower—with scant evidence of the lumbago. The whole discarded lot was brought down, laid out on the church lawn and carefully sized up by the " Steptoes."

The old man's ultimatum was, " Ten bob the lot, gov'nor; they're not a scrap o' use to anybody, mind you, but I'll clear 'em away for yer. I suppose you ain't changed yer mind about that there old tank o' yorn? No? Well, 'ere's ten bob for the rotten old brass."

John was satisfied that ten bob for the new organ fund was better than an assortment of redundant lamps in the belfry.

Off the dealers went; that was the end of them, we imagined.

But a week or so later, on a day when John had gone to London and I was housebound with a sore throat, they returned.

As I opened the door the old father began, disarmingly, " I've brought yer new tank, ma; it's on the van."

" New tank? But we don't want one, thank you! "

" Oh, don't tell me that, lady [he could hardly conceal the sob in his voice]; not now I've gorn and brought it all this way special for the gov'nor. I told 'im 'is old one wasn't no good, an' as I was comin' this way again I thought I'd swop it for this brand-new one."

" No you jolly well won't! The vicar's out at the moment, and it's entirely his affair. I've no authority whatsoever to part with his tank."

" But, lady, when I've brought it all this way," he pleaded. " Cor! Look, just come out to the van and see it for yerself; brand *new*."

When I refused to budge an inch he asked when the vicar would be back, and I—not choosing to disclose that I would be there alone until 10 o'clock that night—said " Can't say exactly; he comes in at any old time."

A brief cogitation; then " I know wot, ma; I'll 'phone later to see if 'e's back."

I thought he must have a screw loose; I'd certainly never met his equal for tenacity of purpose.

Sure enough, within a couple of hours he had telephoned, and, drawing a blank, promised to do so again next morning.

Long before breakfast our telephone bell was tinkling.

" About your old tank, gov'nor; I told yer missus yesterday that I've got a lovely brand-new one for yer, and I'm willing to swop it for yer battered old thing."

John answered crisply " You're wasting your time; nothing doing! Goodbye."

But we could no longer curb our rising curiosity, so we went in search of Uncle and told him the whole rigmarole.

He gave us a knowing look, opened his pruning knife and began scratching hieroglyphics on the exposed side of the tank—like an oriental sand-writer tracing something deeply significant. Then, extending his foot-rule, he measured the tank, and finally did some laborious calculations on a scrap of paper.

" Well," he summed it all up, " at today's price for lead that there tank's worth at least £20," adding as an afterthought " You'd better lock it up."

Shrewd old Uncle! We were almost tempted to buy a guard dog. That was the last we saw of our " Steptoes."

*   *   *   *   *

As the years passed we became increasingly aware of and perturbed by the immensity of the garden and its related problems. The sheer physical exertion of tending it was taking heavy toll of our health. We were not getting younger.

Yet ever and anon we were being urged by well-meaning friends and relations who came to visit us to *expand*; they all had wild schemes for making our fortunes from the soil, though most of them, we noted, made no attempt themselves to cultivate so much as a window-box.

" What you ought to do here," they would recommend, " is to build a hot-house. You could go in for tomatoes in a big way, and lots of out-of-season stuff, lettuce and so on; and with all this space why on earth don't you do chickens? And you'd find mushrooms an absolute winner! "

John tried to hide his impatience. " And when do you suppose I'd do my parish work, pray? " he'd ask.

" Oh, of course, I hadn't thought of that! "

One of the friends was so confident about mushrooms—which nature herself was already supplying in limited quantities on the front lawn—that he presented us with a packet of spawn and wished us luck. I plugged it into the lawn near our existing (negligible) stock. From that day we never saw another mushroom on our land, but the non-edible fungus flourished as never before. Whether there could be any scientific explanation for this phenomenon I've no idea, but when I told our friend he said, reproachfully, " But they were never intended for your *lawn*. I thought you would have enough sense to grow them in the cellar; you've got such vast caverns down there!"

Of course, the reflective satisfaction of gardening is never more piquant than when you are enjoying the vegetables and fruit you have produced yourself—none can taste better; indeed, none can taste half as good. We certainly relished the fruits of our labours and were in full agreement that the abundance of fresh produce brought to our table handsomely justified all the expense, time and care it demanded. But as success-merchants we were admittedly erratic and unpredictable. This was tragically demonstrated in the peach project.

To mark our moving into the vicarage my brother had planted a couple of peach stones in a fine sunny aspect, close by a south wall. In due course two spindly growths appeared, but they inspired us with little hope. Then, year by year, a modest show of the delicate early blossom caused a mild stir, only it never seemed to set. Then one year—miracle of miracles—about four or five small fruits were observed; as far as I remember, they withered and fell off. But the next season, with hope abandoned, we were gloriously rewarded: one of the peach trees was really loaded with healthy-looking fruit. Daily inspections became the drill. Given ideal weather conditions, we envisaged a splendid harvest. They were the very large, deep yellow peaches. The yield was in the region of seven dozen, and I was conscious of an almost maternal pride as I laid them out on layers of cotton wool in a sunny window. They were simply delicious, but I had a hard job to convince my family that they were bona-fide home produce. The following year our wonder tree bore two forlorn peaches, and thereafter, until the time we left, it had not borne again. Judging by the severity of its leaf-curl, I'm afraid its days were numbered. It may have responded to spray and I hope it has, but to my inexpert eye its sickly appearance spelt certain doom.

* * * * *

It was just about the time when our enthusiasm and strength began to show unmistakable signs of wilting that a sweeping suggestion was put forward by the P.C.C. which initially we resisted with bitter indignation. The proposition was to fell many of the older trees in the main garden and remove nearly all the soft fruit, including about sixty gooseberry bushes, and then level and turf the ground to provide one vast lawn. Although we recognized it as a measure to minimize our labours and to achieve a more orderly landscape, we could see it only as an act of gross vandalism. Trees, to us, were living things; the ruthless removal or mutilation of even one for no really sound reason seemed quite indefensible. (The farming fraternity, of whom our P.C.C. was mainly composed, having a trained eye for marginal cultivation, landscape precision and over-all tidiness, naturally viewed the question of spoliation by tree-felling from a totally different—severely practical—angle.)

The entire project, we were assured, would be carried out for us by experts, at no cost to ourselves, and the subsequent maintenance of the then tremendous new lawn would be professionally undertaken.

Because hostility to the P.C.C. was something we were ever anxious to avoid, we reluctantly consented to the scheme, but it was with a *very* heavy heart that I watched one after another of our magnificent old giants being hacked and felled, chopped up and carried away for disposal. I felt like a ghoulish spectator at a major surgical operation callously performed without anæsthetic. We dared them, only over our dead bodies, to fell our beloved copper beech—a superbly majestic giant of a tree, outclassing them all. It was spared, but on an unwilling compromise to amputate its lower limbs. I wished I had gone away until it was all over. While it lasted that part of the garden resembled a bustling Canadian lumber camp, with gangs labouring strenuously from dawn to dusk, and every type of mechanized aid brought into service—mechanical diggers, scoops, levellers and rollers, with tractors chugging around in ceaseless activity like the armoured columns of an invading army.

For the most part it was a meticulously planned and well-organized exercise. There was one major mishap, and that could very easily have been a fatal one.

A particularly tall fir tree—a sixty-foot giant, if not more—was being brought down and some very precise calculation was obviously needed to ensure its fall at the right angle. Actually there was ample lawn space waiting to receive it.

We were not warned when the climax of the operation was imminent; we were just transfixed by the terrifying repercussions of a sudden almighty thud. The whole house rocked in its foundations; in fact, for a second it seemed as if the world had leapt into the air and dropped down again—BUMP! All this was accompanied by a frightening crash of breaking glass. When we could move, John and I crept from the room to learn the worst.

That tall fir tree was lying through the drawing-room window, with its noble head on the Chesterfield settee and its branches sweeping the mantelpiece. The floor was carpeted with shattered glass and twigs; the upholstery glistened with splinters.

It had crashed at the spot where normally I rested for half an hour after lunch—at that very time!—but we had providentially shifted our location that day to the dining room.

*   *   *   *   *

It took a long while to become reconciled to the new, barren scene, and we grieved out of all proportion over the loss of some relatively trivial features—for instance, the marvellous eye-catching clump of wild crane's-bill which year after year had unfailingly provided a vivid cushion of colour up in that old corner. (I could never decide whether this oft-despised weed was really " rich purple "—as the textbooks have it—or " bold blue "—as it appeared in certain lights. To my eye it was a matchless blend of both, belonging only to nature's colour chart.) Behind this cushion tall lupins, in a rich galaxy of shades, had towered haughtily; and then in the foreground was a humble little patch of less voluptuous beauty— narrow-leaved lungwort—for which we had had a growing affection. Here it had spread in welcome profusion, although exiled from its native Hampshire soil. I had loved the muted pinky-blue amid the riot of strong colours. My sentiment for the lungwort may have stemmed from a grievous oversight in the first instance, entitling it, perhaps, to extra favour when its shy presence was finally noticed. It was when visiting a friend one day that the impact of its charm was felt. I raved over her simple arrangement of this pretty little stranger.

" What a little gem " I exclaimed. " What is it called? *Do* let me have a cutting! "

" By all means; you shall have a *root*. It's only lungwort; and let me warn you, it'll spread like a prairie fire. I can't believe you're not already plagued with it. It's just a *weed*." *Just!* Never was the slur of lowly origin less deserved. I came home clutching my promised root; but, sure enough, when I examined that top corner of the garden more carefully a well-established clump gazed up at me accusingly. " And I'm thriving very vigorously, thank you! " it seemed to say; perhaps one of the oldest residents for all I knew. It was awarded an immediate place in my list of favourites for decorative purposes—a spontaneous gesture that redressed, I hope, the former slight.

How easy to overlook the proverbial needle in the haystack, until it pierces your finger! There was the parallel case of the blackberries.

As an inveterate lover of blackberries I could always be counted on to join up with any party out on a blackberrying sortie, no matter how tough and testing the proposed terrain, how uncertain the weather forecast, or how fiendishly prickly and inaccessible the brambles were known to be in that area. For me the whole project had a gravitational pull not to be resisted. So on going into the country I had gleefully tagged on to many such excursions, coming home snagged, lacerated, bleeding, untidy and dog-tired, but triumphantly clutching my little basket—maybe three whole pounds of berries for bramble jelly.

It was in our twelfth year at the vicarage that Uncle said casually one day " I've cleared the path to the blackberries, madam; you'll find I've got most of the undergrowth out of the way."

" Which blackberries? Where? "

" In the orchard, madam, all along the hedge!"—and his tone implied " What a silly, superfluous question to ask."

Well, there they were, in astonishing profusion. I could scarcely believe my eyes. Right at hand, and begging to be picked, we had the most prolific harvest of luscious, large, shining blackberries, all on our own property, demanding no exhausting foot-slogging, no undue stretching and scrambling—and there were no treacherous ditches to fall into.

To think that all these years they had been there, patiently waiting to be gathered, while I, with assumed youthful bravado, had joined the task forces on long-distance endurance tests—all for a pound or two of jelly! Well!

*   *   *   *   *

As I was becoming less equal to energetic gardening and could now manage little more than routine weeding, consolation was found in indoor culture—on a very modest scale. Gradually our wide kitchen window ledge began to fill up with pot plants of every kind and colour—primula, pelargonium, schizanthus, fuchsia, cyclamen, musk, tear-drop, Spanish begonia, and—ever my firm favourite—hot-water plant. No doubt the hot-water plant became prime favourite because it rewarded me with more obvious success than all the others, and with a minimun of effort. I lavished an almost maternal affection on these lovely rich purplish little gems; the slightly iridescent effect of their petals under artificial light always fascinated me. Once I tried to reproduce it in water-colours, but that depth of tone seemed inimitable; at least, it completely eluded me.

One of my hot-water plants eventually won a first at the show, and pride knew no bounds; but my affection for the genus is also linked with faintly amusing associations, and to this day the sight of a hot-water plant evokes a reminiscent smile. I had been at great pains to discover the correct botanical name of my hot-water plant; nobody seemed able to help me. It was almost incredible that quite skilled veteran gardeners shared my ignorance on this point, but they all looked blank and shook their heads. Then we had an unexpected visit one day from one of the Mirfield fathers, and he, as I already happened to know, was the recognized gardening authority at the community house; so, seizing what I estimated to be a golden opportunity for enlightenment, I asked " Father, do you happen to know anything about hot-water plants? "

He shook his head a trifle dolefully. " I'm so sorry, Mrs. Green, but that's something quite outside my province; I'm no plumber and engineer! "

When I made myself a bit clearer he joined in the joke with great gusto.

We were still laughing over this when a visitor called to see John. " What's all the fun going on here? " he wanted to know. We told him about our little misunderstanding, and he was downright scathing with his superior knowledge. " Why, that's *achimenes*; I thought *everybody* knew that! "

*   *   *   *   *

This was not the reverend father's first visit to us; in fact a few years before, when he had been conducting a parochial mission for John, the vicarage had been his home for a fortnight, and an extremely delightful guest we had found him.

The wonder is that he ever favoured us with a second visit, seeing that he had suffered a shameful leg-pull at the hands of my villainous brother, who was spending a day or two with us at the time.

Sitting round the tea table, conversation had drifted—via fresh young lettuce and home-made jam—to gardening.

The reverend father had mused reflectively: " Next year I think I shall have to reduce the soft fruit stock at Mirfield—especially the black currants. There's such a big quantity to attend to, and the worst of black currants is their susceptibility to big bud. A lot of our black currants now have big bud, and once they get that there's absolutely *nothing* you can do about it."

" Oh yes there is, you know," interposed my brother, who I had judged, by his far-away look, hadn't been paying the slightest attention to the conversation.

" *Really?* " said the father, with the enthusiast's alertness for new discoveries. " I've never heard of it. What is it, may I ask? "

" Grow red currants! "

I was sorry afterwards to have bruised my brother's shin so severely, but the vicious kick which I delivered under the table seemed at the time thoroughly deserved. Anyway, it was not premeditated cruelty; and as summary justice maybe it was fair enough.

CHAPTER 12

The Puddings

LOOKING back over the years, it would be impossible to say exactly how many Puddings, all told, we had at the vicarage, because we omitted—very shortsightedly—to keep a register of births. At a very conservative estimate, however, it must have run into quite five dozen, though not, of course, all at once.

The two " permanents " were the original Suet Pudding—heavy matriarch of this feline family—and her eldest daughter, Christmas Pudding, known more familiarly as " Chrissie." All the rest constituted the steady stream of their prolific progeny. With their constant comings and goings, we found ourselves surrounded by an ever-fluctuating cat population, and it would have required a trained statistician to keep pace with their census figures.

Eventually even their christenings presented a problem, as we gradually exhausted all the puddings we knew. With a break in the Pudding tradition thus forced upon us, we resorted to the cake class, and the first of *that* dynasty, I remember, became *Victoria Sponge.*

When I say that Suet was the heavy matriarch, I mean only in her undisputed position of authority as head of the Pudding clan. She appreciated and exercised her sovereignty, asserted her rights, and tolerated no daring interference with them. She certainly refused to put up with any nonsense from the younger element, and she had her own method of dealing summarily with the first sign of juvenile delinquency—a sharp, well-directed right hook to the offender's nose.

Physically Suet was anything but a heavy matron ; she was, in fact, the sleekest, the most graceful and elegant cat you ever saw, whose vital statistics would have secured her instant stardom in the Hollywood of the cat world. She sacrificed her fine figure only for motherhood, never for gluttony. Suet's coat was mainly black and *very* silky, with a fascinating white parting on the top of her head, well-defined white chops, and a whiter-than-white undercarriage, to which she devoted hours of patient semi-dry-cleaning. There was no gainsaying her vanity, but she had outstanding qualities to counterbalance this failing. It was in her shrewd eyes and the proud tilt of her head that her better self was unmistakably reflected—her purposeful intelligence (I nearly put *purr*poseful!), her inflexible will-power, her magnificent independence and, above all, her staid dignity.

One look at Suet Pudding as she picked her way daintily to the middle of the hearthrug by the fire, or, of course, to the sunniest spot by the open window, and you knew without a doubt who ruled the vicarage waves.

Suet had come to us as a tiny bundle of fluff, only eight or nine weeks old but already a spirited and accomplished acrobat. Her name at that stage had been *Plum* Pudding, chosen by her original owner; but John, with a strong aversion to plums at any time, but particularly so at that moment when we were wearily completing the picking of ten irksome bushels of Black Monarchs, declared his revulsion to such a name.

" Something *must* be done about that cat's name; I can't stand any more plums about the place " was his ultimatum. With that he carried her to the scullery trough, turned on the tap and gave her conditional baptism, bestowing the more acceptable name of Suet.

The circumstances in which Suet was presented to us were common enough. We had recently lost our previous puss—the rather stolid, lethargic little Nigger, whose all-black beauty was relieved only by a stubby pink tongue, which he had an endearing habit of *always* poking out; the little pink tip displayed against its black surround imparted a look of adorable soppiness. Nigger, alas, had gone off one day in hot pursuit of a rabbit; with a stab of fatalism, we watched him disappear through the hawthorn hedge. I had a premonition that we would never see him again—a hunch that proved all too true. We organized a full-scale search, tramping many hopeful miles calling fatuously " Nigger! Nigger, dear! Fishy, fishy! " We even exposed ourselves to parochial ridicule (though we never dreamt at the time that we *were* inviting ridicule!) by pinning a notice on the village hall offering ten shillings reward for news of our missing pet. The inducement brought no news and no cat, only a stream of incorrigible children to tell us solemnly that they were looking *everywhere* for it! Was Nigger, they innocently inquired, all black? Or could it, by chance, be ginger, or tortoiseshell, or grey, or tabby? They'd seen every type of cat except an honest-to-goodness black one. One particularly sinister little gang, in dirty jeans, tousle-headed, and their faces awash with lolly dribble, assured me that they had been searching for hours and *hours*—well, at least half an hour! They stood their ground relentlessly, until I weakly went for my purse.

The fact remained that Nigger had gone for good; and then we heard faint echoes of this ridicule: " They must be cracked down at the vicarage; they're offering a reward for a *cat*! " We duly learnt that in the country cats are evaluated only on the basis of their working capacity—to keep down rats and mice. A puss as a pet, it seemed, was a clear symptom of either nauseating sentimentality or mental derangement (or both!)—something to be discouraged at all costs. And as for buying regular supplies of fish for puss— well, " those Greens must have more money than sense."

Bereaved of Nigger, we had vowed that we would never have another cat; we were not the right type to keep pets; we allowed ourselves and our feelings to become too deeply involved!

But when Mrs. Briggs-Hamilton had pleaded for a good home for her little Plum Pudding (*the* most enchanting kitten and already a perfect little acrobat, Mrs. B-H had boasted; and if she couldn't place it it would have to be put down, she threw in artfully!) John and I capitulated—but with mutually agreed provisos: we would *not* make a fool of this one; we would *not*, out of mistaken kindness, be fabulously indulgent; nor would we get ourselves emotionally entangled.

That sounded fine, but we had reckoned without the seductive personality of Suet herself. She quickly sized us up, played her cards intelligently, and won a resounding victory—all paws down.

Mrs. Briggs-Hamilton had made no idle boast in claiming that young Plum, for its age, possessed the most remarkable acrobatic skill; it seemed destined for a sensational career under the inter-national big top.

Within seconds of its installation at the vicarage it began to run through its repertoire, first sitting bolt upright in a begging attitude —a posture which it maintained with casual ease for several minutes. To us it was a spell-binding feat for a kitten of only a few weeks. (I have been told, though I have no proof of its accuracy, that if cats perform in this way it is evidence of congenital ability, which they

Q

could never be taught; and from this we deduced her royal descent from circus cats of ancient and distinguished lineage.)

As she grew older she appeared to have no difficulty in maintaining the begging posture for any length of time she chose—an accomplishment which she turned to good account every morning as she took her place beside John at breakfast and effortlessly wheedled out of him the best part of his bacon rasher and titbits of buttered toast and marmalade. Her other obsession was Swiss roll!

For apparatus Suet used the kitchen clothes-horse—a tall, old-fashioned threefold model—and on this she demonstrated her proficiency so convincingly that we were tempted to reward her with a real miniature trapeze suspended from the ceiling.

Baby that she was, Suet would take a flying leap at the " horse," scamper up to the top rung like a streak of lightning, then perform her series of complicated swings, somersaults and simulated tumbles, obviously revelling both in the exercise and in the human adulation which it evoked. In all this she was daring, fearless and supremely self-assured—and quite tireless.

Her other speciality was the strange trick of catching her tail, for which act she always took up the same position in the kitchen— facing us at breakfast—and then, in an excess of feline abandon she whirled madly round and round with dazzling speed in pursuit of her tail. She'll collapse one of these days, we feared, in her mad tarantella. On the contrary, when she estimated that we had been adequately entertained she took her curtain calls and then strolled over to John and sat bolt upright to receive her next bit of bacon.

I can only affirm that Suet seemed indefatigable in her efforts to entertain us, and I do not believe that she went through this gruelling daily ritual from any other motive.

Needless to say, those mutually agreed initial provisos showed early signs of weakening. We were soon her abject slaves.

*   *   *   *   *

When Suet was awaiting her first confinement, John and I were as anxious as the most nerve-strained grandparents. We had prepared for her a suitable maternity wing in our unused garage—airy, spacious and quiet. A chart was duly hung over her delivery basket, and we promised her all the human assistance she might wish; but in the supreme moment of her life her sturdy independence asserted itself—alone and unaided she produced four lusty little Puddings.

The eldest, as I have already mentioned, was Christmas (Chrissie), and the three boys in the quartet were Sago, Batter and Rice.

John and I were the typical, over-fussy, nearly idolatrous grandparents, constantly rushing out to the maternity wing to have a recount and satisfy ourselves that everything was all right—just in case any kitten-snatching was going on. At last Suet began to eye us with a touch of cold disapproval; apparently she concluded that *we* had designs on her offspring, for we suddenly caught her, with Chrissie dangling from her mouth, trotting cautiously upstairs. It was an object lesson in the maternal instinct to watch how carefully she negotiated each stair to avoid banging the baby against the edge.

What was her plan? we wondered. We saw her carry it into a spare bedroom and plant it gently on an old ottoman; then she streaked downstairs and out to the garage to fetch the next infant; and so on, until she had reassembled her little family in the first floor back—out of harm's way. We regretted having to take them all back again—in a little basket—and Suet seemed genuinely distressed. But *we* had learnt our lesson; thereafter we left her and her brood unmolested, except for taking her food.

We decided quickly to keep Chrissie, but as soon as Batter, Rice and Sago could fend for themselves they were sent out into the world to make their own independent way in life. Batter we were only too pleased to place with the Missions to Seamen at Tilbury, where there were apparently plenty of suitable openings for willing young cats—willing, that is, to catch rats and mice.

By the time the next batch had arrived there were further outlets through the same agency, straight on to outward-bound ships; thus the next consignment of little Puddings—Semolina, Tapioca, Coconut and Date—found their way to Australia, working their passage.

By now Chrissie was exploiting her feminine charms and a new problem was facing us: where and how to find homes for all Suet's and, shortly, Chrissie's descendants. Drowning them, we agreed, would be a hideous crime; adoption was the ethical solution, so we were soon dispatching young Puddings right, left and centre; we left no stone unturned in our efforts to find homes for them.

Of course, we were outpaced; so, in desperation and in the interests of family planning, Suet underwent a little operation. To her lasting credit, the surgical details did *not* become the sole topic of her conversation for the rest of her days. She accepted it with characteristic dignity and reticence; but she *did* thereafter nurse an incurable detestation of men in white coats. She would now run a mile if house decorators came decked up in white overalls; and she promptly broke off diplomatic relations with the cricket umpire, who had hitherto been regarded as a friend.

Chrissie, however, remained a coquettish, much-sought-after young lady, whose cynical contempt for family planning was demonstrably clear from her regular confinements and subsequent display of maternal contentment. More and more Puddings entered into circulation.

From the outset Chrissie scorned the garage maternity wing; it was held in readiness for her each time, but she ignored our co-operative efforts and, instead, annexed the large clothes-basket behind the kitchen door. She obstinately refused any alternative; in fact her preliminary inspection in the early days was always the first intimation of her latest pregnancy. I think she hated to be excluded for a second from the vicarage circle, even to have her kittens; so the clothes-basket it had to be, over which John and I kept discreet vigil, offering encouraging endearments at intervals.

The old lady, Suet, and daughter Chrissie were normally on excellent terms and appeared entirely to enjoy each other's company; in fact, they were almost inseparables. Without persuasion from us, they elected to share sleeping quarters—a capacious round basket in the scullery (*with* cushion, of course)—and they normally curled up so amicably that any thought of possible bad feeling between them seemed wholly unlikely. (Here we miscalculated, omitting the one vital factor—the venomous jealousy that Chrissie's " happy events " engendered in the now sterile Suet. I will return to this later.)

The Puddings accepted *our* established bedtime routine without question; no latitude was asked. As soon as they noticed that John was filling hot-water bottles, preparing the early morning tea tray, and putting out milk bottles, they automatically put themselves to bed; after a few preliminary twists and fidgets they settled contentedly in one big curled-up ball of fur. The only variation on this theme was when they were already dozing in another part of the house or were engaged in a last-minute romp in the garden; then John would call, without raising his voice above conversational

pitch, " *Bed!* Come on, you two!" and two drowsy Puddings (or
two breathless Puddings, as the case may be) would obediently
trot along to their basket; they never demurred (theirs not to reason
why!). There was never a visitor who didn't comment on this uncanny responsiveness. But I have to admit that, amenable as the
Puddings were to our domestic routine, they sometimes gave us a
slightly dirty look at being disturbed.

In the wide-open spaces of the garden the Puddings, judging by
their frolics, found delirious satisfaction and infinite outlet for their
energy. Uncle was the one who manifested little or no interest in
their activities. He failed to see why, with acres of lawn and orchard
in which to disport themselves and sharpen their claws, they chose
rather to invade *his* territory, methodically scratching up the seeds
he had just painstakingly planted. Nets, far from acting as a reasonable deterrent, positively invited special attention—here was a
puzzle to be investigated: " If we can't get to the bottom of it, at
least we can roll over on our backs and flatten whatever is
underneath."

But they had other haunts as well, and their favourite was the
churchyard. The headstones afforded them endless scope for hide-
and-seek. They invariably accompanied me to church—right up to
the vestry door. At that point they were dismissed and withdrew
discreetly behind a headstone while the service was on. Afterwards
they bounded joyously to meet me, confident, I verily believe, that
they were giving me a huge surprise. Then they would follow me
home, gambolling and hopping excitedly over the graves and
suddenly darting through the hedge ahead of me to take up their
accustomed position on a ledge in the porch till I came with the key;
never a deviation in the procedure.

Parishioners told us that they always knew when we were away
for the day, because the Puddings, having seen us off in the morning, would wait patiently by the bus stop hour after hour, determined
to greet us on return. It is a fact that as we got off the last bus Suet
and Chrissie would emerge from the shadows, frisk towards us and
begin rubbing themselves against our ankles; but it had never
occurred to us—until the parishioners commented about it—that
our deserted pets had kept a day-long vigil.

I can remember only one occasion when they so far forgot themselves as to come inside the church. It was not during a service.
John and I had gone in to change the altar frontals and suddenly

The Puddings' favourite haunt.

became aware that we were not alone. There were Suet and Chrissie parading soberly up the centre aisle, at the hesitant pace usually adopted by the approaching bride and her father.

We rebuked them—very mildly—for unauthorized trespass, and they retreated in acrobatic style, leaping cleanly and with grace over the pews, with a margin of at least a spare inch, to emphasize their agility.

* * * * *

The only observable rift in the lute between these two inseparables, Suet and Chrissie, was when—as I have already hinted —the latter continued to increase her progeny after her mother's terminated fertility. Always at the approach of the happy event Suet tended to sulk and show signs of consuming jealousy. Immediately after the event, while undue attention was still focused on the new little mother, Suet assumed a chilly indifference which she clearly did not feel; and the moment the nursing mother had sufficiently recovered to pop out for a stroll to stretch her legs sly old Suet would creep stealthily up to the maternity basket, glare critically at the ugly, blind little objects within, and—if she had half a chance—she would shoot out a paw with rapier-like swiftness and try to claw them. We had to be really on our toes to stave off murder. A glint of insane jealousy shone in her green eyes.

The strained relations between mother and daughter would persist right up to the day when the latest batch of Puddings was sent out into the world (a pet shop in the nearest town became eventually our best means of disposal; they seemed willing to absorb —gratis and for nothing—our entire production, an admirable arrangement all round); once the youngsters were safely out of sight harmony was restored between their elders and they would again be almost living in each other's pockets—until the next happy event. That became the recognized pattern.

It is remarkable that there were not more skirmishes between them, because Chrissie became a brazen, bare-faced little thief, who greedily raided Suet's dinner the instant their dishes were put down. On this issue Suet was a stupidly unassertive, self-sacrificing old thing, but possibly she always had those vital statistics at the back of her mind; slimming, within limits, appeared an accepted discipline.

Like all cats, they demanded comfort and disdained minimum

standards; hence the extreme luxury of their winter sleeping quarters. On either side of the kitchen stove was a deep recess, and here on cold nights they lay, as near as possible to the warmth. Each had her own recess, furnished with her own big, cosy cardboard box —with cushion. At the familiar word " bed " they made promptly for the stove, climbed into their draughtproof cartons and snuggled down. An amusing and inexplicable feature was their habit of occasionally swopping beds, without any obvious signal of their intention. They seemed to read each other's thoughts: one minute they would be sleeping soundly; the next, as if by sudden, tacit impulse, they would drowsily change beds and be soundly asleep again in no time.

*   *   *   *   *

One way and another they were a source of endless amusement to us—also, sometimes, of mild anxiety, for they had their little illnesses and accidents. The most serious was when Chrissie got her paw caught in a gin trap and was pathetically incapacitated for several days; but how she *loved* being the spoilt darling of the vicarage ménage while the contingency lasted, receiving unremitting attention and sympathy, a good deal of unwise pampering, and all the cream off the milk—to offset the shock she had sustained.

It was a sad day when Chrissie, like Nigger before her, vanished through the orchard hedge after a rabbit and never returned.

From then owards Suet reigned supreme, and certainly made the most of her unchallenged rights and intensified spoiling. Age was catching up on her, and she was losing her former agility. No longer would she leap recklessly from the stable roof into the yard; she devised a short cut across the low corrugated-iron roof of the tool shed, where she waited, with a hint of humiliating surrender, for us to reach up and lift her down. Her acrobatic performances were drastically curtailed; she inclined more and more to leisurely drowsing, annexing now the *inside* of the hearth rather than the rug. It all pointed to a slowing down of the pendulum.

Over the years she had steadily insinuated herself into the toils of our heart-strings, which made it all the sadder when, shortly before we left Upper Bellpull, she fell mortally sick; the vet diagnosed leukæmia and, on his verdict and advice, we had no alternative but to have Suet put painlessly to sleep.

How we lamented her passing! I shudder to this day at the remembrance of it.

* * * * *

How many Pudding descendants now populate the cat world is anybody's guess; certainly a prodigious number.

We accepted with mild toleration the pointed jibes directed at us on account of our admitted obsession for cats; and, of course, it didn't surprise us that our choice of names evoked much facetious comment in the village—and some mild confusion! I recall the day when the butcher's man was delivering my order and was standing in the scullery, receipting the bill. I saw Suet streak into the larder, which was forbidden territory. I exclaimed peremptorily " Suet! "

The butcher's man paused in his scribbling, looking so utterly surprised, and said " But you didn't order any, did you, ma'am? "

" Any what? "

" Suet."

" Oh, no, that wasn't meant for you. I'm only speaking to my cat."

I was sure by his look that he placed me there and then on the lunatic fringe, if not well and truly within it.

But I just grinned sheepishly and wondered whether, in rather similar circumstances, the greengrocer had found himself at cross purposes at a house not far from the vicarage, where the son lavished affection on a couple of fine pigeons—one called Chou-fleur and the other Epinards!

I once asked the child what had inspired his choice of names. Were these his favourite vegetables?

" Oh, no; *I* didn't choose them; it's because they're thoroughbreds. Those are the names written on their pedigrees."

" Thoroughbreds, eh? You must be jolly proud of them. Are they husband and wife? "

" No, no! " Paul quickly corrected me; " They're a wife and her brother-in-law "—which struck me as a rather dubious set-up for a respectable loft.

Paul eventually lost his pets through wilful disregard of mature advice. He let them out one day on a freedom flight while he went off to play cricket, leaving his mother to keep watch.

I had popped over to see her with a few apples, and the strangest sight met me. I was baffled. There she sat, poor woman, in the middle of the garden—if " seated " is a word that can be used for a sort of ceaseless rotating movement of head and trunk, operated from the central pivot of the hard chair to which she was anchored. As her body swung round and round her eyes swept the heavens with an intense gaze.

Without disturbing the rhythm, she flung me a cordial greeting: " Hello; do come in [she obviously meant in the garden, for she didn't attempt to desert her post]. So sorry I can't look at you, but I promised Paul I'd keep my eyes on Chou-fleur and Epinards; and they keep going round in circles, the little blighters. I daren't take my eyes off them; he would be so annoyed with me."

Well, he lost them, anyway.

My sympathies were entirely with mum, on whom an unduly tough assignment seemed to have been fastened. She was expecting her next baby in a few days, and it occurred to me that an after-noon's siesta would probably have done her more good than a bird-watching session.

Anyway, I dumped the apples and for a while shared her vigil, and we managed to sustain a fragmentary conversation.

The apples were a daily offering because during this pregnancy my friend experienced an insatiable craving for two things: sour apples, with which I was able to keep her amply supplied from the vicarage crop, and the smell of diesel oil, which she was able herself partially to satisfy by making regular excursions to the tractor yard of a highly mechanized farm nearby, where she would stand for long spells ecstatically drawing in deep, intoxicating sniffs.

*   *   *   *   *

For a final observation on the Puddings: of all our beloved cats Chrissie was easily the most winsome, gay, amiable and seductive puss of the bunch—with an almost bewitching smile at times. Even on that unforgettable occasion when our imbecile thoughtlessness must have caused her excruciating pain and indignity her anger against us, although *burning* at the time (literally!), was only momen-tary; she harboured no sullen resentment.

It happened because, due to the severely hard winter that year, we had provided the Puddings with indoor sanitation. In a secluded corner of the scullery we placed a capacious earth box—that is *earth* in theory, but in reality (with the ground outdoors quite glacial) it was an *ash* box, replenished daily as we did the grates.

On this ill-starred day we were alerted by a cry never to be forgotten—a high-pitched, agonizing, lingering *m-i-a-o-w*. Chrissie, who the minute before had been happily playing cat's-cradle with my knitting wool, had suddenly made a frantic dash to the toilet, squatting squarely, but with disastrous incaution, on the *very* recent top-dressing of glowing, smouldering ashes, from which she retired with super-feline speed, sorely singed.

For the next few minutes she performed a sort of frenzied ritual dance, gyrating madly, pausing only to fling us an occasional baleful glare.

In our wild remorse John and I kept trying to assure her that it hurt us far more than it hurt her, but her pained expression seemed to say pretty clearly " Wait till you can speak from experience."

As far as I can recall that was the only time that Chrissie appeared to question our sincerity; and in her own terms she quickly forgave us.

CHAPTER 13

Exit the Greens

AND now it is retirement, with the opportunity to sit quietly back and take an objective look at the broad field of our endeavours—a luxury denied to us while we were in the thick of it. At the time the swift stream of events that carried us along never slackened sufficiently to allow a complete observation of the passing landscape; the prevailing scene seemed always to some extent blurred or distorted by the intrusion of its more trivial features. We were vaguely conscious of trying to weave a pattern without having time to examine the individual threads.

Unlike today's rebellious young men, *we* have neither cause nor inclination to " look back in anger," despite the occasional rubs and pricks; rather, our backward look is sustained by feelings of profound gratitude for the blessed privilege of service.

Quite frequently, of course, we couldn't see the wood for the trees, so feverish was the tempo and intensive the grind. At such times the most we could do was to obey the impulses of day-to-day hoping and coping, deriving considerable comfort from the belief that even the most baffling twist in the parochial maze would lead eventually to the desired opening, depositing us always a little bit nearer to the ultimate goal; and that must suffice. We had become increasingly conscious of a powerful, benign influence guiding and directing all our affairs. To change the metaphor entirely, it was as if a bright, dependable beacon flashed its reassuring beam, helping us to steer our light craft in heavy seas—hidden reefs would be revealed, drifting obstructions strangely diverted, fears dispelled. Never had we cause to doubt that providence " neither slumbers nor sleeps."

The actual events through which we steered could hardly have been more varied and mutable in character and approach. The human situations we were called upon to deal with mirrored every shade of emotion from despair to elation, triumph to tragedy, craven fear to superb courage. In his pastoral capacity the parish priest has to be prepared to contend with the very extremes of human behaviour and stresses: it could be bitter intolerance or unreasoned hostility, inflated arrogance or affected humility, calculated indifference or near-fanaticism. The whims of the capricious may need to be restrained, or the restless endeavours of the zealot might require discreet curbing, but invariably the most intractable symptom of the parochial malady is *apathy*, or hardening of the spiritual arteries.

How best to deal with the current dilemma was not always apparent. There were occasions when John, having used to the best of his ability, yet with no noticeable effect, the conventional weapons of pastoral aid—spiritual consolation, scriptural authority, admonition, encouragement or plain logic as the case may be— resorted finally to the homely panacea of a snug invitation to " come and warm up by the fire and let me get you a cup of coffee," only to find there, by the fireside, the very key to the knotty problem, followed by the unburdening of a troubled soul. It was as if the warmth, the friendly touch and the homely refreshment helped magically to release the flood of confidence that had proved unyielding to priestly persuasion or theological argument.

In my own humble province, reaching a similar impasse with an inconsolably bereaved wife or a distracted mother whose wayward girl was drifting into a disastrous marriage through her foolish indiscretions—well, words were all too often poor vehicles of expression and sympathy; but I could at least offer the distressed one a shoulder to cry on, and then, after the storm had blown itself out, a cup of tea to steady her nerves and a dab of powder to disguise the red rims. It was always the homely touch that seemed to help most.

Scanning the horizon of the past fifteen years, it is surprising how many of the lasting memories, which now stand out like headlands in the sunshine, are in fact the apparently trivial, insignificant happenings—incidents which at the time were taken too much for granted; acts of genuine, warm friendship and compassion. But isn't it a truism that the most significant impressions in life's circle *are* based on trivialities—maybe because our scale of values often needs adjusting?

There was, for example, the simple, unexpected Christmas gift from a dear little old lady—well up in the seventies—whose charming cottage garden had so often compelled me to stand and admire. On our first Christmas Eve at Upper Bellpull she had crept quietly up the drive to deposit her present in the porch, tiptoeing hurriedly away before I could get to the door. It was an enchanting little wicker basket most tastefully filled with exquisite Christmas roses —about half a dozen perfect specimens, their pristine whiteness accentuated by the accompanying sprig or two of scarlet-berried holly, winter jasmine and a touch of mistletoe, which flourished on her twisted old apple trees.

Attached to the handle by a dainty bow of green tinsel was her neat card wishing us " great happiness and peace on your first Christmas together." And every year after that, until she passed away in her mid-eighties, she never failed to bring her fine floral offering—always simple, always perfect in its artistry—to occupy the place of honour reserved for it on our Christmas table.

Another unobtrusive little gesture in our very early days had served almost miraculously to steady me in a moment of near-panic, when John was suddenly stricken with a virus infection. On the Saturday evening I was sitting anxiously by his bed as he lay inert under a morphia injection. In that large, echoing mansion the slightest creaking sound seemed magnified a hundredfold. I never remember feeling more frightened and isolated; as yet I knew so few of my neighbours, and there was no doctor or nurse within easy call. I positively quailed at the chilling prospect of a whole night's vigil. Then there was a ring at the door; the caller was a pleasant-faced, breathless woman—a total stranger to me—who introduced herself so naturally as " Nobby Clark's wife." Nobby was " mine host " at the local. She had obviously run out hurriedly, with a coat flung carelessly round her shoulders. She wouldn't come in. " Can't spare a minute just now," she explained, adding " but I was *so* sorry to hear of your husband's illness. I felt I must come. I've only just heard about it and I thought you might find these few odds and ends useful when he's on the mend again." She handed me a basket. The " odds and ends " consisted of a dozen new-laid eggs, a jar of home-produced honey, a pound of sugar and a similar quantity of butter. (This, remember, was during the rationing period.)

There was no mistaking the genuine warmth of her concern. I asked how she had heard about John. " Oh, they were talking about it in the bar this evening; when I heard them saying how ill he is I thought I'd just pop across. Sorry I can't stay *now*; I've run out and left the bar unattended. Don't forget to let me know if there's anything else you need. If you want me, just 'phone. Ta-ta! " —and she fled back to her job.

I was deeply touched by this spontaneous sympathy from a complete stranger—at the busiest moment of her Saturday evening trade! Nor was she impelled by even nominal allegiance to the vicar, for, as I learned later, she was a practising Roman Catholic.

But what she brought me, had she but known it, was not merely a generous gift of groceries and a kind word, but a much-needed boost to my sagging morale; a reassurance that I was *not* as alone as I thought I was that night. Her gesture seemed to signal that all would be well. And it was.

In fact, in all our domestic upheavals—mostly accounted for by illness—there was abundant evidence of kindly, practical good-neighbourliness, which helped immeasurably to ease the strain and anxiety. Even the local small fry, with their inexhaustible capacity for hatching out diabolical plots, who simply revelled in their reputations for being " tough guys," showed their redeeming virtues when I was laid low and ordered to be " kept quiet." These young scallywags had recently devised a new way of venting their animal spirits; night after night they had been using the vicarage lane for dirt-track racing—with hordes of frenzied supporters screaming and dancing like little dervishes. To avoid being labelled old " squares " we had not complained, until I fell ill and it came to an issue. Then John went down to the boys and explained that I was in bed and needed to be kept quiet. Without demur, the leader issued a peremptory order to his gang to pipe down. They said they were sorry, hoped I would soon be better, and trooped off as docile as lambs, doubtless to make a big noise somewhere else. While I remained on the sick list there was no repetition of their racket within sound of our place. What's more, the little urchins often stopped John to inquire after me!

*   *   *   *   *

Because it is a common human failing to look for results out of all proportion to the reasonable average, I think John was sometimes a little bit sick at heart—if not actually disillusioned—by the seeming lack of response to the call of evangelism. His own zeal was so intense that at times he appeared limp and exhausted by his unremitting efforts to galvanize a laggard following. In his parochial experience there was no hostility to organized religion, but there was undeniable apathy, with, here and there, vague questionings of the old, accepted formulas, the theological jargon and dogma. The open mind was something that John encouraged, for his contention was that a packaged religion necessarily lacked virility, dynamic power and ultimate satisfaction. It could be an affront to truth and was a natural impediment to spiritual growth.

Reflecting on the prevailing symptom of apathy, I found myself more than once wondering how it is that every parish priest, faced with this mass frustration, does not die of a broken heart. But if I mused aloud John would be the first to administer a sharp reminder that it is the drilling and the seed-sowing that constitute the priest's job; that done, he must rest content, for he is *not* asked to do the harvesting.

From observation, I believe that the factor most likely to bedevil the smooth running of any parish is the common failure on the part of the laity fully to appreciate the priestly rôle as such; that is, as distinct from appreciation of the *man*. Because of this, the incumbent is liable to be seen not so much as the bishop's representative at parochial level, charged to minister impartially, without fear or favour, to all alike, from the humblest cottager to the lord of the manor, exercising his own discretion and reasonable authority, but rather as *their* figurehead—acquiescent, malleable, hapless target of all the pressure groups (each sincere enough in canvassing for its own caucus), and target also of the powerfully divisive individualist (" What we want at St. So-and-so's is . . . "—meaning, of course, "What *I* want, and am jolly well determined to see we get, if possible, at St. So-and-so's is . . . "), while to a large extent his priestly hands remain tied by a pervasive hostility to the slightest deviation.

To reconcile the demands of the *high* element, the *low* element and the *central* position, plus the resolute contenders for the *status quo*—all within one parish!—requires the wisdom of Solomon and the genius of the entire Diplomatic Corps. The less militant sector, sensing a contentious atmosphere, may in the end become *uncritically* tolerant, which is a sign of incipient apathy. There is, of course, the odd incorrigible critic who (always on principle!) takes a firm stand anti-everything; the one who when haloes slip usually adds a malicious shove to ensure that they topple.

The dilemma seems to point to more discipline and obedience (not to mention humility!) as the normal obligation of membership of Christ's body.

No matter what the circumstances, John never underestimated the possible outcome of any spiritual project, and when a rather cynical critic questioned whether our parochial mission had served any real purpose at all John parried with " Who is qualified to use the measuring rod? "

John's initial move to hold a mission had not been received with conspicuous enthusiasm, but when he pressed the need splendid co-operation was forthcoming. The three missioners who took entire charge after our own six months of parochial preparation were skilled and unsparing in their endeavours.

Afterwards, the man who had been so dubious about it all was heard to say: " The people who come to church before still come; the backsliders who caused a flash in the pan during the campaign have fallen away again; the rest remain non-committal. So we're all back where we were! "

But we certainly weren't. John was happily aware of profound results in certain undisclosed quarters.

*   *   *   *   *

Like a bolt from the blue we received our marching orders—from John's surgeon. This was indeed a body blow, its effect utterly numbing. For some days we just lived in a state of suspended animation. Then, gradually emerging from this trance-like state, we set to work to make plans for our removal and for the disposal of the bulk of our furniture, for which we would no longer have the space.

Retirement in our case meant not merely the termination of office, but also the lifting of our roots and transplantation to new soil. It meant exile from the very hub of parochial activity to the relative solitude of private life. We foresaw—and naturally dreaded —the inevitable stripping away of primary association with other people. It meant transition from a semi-mansion in a vast garden to a modest flat; from the magnificent freedom of the open country— its flowers, trees, birds, crops, and clean, invigorating air—to the confined atmosphere of an overgrown suburb—noise, crowds, traffic, diesel fumes, towering blocks of flats, supermarkets! How

R

thankful we were, in the sad circumstances, not to be without inner resources—the hobbies that we had hitherto been forced to neglect would in future, perhaps, have a chance to be cultivated.

We were conscious of an instinctive resistance to the prospect of retirement and the radical changes it must inevitably bring. I had always maintained that to grow old gracefully one had to begin *very* young, and at the present juncture I wished devoutly that I had started the process a good deal earlier. As it was, my " grace " seemed sadly unequal to the needs of the moment.

In this miserably unsettling situation it was not surprising that we should be a prey to so many transient thoughts and speculations; a welter of unbidden impressions kept crowding in, like dreams recalled with great vividness on waking, or like thoughts half-buried suddenly bobbing up from the sub-strata and settling on the surface.

We reflected, for instance, on the paradox that in a vocation which calls naturally for so much study and close reading there should be so little time available for it. John had always been keenly aware of the desirability of keeping pace with modern thought, but what time, he often asked himself, had the parish priest for the luxury of serious application after satisfying the clamant demands of a tight programme of preaching, teaching, marrying, burying, visiting, interviewing, letter-writing, form-filling, organizing fêtes and conducting outings, and attending endless committees, rallies, conferences, working parties and discussions (all more or less obligatory) at both deanery and diocesan level? He had more than a sneaking feeling that the Establishment was in grave danger of becoming over-organized; that its gleaming efficiency could tend to blur the vision of the first cause; that the parish priest was liable to be too frequently distracted from his immediate pastoral charge by participation in this or that official " huddle." Could some of this organizing expertise be canalized and used more profitably within the parishes? Was there, in fact, a tendency for organization to become an end in itself—time-wasting, energy-sapping, a shadowy thing altogether too distantly related to true evangelism? Was the parish priest being tempted to side-step, to some extent, his real terms of reference?

I had often felt mildly guilty because John lent a big hand with the domestic chores; yet, with the dual responsibility of a servantless mansion and a palpably overworked wife, he seemed to have little choice in the matter.

The financial grievances of the clergy tend to be aired with monotonous frequency and far too little dignity. *We* certainly felt the burden of struggling to maintain an enormous property on a stipend that was far from commensurate, though I admit that at times we saw it as a challenge to ingenuity and thrift; but what we most deeply deplored was the fact that these conditions imposed a materialistic complexion on so much of our thinking; shoe-string budgeting can easily become obsessional. We would have preferred to set our sights on more exclusively *un*worldly issues; but at every turn we were confronted with the niggling problem of making those two short ends meet.

Then we felt that there was a pressing need, in matters of church administration and finance, for a better-informed laity; in our experience so many grossly mistaken notions persisted and appeared to be quite ineradicable—those fabulous versions of the untold wealth of the Church, of its allegedly questionable (why? I wonder) Stock Exchange dealings, of its alleged ill reputation as property owner and landlord. Specious arguments, indeed, making it all the harder for the poor parson to vindicate the Church's case. And will anything ever kill the fixed image of the large parsonage house as a status symbol? Why must an unwieldy domicile be regarded as synonymous with personal affluence? *We* tried in vain to present ours as the white elephant that in fact it was. Hasten the day, then, when the laity knows more of the true domestic facts of its Church!

And the clergy themselves would undoubtedly profit by better briefing on domestic issues—the care and maintenance of parsonage property, rights and responsibilities, dilapidations, grants, and so on.

Amid these more sober reflections came one entirely frivolous flash-back, recalling the occasion when John returned more than usually tired from evensong and sank into the nearest chair with a prolonged " Whew! " Then " A pot of tea, please; quick! " As I brought it in I remarked " Your sermon tonight, if I may say so, was absolutely the best I have ever heard you preach; jolly good! "

" Honestly? " queried an incredulous John. " Then thank God, for, as it happened, I'd lost my notes! Before we began I was discussing an alternative tune with Houghton, and I must have absent-mindedly put them down. He found them afterwards on the organ seat; he'd been sitting on them all through the service! "

Perhaps the greatest of all fallacies is that a " quiet country living " is a sinecure. True, a country parish can, in reasonable circumstances, be a clerical paradise; but, believe me, it is no place to put a worn-out old parson out to grass!

*   *   *   *   *

The one thing we felt we could *not* face was the official farewell gathering that rumour whispered was being arranged for us. Like most English people, we shrank instinctively from the emotionally charged moment. But, of course, as on all such occasions, we were carried along on the prevailing tide, and to see the village hall on that Sunday night, packed to suffocation, was as pleasing a tribute as any departing priest could wish for.

One of the wardens whispered to me " It's the biggest surprise to me to see all these people; quite half of them *never* come to church."

" Perhaps not, I agreed, " but don't forget that John has always gone to *them*."

And our flock expressed their appreciation tangibly, and very handsomely.

*   *   *   *   *

The final exodus from the vicarage was a major operation, carried out in torrents of rain, which matched our mood and added considerably to the inevitable discomforts of departure. For days past we had been deeply involved in the cruel slaughter of piece after piece of our large period furniture, and these transactions drove home to us very forcibly the fact that, in a " contemporary " age, one man's treasure is another man's junk. There had seemed no end to the sad disposal of valued books and records, pictures we had grown to love, and even prized heirlooms. It was a vast, ruthless exercise, but there was no alternative.

Having eaten our last meal, standing up in a desolate, empty dining room, using the mantelpiece as a table, John decided to take a last quick look round—just to make sure we hadn't overlooked anything. With so much parish property being always parked at the vicarage, he had been meticulously careful to get this segregated from our own belongings; it took hours the previous day labelling and stacking this lot in a corner of the study: " Church property; don't touch."

At the very point of locking up and leaving, my dumb dejection was shattered by John shouting to the men " Hi! Where's all that stuff that was piled up in the corner over there? "

" It's all safe in the van, gov'nor "—and so it was! To make matters worse, it was well and truly wedged in the forefront of the van. So there we were stuck, miserably bogged down, while the furniture was unloaded into the mudddy, melancholy puddles flooding the drive, until all the church pieces were finally located, manœuvred out of the van, and hauled back into the house. It was a scene of utter desolation.

We were *not* amused; nor were the men!

* * * * *

Since our début, fifteen years before, we had widened our experiences considerably and learnt at least *something*; but we remained convinced that in the life of the Spirit one just goes on learning, learning, endlessly learning; taking test after test, but never becoming proficient enough to take down the " L " plates.

Perhaps this is not so much through failure to study the Highway Code as through general unwillingness to recognize and respect the motives of fellow travellers; and also, of course, through a common reluctance to give way to reason if there is the slightest chance to streak past or jostle a way through the main stream.

Knowledge of the code is one thing; its practical application is another.

* * * * *

To sum up, the Greens, in their approach to Upper Bellpull, were undoubtedly *very* green. They were, I earnestly hope, a few shades less verdant at their departure.